PRAISE FOR THE NOVELS OF AMY DAWS

"I dare you not to fall in love with the Mountain Men Matchmaker series!"

—Lucy Score, #1 *New York Times* bestselling author, on *Honeymoon Phase*

"Deliciously funny and spicy."

—Elsie Silver, #1 *New York Times* bestselling author, on *Seven Year Itch*

"A hilariously fresh and spicy rom-com that I couldn't put down!"

—Meghan Quinn, *New York Times* bestselling author, on *Nine Month Contract*

Bad Boy Era

Dear Reader,

You have officially entered mountain man territory!

Check out the other hilarious and emotional love stories in the Mountain Men Matchmaker series by Amy Daws, starting with *Nine Month Contract* (Wyatt's story) and continuing with *Seven Year Itch* (Calder's story) and *Honeymoon Phase* (Luke's story), available now from Canary Street Press.

And look out for their CEO brother Max's single dad boss/nanny love story, *Last on the List*, available now in all formats!

If you want more sexy rom-coms with humor and heart, check out the other stand-alone stories in the Wait With Me series by Amy Daws, releasing in print in 2026 from MIRA Books, and available now in ebook and audio!

ALSO BY AMY DAWS

THE MOUNTAIN MEN MATCHMAKER SERIES

Nine Month Contract

Seven Year Itch

Honeymoon Phase

THE WAIT WITH ME SERIES

Wait With Me

Next in Line

One Moment Please

Take a Number

Last on the List

THE HARRIS BROTHERS SERIES

Challenge

Endurance

Keeper

Surrender

Dominate

THE HARRIS BROTHERS SPIN-OFF STAND-ALONES

Payback

Blindsided

Replay

Sweeper

Strength

For additional books by Amy Daws, visit her website, amydawsauthor.com. For exclusive news on upcoming releases and updates on all your favorite characters, sign up for her newsletter at amydawsauthor.com/newsletter.

Bad Boy Era

AMY DAWS

MIRA

MIRA™

ISBN-13: 978-1-335-21997-8

Bad Boy Era

For questions and comments about the quality of this book, please contact us at CustomerService@Harlequin.com.

MIRA
22 Adelaide St. West, 41st Floor
Toronto, Ontario M5H 4E3, Canada
MIRABooks.com

HarperCollins Publishers
Macken House, 39/40 Mayor Street Upper,
Dublin 1, D01 C9W8, Ireland
www.HarperCollins.com

Printed in U.S.A.

26 27 28 29 30 LBC 5 4 3 2 1

To everyone who dares to be cringe instead of cool.
It's never cringe to try.
It's the reason love stories exist.

Prologue

The Matchmaker Manifesto
by Everly Fletcher

Rule #1: A first date should feel like a fan-made edit of your favorite rom-com. Short, stirring, full of butterflies, and backed by a Taylor Swift power ballad. *Bonus points if there's slow-mo laughing.*

Rule #2: Everyone has a type. Sometimes they just need an expert to tell them what it is. Spoiler alert: Your "type" is usually connected to unresolved childhood trauma. *Who needs therapy, amiright?*

Rule #3: Background checks are optional. Deodorant is not. Hygiene is the only love language that matters.

Rule #4: Send a text to your date the day after. Show them you're thinking about them. We're ghosting ghosts in this economy.

Rule #5: Eye contact is everything! The eyes are windows to the soul, but also the fastest way to tell if someone wants to bang you or if they're just in it for the food. *To be fair, both are valid desires.*

Rule #6: Find a balance between listening and sharing. No one wants a podcast episode on your mommy issues.

Rule #7: Must kiss on the first date. If you ain't locking lips night one, you ain't locking hips ever.

Rule #8: Chemistry can be created. A hot Spotify playlist, warm lighting, and a healthy dose of delusion can really set the mood.

Rule #9: Make plans to see each other again before the end of the date. Games are for PlayStation.

Rule #10: DTR. Define the Relationship. If you're swapping memes at midnight and wearing each other's hoodies, it's time for some labels.

Bonus Rule: Never under *any* circumstances fall for your best friend's grumpy brother with a sexy thigh tattoo. It won't end well.

Chapter 1

Kickoff: *A rugby term used to identify the start of a game.*

Translation: *Is it too much to want to kickoff people's faces?*

Everly

"Oh my God!" I growl as I glance at the tagged post notification that just popped up on my Instagram.

"Are you talking to me?" my roommate, Cliona, asks from her twin bed across our dorm room as she slides off her white headphones.

I blink rapidly at my phone screen. "That guy I went to the Trinity Ball with last week just one-starred me on Instagram."

"The bloke you said had food stuck in his teeth the whole night, even after you tried to politely tell him?"

"Yes, that guy!"

"What do you mean he rated you? You can't rate people on Instagram." Cliona frowns, her Irish accent getting thicker with her confusion.

"No, but you can make a scathing public post about them," I argue, flashing my screen to her. "The asshat even included a photo of me." I zoom in on the shot he snapped when I wasn't looking. In it, I'm wearing a lush white gown for the ball, something Cliona and I spent hours shopping for. My blonde hair curtains my face as I stare down at my phone, clearly deep in thought.

"I need to take a closer look." The bag of ice on Cliona's leg crinkles as she slides it off her knee and gets up to hobble across the room toward where I'm sprawled out on my matching twin bed. Cliona's back is hunched like an old lady as she struggles to find her balance. She calls this the "rugby walk" and says it's part of the fun of the collegiate sport she willingly participates in, but nothing about walking like an eighty-year-old looks fun to me.

The scent of Icy Hot permeates my nose as she grabs my phone and squints at it. "*One-Star Review for the Campus Matchmaker. Would not recommend, not even to my worst enemy.* Bit dramatic of a start if you ask me."

"Keep reading," I growl and cover my face.

"Can someone explain how the blonde American lass that swans around Trinity campus and calls herself a matchmaking mastermind manages to be an absolute car crash on a date for herself? I know it's not decent to go reviewing people online like they're takeaway curry, but since this one fancies herself as some sort of love guru, I reckon the student body deserves a heads-up: She's a disaster. Full stop."

"What a fucking arsehole!" Cliona growls, her brown eyes lit with rage. "I'll kill the fecker myself. Where's he live?"

"Just keep reading," I groan, rolling over and hugging a pillow over my head.

"I met Everly Fletcher at one of those speed dating events she runs at Mulligans. She wasn't participating in the event, but she's not bad to look at, so I decided to shoot my shot with her instead of the D-list girls she had there. She agreed to go to the Trinity Ball with me. Bit of craic, right? Well, while we're at the festival, she barely looked up from her phone the whole time. I swear I had to beg her to dance with me. That's not a date, that's making me feel like a distraction."

"Everly!" Cliona chastises, likely looking at the photo as evidence.

"I had a crisis going on," I exclaim defensively. "Mulligans

Pub was trying to cancel my final matchmaking event, and I had already ordered those cute little graduation hats for everyone to wear that were seasonal and . . . just keep frickin' reading."

"Fine, fine. But I'm starting to see this guy's point."

I scowl at my roommate as she continues. *"Then out of nowhere, she starts telling me this story about eating her flatmate's laxatives because she thought they were chocolates. Three days of her shitting herself before she told me she ended up in the campus A&E getting an IV and cream for her raw arse. Thought she was winding me up. She wasn't. I tried not to judge, but surely the Saints wept for me."*

Cliona's lips part in horror. "Fletcher, why the bleedin' hell did you tell him about shitting your trousers?"

"It was a funny story," I defend, my head jerking back. "You and I died laughing about it! I was trying to be relatable. That's one of my dating rules, you know."

Her face twists. "Would you ever in your lifetime tell one of your matchmaking clients to share a story about shitting their face off on a first date?"

I swallow the lump in my throat. "No."

"So why did you tell the food-in-teeth guy?"

"It just . . . came up. Context matters."

"Contextual shit?"

I curl my shoulders in as I press my back to the brick wall. "Okay, upon reflection, I can see how that was maybe an off-color story."

"Off-color? It was a shit color!"

"I'm sorry! I was just trying to make conversation."

"About pooing so much you needed to go to hospital? Fletch, this is bad. This is why you never get any second dates. I've just never seen it spelled out so specifically before."

"There's more," I murmur, pulling my legs in to sit crisscross on my bed. It's times like these I realize that perhaps I hung out with my uncles a bit too much in my youth.

"Christ, I don't know if I can take much more." She sighs heavily and continues. *"The real deal-breaker was that she would not stop banging on about her family back in the States and the gorgeous mountains and how her uncles all live up there and she's going there after graduation. Made them sound like they'd walked straight out of a Pixar film. Has she not made it outside of Dublin? Ireland is no snore. Either way, I didn't buy it. Nobody likes their family that much. So now she's not only stomach-churning and rude as sin, she's also creepy close to her family. Bottom line? Taking dating advice from the American, Everly Fletcher, is like letting your mam teach you how to wank. Just wrong on so many levels. If you're in a relationship thanks to her, best get out now while you can. Girl's got no clue what she's at."*

Cliona finishes reading, and the silence in our tiny little dorm room is deafening.

I deserve a quiet moment of shameful reflection. I took what's supposed to be a beautiful, elegant Trinity College in Dublin experience and fumbled it so hard.

"Oh, Fletcher . . . I'm sorry," Cliona says, handing me my phone back and noticing the tears welling in my eyes. "You want me to get my rugby teammates together and go turn his face into a rugby ball? Knock him around until he has no teeth left to get food stuck in?"

I offer a watery smile at my wonderfully savage roommate. "Don't bother. I'm only here for another month, and then I can go back to Colorado and be a social failure there while the whole of Ireland can forget I ever existed."

I press my head to the wall and wallow over the fact that I didn't succeed at taking any of my uncle Luke's advice. In fact, I lied my ass off every time I updated him on my goings-on here.

I said I was going on amazing dates . . . Lie.

I said I was going to loads of parties . . . Lie.

I said I was making tons of friends . . . Lie.

I said I wasn't matchmaking anymore . . . Lie!

I'm a fraud. A phony. A loser who lived in Ireland for four years and only managed to find one close friend in the nth hour because she was forced by the university to have a roommate.

Sure, I connected with a few people over the years. Had coffee, studied, and did some sightseeing with a few willing participants, but forming tight friendships with people my own age has always been hard. I always felt like I was on the outside looking in, no matter which country, it seems.

Cliona's face drops at my destitute look. She points to her chest. "This Irish girl is never gonna be forgettin' ya."

She ends the sentence in that musical, playful accent that people from northern Dublin have where you're not sure if they're teasing you or threatening you. It's a lot of flat vowels and dropped endings on certain words. It's a voice that's become familiar and comforting to me.

A lump forms in my throat over that realization. To think I nearly left Trinity and never truly knew Cliona Reilly is a horror I can't fathom.

She says it was Irish luck that brought us together.

My money is on my grandfather from up above sending me a Hail Mary. He was a bit of a mastermind meddler, just like me, and I think he knew I needed a friend.

And apparently, he thought Trinity College women's rugby legend Cliona Reilly was just the ticket.

She is a beast in so many ways. Not to mention a giant flirt who's shredded with more muscle than my arms have ever dreamed of.

Normally, the rugby players all live in reserved athletic housing off campus, but Cliona had a conflict with one of her teammates last year and had to move out. I was irritated when the university randomly matched us together in a double suite because I'd had a single all my other years going to school here . . . but it turned out to be the best irritation that ever happened to me.

We live together in the Rubrics, which is a stunning red-brick building right in the historic part of Trinity campus. It's an old stately Georgian structure from the 1700s with tall windows and a weathered edge to everything that makes you wonder if it's haunted about nine times a day.

Real talk, it's like living in a storybook.

This building is usually reserved for postgraduate students, scholars, or students with specific needs. My specific need was my controlling father back in Colorado making an obnoxious donation to the campus to secure me a room here so he didn't have to worry about me walking to class from off-campus housing in a foreign country.

The first day I met Cliona, she asked me to rub out a knot in her shoulder with my elbow. I thought she was a weird jock with boundary issues, who was possibly into girls. But I couldn't have been more wrong. She is just a no-boundary bruiser who is hard not to love.

With a sigh, I grab my Irish roommate by the wrist and yank her down onto my bed. "Don't worry, I'll save all my best bowel movement stories for you from now on. I'll even text you photos of them once I'm back home in Colorado so you can really remember all my essence."

"Please don't." Cliona giggles as she shoves me away from her.

"It's only fair after being subjected to your rugby stank all year," I volley back. Her gear bag is a mixture of body odor, grass, and mud. She tries to cover it up with lavender oils, but it doesn't work. This Irish girl has imprinted her scent on me this past year, and I hate how much I'm going to miss it . . . and her.

But I always knew I'd go back to Colorado at the end of my

studies. It's home. My family is the only place I feel like I can be my true self.

Even so, I'm still going to miss Ireland something fierce. There's something about Dublin that feels alive in a way I've never experienced. The slippery cobblestones after a fresh rain, or the way the Liffey River twinkles with gold at sunset. And the coziness of every crowded pub is like a dream. You can be all alone and still feel right at home in an Irish pub.

And Trinity. I'm going to miss it most of all. The library that smells like musty paper. The quad where the bells chime just to stress you out when you're late for class. The oak trees that turn the walk to lectures into a canopy of gold in the fall. Or the hush of campus during rugby matches. This campus was my comfort blanket whenever I felt uncomfortable. I'm going to miss the feeling of walking around an important piece of history.

But it's time to trade university life for Fletcher Mountain. And up until Cliona, I thought it was going to be the campus I'd be missing most. Now I'm prematurely mourning the scent of rank rugby cleats.

Thanks, Grandpa.

Cliona readjusts so she's facing me, and I stare at her to catalog a mental picture of this dark-haired, brown-eyed, five-foot-ten stunner with freckles that dot her nose. I can't believe I was here for three years and never met her. She's the sister I never knew I was missing. If either of us batted for the other team, I'm pretty sure we'd choose each other.

Instead . . . I've just labeled her as my Irish Twin.

Except she already has a twin. Her brother, Conri, *pronounced Con-Ree*, plays rugby for the men's team at Trinity. His vibes are nowhere near as fun as Cliona's. Where she is bold and easy-going, he's broody and in a permanent state of irritated. And he's a giant, which is saying a lot, coming from me. I'm six feet tall, so there aren't many people who make me feel small, but Conri Reilly, who the entire school refers to as "Wolf," stands at six foot five and has the muscle to fill out that massive frame.

Pair that with his molten whiskey-brown eyes, dark hair, and that harsh, punishing glower of his, and he's basically the complete opposite of any of the guys I've tried to date during my time here at Trinity.

Tried being the operative word.

Thankfully, Conri seems to barely notice me, so even considering him as an option is laughable. And the fact that he's my roommate's brother puts him in the do-not-consider category. That's just basic girl code.

"I truly don't understand how you've spent most of your time here at college matchmaking fellow students but are still so shite at dating yourself. It's quite impressive if you really think about it."

I sigh heavily and turn onto my back to stare up at the ceiling. "I've accepted that those who can't do . . . teach."

Cliona would have been a fun one to match, if she had ever let me. But she was fresh out of a one-year relationship that exploded when she moved in and said she was off boys for the foreseeable future.

"What are you going to do back in America?" she asks pointedly.

"What do you mean?" I turn to frown at her. "You know I'm helping out at my aunt's animal rescue facility."

"I mean romantically. Maybe you should try the dating apps?"

"I am not dating anyone back in America." I wave her off. "I'm planning to live in my dad's new cabin that he built up on my uncle Wyatt's mountain, which means I'll be neighbors with all three of my uncles. And bringing a boy up to Fletcher Mountain would be an act of *war*. I'd be feeding the poor guy to a pack of wolves if the wolves had beards, weird obsessions with their pets, and a penchant for wearing flannel in the summertime."

Cliona giggles. "I hope to come to America someday to meet these overprotective uncles of yours. They sound like total nightmares."

I smile softly. "Naw, they're great. They just never think anyone is good enough for me. My high school boyfriend of two years was nearly chased away by the three of them the night he tried to pick me up for my senior prom. And he's what you'd call a tragically nice guy."

Cliona makes a noise in the back of her throat. "At least you had a nice boyfriend and not a cheating arsehole."

"Yeah, there is that . . ." My voice trails off as I work to hide my outward reaction. You'd think dating a guy for two years would give me lots of relationship experience, both intimately and socially. Unfortunately, dating the nice guy can be painfully boring. But I'm not about to complain about that to Cliona after everything she went through with her ex.

"And at least your family cares," she adds wistfully. "My parents don't even come to me and my brother's rugby matches. I think in the four years me and Conri have been playing for Trinity, they have attended a total of three games. It's pathetic. And tomorrow is a huge match for Wolf."

"I'm sorry, Clio," I say, watching her eyes tighten.

She shrugs dismissively. "They're the only Irish people in the country who don't fancy rugby. It's a pain, but we don't get to pick our family, do we?"

I watch her quietly for a moment. Cliona is the grin-and-bear-it type, and normally nothing gets her down, but I know she's anxious about finishing school. She's finally going to be able to fulfill her big dream of playing rugby professionally, as she's signed a contract with Leinster Rugby, an Irish provincial team in Dublin. She's gearing up to play at the highest level, and she's absolutely thrilled about it.

However, her parents' top priority has always been her and her brother's education. They run a corner shop in Ballymun on the north side of Dublin and work really long hours to keep it afloat, often missing out on games and special events because of it. They have big career aspirations for their children, which is why they enrolled them in the FESS program at Trinity.

FESS is a finance, economics, and social studies program. A lot of people who graduate from FESS go on to get careers in finance, consulting, law, and business. It's also good for people interested in media, communication, and marketing, which is definitely my thing.

It was the FESS program that drew me to Trinity. I liked that it seemed to combine my two favorite things: people and numbers. I've always loved figuring out what makes people tick, but I wanted to understand the data behind how the world actually works to back up my findings. It's amazing how easy this kind of data can apply to matchmaking. Whether I can make a future out of that remains to be seen.

But, if you're going to spend your college years buried in books, you might as well do it somewhere as beautiful as Trinity.

Clio's parents' dream is for both their children to become lawyers or "solicitors" as you call them in Dublin. It's the ultimate success story they never achieved for themselves. They see rugby as just a hobby, which is wild when Cliona has achieved the level she has in the sport.

I don't even know much about rugby, but I know she's remarkable. Everyone on campus talks about her.

After uni, the plan is for her and her brother to play rugby professionally. And if they aren't raging successes after their first year, they're going to take their law exam and let rugby go to start training in corporate law. To be a rugby player and a lawyer would be next to impossible.

The pressure is on for my dear Irish friend. And if anyone knows a little something about pressure, it's me.

I'm still not certain what I'm going to do with my future. A future in matchmaking doesn't seem like the most responsible choice, but I'm not sure what else would fit me. It's why I prefer to distract myself with other people's problems. They seem far easier to solve. Hence, the plan to help out my aunt Trista.

"Want me to come with you to your brother's match tomorrow?" I offer, giving her arm a little squeeze.

Cliona's eyes widen. "You've never even come to a match of mine!"

"That's your fault," I retort with a gentle shove. I tried to come to some of my roommate's matches initially, but she told me she liked that I existed outside of her rugby world. She said she wanted our friendship to be devoid of rugby as much as possible. Other than the smell, I guess. "But if I come, I'll get to spend more time with you before we leave school in a few weeks, and that's reason enough to break our rugby-free rule, don't you think? Not to mention, I'll need to know a little something about rugby to keep tabs on you from America."

"Oh, go on! I'll teach you everything!" Cliona grabs my arm and playfully wriggles me around like a rag doll, always having no idea how strong she is. "We'll hit up a pub after, and it'll be grand. Let me find you something to wear so you look like a proper Trinity Rugby fan at this match."

I laugh as she hops up off the bed and begins rummaging through her closet, favoring her sore knee. My Irish roomie dressing me for a rugby match—at least this is one fun story I won't have to lie about to my family.

Chapter 2

Red Card: *Red cards are shown to players who have been ordered off the rugby pitch for foul play, violent conduct, or for committing two offenses resulting in yellow cards, which results in the team playing one player down.*

Translation: *Only complete psychopaths get red cards.*

Everly

Being inside College Park for a rugby game is like stepping straight into the world's most charming, slightly insane, and oddly smelly postcard.

You've got these grand old Trinity buildings towering over you like grumpy ancient professors, but then there's this bright, lush stretch of green field that seems to glow under the hazy Irish sun.

That glow must make everyone high because I swear the people around me are on some sort of acid trip as they scream and thrash around every twenty seconds about God only knows what.

Some twenty-year-old guy with mutton chops dumped his drink down my back earlier while screaming at the refs, and Cliona looked at me with tearstained eyes like I was just anointed with holy water.

And when Trinity scores, I seriously fight the urge to hide under my bleacher and cry a little.

This is rugby.

Who the hell came up with it?

At a glance, it's a bunch of barbaric-looking guys in way-too-short shorts and jerseys that are two sizes too small feeling each other up and doing Cirque du Soleil acrobatics just to catch an overinflated football. Seriously, if I wanted to watch thirty guys hugging for eighty minutes, I could have stayed in my dorm and watched gay porn. At least then my back would be dry.

And the fact that these men bash into each other with no pads on is absolute lunacy! They wear fewer clothes than I do to bed and take hits so hard I swear I hear their bones crunch. And they do this all while clutching an egg-shaped ball and trying not to die? What the actual fuck?

Cliona called one weird maneuver a *scrum*, like that simple word somehow makes this all make sense, but the reality is rugby is straight violence.

And completely erotic.

When they do that hoisting thing where they lift one of their teammates up into the air? I think it's called a "lineout"? That's just an excuse for a man to show what he's packing in his tiny shorts. Total grape smugglers, these rugby guys. Whatever nut protectors they wear leave very little to the imagination. I could guess every single one of these dudes' condom sizes after watching just the first half.

And why is the ball shaped like an egg? No one knows. It just is.

Rugby is quite simply just hot, sexy, violent nonsense.

But if I breathed a word of this out loud here in College Park, it would be off with my head. Seriously, I would probably be kicked out of Trinity, stripped of my degree, and deported from Ireland. And that's only if Cliona didn't kick my ass first!

"Jaysus, this match is feckin' mental!" Cliona screams, her eyes bloodshot from how feral she's been during this entire game. She slices her fingers through her long, dark hair, which started off so cute and curled into wavy tendrils but now is a frizzy disaster. The rest of her is still somewhat adorable. She's wearing her rugby jersey, and she paired it with some baggy jeans. She looks effortlessly cool.

I, on the other hand, look like I'm cosplaying as a rugby fan. She forced me to wear one of her brother's hunter green Trinity Rugby T-shirts that's enormous on me. I tucked it up into my bra to have a sort of baggy, cropped look, but I can't stop fiddling with it, fretting that people can tell I'm a rugby virgin . . . which, in fairness, I am. But I'd at least like to look the part.

Oftentimes, people think I'm athletic because I'm six feet tall, and standing next to Cliona, they maybe assume I'm a student athlete as well. But they couldn't be more wrong.

I was in gymnastics when I was little and wasn't half-bad until I hit a crazy growth spurt, and my height made me lose whatever coordination I had. My uncles called me Baby Giraffe when I was a teenager for a reason.

Now, after four years in college, I've lost a lot of that gymnast body definition I once had, but I still manage to feel relatively confident in my own skin. I've just never worn a men's shirt this big before. The sleeves go past my elbows, and I swear the fabric still smells like Cliona's brother, even though I know it's clean. I get hints of cedar and soap and something darker I can't name, but it causes a tight ache between my legs every time I breathe it in.

God, why do some guys smell so fucking good? Like excuse me, I don't need to feel the exact location of my ovaries in the middle of a rugby match, thank you very much.

It's ridiculous how something as simple as a giant T-shirt can elicit such elemental sensations. It's just too big, too boyish, too much of *him*. It inspires thoughts of prehistoric gender roles—me getting knocked over the head and carried back into the big, strong caveman's lair. You, Tarzan. Me, Jane. Me, horny for big, strong thighs.

Gross, Everly! Get your shit together. You're more evolved than this.

I push my long blonde hair behind my shoulders and force myself to stop messing with Wolf's giant shirt to refocus on the field. This is apparently a big game for the men's team. Cliona said this is the semifinal match that earns Trinity a chance to play for the Bateman Cup, also known as the All-Ireland Winner's Cup. And knowing the Irish after four years of attending university here, I'm guessing the cup will be filled with booze if they win.

Partying is one thing the Irish do exceedingly well.

That and apparently rugby.

So here I sit, wide-eyed and clueless about what exactly is going on down on that field, but no less turned on by the feral magnetism the game emits. It's bizarre to be terrified and aroused in equal measure.

"What do you think?" Cliona asks with a hopeful smile. "Grand, isn't it? You couldn't have picked a better match to pop your rugby cherry with."

I smile and nod, blinking back at my Irish bestie. "I still have no idea what's happening."

She rolls her eyes and drapes her arm over my shoulder, pulling me in close so she doesn't have to yell so loud. "Alright, Fletch, let's go over this one more time, yeah? You've got fifteen players on each side. The main goal is to carry or kick the ball over the other team's try line and touch it down. That's called a try, and it's worth five points. After that, you get a chance at a conversion kick for an extra two points. You can also kick for penalty goals or drop goals during open play. Those are worth three points. The tricky bit is you can only pass the ball backward or sideways, never forward. To move the ball forward, you must run it or kick it."

"Why is there so much hugging?" I ask, glancing down as a group of guys form a sort of dome-shaped igloo of bodies and arms.

Cliona's lips thin. "Those are called scrums. It's how we restart play after a minor foul. Then there are rucks and mauls, basically everyone piles in trying to win the ball back either off the ground or in a player's arms."

"This is kind of like American football and soccer had a baby," I exclaim with a cheery smile, feeling like maybe I understand a bit more now.

"And the Saints wept," Cliona murmurs, her head jerking around in fear of someone overhearing what I just said. "Of all the roommates I could have been paired with my final year at college . . ."

I frown and smile and then frown again because I can't tell if she's saying that in a bad way or a good way.

Cliona licks her lips and grips my shoulders. "Rugby is ten times more physical than soccer. And it's been around for ages. It was a hooligan's game played by gentlemen. Though admittedly, there's not much gentle about Wolf. But all these other sports have just stolen bits from rugby. And American football is a joke. All those pads and the constant starting and stopping to hold a wee committee before every play. My God, what do they always have to talk about in those huddles?"

I shrug. "I don't really know much about American football either."

Cliona pinches the bridge of her nose and looks back toward the field, clearly giving up on me. I laugh and wrap my arm around her elbow, knowing full well this girl will forgive my ignorance. She once told me she loved that I didn't know or care about sports because she needed one part of her life to not revolve around athletics. Apparently, that appreciation is waning today for reasons I still don't understand because . . . rugby.

"Come on, Wolf! Finish this!" Cliona screams and points to where he's at on the field. "My brother has been running the pitch today in the no. 8 spot, which is brilliant because Trinity has been bolloxin' it up the whole feckin' game. We were a lost cause until Wolf turned things around. The timing of this couldn't be better for him."

"Why is that?" I ask, turning my attention back to the field, and my eyes can't help but fall on him. My eyes haven't left him for most of the game, I'm afraid. He's magnetic on that grass. Nimble for a guy of his stature, and he's easily the biggest on the team.

The dirt and sweat clinging to his body is mesmerizing. His dark, nearly black hair, which is normally this floppy, unkempt mess, gets curlier the more he sweats. It's very human of him when he's down there looking *inhumane*. The rage on his face when he's doing that hugging thing?

It sends shivers down my spine.

Also, what is it with rugby boys and their thighs? They're friggin' tree trunks! And the fact that they wear such tiny shorts means we can't help but gawk at them. They ripple in places I didn't know thighs could ripple. Wolf's legs are especially interesting because he's got a full display of ink on his left quad that gives him such an edge. Plus, he has a half sleeve on the lower half of his opposite arm, which means he's playing the part of "Conri the Wolf King" very well.

I find myself almost regretting coming to this match because now I won't ever be able to get this mental image of him out of my head. My best friend deserves far better than her girl lusting after her brother. And I deserve better than ogling over the cliché campus bad boy.

Cliona's eyes scan the crowd. "There are scouts here today to watch Wolf specifically because he still doesn't have an invite from a provincial team yet. They've scooped up their players from Trinity ages ago, but they're giving him one last look today. He's incredibly talented, but his bad reputation on the field holds him back."

"Why does he have a bad reputation?" I ask, even though I think I could have guessed that in the brief interactions I've had with him. He doesn't give I'm-a-team-player sort of vibes.

Cliona purses her lips. "He has a bit of a temper on the pitch. Basically, he's gotten into more fights on the pitch than half the pubs in Dublin see on a Saturday night. Red cards are a regular occurrence for him, I'm afraid. He's gone to therapy and gotten better the past couple of years, but most teams still feel he's too unreliable. However, a game like this could certainly help change their minds. Jaysus, I'm fierce proud." Tears form in her eyes as she marvels at the field. "I get that you don't know rugby, Fletch, but this here isn't just rugby. This is a feckin' miracle we're witnessing, and that's Moon creating it."

I smile at her term of endearment for her brother. Cliona told me that her nan calls them her Sunshine and Moon. Light and dark. And when you see the Reilly twins together, it makes perfect sense. Where he's quiet, dark, and brooding, she's light, smiling, and expressive. Polar opposites.

Their relationship is unique. They're close but in a casual, almost automatic sort of way. They check in with each other a lot and do that automatic twin dialogue. They support each other without hesitation, almost as if they're making up for their parents' lack of enthusiasm. And just to have terms of endearment for a sibling shows they mean a lot to each other.

My term of endearment for my little brother would probably be something slightly less meaningful, like Little Shit.

I should really reflect on why I reference poo so much.

Wolf being compared to a dark, ominous moon makes sense though. I actually met him long before I met his sister. It was my first year here at Trinity, and we had a class where we worked on a group project together. Had several meetings at the local pub all the students frequent called Mulligans. He was obviously handsome in that rugged, silent, rebel-without-a-cause way about him, but not at all my type. Not that it even mattered. The asshole acts like he doesn't remember me every time I see him. Like he didn't peg me with a nickname the first time we met.

"Stretch."

Real original label for the six-foot-tall girl.

I should call him Loom because that's all he does. Loom over everyone, all while saying nothing. Creepy, really. The first time I saw him in our dorm room after I started rooming with his sister, I was fresh out of a shower and wrapped in a towel. I walked in to find him standing by the window, looking completely unbothered. Meanwhile, I damn near broke out in hives from embarrassment. I tried to overtalk myself out of the awkward situation. I think I babbled something about hoping his sister doesn't have athlete's foot because I'm not about the sandals-in-the-shower life, while he said nothing. He just clenched his jaw in disgust.

Clearly, me in a tiny towel had absolutely no effect on him. Unless perhaps I offended him with the athlete's foot joke. He is an athlete. I'm sure they get it more often. That's just science.

This is why I matchmake.

I just don't seem to ever have any genuine chemistry with the opposite sex. I'm "too much" for most guys to handle. Perhaps being raised around mountain men and lesbians made me a bit too blunt and never taught me the art of subtlety. Even if I try to follow my own matchmaking rules, I fumble it. It's why

I've learned I'm better off serving others. At least then I get to experience love adjacency . . . if that's a thing. It fulfills me in a way that makes me happy. Gives me purpose.

The crowd swells as Wolf charges through and touches the ball down to score for the second time just before the whistle blows. He roars in the end zone like a man possessed—veins popping out of his neck, arms, and legs. His teammates maul him in celebration, looking like children hopping up and down next to this God-sized man.

Tears stream down Cliona's face as she stands beside me, frozen in shock. Fans jostle and pat her on the back all around us, everyone acutely aware that it's her brother out there nearly winning the game for Trinity.

"All Trinity has to do is nail this conversion and we've won," she says quietly as she folds her hands into a prayer and closes her eyes, refusing to watch.

The whole stadium is racked with emotion as a hush falls over the crowd. You could cut the tension with a knife it's so thick. And just before the team gets set to do the kick, a scuffle breaks out, and my eyes swerve to the sound of shouting coming from down below.

It's then that I spot Wolf standing toe to toe with a player from the other team. Well, not quite toe to toe as Wolf towers over him. The two of them are sniping at each other as Cliona's brother leans in and presses his forehead into the other player's, their lips dangerously close to each other as their communication escalates.

"Christ, not him," Cliona gasps as she grips the sides of her head and her eyes laser-focus on her brother. "Walk away, Conri. Just walk away."

The forehead pushing reaches a breaking point as Wolf lifts his hands to the other player's chest and shoves him.

The guy stumbles backward, regaining his balance before he

comes charging back, and the entire crowd gasps when Wolf pulls back his fist and sends it right into the player's face.

Instantly, a whistle shrieks, but it's too late. Fists start flying between the two players. In seconds, guys from both teams swarm in, trying to pull the two apart while also getting in scraps themselves.

The howl of the crowd rises sharp and primal as bodies crash together on the field, but not in the cute huggy way they were doing before. Everyone is going after everyone, but Cliona's giant brother is the standout. He is a terror out there, still charging full speed after the guy who started in with him. And when a referee steps in front of him to try to stop his momentum, that's when things take a dark turn.

A collective outcry tears through the stadium when Wolf does the unthinkable. He shoves the ref so hard the man's feet sweep out from under him, sending him tumbling backward onto his back with the whistle still tight between his lips.

Complete chaos erupts around us in the stands next. A guy grabs Cliona harshly on the shoulder, cursing out her brother, and another person grabs that guy, helping Cliona break free of him. Except Cliona doesn't want to be free. She stands up on her seat and shoves the man who touched her, thrusting her finger in his face to tell him off for putting his hands on her.

I glance down at the field to see the refs have ended the game due to the offensive behavior, resulting in a loss for Trinity. Someone asks Cliona how much money her brother was paid to throw the match, and it's then that the entire crowd begins to turn on her like a living beast. Several people thrust their fingers aggressively at her, one woman even throwing her drink at us. Cliona yells back at them, her voice hoarse with panic as she grabs my hand and drags me out of our seats, while struggling to make a call on her phone.

When we finally get out of the stands, a match steward

appears beside us suddenly, and I frown, wondering if Cliona and I are about to be kicked out. It takes me a second to realize that this guy is here for our safety. People know Cliona. The Reilly twins are somewhat famous in the world of rugby, even if they only play at the collegiate level, and apparently, whatever her brother just unleashed on that field has escalated us to the point of needing protection.

The steward escorts us through the concourse, past some refreshment stands, until we reach a set of double doors. He uses a card to buzz us through, and the dull roar of the crowd becomes muted as we're marched down a long concrete hallway. I hear Cliona's dad on the other line yelling back through the phone, and Cliona seems to be agreeing with everything he's saying.

A deep voice thunders down the hallway and becomes even louder when we're guided into what appears to be a men's locker room, where I find Cliona's giant brother sitting on a medic table being screamed at by the man who was coaching the team from the sidelines only moments ago.

Wolf is covered in dirt and grass stains, his body drenched with sweat as he breathes heavily and ignores the trail of blood sliding from his eyebrow over his cheekbone.

"You had one feckin' job!" the coach roars, thrusting his finger as he paces in front of his player. "You needed to play like your life depended on it. You knew the winner of this game gets to play for the Bateman Cup next week. You knew this, and you still acted like a fucking eejit! This was a do-or-die situation, and you just forced the ref to end the game and handed the other team our shot. What the hell were you thinking?"

Wolf's eyes stay focused on the ground as he says nothing, and I suddenly wish that Cliona had left me outside the door to wait. This isn't a place for me. I still don't know what a damn scrum is. I certainly don't belong in the Trinity Rugby men's locker room witnessing a coach discipline his athlete.

"You're going to be banned from playing rugby in Ireland for at least six months, you fucking knobhead! One-month suspension at the very least. This is how you're ending your career at Trinity. Not to mention this was your last chance. We had the scouts here just for you, for Christ's sake."

Wolf continues to stare at his cleats, doing that unbothered, irritating thing he does as he swipes away some sweat from his brow. I guess I feel better knowing it's not just me he gives that kind of emotionless reaction to.

"Do you really have nothing to say for yourself?"

"I'm sure if you—" Cliona tries to interject, but the coach turns murderous eyes to her.

"You stay the hell out of it, Reilly!" the coach snarls at Cliona, his tone echoing in the room.

In an instant, Wolf vaults off the table and closes the distance between him and his coach in three thunderous strides. My breath hitches as the muscles in Wolf's back coil, his chest heaving as his eyes flash with rage. He looms over the older man with a lethal kind of calm, like those silent dogs you never expect to bite but then end up ripping a person's face off. Is he going to do to his coach what he did to the ref? I wouldn't put it past him, I guess.

Wolf doesn't say a word. He doesn't have to. The look he levels at the aged man is a clear warning that if he ever speaks to his sister like that again, Wolf will bite back.

And strangely, that primal reaction in him scares and settles me. I like the confident, overprotective power he emits. It makes my skin heat to watch him defend something so violently, and it's not even me he's protecting.

God, what is wrong with me for being turned on at a tense moment like this?

"Go on, then, lad," the coach croaks, jutting his white, bearded chin upward. "Hit me too. End your career in rugby full stop after I gave you a chance. Then we can be done watching you waste all that God-given potential . . . and breakin' my damn heart."

The sweet Irish lilt of the coach's words causes my eyes to well with tears. I glance over to see Wolf's brows furrow as the two men exchange more silent words. It's clear there's a relationship here that isn't just a coach and athlete. This man cares about Wolf. He cares about his future. And Wolf seems to be fighting to accept that fact.

Cliona's gentle plea breaks the tension. "Moon, please," she begs, her voice barely above a whisper.

After a beat, Wolf turns to look at his sister. Only his eyes don't stay on her. They slide over right to me, clearly just now realizing that I'm in the room too. And the force behind his harsh gaze sucks the breath clean out of my lungs. A hot flush crawls up my neck while shame and dread tangle tight in my chest. I wish like hell I had the ability to disappear entirely. Why can't I be five feet tall? Just small enough to duck behind this steward and hide from the terrifying storm that is Conri Wolf Reilly. Because it doesn't take a genius to fill in the blanks of what he is silently saying to me.

Why the fuck are you here at the worst possible moment in my life?

My eyes are pleading with him while silently replying, *I'm sorry. This wasn't my idea.*

The tension breaks when Wolf takes a step back, dropping his head and showing some semblance of remorse.

The coach sighs as he slumps his shoulders. "The worst of it is I still had hope for you after graduation, lad. Leinster was here, and you had a real shot . . . but now . . . Jaysus. It'll take a miracle for anyone to want you."

Without another word, the coach turns to walk away, and the steward follows him out, leaving me, Cliona, and Wolf alone in the smelly locker room.

After a long, pregnant pause, Wolf's stony posture buckles as he flings his hand out and sends a stack of medical supplies flying into the wall. I jump at the noise, but not necessarily the outburst. I've seen my uncles lose their shit over far less, so this level of anger doesn't feel all that shocking to me.

Once the last roll of tape has stopped rolling on the floor, Cliona bravely asks, "Feel better?"

My eyes widen because this does not seem to be a good time to taunt the wolf. Then again, Cliona has never been one to hold back.

"Get your shite, and let's get out of here. Mam is driving down to collect you. You better not have fucked this up for me too, or so help me God, Conri." She turns on her heel and walks past me without a look back.

I hesitate in the room, tugging on Wolf's shirt I'm embarrassed to be wearing right in front of him. *Jesus, I probably look like one of his stalker groupies.*

I should say something, anything to acknowledge the difficult time he's going through, maybe even apologize for being here or offer some words of encouragement and hope. Help him see the bigger picture.

Instead, the drivel that comes out of my mouth is something that will haunt me until the end of my days.

"If it's any consolation, I think half the crowd is pregnant from watching your thighs out there today."

Wolf's face is completely unreadable as he stares back at me for an eternity. I offer a wobbly smile before he turns on his heel and makes his way over to the lockers, dismissing me like I don't even exist.

So, I do what I should have done before I opened my mouth. I scamper out of there with my tail tucked between my legs, cursing myself for that stupid, stupid joke.

But at least I didn't tell him about shitting my pants.

Chapter 3

Conversion: *Trying to turn one score into something more.*

Translation: *Desperate times call for desperate measures.*

Everly

"Well, are you all packed up?" my stepmom, Cozy, asks over the phone as I tape a box of my clothes shut.

"As much as I can be." I blow a strand of hair out of my face and pull the lid off the marker to write down my new address at Fletcher Mountain. "The rest I should be able to fit in the three suitcases I'm allowed on the plane."

"Good, good," Cozy replies cheerily. "How about finals? Are you ready for those?"

I groan. "I'm ready to be done with uni and studying if that answers your question."

"I'm ready for that too," she confirms. "It will be nice to have you home for good. We've missed you in Colorado, Sea Monster."

I smile because that's the nickname Cozy gave me back when she was just my nanny, and I was a mere eleven-year-old, bullheaded little terror. She was the last name on the list of people my dad and I were interviewing, but I knew the moment she walked into the boardroom wearing an orange tie-dye matching set that she was perfect. Not only for me, but for my dad.

My matchmaking origin story.

Now they're married and have my brother, Ethan, who's twelve, and they're in the process of building their third home up on Fletcher Mountain next to my uncles. If that's not a rave review for my matchmaking skills, I don't know what is.

"Are you bummed I'm moving straight to Fletcher Mountain and not coming back to Boulder for a bit?" I ask as I click the speaker button on the phone to have both my hands free to stack my box on top of the others I'll be mailing out tomorrow.

"Not at all," she answers genuinely. "I get it. You're twenty-two years old. You don't want to move back into your old childhood bedroom. Plus, if you're working on the mountain, it makes sense for you to live up there." Her tone shifts to one of teasing when she adds, "Not to mention, you moving into our cabin is the only thing that motivated your father's brothers to actually get some work done on our new build. I've been hounding them for months to make some progress, and they keep pushing me off, but the minute I inform them you're going to move in there when you get back, suddenly, the Fletcher Family Getaway is nearly complete. Those three uncles of yours are super excited to have their niece up there with them for a while. We've all missed you something fierce."

I smile at that, feeling an ache in my chest as I long for the comfort of my family. I've been abroad for a long time, and I can't wait to feel settled and grounded again. "I'm excited too. It'll be an experience to fully immerse myself in the mountain living. I can't wait."

"Trista can't wait either. Poor thing needs all the help she can get. She is drowning with how quickly her rescue is growing. She just got a donkey at the center."

"Oh, I know," I exclaim excitedly. "I'm fully informed, and I've already drafted up a plan of action for the summer. I'm hoping the guys have made progress on that lane I requested they add from the highway that gives more direct access to Mount Millie. That's a big part of my master plan."

"Putting that FESS degree from Trinity to good use already."

"Damn right," I confirm. "Mount Millie Rescue Center is going to be my bitch this summer."

"Some things never change with you, Sea Monster." Cozy laughs, and my head jerks up when Cliona opens the door to our room, her face red and blotchy, her posture slumped and defeated.

"Hey, I gotta go, Cozy. Did you need anything else?"

"Nope. We'll see you when we come out in a couple weeks to bring you home! Save me a pint of Guinness."

"Will do . . . Talk soon!"

We hang up, and I jump up from the ground and rush over to Cliona, who looks worse than I've ever seen her. And that's saying a lot because some of her rugby matches make her look like she was hit by a truck.

"What happened?" I ask, my voice trembling with concern. Cliona has been gone all weekend, back home with her parents and Wolf after the dreaded rugby match. We've texted a few times, but it seemed bleak with her parents, so I didn't have the heart to tell her that the whole campus is calling her brother Conri the Convict.

Not much of an upgrade from Conri the Wolf, I fear.

"Worst weekend of my life," she says and flops face-first onto the mattress.

"Why? You didn't do anything wrong."

"No, but this drama with Conri is bad. Thankfully, they ruled that his shove against the ref was accidental, but he's still banned for six weeks, which is just reaffirming my parents' hatred for rugby." Her face twists in pain as she fights back tears. "They don't want me to play for Leinster now."

I gasp. "But you already have a contract."

"They want me to decline it." She turns over and scrubs her hands over her face, wiping aggressively at her tears spilling down.

"But, Cliona, you're an adult. You can make your own choice in all this, right?"

"Oh, sure, and then just devastate my parents until the end of time." She scowls up at the ceiling. "I don't know what it's like in America, but in Ireland, a mam's guilt is about as bad as it can get. Like a rosary wrapped around your throat, meant to save you, when in fact it's just choking the life out of you."

I tilt my head to the side. "American guilt isn't real fun either."

"And, Everly, can I be honest?" she says, sitting up to look me straight in the eyes. "I don't know if I even want rugby without Wolf. To go play for a club while he's stuck working for the corner shop and studying for his law exam feels like such a shite thing for me to do to my brother, especially when he got into that fight because of me."

"What do you mean because of you?"

She winces as if she said too much. "It was my ex he got into it with on the pitch."

"Oh," I reply gravely. "I didn't realize."

"I don't even care about my ex. It's my brother I'm wrecked about. I have to save his career. We're the Reilly Rugby Twins. I don't want to lose that." She touches the sun and moon tattoo on the inside of her wrist.

"What can be done, exactly?" I ask, feeling my blood pressure rise with the desire to problem-solve this situation. I don't know Conri enough to really feel called to help him, but I'll do anything for Cliona. "Is there really no club that wants him?"

Cliona chews her lip thoughtfully. "As it stands today, there is still one club on the table. It's one that Wolf wasn't interested in before, but now, it's his only option. He just has to show proof that he's working on his anger."

"Okay, that sounds promising." I jump up on my feet and begin pacing the room. "We just need to do a bit of image rehab for him. Prove to them that he's not the animal he appears to be. Maybe he can do anger management classes or go to therapy. Or volunteer to help those less fortunate. Something that shows he's working on himself more than just the physical ways that rugby requires of him." My body shivers as I think of those incredibly thick thighs of his, and then I shake my head to get back on task. *Mustn't think of best friend's brother's thighs ever again.* "I can come up with an action plan tonight. I can even write him a letter that—"

"Fletch . . ." Cliona cuts me off, and I turn to find her sitting up and staring at me with a huge, bright smile. "Can you get him a job at your aunt's rescue center?"

"What?" I ask, my mind spinning at the bizarre words that just came out of her mouth.

"The place you're going to work after uni. It's a charity, right? A nonprofit? Could Wolf work there for your aunt?"

"I mean . . . maybe, but why would he want to? It's all the way in rural Colorado."

"The club that has interest in Wolf is in Denver."

I lower myself onto my bed to stare back at my roommate. "My Denver?"

"Are there any other Denvers?" Cliona laughs.

"I don't know." I struggle to blink away my shock because this is a weird merging of worlds right now, and I'm not sure how I feel about it all. To think of Wolf in my life back in Colorado feels intimate and bizarre. Like he's seeing inside my panty drawer.

God, "panty" is such a gross word. "Underwear" feels weird

too. Like something for old people. "Knickers" is more common over here, but that feels silly. Wolf will certainly think I'm silly. He'll take one look at me with my family, and it'll confirm everything he probably already thinks of me. Dumb, silly girl with a peculiar panty drawer.

Why aren't there better names for our undergarments in times like this when I'm having a little mental breakdown?

"Wolf's coach called in a favor to this Colorado team, and they said they'd consider him if he attends their summer training camp and proves himself. Show them that he's not—"

"Conri the Convict?"

Cliona's head jerks back. "A bit harsh, isn't it?"

I clench my teeth and wince. "That's what the whole campus has been calling him."

She rolls her eyes. "Of course they have. Traitorous eejits. Couldn't tell a rugby ball from a weak Guinness, but yeah, go ahead and take a grand dump on my brother, who's the only reason Trinity even had a chance at winning that match. Gobshites."

The room goes quiet for a long, awkward moment.

"Fletch, you have to help my brother. This is what you do. You help people. Only instead of matching him with the love of his life, you're matching him with a situation that could help his last chance at playing the sport he loves."

"Oh, Jesus, no pressure there." I chew my lip nervously.

"If he can prove himself in America, then he could eventually be picked up by an Irish provincial team. But he needs this first. I need this. I don't want to play without him. He's my brother. My best friend."

"I thought I was your best friend," I murmur pathetically.

"Ya can't be my best friend when you're already my soulmate." She smiles softly, and I feel that sentence like a healing balm to my troubled soul that I hide from the rest of the world all day, every day. I never had to hide anything from Cliona. From day one, she's just understood me. I'm not too much for her. I'm just enough.

"Can you talk to your aunt and see if she'd be open to a work program for him?" she asks again, getting us back to business. "It'd be like a J-1 student work visa thing. They wouldn't have to pay him much. And if they have room and board, that would be grand. Working for a rescue center would look great to his potential team, don't you think?"

I lift my brows, hating the fact that this would work great for Trista too. Laying it all out like this, I'd be an asshole not to at least ask about it. But the idea of spending the summer near Wolf, as his neighbor, working with him . . . it's turning my mind into a total blizzard.

"Does he even have any experience with animals?" I ask dejectedly.

"Course he does," Cliona peals, her voice pitching so high only dogs can hear it.

I can't help the hyenic laugh that bubbles up from my throat. "Sure, what the hell. I don't see why I couldn't convince my family to host a problematic rugby player who's been ousted from European rugby, who is also your terrifying, grumpy brother, for a summer. What's the worst that could happen?"

Cliona's smile is genuine. "If anyone can pull it off, Everly Fletcher . . . it's you. You are a mastermind, after all."

Chapter 4

Lineout: *The forwards from each team line up, and the ball is thrown in between them. Players are then lifted into the air by teammates to catch or tap the ball back to their side.*

Translation: *It's basically a buffet of sweaty, bulging man muscle.*

Everly

"Dad!" I yell from across the grass when I lay eyes on the man I owe the past four years of my life to. Hell, all my life. He's propped under a thousand-year-old tree, dressed in a crisp, gray suit and a black tie, looking like the perfect, put-together businessman he always is. However, the moment he spots me through the sea of students, his face contorts with overwhelming pride and sadness.

In seconds, he's closed the space between us and scooped me into his arms, squeezing my guts like he hasn't seen me all year.

Because he hasn't.

For the first time, I didn't come home over any of my holiday breaks. Cliona and I did a bunch of European excursions every chance we got. We backpacked in Greece and toured all the areas of Ireland I hadn't seen yet. We roughed it at a hostel in Barcelona and accomplished more travel in my last year than I did in my first three years in Dublin. But it was my final year, and I wanted to see all that I could before coming home. I was so busy I didn't even have a window for my family to come see me. It's incredible how easy it is to be adventurous when you have a great friend to travel with.

However, all that waiting makes this moment feel ten times more extraordinary.

"Damn, I've missed you, kid," Dad murmurs into my hair, lifting me up off the ground as he crushes me to him.

"Evie!" Ethan yells, and his arms wrap around my waist as Dad releases me. "What did you do to your hair?"

"Hey, butthead!" I tease and bend down to give him a big squeeze. "What did you do to your body? You're huge!"

My mom, Jessica, and her wife, Kailey, find me next, pulling me in for long, lingering hugs. They both play with my newly chopped hair—I cut it into a bob last week after finals. It was totally unplanned, but one second, I was watching this video online of a girl with my kind of hair looking fresh and fabulous, and the next, I was squealing in my bathroom as Cliona cut my long ponytail off. It ended with a trip to a hair stylist to give the bob some shape, but now I love it.

When my moms have finished obsessing over how great my hair looks, I glance around and find Cozy standing back in the distance, awaiting her turn. She does that a lot to be respectful to my mom, but it's totally unnecessary because everyone loves Cozy, practically as much as my dad does. She's impossible not to love.

With a laugh, my mom grabs Cozy's arm and pulls her into the group so I can assault my stepmother with a hug too. Three moms, a dad, and a brother is quite the unconventional family, but I wouldn't trade them for anything in the world.

"I'm glad you made it," I say, turning to look up at my dad.

"Damn flight delay," he mutters, his face tight and irritated.

"Don't get him going again," Cozy chides and looks to me. "Your dad was literally trying to book a private plane at the airport while we waited."

"If my plane was big enough to do international, I would have fired that up, believe me," he growls seriously. "They make it way too difficult to book last-minute private flights. I'm going to write a strongly worded email to that charter plane company."

"You do that, Max." Cozy pats my dad on the chest, and he glowers down at her, fighting back a smile that only she puts on his face like that.

"Fletcher!" a female voice calls out, and my whole family turns to see Cliona running toward me. It's move-out weekend at Trinity, and the whole campus is abuzz. Finals results and graduation ceremonies don't happen for a few months, so it's just a lot of families showing up to help get their kids home. "Your family made it, I see."

"Just barely," Dad grumbles under his breath.

"You must be the roommate," Cozy peals excitedly. "Everly has told me so much about you."

With a firm yank, Cozy pulls Cliona into a hug, and my roomie looks shocked at first but then sinks into it as everyone does with this woman. Cozy gives the best frickin' hugs. She says it's because she's plus-sized, and plus-sized people are cuddlier, but I think it has far more to do with her heart than her body.

A shiver runs up my spine when I spot Wolf approaching at a slow, leisurely pace toward us. He was in our room this morning, helping Cliona with her boxes, and I couldn't help but admire his huge muscles flexing around every load he hauled out in his silent but grumpy way that is his standard mood, it would seem.

His gold cross necklace shimmers over top of sleek black button-down. I'm shocked to see him dressed so formally for this meeting. He looks almost proper with his ink and thick thighs covered up. It contrasts greatly with the version of him

I've become used to on campus. This is definitely a version of Wolf I like seeing.

Feeling suddenly parched, I turn away and clear my throat to do quick introductions, avoiding eye contact with the terrifying Irishman who's about to fly over an ocean with me and spend the entire summer in my vicinity.

"This is my dad, Max. My moms, Jessica, Kailey, and Cozy. And my brother, Ethan."

"Oh, go on." Cliona balks. "You have quite a crew here, Fletcher. And this doesn't even include those crazy uncles you told me about."

I laugh and shrug. "Yeah, everyone wanted to get one last glimpse of campus before I say goodbye."

"That's lovely," Cliona says with a smile. "This is my brother, Conri, by the way. Everyone calls him Wolf."

All eyes move to the goliath beside Cliona and then shift upward in unison.

"Must be all those Irish potatoes!" Cozy says with a laugh as she yanks Wolf down for a hug next. I fight back a laugh as his face tightens with irritated confusion. "Why do they call you Wolf, then?"

He clears his throat like it's sore. "Conri means Wolf. Something my gran started when I was little." He shrugs like he's sorry he had to say that.

"Nothing little about you!"

"He used to be a runt," Cliona laughs and then winces when Conri cuts her a menacing glower.

"You're the one flying home with us tomorrow, I take it?" Dad steps forward.

Wolf frowns at my dad's offered hand but thankfully reaches out to shake it. "Yes, sir."

"Took an act of Congress to get the J-1 visa approved so quickly, but sounds like you're all set now."

Wolf clears his throat and forces a smile that looks painful. I have to cover my mouth to hide my amusement because, I have to admit, it's fun to see Wolf being the uncomfortable one for once instead of making everyone else feel uncomfortable.

The past several weeks, I've had to text him with all the things that he needed to send my family back home in order to get his work situation set up, and I swear the guy has a character limit on his text plan because all I ever got back was "K." I assume he uttered a few more words to Trista when he interviewed with her for the job. In all honesty, I was surprised she said yes to it all. But that's Trista. The girl is a think-outside-the-box type of person, and hiring a bad-boy rugby player to be her farmhand for the summer is way outside the box.

It's all maddening because if the roles were reversed and it was Wolf doing me this massive favor with his family and getting me set up with a huge opportunity, I would certainly find some modicum of dialogue for the host family.

"We so appreciate your help with everything, Mr. Fletcher," Cliona says cheerily. "Wolf is thrilled at the opportunity to attend the rugby camp in Denver, and it wouldn't be possible without your family—"

"Thank you for saying that," Dad interjects, offering Cliona a polite smile and then directing it to Wolf. "But you can thank my sister-in-law, whose rescue center it is. I merely just helped with the paperwork."

"And booked Conri's flight," Cliona adds with a wobbly smile. "That was extremely generous, Mr.—"

"Please call me Max. Not even my father went by Mr. Fletcher."

The mention of Grandpa causes my heart to squeeze inside my chest. It's been five years, and it still feels weird that he's missing all of this. If it's this hard for me still, I can't imagine how my grandma must be feeling back home. I make a mental note to carve out some quality time with her upon my return. We've been emailing during my time here, so she's well updated on my life and me on hers, but I still miss seeing her in the flesh.

As if Cliona senses my shift in mood, she reaches out and grabs my hand, pulling me close to her.

"I'm sorry we couldn't meet your parents today, Cliona and Wolf," my mom says with a soft smile.

"They couldn't leave the shop, I'm afraid, but we'll be home tonight for a big family dinner. Mam's doing a proper roast." Cliona smiles nervously at all four of my parents. I'm sure it's a weird feeling for her to be leaving one of the most prestigious colleges in all of Ireland and not have her parents here to even take a photo of her and her brother. Cliona shakes her shoulders and releases my hand to give everyone a wave. "We best get going so we're not late. Should we do our final goodbye now, Fletch?"

"I guess," I reply, a knot instantly forming in my throat.

She pulls me in for a bone-crushing hug that radiates through every part of me. I thought Clio and I shed all our tears last night as we spread out in our tiny, dilapidated dorm room. We shoved our mattresses together on the floor and reminisced about our college and travel experiences over takeout and macaroon bars until neither of us could keep our eyes open a moment longer. This morning, we cried as we packed our last few items, and then we cried as Wolf took pictures of us in front of the Rubrics building and Campanile—the same Campanile that we couldn't walk under before finals, or we would have failed all our tests, according to a campus superstition. We even cried at Mulligans over a morning pint. We've cried all over campus today.

Yet here I am . . . blubbering again.

I blink away the tears blurring my vision and catch Wolf

frowning down at me. That irritating pinch between his brows is permanent at the ripe age of twenty-two. I guess that's what he gets for being such a moody grump.

I sniff loudly and pull away. Cliona looks just as bad as me, and the two of us erupt into hysterical giggles. "We're a bleedin' mess, we are," she says, her accent thick.

"I know," I croak, wiping my nose off on my gown. My eyes start stinging again as I say, "I don't know what I'll do without you."

"Aye, you'll be grand." She glances at her brother, who has that same unreadable expression. "I'm sending a piece of me with you back home until we meet again."

I nod and meet eyes with Wolf, whose gaze is venturing on tender, which I didn't even know he was capable of. He looks away suddenly, so I turn my watery smile back to my soulmate. "Until we meet again, Cliona Reilly."

And without another word, she turns and shoves her brother back from our big family moment. Wolf's eyes hold mine again, and just that one searing look sends blood rushing to my cheeks.

When he finally turns and falls in stride with his sister, I take a moment to watch the Reilly twins walk away as I wipe away the last few tears from my eyes. If only it were Cliona coming to Colorado to play rugby instead of her frustratingly grumpy brother. Then maybe leaving Dublin wouldn't feel so difficult.

My dad's arm wraps around me as my brother Ethan's fingers slide through mine.

"Shall we grab some food?" Cozy asks cheerily.

I nod and smile. "I know just the place."

We make our way over to Mulligans on a backstreet near campus. I found this spot early in my time here at Trinity. That was when I learned the students in Dublin spend more time studying in pubs with pints than they do in libraries with silence. Gotta love the Irish.

"This is the pub that hired me to host my matchmaking clinics," I tell my family over a round of Guinness that I made them split the G on. *When in Dublin.*

"And how did the Irish enjoy your mastermind scheming?" Cozy asks with a knowing wink.

I point to a couple who are sitting in a booth in the corner. "I paired them up my second year, and they've been together ever since." I point to the female bartender behind the counter. "And last I heard, she was still with the guy I matched her with last Christmas."

My mom's all laugh. "How many people did you actually match up?"

"My Excel spreadsheet says sixteen couples." I smile proudly and push the fact that I failed on my own adventure deep down to the pits of hell. *Focus on the positive, Everly.*

"That's thirty-two people," Ethan says around a french fry.

"You bet your ass it is." I high-five my little brother. "Of course, it's possible I don't have updated information on all their relationship statuses. I try to check in every quarter, but this last year, I was kind of busy."

"Cliona seems wonderful," Cozy says, knowing that's why I was busy. "Did you ever set her up?"

"Naw, she had a bad breakup with a guy last year and said she's off men for the time being."

Cozy nods thoughtfully. "Her brother is a bit different. Quiet, isn't he?"

"Yeah, he kind of keeps to himself. You know how Cliona and I did a lot of traveling together this past year. Well, she always invited him, but he never wanted to come. Very much a homebody."

"He's gonna be a long way from home come tomorrow," Dad says, taking a sip of his pint. "I don't know if I like the idea of you living up on the mountain with him."

"Dad, I'm not going to be living *with* him. He's going to be in the barn apartment. That's on the opposite end of the compound. We'll barely see each other."

"Except you'll have to work together, right?" My father scowls.

"Maybe a little, but he's going to be doing maintenance and animal care. I'll be doing administrative and marketing stuff. Totally different departments. Not to mention, the guy can barely speak in full sentences . . . Hardly my type. You have nothing to worry about."

My father hits me with a flat look because Mount Millie isn't exactly a high-rise in Denver where we'll be operating on different floors. And I'm sure our paths will cross, but probably not that much. Plus, Wolf barely acknowledges my existence. To him, I'm just Cliona's perfectionist type-A bestie who excels at her own public humiliation. Whatever this overprotective father bit my dad has going on right now is for nothing.

Plus, even if Wolf were my type, I'd probably just figure out a way to sabotage that as well. Conri the Convict and Everly the Extra would *never* be a match in one of my spreadsheets.

"And not for nothing, but his sister is my best friend," I state pointedly. "She loves and trusts him, and I trust her, so we have to give him a chance."

My dad purses his lips, and I see Cozy hit him with her elbow. "Max, in case you didn't know it, this daughter of ours is an adult now. She can handle herself."

My mom shoots me a knowing wink from across the table, clearly much less concerned about all of this. She's probably grateful that Cozy is around these days to talk Dad down off his high horse.

My mother is a professional travel photographer and a major free spirit. Total opposite from my dad, but in more stark ways than Cozy is different from him.

Sadly, my parents separated when I was a toddler, so I have no memory of them together. In fact, I don't even have a memory of my mom being with a man. She and Dad got together in college, and I was a bit of a whoopsie. I think they tried to make a go of it but were never successful. After they split, she found Kailey, so my mom being married to a woman was just something that always existed in my life.

It wasn't until I was older that I realized my family situation was unique. I distinctly remember a conversation my mom and I had when I was ten years old about how she loved Dad romantically at the time I was conceived but later began to accept her true sexual preferences. I remember feeling amazed at the idea that she could like both boys and girls. It felt so comforting to me. I liked the idea that the world is full of possibility for people to find their perfect person, regardless of gender.

Not that that information has gotten me any closer to finding my person. I'm like a Michelin-star chef who makes award-worthy meals for others but manages to burn frozen pizza rolls for herself. Sad, pathetic, exploded pizza rolls.

Either way, I'm lucky with how well my parents get along. To have them both here, as well as Cozy and Kailey, is such a gift. I'm surrounded by great love stories and will be coming home to awesome relationships I helped build for all three of my uncles.

Sorry, but *I am a friggin' mastermind!*

"You're going to love the cabin," Cozy says excitedly, trying to change the subject. "It'll be some time before we're done with the mother-in-law suite for your grandma that we're building on the back, but the main part is fully done, and I've got it all furnished and decorated for you. It really came together nicely."

"Cozy, I told you not to go to any trouble for me." My eyes move to my dad, who just shrugs.

"You need a bed, Everly!"

"Well, thank you." I sigh heavily. "But I'm still guessing you went overboard."

"I didn't . . . not really. I kept it simple."

My dad makes a noise in the back of his throat, and the two exchange teasing smirks.

"I wanna live up on Fletcher Mountain too," Ethan says, crossing his arms with a dramatic pout. "Can I stay with you, Everly?"

I laugh and ruffle his hair. "I think Dad and Mom would miss you too much if you lived with me, buddy. But I promise once I get settled, we'll pick a weekend, and you can come up and help with all the animals. Sound good?"

He shrugs with an exaggerated nonchalance. "Fine, but only if I get to name the next rescue."

"Did you have a name in mind already?" I ask, because I know my brother all too well.

An evil grin spreads across his face. "Sir Poops a Lot." *Guess mentioning poop does run in the family.*

The table laughs as Ethan smiles proudly, and then we all tuck into our food while I share with them some of my plans for Mount Millie Rescue Center. I'm going to miss Dublin something fierce, but I know there is no place like Fletcher Mountain.

Chapter 5

Try: *A bold move pays off—crossing the line in more ways than one.*

Translation: *Wheels up, Conri the Convict.*

Wolf

I frown as the flight attendant directs me toward the front of the plane, up by those lay-flat pods that I've only ever seen on TV shows. Surely, this area can't be for me. There must be some mistake. Or maybe there's some cheap seats in the front I don't know about. Hell, I wouldn't be surprised if I had to ride at the bottom of the plane with the dogs. I'm a bleedin' fish out of water, and every person in the cabin of this plane can probably tell I've never even left Ireland.

I don't have the travel bug in me that Cliona does. I spend my summers working at my parents' shop and volunteering at these youth rugby camps in my neighborhood. The only reason I even have my passport was in case I was recruited to a European team. I bollixed that up good and proper, didn't I? Now I'm on my way to America to train with someone I've never even feckin' heard of.

As I draw closer to my seat number, my gut sinks when I see a familiar blonde in the window seat right beside mine. She's got sparkly silver headphones on, a fluffy blanket draped over her body, and a silk eye mask already propped up on her forehead.

Jesus ever-loving Christ.

"Oh, there you are!" Everly peals excitedly, waving at me like a maniac. "We wondered when you'd get here. Glad you made it to the gate okay. Didn't you see my texts? I was trying to find you in the airport."

I wince and look across the center row to spot Everly's family several rows up. Her dad gives me a tight smile that I know he doesn't mean.

I knew I'd be on the same flight with all of them. I just didn't know I'd be seated right beside the one girl I can't seem to ever get away from.

"What's wrong?" she asks when I make no move to sit down.

I clear my throat. "There's been a mistake with my ticket."

"What do you mean?" She rises out of her chair and makes her way over to grab the stub out of my hand. I can't help but eye the velvet rainbow-print pillow around her neck.

She's a lot, this one. She's like one of those glitter bombs that goes off and you find yourself picking glitter off your body for the rest of your life.

But her scent hits me all at once, and my eyes close as I drink it in. I could pick Everly Fletcher out of a crowd blindfolded because of that smell. It's this warm mix of vanilla and something soft and floral, like jasmine. It clings to her clothes, her hair, the room she shared with my sister. It's frustratingly appealing.

"This is right," she says, handing me my ticket back.

"You sure I didn't get swapped with your brother?" I glance through the doorway that leads to the standard-class seats. That's where I was mentally prepared to be. I was ready for my knees to be jammed against the seat in front of me or spread out so wide I'd get dirty looks from the person next to me for encroaching on their space. That's what a guy like me deserves. It's what I'm used to.

Everly buzzes her lips. "Wolf, my dad was trying to book a

private plane to Dublin because of a sixty-minute flight delay. He wouldn't fly anyone in economy."

I clench my jaw and frown. I knew Everly Fletcher was loaded. You can tell by the way she dresses with her fancy headphones and trainers. But booking a business-class flight for a perfect stranger who's meant to be the hired hand this summer on a farm is an obnoxious display of wealth. I'll just go ahead and add it to the list of things that irritate me about Everly Fletcher.

My teeth crack as I toss my carry-on into the overhead and begrudgingly lower myself into the posh seat. When I spread my legs out straight, I can't help but sigh with appreciation. It's decent, to be sure, but I wonder how much it cost. I would have rather had a cheap seat and the money in my pocket if anyone was asking . . . but of course, they didn't.

I'm not sure anyone has asked me anything in the past several weeks. One second, I'm getting screamed at by Coach Flannigan. The next second, my parents are telling me that I'm done with rugby and it's time to prepare for my law test. Then my sister is begging me to accept this pathetic Colorado team offer so she can play for her team, and Everly is blowing up my mobile with forms I need to fill out for a J-1 visa work program.

Bloody hell, I buggered up my life properly, didn't I?

Now I'm set to go to a training camp for a Major League Rugby team in Colorado that no one has heard of called the Denver Grizzlies or some shite. Cliona thinks it's destiny that the one team that invited me is the one team she has a friend living nearby that I could stay with.

I think it's the universe having a go at me.

Especially because the few phone calls I've had with the coach don't seem all that optimistic. He basically told me that if I can get my ass to Denver and show him I'm not a waste of God-given talent, I can have a spot on the team in autumn. So, nothing is even guaranteed at this point.

And not only do I have to train with their team all summer, but I'm also supposed to log community service hours like I'm some sort of delinquent. I have to prove that I can play the poster boy for the league's big push to grow their rugby fan base in Colorado. And if bad press is good press, they're already smashing that with the addition of me to the squad. My sister sent me a social media post with my name on it this morning from some local sports news station:

Denver's Bold Bet: New Rugby Franchise Banks on Ireland's Most Controversial Rising or Falling Star. Conri "Wolf" Reilly May Soon Become a Denver Grizzly Despite His Questionable Altercation with an Official

This is why I don't do social media. It's brutal for the mental health. It's all just a shite show of anxiety, depression, and cyberbullies tearing people to shreds for the craic. Suicide rates have only gotten worse with the growth of online living . . . and there's a reason for that.

Regardless of the latest headlines dragging me through the mud, here I am, flying to America and hoping I can fit in with this team well enough to earn me that elusive spot by summer's end. That kind of pressure isn't exactly good for the mental health either.

If it were up to me, I would have called it quits after Trinity. I'd have come home, worked for the shop, taken my law exam like my ma and da wanted, found a contract training program with a corporate firm in Dublin, and been done with it all.

But I'd be sabotaging my sister's mental health in the process, and I won't do anything to make her life harder than it's been. She's been through a lot the past couple of years with her breakup and is just starting to behave like herself again. She's feckin' brilliant at rugby, and women already have a tough enough time getting the recognition they deserve. So, if I have to keep playing to give my sister the confidence to go for it, then so be it.

Not to mention, if I give up on rugby now, then all the shite that I sacrificed when I was younger would be for nothing. I lost deep, meaningful friendships because of rugby. My mate Finn still doesn't speak to me for leaving him behind to join the team. This sport, frustrating as it might be, has still given me a lot. It gave me a sense of purpose when I had nothing. I can't just give up now when things get a tiny bit hard.

Which means I'm spending the summer biting my tongue, playing nice, and trying like hell not to come undone over the girl beside me, her scent all summer and sin and the sort of temptation I've spent years denying.

Should be grand.

"This flight is painfully long, but at least it's direct," Everly says with a bright, cheery smile as she sprays some sort of mist on her face and then offers it to me like it's fucking normal to spray shite on my face for no apparent reason. "Are you excited to see America for the first time? Are you leaving some girl back in Dublin brokenhearted? What even is your current relationship status, Wolf? Cliona never said."

I stare at the bubbly lass that I've not been able to escape in my four years at Trinity. My eyes do a cursory sweep of her hair. It's taking some getting used to since she chopped it all off.

Admittedly, I often admired Everly's blonde hair when it was long and wavy. It's this light, glossy platinum shade that complements her fair complexion. I saw the back of her locks more times than I will ever admit.

But now it's all different.

It's short and bouncy and full of attitude. Like it doesn't know how to behave, which bloody well suits her. She's constantly flipping it over from one side to the other, clearly still not used to it herself. And when a pale, nearly white strand falls around her face and clings to her full peach-colored lips? I have to look away, it's so disarming.

Frankly, it's frustrating how beautiful Everly Fletcher is. Not only does she come from what appears to be gobs of money, but she looks like it too. She's the kind of lass who would fit right in at a posh dinner party. That angelic look of hers was intended for the Victorian era with corset dresses and proper table manners. Not flopping around next to a filthy rugby player. It's why I've avoided her for all these years. I'm not into the princess do-gooder types, and she'd only distract me from my goal in life, which is to find myself a damn rugby team.

Her face falls when she realizes I'm not going to answer her question about my dating life. It's really none of her bleedin' business. With a roll of her eyes, she murmurs under her breath, "Excuse me for trying to make small talk."

I shake my head and look forward. I'm not doing this. I'm not getting more personal with Everly Fletcher. I've done a good job not speaking to her for the past four years, and I can keep that up now. I have a job to do in America, and I need to focus on that.

Just because she's mates with my sister and I had to take a bunch of photos of them crying all over campus yesterday doesn't mean I'm going to soften toward the American—even if Cliona ordered me to be nice to her before I left.

"We've never lived in different cities before, and now we're about to live in different countries," Cliona says, her voice tight with emotion as we wait for the bus that's going to take me to the airport this morning.

"You need to look out for yourself, alright?" I frown at her, my body

tense with worry. "Don't go out partying too much with your new team. And stick with the no-dating policy for now."

"Ah, go on," Cliona bites back. "I don't need you to tell me that. Don't forget, before your growth spurt, I was the one fighting your bullies off, not the other way around."

"I'd never forget that, Sunny." I exhale heavily and call her by the nickname our gran gave her when we were kids. I don't use it often, but it feels fitting when it's such a monumental moment for both of us.

"We're going to do a video call on our birthday in a couple months, okay?" she says, her eyes filling with tears. "So we can do our cake together like always."

A knot forms in my throat. "Gonna be hard to blow out each other's candles on a video call."

"I know, but we're growing up. We had to miss a birthday together eventually."

I huff out a noise of discontent. "You'll be careful though, yeah? Don't walk alone late at night and all that."

"In case you didn't know, I'm about to play rugby professionally and can look out for myself, ya eejit." She flexes her bicep at me before pulling me in for a hug. "And please be nice to Everly. I know she's a lot, but if you give her a chance, you'll find out she's the perfect amount of too much."

"If you say so," I grumble under my breath, my shoulders tightening at the mention of her name.

"Go on, then. Your bus is pulling up." She breaks our hug and gives me a hard push. "Go kill it for those Grizzlies, Moon."

"You go kill it for Leinster, Sun."

Regardless of what my sister said about being nice to Everly, I'm not letting this American girl natter on for the ten-hour flight from Dublin to Denver. I'll park myself in the toilets if I must. Being nice doesn't mean I have to talk to her nonstop.

So, to make my boundary clear, I slide my headphones over

my ears and yank my hood down across my eyes and prepare to do what I always do: ignore the girl that I met years ago in a business marketing class. The girl who was a pushy pain in my arse then and still is a pushy pain in my arse now.

Though admittedly, she was easier to avoid when I was just staring at her from a distance.

Everly

I've never been a good plane sleeper. I can't seem to get my brain to shut off. I just think about too many things. My doctor back home gave me a few sleeping pills a couple of years ago, but I swear they're horse tranquilizers because the few times I've tried them, I don't remember getting off the plane.

So now I reserve those pills for the minute I arrive home and want to sleep like the dead for eight to twelve hours.

Which means I'm spending this ten-hour plane ride just thinking away. About people, about things I've said to people, things other people have said to me. I think about when the next meal is coming around and the fact that I seem to be the only one on the plane not sleeping. I think about my job and my future and my family and what it's going to be like living on a mountain with them and Cliona's hot, scary brother for an entire summer.

This plane ride in particular, I'm also thinking about how massive Wolf's thighs are. He wore athletic shorts on the plane, which just seems weird to me. Too exposed. Too casual. How is he not cold? I'm tucked under a blanket with thick, fuzzy socks on, and I'm freezing. But he's just letting all that man muscle hang out. I wonder if his buffness has him always running hot? Maybe extra muscle is like a built-in heating blanket? He certainly looks warm.

His thigh tattoo is interesting as well. It's an intricate portrait of a wolf howling at a moon, with Celtic knots wrapped all the way around his gigantic thigh. I assume the wolf has something to do with his nickname, and the moon has to do with the sun/moon labels his grandmother gave him and his sister. Does he like his grandmother more than his mother? I wonder. It's hard to tell. Cliona has shared some of the tension with her overworked parents, but Wolf here feels like a mystery I'd like to unravel a bit more.

There's also what looks to be some GPS map coordinates inked in his tattoo, and I can't help but wonder where they route to. Is it an invasion of privacy to type them into my phone to find out?

I'd love to ask him what it all means, but the guy has been passed out cold since takeoff. He missed meal service and snack service. Lucky for him, I accepted his food and tucked them into the seat in front of him so he can eat it when he wakes up.

His neck is totally going to hurt tomorrow. I can't help but rub my own neck in response. Why did he never lay his seat down? Such a waste of a good business-class spot. Cliona texted me to look out for him because he's never been outside of Ireland. But it's kind of hard to look after someone who literally doesn't even show up to the gate until the last minute and who willingly puts his sports player body in such an uncomfortable position. Does he just not care about being early for an important flight? Or is he just keen on avoiding me for as long as possible? I'm going to guess the latter.

Wolf's head jerks out of nowhere, and he groans a deep, rumbly noise, his brows furrowed as if in pain. This is ridiculous. He needs to lie back, even just a little. He has to start that rugby camp in a couple of weeks. He can't be all messed up from a long flight.

Taking matters into my own hands, I unbuckle my seat belt

and crawl onto my knees to lean over the partition between our two seats so I can access his chair controls. Holding my breath, I bite my lip as I push the button and pray like hell he'll sleep through the decline, but I am wrong. So very wrong.

With a grunt, Wolf shoots up like he's been punched in the gut as he catches me with my finger on his controls. His sleep-filled eyes gape at me like I'm a kid he busted breaking into his cookie jar, and I feel one inch tall in this moment.

God, why am I like this? Why did I care if his neck would hurt? Why didn't I let sleeping dogs lie instead of poking the grumpy wolf with a stick?

I huff out a strange laugh. "Sorry . . . it's just . . . your neck looked cramped, and I didn't know if you knew how to lay your seat flat, so . . ."

My voice trails off as he glowers back at me and slides his headphones off his ears. "I don't need your help, Stretch."

He crosses his arms over his chest and turns away from me while I sit there with my lips parted, staring back at him in shock.

The asshole *does* remember me from class. That's the same nickname he pegged me with my first year here, but he hasn't used it since because he's been too busy . . . pretending not to know me? What the actual fuck? That is crazy work on its own. But couple that with the fact that he's been nothing but dismissive to me for my entire last year of university, and I'm so very done tiptoeing around this Irish jerk. He's not a misunderstood bad boy. He's just a fucker.

With a huff, I jab my finger into his shoulder so he's forced to look at me. "I knew you remembered me. Why have you been acting like you don't?"

His stormy eyes are slits as he glances down my body in a way that makes me feel unnerved. "I haven't been acting like anything. Just let me sleep."

He turns away again and prepares to pull his headphones back up over his ears, but I am not done. This man will not mistake my kindness for weakness. I grew up with fucking mountain men uncles, okay? Not just uncles, but like . . . grown-ass men who let me drive my first ATV at age eleven and told me to aim for the trees because they would slow me down. I am not the pushover that Wolf might think I am.

I reach over and yank his headphones off, which doesn't seem like the smartest thing to do because his nostrils flare with agitation, and that muscle in his big, square jaw twitches.

God, I really hate how hot he looks when he's angry. And considering he's angry all the time, he pretty much always looks hot, which is just how it goes for men. They get to be brooding and sexy, while women get labeled with a resting bitch face if we're not always smiling.

Unfortunately, Conri Wolf Reilly is the epitome of brooding hot. His face is angular and striking, his brown eyes the color of watered-down whiskey. Not to mention, there's something guarded in the way he looks at you. Like he's seen you naked and is judging every square inch of you. The only thing is, I can't tell if he's judging in a good way or a bad way.

And that mouth of his. It makes my insides clench. It's sharp lines and threatening twitches that deliver perfectly harsh replies. But his lower lip has a mind of its own. It's full and soft—completely at odds with the rest of his cruel face. It gives a hint of suppleness that makes you wonder how it would feel pressed against your mouth, your neck, your breasts, your . . .

I expel a strange breath as I realize just how far my thoughts got away from me. Maybe it's the stress of not knowing what's coming next. Or maybe I'm just a sucker for punishment. Either way, I am not ogling my best friend's grumpy brother. I'm here to give him a piece of my mind.

"I would love to leave you alone, *Wolf,* but in case you didn't know, your sister asked me to help you out with this job, and that's what I'm trying to do."

He blinks back at me, his long dark lashes thicker than they have any right to be. "Well, I don't need any help sleeping, *Stretch*. Other lasses a lot less fussy than you have already tired me out proper."

His eyes lick up and down my body, and it takes me all of three seconds to pick up what he's saying before I jerk back with disgust. "I'm not trying to help you sleep like *that*," I sputter, my face heating with mortification. "I'm trying to help you with everything else."

"What the hell are you on about?"

"I mean my family." I seethe, my hackles fully raised now that he's being completely inappropriate. "I thought I could use this plane ride to debrief you on everyone you're going to meet and interact with in Colorado, but you don't seem to give a shit. You're too cool to care about the fact that I stuck my neck out for you with the people I love more than anything in the world, and so help me, Wolf, if you fuck this up and disrespect them or cause problems for me or make a scene or start a fight, I will be the one getting assault charges because I will . . . *kick your ass*."

My voice comes out in a strange, squealy tone that I've never really heard before. But then again, I'm not sure anyone has ever made me as frustrated as this boy beside me. I'm normally someone who keeps the peace, not stirs things up.

But Wolf Reilly makes me crazy.

His face twitches into something I think . . . *no* . . . couldn't be . . . is he . . . ? Is he . . . *laughing at me?* I mean, he's not fully laughing, so it's hard to tell, but whatever his face is doing is certainly not the permanent scowl I've grown accustomed to over the past year.

This motherfucker.

The absolute *audacity* of this asshole cracking a grin over my emotions is enough to make me want to scream into my gay pride ally neck pillow.

With a growl, I turn away from him in my seat and open my plane window shutter to stare into the dark abyss as this tin can I'm trapped in with an infuriating Irish boy continues catapulting us over the ocean. "How you and your sister can be so completely different is really something that should be studied by science," I murmur under my breath. "Cliona is cool and fun and open-minded. She loves talking and pestering me with questions about my life back home. She certainly would never sit on a ten-hour plane ride next to me and not utter a single word. Or pretend not to know me for years at a fucking time."

After a long pause, Wolf releases a heavy sigh beside me. "What do you want me to know?"

"Nothing. You're clearly all good. You know everything." I frown back over at him. "Good luck in America. I hope you have a great trip."

He levels me with an unamused look. "Just get on with it, Stretch. I know you want to talk, and I'll sit here and listen."

My eyes narrow as he stares back at me expectantly, waiting for me to grace him with an answer. Part of me wants to be stubborn and give him nothing. After all, he all but admitted that he went out of his way to avoid me this whole time. But the better part of me knows that the more informed he is, the stronger chance I have of this all working out. So, with one deep breath, I pull my phone out and open my gallery of photos to give him the Fletcher family 411, complete with visual aids.

"You're going to be living on what's called Fletcher Mountain. It's my uncle Wyatt's property. Wyatt is one of four brothers, my dad is the oldest. Wyatt is super passionate about eco-friendly, sustainable living. It's ninety-five percent of what he does with the Fletcher Brothers Construction business that my grandpa started. Wyatt is married to Trista, your new boss and the owner of Mount Millie. They have a daughter named Stevie, who is three and a half years old and has the cutest curly brown hair I've ever seen on a kid."

"Should I be taking notes?" Wolf asks, and I look up from the photo of Stevie on my phone and see a little spark of humor in his eye.

I glare back at him. "Can I continue?"

His nostrils flare, but he thankfully lowers his eyes to my phone again.

"This is my uncle Calder. Don't let the tattoos scare you—he's a total softie. He lives on the mountain too. He just got married to my stepmom Cozy's best friend, Dakota. They eloped to Vegas, despite my constant begging them for a traditional wedding. I'm not surprised they did their own thing since Dakota was married before, and Calder cared more about getting a new cat than having a fancy wedding, but I'm bitter about it still. I set them up, and I feel like they owed it to me to have a wedding, but whatever, it's not up to me, I guess."

"You matchmake your uncles too?" Wolf asks, his eyes blinking back at me. "So, the stuff you did at uni . . . the dating events at Mulligans . . . that wasn't unusual behavior for you?" I can't tell if he's impressed or thinks I'm a nutjob.

"That was just me passing some time, Wolf," I reply with a coy shrug. "I matched my dad and Cozy when I was just eleven years old. This is my life's work."

"Christ," Wolf murmurs under his breath.

"Do you have a problem with falling in love?"

"No," he bites back, his tone deep. "I just think some people aren't built for love. Some of us are just better off in scrums."

I frown back at him. "Oh yes, the rugby hugging thing."

He blinks back at me in horror.

I purse my lips, feeling proud that I knew that term. "Well, to me, a scrum looks like a helping hand, which is very similar to matchmaking."

He huffs out a noise of discontent. "Did any of your uncles *ask* for a helping hand?"

"No."

"My point exactly."

"Can I finish, please? I still haven't told you about my uncle Luke, and he's one of my best success stories, so if you could listen and not judge, that would be great."

Wolf sits back and shakes his head, silently allowing me to continue as I pull up wedding photos from two years ago.

"Luke and Addison are on Fletcher Mountain as well and expecting a baby boy any day now. I had a big hand in their marriage-of-convenience-turned-real-life wedding a couple years ago. I'm thrilled that I'll be just next door to them for whenever the baby decides to come. I know Stevie and this new baby are just my cousins, but my uncles are the big brothers I never had, so I feel like an aunt to them. Seeing Fletcher Mountain turn into a growing family compound makes my romance-loving heart swell with pride."

"Wait, did you say you're going to be living on the mountain too?" Wolf asks, his eyes wide and laser-focused on me.

"Um . . . yes. My dad and Cozy have been building a getaway cabin up there this past year. And since I'm working for the rescue facility this summer—"

"You're working at the rescue center also?" His eyes are the size of saucers now.

"Yes. Did Cliona not tell you any of this?"

"No, she did not." He scowls down at the floor, muttering something under his breath. "Your Aunt Trista mentioned you doing some social media stuff, but I didn't know that meant you were actually working there and living there. Christ." He murmurs the last part under his breath, but I hear it loud and clear.

"I'm sorry, but do you have a problem working with me?"

"No problem," he bites back and turns forward, revealing that muscle in his square jaw again. "No problem at all."

"You certainly *look* like you have a problem." I huff indignantly. However, it feels good to make this guy uncomfortable. He's been making me squirm my whole senior year, and maybe even before then, whenever I'd see him on campus. I didn't see him in our dorm room that often, but he frequented Mulligans a lot, like I did—not that he ever talked to me. He was always just sort of there in the background. Watching. Judging.

"I don't have a problem," he growls and then asks, "Why aren't you working for your father's company? I'm sure he'd give ya a corner office and your own assistant who'll fetch you a fancy coffee whenever ya like."

I glare at his tone but wince at the fact that he's not far off. "For your information, my plan *is* to work for my dad's franchise development company in Boulder eventually. My degree in business marketing will serve me well there. But I need to get three years' field experience first. It's his policy. In the end, it's still nepotism, but at least I'll have some understanding of how other businesses operate before coming in to work for him."

"So, your idea of field experience is to work for another family member's business?" Wolf asks with a pointed look.

"Experience is experience, okay?" I bite back defensively. "My family are all very entrepreneurial, and I like to help. Your parents have a family business too, right?" I ask, tilting my head to eye him with a challenge. "Cliona told me they run a corner shop. That's like what we Americans call a convenience store. Did you really never consider taking it over for them after college?"

"Sure, for a bit, but it's not the kind of place you need a degree from Trinity to run." Wolf's face twitches with irritation. "And I'm not exactly eating from the same silver platter you are, Stretch. The only reason I even got into Trinity was because of my grades and my rugby skills. So don't you go trying to compare your situation with mine. We are very different people. I have had to work for every single scrap that's been tossed at me in life."

His tone is harsh and dismissive and pokes at a part of my past that I've struggled with before. And I hate even saying that in my head because it's giving "poor little rich girl."

But . . . it's weird growing up with money. In high school, kids would often look at me differently for the privileges I had, which was silly because it wasn't like I was driving a Lamborghini or carrying a Prada backpack. I drove a Jeep truck, something sturdy that handles well in snow. And at best, my wardrobe was lululemon leggings or the occasional SKIMS—nothing outrageously expensive or designer by any stretch. And yes, my dad has a private plane, but he uses it for work more than leisure. And I'm far from the only kid whose parents have a ski home in Aspen.

God, I really do sound like a poor little rich girl.

And I hate that because I'm fully aware that first-class flights aren't the norm. I've learned that taking vacations every year is a luxury, or even having an air-conditioned garage. It's crazy the little things you just assume are normal until life shows you otherwise.

Like having a married lesbian for a mother or three uncles all living on a mountain compound together.

The point is, I'm aware of my privilege and insulated life. It's why I thought going to Ireland and broadening my horizons would help me branch out a bit and see the world differently. Maybe figure out how to make new friends.

However, all Dublin did was point a mirror in my face that said: *Everly, sometimes you're just "too much" for people to truly accept.*

My stomach twists with the fact that Wolf so easily sees that in me without even knowing my upbringing. I guess I can be grateful he's making his judgmental remarks to my face instead of behind my back like people in high school did . . . painful as it might be.

I lick my lips and hit him with a challenging glower. "You're right, I've lived a pretty good life. And I'm lucky because my family is super supportive. I know going to college abroad was a big expense, and I'm grateful for the experience. But maybe my gratefulness is why I want to work for family. I like the idea of helping someone I know and love, and I guess I'm fortunate again because I have that opportunity. But that exact opportunity is working out well for you so far, isn't it?"

His brows pop upward as he stares back at me with that frustratingly unreadable expression. His eyes trace over my face like he's committing it to memory. The dark smolder in his brown gaze makes my stomach flutter, and I struggle to put a damper on that feeling because being attracted to my best friend's twin brother is not the vibe I'm going for this summer. Especially one who so clearly despises me.

And honestly, fuck him. He's not going to point at me like I'm the privileged brat when his connection to his sister is what got him on this flight and gave him the chance to rehab his image. The one he screwed up by turning into a rager on the field. Life is all about connections, and he's not completely innocent in that.

"I suppose you're right," he replies through clenched teeth, his eyes staring right at my lips. "I guess we'll just have to make the best of this summer."

With a heavy sigh, he turns away, yanking his hood back up over his head as he folds his arms tight across his chest like he's rebuilding that wall that was between us all this time. His voice is deep and rumbly when he adds, "Thanks for the family connection, Stretch. I'll try my best not to embarrass you."

He turns his back to me, and I release the breath I didn't even realize I was holding as I wonder for the hundredth time how I'm going to get along with this rugby boy I'm saddled with for the summer.

I'm usually pretty good at figuring out what makes people tick. I consider myself an empath of sorts, which is what makes me so good at matchmaking. But Conri Reilly is a horse of a different color. I don't even know who I'd match him with if I had to pick someone. No one back at Trinity comes to mind.

Not that matchmaking is what this summer will be about anyways. I'll be working full-time and enjoying family time. Certainly not focusing on a burly Irish boy who hides under a big chip on his shoulder.

Am I curious about that something deep and a bit scary that I see in him? Yes. Am I slightly determined to find out what that something is? Yes.

But that's not what Cliona meant when she asked me to look after her brother. He's not a project for me to fix or someone I should be determined to make like me by the end of summer. That's not what the next three months will be all about. *Just keep reminding yourself of that, Everly.*

Chapter 6

Maul: *When the ball carrier is held up by opponents but stays on their feet, and teammates pile in to push them forward, a moving, heaving contest for control.*

Translation: *The two are bound together whether they like it or not.*

Wolf

I left Dublin, Ireland, at 3:25 p.m. on a Friday, and I ended up in Denver, Colorado, at 5:56 p.m. on a Friday, which means I took a flight back in time. A flight that was far chattier than I expected, but that's Everly Fletcher for you. Cliona is right—Everly is a lot.

Little does she know, I knew that information long before she did.

Since the moment I met her first year, I could tell she was a typical, over-the-top American. Like a walking greeting card. Always chipper. Always happy. Always smiling. And far too trusting of people. She moves through life as if she's never been hurt, and for girls like Everly, they probably haven't. That's privilege for ya. If only we could all be so lucky. I knew then, as I know now, that we'd never be friends. She's sunshine and rainbows, and I'm dark and cloudy storms.

The Fletcher family is quiet as we all load into a large black Sprinter van that Everly's father booked. I'm sure renting this big thing cost more than the single vehicle my parents own, but I suppose I'll have to get used to being around people who are comfortable having money.

It has perimeter seating, and I snag a spot behind the driver, only to have Everly's brother sit right beside me. It wasn't ten minutes down the road before the wee man they call Ethan managed to fall asleep leaning against me.

"Oh, I'm sorry. I can move him," Cozy offers, clearly jet-lagged herself. I hold my hand up to stop her from getting up.

"He's no bother," I murmur, and she smiles a silent thanks as she leans on Everly's dad.

I turn, and my eyes snag on Everly seated across from me. She looks away quickly like she wasn't gawking at me like I'm an alien, so I turn my gaze to the window to do the same.

Colorado is a far cry from home, to be sure. Everything is bright and new and covered in fresh pavement. Ireland is ancient everywhere you go. Damp and green and mossy and damn near tilted like it's drunk all the time. Here, it's all wild and sharp. Bigger skies, taller mountains, wide-open spaces with air so dry I crave a pint almost instantly.

As we make our way toward Boulder, Everly's father points out something called the Flatirons. The only way I can think to describe them is tall, slightly smashed mountains—almost like an incomplete painting. Like someone was drawing out a mountain landscape and then got frustrated and swiped their hand along the side of it to start over. They could be compared to the Cliffs of Moher, maybe, but flipped on its side and blasted with far more sunshine. Reminds me of me and my sister. She would be the Flatirons, and I would be the Cliffs of Moher. Bit of light and dark vibes. Sun and moon.

The van pulls through the city of Boulder, where Everly grew up. It's a posh place that seems very well kept up. Another complete opposite of Dublin. I expect this is the kind of place that serves oat milk in all its coffee shops and has a yoga studio on every corner. It's also clearly a pet-friendly town because there are people with dogs everywhere I look. I even saw a bloke walking around with his cat strapped to his chest.

Dublin is messier. Louder and more run-down with its age. Where Boulder smells of fresh mountain air and new trainers, Dublin reeks of chip vans, spilled pints, and regret over drinking too much the night before.

But don't get me wrong, I fucking love Dublin. It's that dirty grittiness to it that feels like home. This place feels like existing inside a film.

We stop at Everly's father's giant house, and everyone piles out, saying their goodbyes to their daughter and offering polite waves to me. They apologize for not seeing us up to the mountain but assure Everly that they'll be by tomorrow with more of her things and to celebrate her homecoming properly. She kisses them all goodbye, and when the door closes, leaving just the two of us in the van, she slumps back in her seat, looking wrecked with exhaustion.

It makes me feel bad.

I could have been kinder on the plane. She didn't deserve my harsh attitude. And she's right. I should be grateful for her and her family's help with all of this. It is my mess, after all. If I'm going to be forced to be around her all summer, I probably should try to be . . . well . . . friendly, I suppose.

"Hey there, Stretch?" I croak, and she turns her eyes from the road to look at me seated directly across from her. "Sorry for being a dickhead on the plane, alright?"

Her brows furrow, and when the setting sun blasts through the window and illuminates her face, I see that her blue eyes are wet and red-rimmed.

My heart lurches as I stand up to move over to her. "Fuck, I didn't mean to make you cry."

"You didn't make me cry," she snarls at me like I'm an eejit, so I sit back down. "I'm just . . . exhausted . . . and homesick."

I tilt my head and look around. "But you are home, aren't ya?"

"I know that," she growls and turns away to dig into her purse. "I just regret committing to going to Fletcher Mountain first. I would have loved a night back at my dad's, but then I make my mom feel bad if I don't stay at hers, and it becomes a whole thing." She pulls out a wee bottle of pills and tosses one into her mouth, swallowing it down with a quick drink of water. "Forget it. You wouldn't understand."

She pulls her legs up and tucks them under her chin, and I can't help but marvel over her. To care about everyone else's feelings all the time must be exhausting. No wonder she's shattered.

Not to mention, we're both on the precipice of big changes in our lives, not knowing exactly what the future holds. Transitioning from university life to a real life. And Everly perhaps has it even worse, going from her old life in Boulder to a new life in Dublin and back to her old life, but slightly different. It's a lot.

I clear my throat and offer, "I can understand being overwhelmed if that's what ya mean."

She nods woodenly and then sighs, resting her cheek on her knees. "I just need to crash."

"Maybe close your eyes for a bit. My gran always said things have a tendency to look better in the morning."

She shoots me a wobbly smile and then lies down on the bench, stretching those long legs of hers out to get more comfortable. I turn away to let her rest and watch the view slowly shift from city highways to steep mountain canyons. There are loads of trees and forestry up here too. A beautiful sight that I think I could get used to.

After about thirty minutes of winding roads, I see a quaint little cutout of a black bear next to a sign for Jamestown.

WELCOME TO JAMESTOWN
EST. 1883
ELEV. 6926'
POP. 250

It's one of those tiny communities that you could blink and miss entirely. Lots of those in Ireland too, not that I've ever spent much time in any of them. I spot a wee pub on the left where the sign reads:

THE MERCANTILE
WHERE EVERYONE IS A LITTLE FERAL

I can't help but smile at that. It looks relatively decent—nothing like our old brick pubs in Dublin, but there's at least no men with dogs outside of it, so I already like it better than what I was spotting in Boulder.

The van slows and takes a sharp right, and I spy a small wooden sign that says Fletcher Mountain. Christ, is it that easy to buy mountains in America that you can give them your surname? You'd never get away with that in Ireland. Everything has some sort of historical relevance to it that protects it from the likes of capitalism. This truly is the Wild West out here, isn't it?

We lurch up the gravel lane, the setting sun slicing through the thick forestry. I wince as we take a sharp curve that has no guardrails at all. Back in Ireland, we have our share of rough country roads, but they at least have the decency to be flat. This feels like off-roading on the back of a bleedin' dragon.

I glance over and am shocked to see that Everly is sleeping through this treacherous journey. I half wish she were awake to help calm my anxiety a bit. If she were, I'm sure she'd be insufferably talking nonstop, pointing out everything with teeth-gritting details. Her nattering on has this annoying and calming effect I can't explain.

Surely, this driver knows what he's doing, right?

I turn back to look out the window and force myself to enjoy the views and stop fretting about the driver. Tall pine trees press in from both sides as streams of sunlight bleed through the canopy overhead. I swear the air shimmers like it's half-magical or something. I sort of hate how fascinated I am by it. I'm proud to be Irish, and I never imagined I could be impressed with anything more than my home country, but this here . . . this is proper beautiful.

I spot a wee sign and a turnoff that says Mount Millie Rescue Center and crane my neck to get a better look. That must be where I'm to spend my days working this summer. Should be interesting. I grew up just north of Dublin, so I'm pretty much an urban boy through and through, but I'm no stranger to hard work. So long as I don't have to handle the animals too much, I should be just fine.

We crest over a steep incline, and my jaw drops when I see the wide, sunlit clearing ahead that reveals what must be the Fletcher compound.

"Christ, this is like another village up here," I murmur to myself as we bypass a large red barn and a pasture on our right. The driver continues up the gravel path that leads us toward three unique cabins, all spaced far enough apart to give a guy some space, but close enough together you're still very much neighbors. The first one has striking, angular windows and looks like it was built right in the thick of the forests. There are giant panels on the roof that I assume are solar. I remember reading up about Mount Millie before I said yes to the work visa opportunity, and its headline on their website said that it was Colorado's first fully sustainable rescue center.

The next home is a rustic, more modest log cabin with a front porch that has some nice rocking chairs out front. It's similar to the third one, except the third has flat wood siding, but it's also somewhat modest. My eyes snag on a chicken perched on its porch railing, like the damn thing lives there or something.

When I turn my gaze to the final cabin tucked in the back and nearly concealed by the trees . . . my jaw can't help but drop.

Holy Christ on a bike, it's something.

It's a glass, modern, boxy sort of structure that's perched near the edge of the ridge and wrapped in a wide cedar deck that looks out over the canyon below. It's all clean lines and dark wood siding that blends into the trees on one half, but then the other half is entirely large square panes of glass that reflect the pine trees and pinkish-purple skyline like a damn painting. The cabin, if you can even call it that, is tucked away, almost separate from the rest of the compound, but still very much a part of everything. Like a fancy star on top of a Christmas tree. I even spot a bubbling stream running down a small slope behind the cabin and a walking path that looks like a perfect place for me to run.

If this is what money can buy, I reckon I'd like to say fuck all to rugby and becoming a lawyer and work for Everly's father.

"I'll get the bags," the driver says as he comes to a stop in front of the large double-door entrance.

"Right. Sure. Thanks," I reply, not bothering to tell him I'm not staying here. I've only got my two bags and a carry-on, so I can manage it back down to the barn after we get Everly dropped off.

I glance inside and can just make out the warm glow of pendant lights and exposed beams above polished concrete floors. A curvy woman with wild, curly hair steps out of the front doors of the cabin and waves eagerly in my direction. I recognize her as Trista from our video interview we did a few weeks back.

I turn on my heel and lean over to give Sleeping Beauty a gentle nudge. It's strange to see her in such a vulnerable way. She inhales deeply and makes a funny kissing noise with her lips, not even remotely waking up. I fight back the urge to laugh because she looks a hell of a lot more peaceful now than she did an hour ago.

"Hey, Stretch, we're here," I say softly as I glance over my shoulder and see the woman letting the driver inside with all our luggage.

"Everly," I state a bit louder.

"Mmm . . . thunder thighs of destiny," she murmurs.

I jerk my head and frown. Is she talking about me? Surely not, right? Then again, this wouldn't be the first time she's remarked on my thighs.

"They could definitely crack a watermelon," she coos and giggles in her sleep, and I have to cover my own mouth to stop myself from laughing as my stomach swirls with amusement. Whatever that pill was that she took has messed her up properly, no doubt about it. But bloody hell if there isn't a dark, quiet part of me that likes the fact that I'm seated so firmly in her subconscious because she's been in mine a time or two as well.

I turn to see the driver accepting a tip from the woman and beginning to make his way back to the car. With a growl, I grab Everly's white tote bag and throw it over my shoulder before bending down to pick her up. If she's dreaming about thighs of destiny and refusing to get her arse moving, I'll move it for her.

I grunt as I stand because she's an awkward-as-fuck load. All dangling, long limbs and arms flung out like she's dead. When she first came to Trinity, she was skinny. A bit too skinny, if you ask me. But she's filled out some in the four years I've seen her around. Her arms have thickened, along with her hips and legs. She's got a bit of a belly too, and I like that look on her. She's healthier at this size and looks less like a faint wind could blow her over.

With a jerk, she curls in and nuzzles her nose against my neck like I'm her cuddly teddy bear, not the arse she was snapping at on the plane just hours ago. The scent of jasmine wafts over me, and I feel my body shudder over the close proximity to her. I've never touched Everly Fletcher before, and I know instantly I'm going to have to wash this bleedin' shirt to get her scent off me.

I carefully make my way out of the shuttle, turning sideways to not whack her against anything. When I come around the front of the van, Trista's eyes go wide.

"Is Everly sick?" she exclaims and rushes down the long flight of steps to greet me.

"Not that I know of. I think she's just jet-lagged to oblivion." I offer a rueful smile. "I tried to wake her, but she's out of it. I think she took a sleeping pill."

"Oh, my gosh, let me get the door for you." She hustles up the steps ahead of me, opening the glass-paned doors to allow me to carry Everly inside.

"Cozy said she's going to be sleeping in here. Just follow me. I'll get the covers pulled back." Trista rushes past an elegant but simple kitchen on the right and down a hallway through the door at the end. Everly squirms lightly in my arms, making the most dick-rising noise I've ever heard. I stop for a second to get my head on straight when her hand slides up the back of my neck and tugs my hair, making me physically flex every muscle in my body as I hold my breath. I must be fucking tired if this is all it takes to almost bring me to my knees.

I release a slow, controlled breath and double-check she's still unconscious and sleeping and not awake, about to lay into me.

Growling softly at the knackered, infuriating girl, I finally step into the bedroom, doing a sideways move that has me almost smacking her head on the doorframe.

My brows lift. I shouldn't be surprised that it's just as stunning as the outside. It's got giant windows that overlook the stream out back, and I can't help but think how easy it would be for someone to stare inside at her. My throat tightens as I glance at the big white bed in the center of the room. Will she have men in here? *Why is that any of my fucking business?*

I shake away that intrusive thought and turn my focus to the large printed photograph of the Rubrics building at Trinity. It's placed on the wall opposite the bed and wrapped in a thick, studded leather frame, adding a richness to the photo and making me wish I had something like that for my own space. I hadn't lived in the Rubrics, but I sure looked at that building enough for it to leave its mark on me.

"Here you go," Trista says, folding back the blankets for me to lay the girl my sister befriended her last year of college down onto the bed.

The sheets brush the backs of my hands, and I fight the urge to crawl inside and make room for myself. *Christ, I must be tired if I'm fantasizing about falling asleep with Everly Fletcher in my arms.*

When Trista begins pulling off Everly's shoes, I make a hasty exit to give them some privacy. Me being in Everly's bedroom is not a good idea. Not ever.

My eyes sweep the living room. It's clean and simple. Long black leather couch. A telly and a couple of end tables and lamps. Everything looks expensive. I refuse to sit down because I'm sure I'd ruin something just by existing.

Moments later, Trista comes rushing toward me, out of breath and pushing her curly hair back behind her ears. "That girl always knows how to make an entrance," she replies with a laugh and then smiles warmly at me. "Hello, Conri. It's nice to finally meet you in person."

I grip the back of my neck, trying to rub away the feeling of Everly's hands that were just there, and nod. "You can call me Wolf if you like. Everyone does."

"Wolf it is. You can call me Trista." She reaches out and shakes my hand. "Welcome to Fletcher Mountain."

My brows lift as I take in the full view of the sweeping mountain canyon and all the cabins and the red barn downhill. "It's really something."

"It is, isn't it?" Trista stares out at the view like she doesn't live here and see it every day. "Can I show you to your place?"

"I'd appreciate that."

She grabs my smaller suitcase despite my protests, and we lug them down the long steps to load them into a Ranger ATV she has parked beside the house. I slide into the passenger seat, feeling so weird not having a steering wheel in front of me. I can only imagine how odd that's going to be, driving on the wrong side of the road, and she zips us down the gravel lane headed toward the barn just as darkness sets in. I glance at the three glowing cabins as we drive by and swear I see people in the windows duck and hide. Not just in one cabin either. All three of them seem to have someone inside trying to have a nosy peek.

I suppose I'd be curious about an Irish rugby player moving onto my mountain as well.

I really hope I get on with this family, or it's going to be a long bleedin' summer.

Trista parks in front of the red barn and once again fights me on taking one of my suitcases, even though I'd really prefer she carry nothing. We step inside the dutch doors, and she flicks a light on, bringing the quaint barn to life.

"Just a couple introductions, and then I'll show you upstairs."

I frown and twist my head around, looking for any other people in the barn. Trista marches down the long alley between the stalls and stops at the far pen on the left. "This is Millie, the queen of Fletcher Mountain and the namesake for which Mount Millie Rescue Center was founded."

I walk to where she stands and lean over the gate. A brown-and-white goat hops up from her spot in the corner to greet us. "She's a Nigerian dwarf goat and the beloved rescue belonging to my husband, Wyatt. If you want brownie points with Wyatt . . . feed Millie snacks any chance you get. She loves veggies. Carrots, celery, that sort of thing. I put some in your fridge upstairs. Millie and the rest of the mountain think Millie is the number one guy in the group, but actually, it's this handsome fellow." She pushes off the gate to cross the alley to the opposite side. "This is Sir Reginald. The true number one guy in the group."

I frown in confusion.

"Do you guys not have *Vanderpump Rules* in Ireland?"

I shrug because I have no idea what she's saying.

"It's reality TV magic—a cultural institution. You have to watch it, Wolf. Promise me." She grips my face earnestly, squeezing so hard my lips form a round O shape. So I nod woodenly, having no intention of following through with this promise . . . but I'm not sure I'll make it out alive if I don't agree.

She sighs and glances down at what appears to be a small pig. I can't actually see much of him because he's lying on some sort of mattress and covered in an orange felt blanket. "Sir Reginald is my baby. He's still bitter I didn't name the rescue center after him, but Mount Millie was here first, so we had to pay respect, you know?"

I know my new boss is speaking English, but I can't understand a word of what she is saying.

"This here is Handsome," she adds, shooting across the alley again and petting the miniature horse who is struggling to get his head over the gate to say hello. I recoil when I see his fleshy tongue hanging lifelessly out of his mouth. Trista must notice my reaction as she pets him and adds, "He has a tongue paralysis that is a permanent medical condition, so he's always in a constant state of emoji. Handsome, isn't he?"

I frown, not sure *handsome* is the adjective I'd use to describe this animal, but I force a smile to play it off like I think he's indeed . . . handsome.

"And this is Butterscotch. She's a sweet little miniature Highland cow—do Irish people hate Scottish people?"

"What?" I ask, jerking my attention away from the cow to Trista.

"Is there like a rivalry between you guys? Or is that just with England because they tried to colonize you and force you to change your religion?"

"Umm . . ."

"Never mind, we have all summer to cover that." She sighs happily and glances around the barn. "Chickens are out back in their coop. I can introduce you to them tomorrow in the daylight. Hard to remember their names if you can't even see them."

Her chickens have names?

"This barn used to be heaping full, but a lot of the animals have been moved down the peak to the rescue center now that it's fully operational." She purses her lips sadly. "Only personal pets up here. Rescue pets we're working toward rehoming live down there now. I hate it. It feels like segregation, but it's really just an insurance thing.

"As we discussed, part of your job will be to muck out these pens a few times a week and collect eggs from the coop in addition to the Mount Millie stuff. You can do everyone except Millie. Wyatt takes care of his own goat. And if you try to help too much, he goes from Papa Bear to Grumpy Bear really quick. Trust me, you don't want to see Grumpy Bear. Anyways, your place is up this way. Follow me."

She leads me down the alley to a set of wooden steps that run down the center of the barn. I follow as we haul my bags all the way up. When she opens the door at the top and steps aside to reveal the space, I can't help but feel impressed.

It's a large loft setting with a kitchen, round dining table, living area, and a big bed on the far wall below some wide windows. A decent-sized bathroom is to the right, and along that wall is a large desk with various papers and a computer on it. The wood floor is covered in red patterned rugs, and the ceiling is exposed natural wood with beams.

I knew when I got this job that I was going to be living in a barn above animals, but I expected it to be much more run-down than this. This is properly decent and more my style than the fancy place we dropped Everly off at.

"That bed has a remote and is adjustable," she says, pointing to it. "Super-duper comfortable. Like sleeping on a cloud."

"Sleep out here a lot, do ya?" I joke.

"I lived out here."

My brows lift.

"Did Everly not tell you how Wyatt and I met?"

I shake my head. The girl told me a lot, but we shockingly did not cover that part, I guess.

She laughs and shakes her head. "Another story for another day. Anyways, sorry about the desk and computer, but we were kind of using this as an office before you came along, so hopefully you don't mind us leaving this up here. We do most of our work from the shelter now, but occasionally, we might need to pop up here to do some bookwork stuff. Is that okay with you?"

"Of course, of course," I state with a nod. "I, um . . ." I clear my throat and squeeze my hands into fists, summoning my sister Cliona's extroverted nature to say the next bit out loud. "I really appreciate all you've done to make this possible. I know it was a lot of work to make it happen, and it means a great deal that you took a chance on me."

Trista smiles warmly. "The rugby thing sounds like a great opportunity, Wolf. I'm happy for you. And honestly, I think this is a win-win situation because I just don't have time to do it all, and we need more muscle around here."

I nod. "I can certainly give you that."

She reaches out and pats my arm in a nurturing way. "I hope you fall in love with it up here just like I did. This apartment has a very special place in my heart." She spins on her heels and glances around, getting a soft look in her eye. "Anyways, I'll let you get some rest. You don't start work until Monday, so sleep the day away. Shake off the jet lag, and please let us know if you need anything. I know you don't have a car, but there's plenty of people around here that can run you anywhere you need to go. Just shoot me a text. You have my number."

"Thanks much."

She makes her way toward the door and stops to add, "Oh, and I loaded the fridge and cupboards for you, so please eat if you're hungry. You said no allergies, so I went a little nuts. Frozen pizzas in the freezer, chicken nuggets, Popsicles. All my favorite food groups."

I blink back my shock. "Wow, thank you. You didn't need to."

"It's a big deal moving to another country. The least I can do is make sure you're well-fed." She smiles again, and I feel a tightness in my chest over her generosity.

"I'll try not to let you down, Mrs. Fletcher," I state seriously because I mean it. I genuinely don't want this trip to be a complete failure. I don't want to self-sabotage like I have so many times before. There are a lot of people depending on me to make the most of this, and I don't want to fail them.

"As much as I love being called Mrs. Fletcher, please stick with Trista. We're not formal around here." She glances around briefly. "And I'm not worried about you letting me down, Wolf. This mountain has a way of healing things you don't even know need healing."

She winks before marching out, leaving me in my new place in a new country with a full fridge, feeling like I'm in for one heck of a ride up here on Fletcher Mountain.

Chapter 7

Knock-On: *When the ball is accidentally knocked forward resulting in a penalty.*

Translation: *Like accidentally passing out and having to be man-handled off a van by your best friend's hot brother.*

Everly

I feel like I was hit by a bus, I think to myself as I wake up, not knowing where the heck I am. I sit up in the big white fluffy bed I find myself in and glance around the room that's drenched in broad daylight. My eyes move to the window as I hear a creek bubbling outside. I would swear I was dreaming if I didn't feel so fucking awful.

"Okay, that Ambien was a bad life choice, I think," I croak as I lick my dry lips and crave water something fierce.

I thought taking it on my way up to Fletcher Mountain would mean it would kick in just after I got settled. I guess I was wrong because I don't even remember coming into this house.

And what a house it is! My dad and uncles didn't start building this place until after I went off to university, and it was declared move-in ready right before I graduated. I glance into the attached bathroom and note glossy white tile and double sinks. Everything is so shiny and new. The smell of bacon permeates my nose, showing other signs of life in this house, so I yank the covers back and crawl out of bed to investigate.

"Ew . . . I'm in my airport clothes still." I wrinkle my nose and jerk my head up when I hear loud footsteps thundering down the hall before the door bursts open.

"Mom, she's awake!" Ethan screams loudly, his dark hair flopped over his eyes.

"Where am I?" I ask my little brother.

"The Fletcher Family Getaway . . . duh." He rolls his eyes, clearly annoyed by me. "Come on. Mom's making breakfast."

He turns and walks away, so after taking a moment in the attached bathroom, I follow him through the hallway, taking in my new digs that I have no recollection of seeing last night. There's a slew of boxes lining the wall filled with my stuff from my bedroom back at my dad's, and I wonder what time it is and where my phone ended up.

I emerge to find Cozy at the stove in the kitchen, turning bacon, and my dad is at the white quartz island, reading a paper. Glancing around our new home, I wince against the bright sunlight pouring in through all the giant windows everywhere.

"I have no memory of getting into that bed." I point down the hall, and my parents both swing their heads to me. "Or this house."

"Good morning!" Cozy says cheerily as she bustles over and gives me a big hug. I wish she wouldn't touch me because I feel filthy. She chucks my chin playfully. "Trista said you were pretty out of it last night. That boy Wolf had to carry you inside."

"He carried me?" I gasp, my jaw permanently on the floor as my body erupts in chills. Oh, God, maybe it's good I don't remember any of that. I'm sure he scowled the whole time, pissed he had to be so close to me.

"You don't think he drugged her, do you?" My dad directs this question to my stepmom, his brow furrowed with worry. "Dammit, I knew we should have come up the mountain with them."

"I took a sleeping pill, Dad." I groan and pinch the bridge of my nose. *And then he fucking carried me to my bed. When I wasn't even conscious enough to enjoy it.*

Cozy tsks knowingly. "Everly, I told you those things are strong."

"I'm gathering that." I blow out a long breath and rake my hands through my disastrous hair. "I need a shower. I can't think straight."

"Food will be ready when you come out. Go feel human again."

I turn to make my way down the hallway and then pause to confirm one more time. "He actually carried me?"

Cozy winces and nods. "I'm afraid so, Sea Monster."

I groan and tip my head back. "This is so embarrassing."

I emerge twenty minutes later in a clean pair of leggings and a Trinity T-shirt that I found in my suitcase. Someone must have left it in my room along with my tote bag and phone, which is now charging on the wall.

Cozy has just dished the last plate, so I join them at the counter to eat. "Um . . . love the house," I say around a mouthful of bacon, feeling mildly more awake. "That shower is amazing."

"Right!" Cozy smiles triumphantly, glancing up at the lofted area above us that overlooks the living room and glass side of the house. "The one upstairs is great too. There's two bedrooms upstairs with a Jack and Jill bathroom. And there's another full bathroom around the corner there off the living room, with a soaker tub. I'll give you the full tour after you've eaten."

"Amazing," I reply with a sigh. "I should sleep upstairs though, yeah? I don't want the primary room in case you guys want to come up on a weekend."

"Oh, don't be silly," Cozy says with a wave of her hand. "We can sleep upstairs if we come up. It makes no sense for you to take a smaller bedroom when you're living here full-time."

I sigh heavily. "It's too much. I'm going to pay you rent."

"No," Cozy argues.

"Deal," my dad says over top of Cozy's no.

"Max!"

"She can contribute to the household expenses, Cassandra." Dad pushes his eggs around his plate. "I know Trista isn't paying her much, but a little rent will be good for her. She already has a free car, free insurance, free cell phone."

Cozy hits my dad with a stark look. "Are you going to tell her what's sitting outside?"

My eyes snap to my dad. "What's sitting outside?"

"A new car," Ethan answers casually.

"Ethan," Dad growls, looking over his shoulder. "It was supposed to be a surprise."

Speechless. I am speechless.

I rush out the front door onto the deck, and my jaw drops when I see a pearly white Range Rover sitting in front of the cabin with a big red bow on it. I hear my family joining behind me, and I turn around, shaking my head from side to side.

"I know you liked your truck, but it needed new tires, and it was time for an upgrade. This has four-wheel drive, so you won't have to even think when you're driving up here in bad weather. It has a five-star safety rating and is fully electric with hookups just over—"

My dad's voice is cut off when I barrel into him, hugging him like I did when I was eleven years old and leaving him for the week to go to my mom's. Back when I used to worry about him being lonely and sad and thinking he'd never find love again.

He grunts, clearly caught off guard, but in seconds, his arms bind around me, tight, familiar, and so incredibly safe.

"Thank you, Daddy," I say, my body shaking with the tears flowing freely down my face. "You didn't have to do this."

He releases me, and when I back up to look at him, I see his eyes are red-rimmed. "I'm proud of you, kid. Going to school in Dublin took guts, and you stuck with it, even when it was hard. You're lucky I didn't buy you your own mountain."

I expel a garbled laugh and look over to Cozy, who's full-on crying just like me. I close the distance between us and hug her just as fiercely, her warmth radiating straight through my heart. "Thank you, Mama Cozy," I croak, using the name I gave her after she and my dad got married all those years ago. "You guys are too much. I've missed you all so much."

"You can say that again," Dad huffs knowingly. "No more going several months with no visits, okay, kid? I'm not too proud to call this car a bribe for quality time."

"I'm home for good, I swear." I grin back at him, and he shoots me a wink.

"Tell her about the party," Ethan blurts out as he stuffs a pancake into his mouth.

"What party?" I snap my head back to my stepmom.

"Ethan," Cozy chastises. "That was also supposed to be a surprise."

"What party?" I ask again, my interest piqued.

"Your uncles are hosting something for you tonight down at the Mercantile," Dad answers with a shrug. "You can't honestly be that shocked."

"Seriously?"

"Yeah, are you up for it?" Cozy asks, inspecting me in that motherly way she has about her. She reaches out and tugs on my short locks, marveling over my hair just like my mom did.

"Yes, absolutely." I smile brightly.

"Your Ambien hangover is magically cured?" my dad drones, pulling the keys out of his pocket and dangling them at me.

I rush over and grab them out of his hand. "Yes, definitely! I am dying to see everyone. I bet Stevie is so big now, and I want to see Addison actually pregnant. I can't believe no one is over here knocking down the door already."

"Dad told them not to come." Ethan shoots a glare at our father.

He frowns back at him. "My brothers will have her up here all summer long. I can claim her first day back home."

My chest swells at my dad's sweet sign of affection, so I pocket the keys and walk over to give him a big hug. "Love you too, Dad," I say with a quick kiss on his stubbled cheek. "Want to go for a drive with me?"

"You bet I do." He huffs out a noise before pulling me back in for one more hug. "It's good to have you home, kid."

I stand outside the barn, anxiously trying to find the nerve to go upstairs and invite Wolf to the gathering tonight. It was Cozy's idea, and I know it's the right thing to do. He doesn't have a car, he has no friends, he's probably hungry. It's the decent thing to do.

Just go and invite him.

Only now that I know he carried me into my house last night, I feel all types of mortification stopping me in my tracks. At six foot tall, I'm not exactly light as a feather. Never have been. In fact, I remember a doctor giving me a speech once about how I shouldn't compare my weight to my friends' weights because they're so much shorter than I am. Not to mention, I've put on a few pounds over the last four years. I hate thinking about my jiggly, travel-stinky body in his arms.

As he remarked on the plane, he's never had issues attracting female company, so I just feel a bit . . . embarrassed. Disappointed. I know he'll never see me as attractive, for reasons that probably have nothing to do with my looks, but still. A girl has her pride.

"Just go in there," I tell myself by way of a pep talk. "Go in to say hi to Millie and Handsome and Reggie. Start with the animals, and then you can march upstairs and knock on his door. Just knock on his door. It's that easy."

"Knock on whose door?" a deep voice booms from behind me, and I swerve around to find Conri the Convict standing before me in nothing but a pair of rugby shorts and sneakers.

His chest is heaving and drenched with sweat as he struggles to catch his breath. He pulls his headphones down around his neck, catching me staring at his corded and ink-covered muscles like I'm committing them to memory to draw in my furry notebook later. Maybe I am. And maybe I am mortified for the second time in less than twenty-four hours, but I can't seem to tell myself to stop the staring.

"Handsome's door," I blurt out. "The horse. Handsome the horse. I don't know if you've met, but I was just getting ready to knock on his door and, um . . . reconnect." I swallow the painful knot in my throat as I try and fail to tear my eyes away from his massive thighs in those damn shorts of his. *Talk about reverse sexism here,* I scold myself and finally meet his gaze.

"Knock on his gate, you mean?" Wolf side-eyes me.

"Yeah, you could call it that. In America, we call them doors . . . sometimes. Just a cultural difference . . ." My voice trails off as I debate flinging myself off this mountain.

"Okay, I'll leave you to it, then."

Wolf makes his way past me before I open my mouth and blurt out, "Are you all settled, then?"

He stops and turns on his heel. "Yeah, just about. My sister is shipping more of my stuff, but I'm sorted enough for now."

"Do you like the apartment?" I glance up at the little window where the bathroom is that looks down over the mountain compound.

"The flat? Yeah, it's grand. Trista said if I keep the pens mucked out, my stuff won't smell like a barn too awful."

"Oh, so you met Trista in person, then." I glance back at my uncle Wyatt's house. It was the first house they built up here since this land is technically all his. It was just a few years later that my uncles Calder and Luke added their homes up here. And now my dad too.

"Yeah, I met her last night."

"Did you meet my uncles?" I bite my lip in preparation. I can't imagine how that first greeting would have gone.

"No, not yet. It's been a bit quiet up here. I thought there'd be more people around."

"Um . . . yeah, I guess they're planning a big surprise party for me tonight down the mountain at the Mercantile. It's the pub in Jamestown."

"Oh, I saw that place when we arrived last night. Doesn't sound like much of a surprise if you know about it, does it?"

"Ethan kind of spilled the beans."

"Ah, sure."

"Do you want to come?" I ask, feeling blood rush to my cheeks. "I mean, you don't have to, but you could meet everybody, and I can show you a bit of Jamestown beforehand if you want."

His eyes narrow as his brows twitch with a flash of discomfort, like he's not sure he wants to say yes. Then it's gone and replaced with something more guarded. "Sure, I'll come. What time?"

God, why did that make my heart nearly skip a beat. "Um . . . we could leave in like an hour?"

"Perfect. I'll have a shower, then. Thanks much."

I exhale a huge breath when he turns to make his way inside, grateful I got through that interaction without having to discuss what happened last night. I turn to make my way back toward my cabin but stop dead in my tracks when he calls out to me one more time.

"Oh, and Stretch?"

"Yeah?" I turn and smile brightly at him.

"Were you aware that you talk in your sleep?"

A pit settles in my stomach. "Um . . . your sister mentioned it a time or two. What did I say?"

"Something about a watermelon," he replies with a quizzical brow. "It was very flattering, though I'm not sure it's decent to repeat within earshot of the precious animals."

My cheeks flame with humiliation, but then another thing causes my body to physically react in a different way.

The rugby bad boy is . . . smiling.

And dare I say . . . chuckling?

It's low and rough, and it sends a rush of warmth over my skin that gives me goose bumps. His eyes are practically twinkling with mirth. I've rarely seen Wolf smile. I've certainly never heard him laugh. Who the hell is this guy in front of me? And is he acting like he likes what he heard?

I blow out a long breath and lift my arms into a shrug, trying to feign confidence I just barely feel. "Maybe if you weren't so boring, I wouldn't have fallen asleep on you."

"Oh, so that's how it is?" He chuckles softly. "Very well, then. I'll try to be more *stimulating* company tonight."

He taps the barn gently with his fist and shoots me a dark look before heading off and leaving me positively swirling with emotion.

Stimulating company, indeed.

Chapter 8

Offside: *When a player is farther forward than the teammate who is carrying the ball.*

Translation: *The condom section of the grocery store is definitely offside.*

Wolf

"My uncles are volunteer firefighters," Everly says, pointing to the Jamestown fire department building as she drives by a dilapidated-looking structure that leaves a lot to be desired. "It's a really important job out here because any type of fire situation can escalate to catastrophic levels quickly."

I glance up at the mountain canyon above us. "We have those in Ireland too, even though it feels like it pisses rain all the time."

"Oh, yes, that was the first thing I noticed when I came to Trinity. Everything is always wet."

She laughs, and my mind can't help but picture Everly on campus again. She has an angelic look to her. Perfect creamy porcelain skin that flushes easily and light blue eyes that shock you when she wears a little extra makeup. But her style isn't what I'd call girlie. She dresses like a bird who could beat you in darts, but you'd still want to buy her a drink after. Usually, some trainers on her feet and well-worn jeans that hug her arse, but then she adds in a cropped tank that reminds you she has curves. And she's soft in all the right places.

My eyes glance down at Everly's legs on full display in the little white shorts she came out wearing tonight. I'd walked up to her cabin to wait for her by her brand-new Range Rover, a slick hundred-thousand-quid beast, depending on the trim, and had to look away when she came down the stairs. She looked good at Trinity, but something about her on the mountain looks even better. Fitter, even.

At Trinity, I could ignore her, hard as it was. Here, that's proving to be impossible.

"What's the population of this town again?" I ask, desperate to distract myself from the scent of her engulfing me inside this SUV because it's clearly letting my mind wander to places it has no business wandering to.

"I think it's like three hundred people. It's not much, but it's a pass-through town for bikers and travelers. We're lucky to have the Mercantile. The owner, Judy, expanded it from a pub to a grocery store ages ago, so if you need anything, you can likely find it at her place. And it's walkable from the mountain if you don't mind a steep mile-high hike home."

"Yeah, I can manage that." I hold my hand out the open window, testing the air. "It's warmer down here than it is on the mountain, isn't it?"

"Yeah, the elevation is trippy."

I nod because I learned that the hard way on my run earlier today. This oxygen is going to take some getting used to. Back home, I could knock out pitch sprints all day without breaking a sweat. Here, I felt like I was breathing through a straw after getting punched in the guts. Miserable feeling.

Fletcher Mountain clearly doesn't give a toss that I played rugby for Trinity or that I log countless hours in the gym and flatten blokes in a ruck. The Colorado Rockies make a mockery of my previous training.

But I was too stubborn to give up. I have two weeks before my training camp starts with the Grizzlies, and Coach Flannigan told me to give myself time to adjust to the altitude before camp. That's why I came out early. I can't be the first one on the ground gasping for breath, or they'll be forgetting why they decided to take a chance on me in the first place.

But the views on my run were a nice distraction from my burning lungs. It was pleasant not seeing any traffic or hearing the hum of the city. Just the wind in the trees, the thud of my trainers, and the occasional call of a bird that sounded like it wanted to finish me off.

"Elevation sickness is a real thing too, so be sure to stay hydrated," Everly says as if reading my mind. "It's June now, so it's not too terribly hot yet, but by July . . . it'll be scorching, especially in Denver, where your camp is."

I nod, and my phone chirps in my pocket, distracting me. I pull it out to see a text from Cliona asking how my first day is going and if they've caught on that I've never set foot on a proper farm before.

"Clio?" Everly asks knowingly.

"Yeah, she's blowing my damn mobile up."

"Mine too." Everly laughs. "I'm sure she's lonely. This is probably the farthest you guys have ever been apart from each other, huh?"

"It is, actually," I reply and then look out the window, shifting in my seat.

"That twin connection must be a totally different experience than me and my brother. I love Ethan—was obsessed with him when he was a baby. But the older he got, the crazier he got, and while I was sad to leave him for Dublin, I wasn't too sad . . . if you know what I mean."

The corner of my mouth tips up as I recall the lad falling asleep on me last night. He didn't seem too crazy to me.

"Well, it's about time for the party, so I suppose I'll head back and prepare myself to be fake-surprised."

She turns around in the post office car park and backs up to get her vehicle headed the other way. It's quite a sight to watch Everly drive. She maneuvers her SUV like it's nothing, despite the fact that it looks like it belongs in outer space, not a small mountain village. I don't think I've ever even been inside a car this nice. And I still expected to see the steering wheel in front of me when I got in the front seat. So strange.

Growing up in Dublin, there was never a need to own a car because public transport was cheaper and more convenient. None of the kids I grew up with drove either. My parents have a car the family all shares, but that's it.

It's going to be a bit more difficult getting where I need to go here. I am capable of driving, but hiring a car for the long term would cost a fortune, and since I so rarely drive, navigating a car on the opposite side of the road sounded like a bad idea.

Luckily, there's a bus that runs from Boulder to Denver that costs three dollars a trip, so Trista said that someone from the mountain will drive me to the bus stop in Boulder the three days a week I have training. Apparently, the Fletcher Brothers Construction business is in Boulder, so someone is always headed into town. Can't wait for those awkward rides.

"No turning back now," Everly says as she parks outside the Mercantile.

There's a good number of cars scattered throughout the car park, and I can't help but feel anxious. "Why don't you go in first, and I can join a bit later."

Everly frowns. "You don't need to do that."

"I'd prefer it, actually. I don't fancy attention, and this way, I can work my way in slowly."

"You don't fancy attention, but you start fights on the rugby pitch?" she asks boldly, her blue eyes pinning me in my seat.

I tilt my head at her, stunned a bit by her brazen statement. "You think I'm doing that for attention?"

Everly's shoulders lift. "I'm sure it doesn't hurt with the

ladies." She taps her nails on the steering wheel as her cheeks flush a rosy hue, and I wonder what she's getting at here.

"Do you have a question mulling around inside that noisy head of yours, Stretch? Because if it's all the same to you, I'd rather you just ask me what you're thinking instead of river dance around it." My tone is harsh and punishing, but my hackles are raised at her insinuation that I'm picking fights as a means of bagging birds.

"I tried to ask you directly on the plane," she snaps, looking at me with a challenge.

"Ask me what?" I snap back.

"If you had a girlfriend back in Dublin." Her nostrils flare in a rather comedic way. The girl doesn't do angry very well. She's just too cute and sweet-looking. Like a puppy.

And apparently, this cute, sweet thing is desperate to know my relationship status. Satisfaction curls inside my belly over her admission. I'm under her skin, and it feels good because she's been under mine for going on four years.

"I don't do the girlfriend thing," I reply, leaning in closer to her, my eyes dropping down to her lips. "Never have. Never will."

I look up and see her brows pinched together. "Why not?"

I shrug dismissively. "I'm trying to make a proper go of this rugby career, and I can't have some bird messing with my plans. The hope is to do well here and get noticed by a team back in Dublin."

Everly's brows lift, her face looking almost devastated if I didn't know any better. "What if you really like the Denver team?"

"I'm not going to like anything more than getting home to Ireland."

Everly's cobalt-blue eyes flick back and forth between mine.

"What if you meet someone? What if I could find you the love of your life? Would that change things?"

I shake my head. "I didn't want you to matchmake me in first year, and I certainly don't want you to matchmake me now, especially not here in America. This summer is my comeback season for rugby, and that's it. Anything outside of that would just be a distraction."

She sniffs and looks forward, her chin jutting up defiantly. "Can I ask what happened to cause you to need a comeback season in the first place? Or did you always pick fights on the rugby field?"

I inhale a sharp breath through my nose as she so casually asks a question that is anything but casual. "You have no clue what you're talking about."

"I'm just trying to understand you a bit more." She arches her brows like she's solving a crime. "Everyone has a story. What's yours, Wolf? My theory is some girl broke your heart. Am I warm?"

My teeth crack as I fight back the outward reaction I want to have over her poking and prodding at me like a bloody science experiment. I want to snarl back at her and tell her to fuck off because she doesn't even know me. Instead, I grind out, "It's none of your business."

Her breath catches in her throat, and I can't help but see the hurt in her eyes. I bet Everly Fletcher isn't used to people telling her no. The girl probably gets her way a lot in life if this fancy new car is any indication.

But she's not going to dig into my past. Not now. Not ever.

Awkward silence descends over us as she stares forward and chews her lip, like she's having a whole conversation in her head. I'm sure she wouldn't like it if I reversed the question on her. Pestered her about her dating history and love life. As far as

I can tell, the girl doesn't date very often. And when she does, it apparently doesn't go well, if Instagram posts from prats on campus are any indication.

She seems much more focused on obsessing about everyone else's love life.

What on earth could she possibly gain from matchmaking people? And why all of this focus on falling in love? She could use her irritating, helpful tendencies for so many other things, but instead, she chooses to funnel it all into meddling in other people's love lives.

Yet another thing I don't understand about this girl.

But I know better than to ask any of these questions. I already know too much about Everly Fletcher. More than anyone realizes.

"You better head inside. You don't want to be late for your own party," I state, pointing to the pub entrance.

"Okay," she says as we both slide out of the SUV. She tightens the flannel wrapped around her waist. "See you in there?" She says it like a question, like she doesn't believe I'm going to join her. Like I might just bugger off back up the mountain and forget all about this party tonight because she poked the wolf and the wolf bit back.

For some strange reason, the thought of disappointing her needles something inside me, so I nod and offer a half smile over the hood of her car. "Yeah, I'll be right there. I'm just going to pop next door and poke around a bit. I'll see you in a few, Stretch."

She smiles at my use of her nickname. Like it soothes her in some bizarre way. She gives me a little wave before heading toward the door on the pub side, so I walk over to the grocery side, my mind wrecked with how weird this is all becoming.

In less than twenty-four hours, I went from barely speaking to my sister's American roommate to snarling at her on the plane and to now worrying about disappointing her. I'd better get a fecking grip.

The bell above the door jingles as I walk into a shop that feels a heck of a lot different from my parents' shop. The scent of pine and beef jerky hits me as I make my way down the aisles, perusing what they have to offer. It's not much, but there's some fresh produce in one area, milk, snacks, and canned goods in another. Not to mention alcohol and tobacco. I head over to the health and wellness section, where I find a few bars that look like they might contain protein, so I grab a couple and continue down the aisle in search of some pain meds. My lungs are still burning, and this headache I've had since my run doesn't seem to be leaving despite the copious amount of water I drank. It's then that I stumble upon a very different section of the store.

The adult section.

More specifically . . . condoms.

Or "johnnies" as we sometimes refer to them in Ireland.

I realize that I did not pack any of these, and I wonder if I should grab some while I'm here, just to be safe. It's not as if I know any women in the area, and I'm certainly not going to let Everly set me up. But once I start working out with the team, it's possible we could start going out after training. Or maybe I meet someone next door at the Mercantile. Things happen, and it's always good to be prepared.

My sex life at Trinity was decent. Nothing outrageous, but I did a proper job of making up for the time I lost growing up as a scrawny kid through most of my younger years. Even in secondary school, when I finally shot up in height, I was still so thin my mam used to say I could fall through a crack on the pavement.

Playing rugby changed that.

The weight room became a second home to me. Pair that with team training, and after a couple of years, I could finally fill out a T-shirt and shorts decently.

The girls took notice of that at Trinity. They took notice of the whole rugby team, if I'm being honest. Whenever we won a home match, there would be these giant "house gaffs" or house parties as they refer to them in America. The houses were packed, messy, and loud, and all I really had to do was show up, sit on a sofa, and nurse a beer before some lass would come over and join me.

Socializing is easy when you realize all anyone ever really wants to do is talk about themselves. I'd let the girl tell me her whole life story, and then eventually, we'd be snogging our way out the door to wherever her flat was.

It was meaningless and just a bit of fun. That's all I was ever looking for because it was college. No sense getting tied up in a serious relationship when our lives had barely started. I had enough to manage with my sport and my studies. The last thing I needed was a relationship taking my focus off that.

It's why Everly's matchmaking shite on campus irritated me so much. *Why did an eighteen-year-old American think she knew all there was to know about love?*

Trinity College | Dublin, Ireland
Four Years Ago

"What's your relationship status, Conri? If I had to guess, I'd say you have a bench full of ladies you sub in whenever you feel like it. Am I right?" Everly Fletcher sits down beside me at Mulligans Pub with a furry notebook in hand, brows arched with cheeky challenge.

When I say nothing to the annoying American girl I was paired with for a class project, she asks, "Bench full of guys, maybe?"

My gaze sharpens.

"Definitely heterosexual. Good to know." She scribbles in her furry notebook, her mouth quirked with excitement. When she's done, she

drags her gaze up and down my body. "How tall are you, exactly? You know what? It doesn't matter. Any guy over six foot two wins everything. You could list 'just vibes' for your career aspirations on a dating profile, but if you're well over six foot, girls will say that makes you mysterious, not lazy."

I lean in just close enough to see that peach gloss on her lips. "You done talking yet?"

"Not even close," she chirps back. "I want to invite you to my first speed-dating clinic I'm hosting here at Mulligans. The girls would flip if I had a rugby guy show up. I know I could match you with someone amazing!"

I look her hard in the eyes. In those bright blue and naively innocent eyes that make me ache for the fact that I've never looked at the world like it was all shiny and new, and reply, "There's absolutely no way in hell I'd participate in your matchmaking shite."

"Why not?" she asks, leaning in close enough that I can smell her perfume. "It could be fun."

"There is nothing fun about sitting at a pub table being forced to talk to someone on command like I'm a trained dog."

She leans close and gives me a wee poke on the chest, bathing me in her scent for a second time and causing my cock to twitch. "But what if you find the love of your life? Then wouldn't that little bit of awkwardness be worth it?"

I trace the place she touched on my body and release a breath that's weighted and full of way too much shite for a guy in his first year at university. "Maybe some of us don't deserve a happily ever after."

Present Day

I scoff and shake my head at that memory. Everly's whole personality was matchmaking, which just angered me. Love doesn't protect you from being poor or struggling. Doesn't mean that your life is worth it or that you've achieved your goals. It angered me that she thought happily ever afters were the be-all and end-all for everyone.

This American girl flittered around that university pub like she was somehow divinely gifted at finding love for people. It was laughable. She even had a poster up on their pub wall for her dating clinic schedule at Mulligans. Ridiculous.

The craziest part? She did it all for free. It was clearly something a girl with too much money and not enough real-life problems did with her free time.

Cut to my sister becoming roommates and fast friends with her our final year to now with me living just meters from where she sleeps at night? It feels like the universe is having a proper go at me because no matter how hard I try, *I can't escape Everly Fletcher.*

And if I want to get my brain off her and the way she subtly needles me for information while blinking that doe-eyed look at me, or how she absentmindedly licks her lips when she's thinking, or how her clothes show off just enough to give a view of her curves, but not enough to be blatantly trying to show them off . . . I need to get with someone else the first chance I get. Preferably, someone who isn't obsessed with happily ever afters.

I reach to grab the box of condoms and freeze when a deep voice growls behind me. "I'd think long and hard before you grab what you're about to grab."

My back tenses as my fingers brush the box of johnnies.

"At least he's being smart," another voice grumbles, this one deep as well, but a touch more playful.

A third chuckles. "It's not smart to buy these here. The whole town will know before he's even checked out."

"So long as he's not thinking about being *smart* with anyone we know," the first voice chimes in again.

I slowly lower my hand and swallow the knot in my throat before turning around to face whatever fucked-up small-town shite I just dropped myself into with very little effort.

My eyes lift to find three broad, bearded beasts standing shoulder to shoulder, shooting daggers at me. They're dressed in various shades of flannel, all three of their arms crossed over their chests like they're guarding the gates of hell, and I know instantly . . . these are the Fletcher brothers.

And they're scowling at me like I'm the shite they scrape off their boots after a long day wrestling mountain lions. Right now . . . *I think I'd choose the mountain lion.*

"Are you sure this is him? He doesn't look Irish," the one in the middle asks, his nose wrinkling. "And fuck, did none of you ask how tall he was? This guy is huge."

"Why does Everly always find the tall ones?" the one on the left with longer hair asks, turning to look at the two men he's standing with.

"It's three against one," the scary one on the right croaks. "Doesn't matter how tall he is." Silence falls over us for a moment before he barks, "Who are you?"

I jump and clear my throat, rolling my shoulders back to feign confidence. "I'm Wolf . . . or . . . or Conri."

"Don't know your own name?" the scary one asks.

I shake my head firmly.

"Then what is it? Wolf or Conri? Which one we using."

I flinch as a flash of my past rushes to the front of my mind.

"Oi, Wolfhound!" the kids at school jeer, circling like a pack of scraggy terriers. "Bet ye sniff out yer dinner in the bins like the rest of the mutts."

I'm eight and all knobby knees and tiny fists balled tight enough to leave crescents in my palms. Mam has patched my jumper three times this term alone, and every stitch feels like a sign on my back saying Kick Me.

One of the boys shoves my shoulder hard enough to send me skidding down to the gravel. The sound of lads laughing at my expense echoes in my ears as I taste blood in my mouth and a sharp sting burns from where I bit my tongue.

"Say something, Wolfhound!" another sneers, taller than me by a head, reeking of crisps and body odor.

Heart hammering in my chest, I do what he asks. I wipe my mouth on my sleeve, look him dead in the eye, and say, "Steady on. Even a hound will bite if you back it into a corner."

My reply is a bad idea because even though I got one swing in . . . they get in ten times more, making that blood in my mouth triple in volume by the end of it.

I blow out a long breath and force myself to stand tall and not allow myself to be triggered back to memories of schoolyard bullies. Back to memories when I was begging for puberty to hit while the rest of the lads in my class towered over me. But I haven't been that young, weak boy in many years, and I'm not about to let these bearded brothers get a leg up on me.

"My name is Wolf," I state confidently as I straighten to my full height.

His eyes twitch. "Wolf Reilly?"

I nod and then flinch when the guy's hand comes toward me, but then I see that he's just offering it for me to shake. "I'm Wyatt Fletcher. Welcome to my mountain."

His grip is bone-crushing, but I meet it back with my own strength, summoning my years of rugby training. They caught me with my trousers down a second ago, but I'm recovered now.

"Thanks for having me," I reply with a bit more pride in my voice.

"I'm Calder," the middle one says jovially, like he wasn't just eyeing me into an early grave moments ago. He grabs my hand and gestures next to him. "This is Luke. You can ignore him."

"No, you can't," Luke says, shaking my hand next. His eyes narrow as he leans in close. "My cabin is closest to Everly's, and I'd like to inform you that I've taken up birdwatching, so watching is all I do."

"That's not creepy at all," Calder says under his breath.

"How old are you?" Wyatt asks, his brows furrowed as he eyes me up and down.

"I'm twenty-two," I answer honestly.

"He doesn't look twenty-two." Calder steps back and tilts his head. "Fuck, man, what's your workout routine? I didn't look like this at twenty-two. Is this all from rugby, or do you do weights too?"

"Bet he can't grow a beard," Luke mumbles petulantly.

"Go ahead and buy those condoms." Wyatt's eyes twinkle with death. Straight murderous death.

"Yeah, don't let us stop you." Calder chuckles and covers his mouth with his fist.

A hush falls over us as they all wait to see what I'm going to do. This is a test. A test that I'm probably going to fail because I have no idea what the fuck is going on. I'm just about ready to reach back and grab them to show these guys that I won't be intimidated when a shrill voice yells, "Hey!" and breaks all our focus.

I turn to see my new boss marching toward us, practically dragging a toddler by the hand behind her. She stops right next to me and directs her ire toward the flannelled terrifiers.

"What the hell are you three doing? You were supposed to pick up the cake. Did it really take all three of you? Everly already arrived, and you missed her big entrance."

The three mountain brothers step back and drop their heads in shame.

"I see what's going on here," Trista says, pointing to me and then back to them. "They freaking you out? Trying to scare you off?"

My jaw clenches as I glance back at them, unwilling to confirm her accusation but unwilling to deny it either.

"Look at me. All three of you," she snaps, turning her back to me as she addresses the three grown men in front of her like they're the wee little girl she has clutching her finger. "We talked about all this. Wolf is my responsibility. None of yours. You're not doing that scary-protective-uncle bit with him, okay? He's my employee, and he's here to work. He's not here to screw your *adult* niece. And he's certainly not here for you to terrify. Got it?"

They begin to argue back with her, but I'm distracted by the conversation when something sharp presses into my quad. I look down to see the child that Trista is holding on to is now poking the wolf tattoo peeking out from my shorts on my thigh. She's all chestnut curls and chubby cheeks and stares up at me with the kind of confidence that suggests perhaps she runs the mountain, not these three uncles of Everly's.

The corner of my mouth tips up into a smile, and she grins back, the two of us having a quiet moment before her mam bends over and picks her up. "Go to Dad. He needs a chaperone, apparently."

"Way to go, Papa Bear. You got us in trouble," Calder grumbles.

"I didn't drag you in here with me," Wyatt barks as he hoists the little girl up on his shoulders as they begin to walk away from me.

"Birdwatching is not creepy . . ." the third one named Luke adds, following them down the aisle.

Trista turns on her heel and blows a curly strand of hair out of her face. "Three grown men to pick up a cake." She offers me an apologetic smile. "You okay? You need a cookie? A therapy session? A time machine to take back the decision to move here?"

I sniff and shake my head. "I'm alright."

"Good. Come on and let me take you next door to the party. You'll be safe with me." She pauses as she looks around. "Unless there was something you needed to buy first?"

I lick my lips and set the protein bar back on the shelf before giving a lingering look to the condoms. "I can come back later." And I leave those condoms exactly where they are and where they might have to remain.

So much for a comeback season.

Chapter 9

Third Half: *A classic rugby term. The first two halves are the game. The "third half" is what happens after.*

Translation: *Let's party!*

Everly

I'm just about to accept the glass of champagne from the bartender and owner, Judy, when I'm pummeled by a large figure and two giant arms that wrap around my waist.

"Butthead is finally home," my uncle Calder roars as he lifts me up off the ground and spins me around.

Two more arms grab hold of me, and next thing I know, I'm hoisted up even farther. "Evie girl is back!"

I laugh as I hold on to Luke's shoulder and stare down at the bird's-eye view of a room full of my favorite people. "Oh my God, you're going to drop me!"

"We got you, Evs," Calder reassures, repositioning me so one half of me is propped on his shoulder and the other half on Luke's.

Wyatt appears in front of me with Stevie on his shoulders, making us quite the pair.

"Everly!" Stevie cheers as she smiles and claps.

I reach out to give her a little squeeze. "Hi, Stevie girl!"

"Be careful," my grandma Johanna warns from her seat at the big table that's decked out with a red-and-white-checkered tablecloth, flowers, and a Welcome Home, Everly! sign that greeted me when I arrived ten minutes ago. Seated around the table are Dakota and Addison, my two newest aunties-in-law, my grandma, my dad, Cozy, and Ethan. They all stare up at us with completely unimpressed looks. They are clearly far too used to my uncles making spectacles of themselves.

"I think this is a rugby move, isn't it?" Uncle Wyatt asks, shooting me a knowing wink that's his quiet way of saying, "Welcome home, kid."

"This is a rugby move," I exclaim, thrusting my hands up into the air. I flip my hair over to one side as I scratch my head in thought. "Shoot, I just learned this. What is it called?" My eyes search the bar, and I spot Wolf, who has just entered from the store side. He's standing with Trista and watching the scene unfold with wide eyes. "Wolf . . . what's the thing where you guys lift the other guy in the air so they can catch the ball?"

All eyes swerve to the tall, dark, handsome new face who's standing in the doorframe. Well, crouching. He has to duck down to walk through it. I feel like Wolf is getting a bigger reaction to his entrance than I did.

"Holy shit, that's him?" Dakota gasps, elbowing Addison, who lifts her hand and instantly begins fanning her face.

"Has to be," Addison replies with a deep breath.

"I told you guys," Cozy adds while popping a cherry from her drink into her mouth.

"You didn't tell me enough," Dakota deadpans.

"Babe, I can hear everything you're saying," Calder says to his wife.

"They don't even have the decency to whisper," Luke adds with a pout.

"Quiet, boys, I want to hear this fella talk," Judy, the bartender, croaks as she jabs an elbow into Calder's side.

The women all smile dreamily as they gawk at the Irish rugby player who just entered the chat. In all their defense, Wolf does look painfully good. He's dressed in a black T-shirt that's stretched tight over his biceps and chest, where his signature gold cross necklace rests. And he's wearing a pair of pale gray shorts that are short and trim and fitted over his sculpted thighs, revealing all of that infamous ink of his.

He looks like a total fish out of water in this rural mountain dive bar. But he's clearly a fish everyone would like to catch.

Wolf's eyes lock on mine, and my heart rate increases as he answers my question. "It's a lineout lift."

"Yes," I exclaim, clapping my hands excitedly. "And it totally shows what the guys are packing downtown, if you know what I mean."

"Excuse me?" I hear Wolf retort, but my brother distracts me by chucking a rugby ball at my face.

I nearly Marcia Brady it and take it to the nose, but luckily, I haven't had anything to drink yet, so I'm able to react quickly enough to catch it before it makes contact.

Apparently, Ethan made my dad buy him a rugby ball on the way up here today because he wants Wolf to teach him how to play. I fear this Irish boy is going to be integrated into my family whether he wants it or not. I hope he knows what he's in for.

My uncles finally lower me down off their shoulders and give me big hugs, murmuring words of welcome as I move from one to the next to the next. Wyatt holds me just a little bit longer as I squeeze little Stevie as well. "We missed you up here. Welcome back, kiddo."

"Thanks, Uncle Wyatt."

He ruffles my new hair, and our moment of love bombing breaks up when Judy brings out trays of appetizers, forcing all of us to settle down and take a seat.

"I'm so glad you're home, my Evie-girl," my grandma says, squeezing me into her for the third time since I arrived. "You're back for good now, right? You're not about to break the news to me you're getting your master's in Prague, are you?"

"No," I reply with a laugh as I watch Trista introduce Wolf to the rest of the crew on their side of the table. "I'm done with school and ready to work."

"Good." She takes a sip of her drink and smiles. "I'm ready for you to be in the same time zone."

"Me too. How are you, Grandma? What's new?"

"Oh, nothing much. Taking care of this one a whole bunch is a full-time job." She smiles at Stevie, who is currently covered in ketchup. "Ethan and I help Trista out at the center when we can get up here. It's good. I'm busy with everyone! I like to stay busy."

"That's so great, Grandma," I reply and can't help but marvel at how good she looks. Her gray hair is styled perfectly in a short, chic bob . . . much shorter than mine . . . and she looks like she has some sun on her cheeks.

I'm glad to see her doing well. It's been five years since we lost Grandpa, and I worried about how she'd adjust with me not around to stop by every week. Losing him was hard on her. It was hard on all of us. And we all adjusted to the loss in different ways.

For my dad, it made him really latch on to family and finding ways to make more memories with everyone . . . hence the new cabin on Fletcher Mountain and the family trip for Wyatt and Trista's wedding several years ago.

For Uncle Wyatt, it inspired him to finally want to start a family of his own, which shocked so many of us at the time, but ended up being the best thing that ever happened to him.

I smile as I watch Stevie force a french fry Wyatt didn't ask for into his mouth. She's almost four and has softened his grumpy mood more than I ever could have imagined. And if it wasn't her that accomplished that, it was Trista. And if it wasn't Trista, it was the plethora of rescue animals she managed to sneak up into his barn beside his pet goat, Millie. Family and farm life suits Wyatt, and I'm so glad that I found Trista to be his surrogate all those years ago.

Uncle Calder has changed a lot since Grandpa passed as well. And Dakota was a huge part of his transformation. She inspired him to grow his woodworking and furniture-making passion, that was more so a grief coping mechanism, into a full-fledged business that's now so successful I had to pass off my social media managing to a legitimate company. Now they're a happy family with two cats . . . Milkshake and Malt.

And Uncle Luke . . . I smile as I spot him squatting down in front of where Addison is seated. He cups her sides as he rests his forehead against her swollen belly. She slides her fingers into his hair and whispers something that has him throwing his head back in laughter. His story might be the one I'm most proud of. He silently loved the lumberyard girl for so long and never told a soul—though I have a funny feeling Grandpa knew. He often would make Luke go pick up their orders because he was pulling some strings from behind the scenes. I like to think that's where I get my meddling from.

And for Grandma—all these changes in her sons' lives have resulted in her living her best grandma and mother-in-law life she could have ever dreamed of. She's turned into a replacement mother for both Trista and Addison. And she appreciates Dakota daily for keeping Calder in check. My dad is adding on a mother-in-law suite to his cabin on Fletcher Mountain so she can stay with them whenever she wants.

Like . . . this is it. *I've done it.*

I gave everyone in my family their happily ever afters.

If only Grandpa were here to see it all.

I release a trembly breath as I wonder if this is what Grandpa had in mind for me. Matchmaking gave me purpose when I couldn't seem to figure it out for myself. Maybe my big realization after losing our family patriarch is to just continue to be the glue that holds everyone together. Even if I can't easily find love myself.

I can live with that.

Heat spreads across my face when I look up to find Wolf staring at me curiously from across the table. He frowns, almost like he can sense my mood shift, and I shake my head and attempt to refocus on the group.

"So, what's your long-term plan, Ev?" Luke asks, dropping down in the seat beside me as he drinks from his beer. "Are you working at Mount Millie just for the summer? Or indefinitely?"

"She has to work for three years in the field before she can work for Fletcher Industries," my dad replies for me with a firm tone.

"Maybe she wants to come work for Fletcher Brothers Construction," Wyatt says, leaning over the table. "We could probably use some business strategy help."

"You're not seriously trying to poach my first business development specialist before she's even started her job, are you?" Trista calls across the table.

"I have a feeling your dad is going to lose you to Mount Millie forever if you're as good at this job as you were for my furniture business," Calder says with a knowing smirk.

"Guys, guys, there's plenty of Everly Fletcher to go around," I state, holding my hands up dramatically. "Let me get Mount Millie online and see who I can help next, okay?"

"Hey there, stranger," a male voice states from a distance, interrupting my family laughing at my lame joke.

I push my hair out of my face and look up to see the last person I would have ever expected to see at the Mercantile.

"Hilow," Trista exclaims as she jumps up from her seat and rushes over to our side of the table. "Nice to see you made it."

"You invited my ex-boyfriend?" I hiss under my breath to my aunt as she bustles by me.

She smiles through clenched teeth. "Remember, Everly, I told you he's job-shadowing my vet friend, Avery, this summer. Avery, the vet that comes up to Mount Millie for us all the time—free of charge."

Wyatt clears his throat, and Trista rolls her eyes at him.

"I guess I forgot about that," I murmur, suddenly feeling very parched. I reach out to grab my drink and take a long sip. It's been years since I've seen Hilow. We ended on good terms, but it was definitely one of those one-sided breakups.

"I dropped off that probiotic paste for your alpaca at the shelter," Hilow says, hooking his thumb back toward the bar exit.

"Oh, good, thank you. I hope it'll help calm Trumpet down. He weirdly hates the new horse," Trista says, glancing back at me.

They both stare at me like I'm supposed to do something, so I stand up and walk over to give my high school ex a hug. That's what you do at times like this, right? Hugs?

Hilow's long arms wrap around my waist as he hunches down to hug me back. He's easily just as tall as Wolf and my uncles, but nowhere near as built. He's more that nerdy-slender sort with a sweet face and a smile that seems almost permanent. When Trista told me he was training to become a vet, I thought that made perfect sense. He looks like a sweet vet type.

And a sweet, nice first boyfriend.

"You look amazing, Everly," Hilow says, his eyes sweeping over my whole body and then lingering on my head. "I like what you did to your hair."

Self-consciously, I thread my fingers through the front of it and sweep it to one side. "Thanks, it was kind of impulsive."

"It looks great. You look great. Really, really great."

"Okay, we get it," Calder drones, not looking up from his beer. "She looks great. Move on to something else."

Hilow clears his throat as his eyes dart to my three uncles and my father, who have intimidated the shit out of him at least half a dozen times. The worst being my junior-year prom—they almost didn't let him in the front door. It took some time before they saw him for the harmless, sweet creature he is.

"Um . . . how was Ireland?" he asks, his smile forced as everyone continues watching us.

I flush as I feel one set of whiskey eyes laser-focused in my direction. "It was good. Long time no talk, I guess."

"Four whole years," Hilow says swiftly. "Good to have you back for good, finally."

He says it in a way that feels like it means something more to him than I want it to, but maybe I'm just reading into it too much.

The thing about Hilow was, there was never anything wrong with him. He was always happy. Always pleasant. Always attentive and kind. He called when he said he was going to. We were together for two whole years, and he was my first for so many things.

But when I think about the epic love stories or the couples I've matched . . . those descriptors I just listed aren't enough to convince me two people belong together.

So, I did what I thought was right and ended it before I went away for college, even though he really wanted to do long distance. One thing matchmaking taught me was that you should never settle for anyone less than your person.

"Hilow is amazing with the animals at the rescue center," Trista says with wide, eager eyes. "A big help to Avery when he's overwhelmed. I'm so grateful. Hilow, why don't you sit down and join us for a bit?"

He looks to me for approval, and I pause for a moment before snapping out of it. "Of course, yes! Join us."

Trista yanks the back of Grandma's chair, dragging her down toward the end of the table without even getting her out of her seat. She then grabs another chair and plunks it right beside mine with a giant, freaky smile. If she's trying to play matchmaker, her technique could use some serious work.

But, with a polite smile, I lower myself into the chair beside him and do my best to catch up with a guy I would have been fine with never seeing again.

Wolf

"Why they call you Wolf?" Stevie, Everly's cousin, asks as she stands beside me with her elbow propped on the table, staring up at me.

"'Cause I'm scary," I reply curtly.

"You not scary." She pokes my arm, and I frown because it hurts. Why do her little fingers feel like knives? "Why do you have a wolf on your leg?"

Poke.

I hiss and glance around the table, wondering when someone is going to come collect this kid who's bothering me. I'm much more interested in earwiggin' on Everly and that lanky prat who's just shown up out of nowhere. Who the heck is this guy anyway? Is that her type? Why does she look like she'd rather be anywhere else?

The urge I have to get up and push him out of the building is strong, which is highly concerning, considering she has a table full of uncles who are much more suited for that level of protection.

But the way this bloke's presence is triggering me is troubling. This is Everly's turf. She is fine.

We're not at Trinity College anymore.

"Hello?" Stevie reaches up and grabs my face with her tiny hands, forcing me to look at her and thereby breaking my focus on Everly. "Why Wolf?"

"'Cause that's what my nana started calling me as a boy," I snap with irritation.

"What's a nana?"

I grumble under my breath. I'm pretty sure they use this word in America. How does she not know it? "It means grandma."

Her eyes widen. "Can I call you Nana?"

"No."

Her face falls. "Why not?"

"Because you have a nana right over there."

She buzzes her lips and glares at me.

I roll my eyes. "Fine, call me Nana. I don't give a toss."

I straighten when Everly stands up from the table with Hilow and the two of them turn to walk over to the bar. His hand lingers behind her, like he's going to touch her but decides otherwise.

I don't like it, but when I look around the table to see if any of her psychotic uncles are noticing what I'm noticing, they all seem perfectly at ease with her talking to this guy with a weird name.

My eyes can't move away from them. From all my time watching Everly over the last couple of years, I can see how uncomfortable she is standing rigid next to her ex, who has a smug-as-fuck smile on his face as he leans in way too close to her. She always lets people get too close to her. She's too trusting. Too open. She sees the best in people from the jump, whereas I require them to prove themselves first.

Heat boils up my spine as I clench my fists on the table.

"Where are you going, Nana?" Stevie asks as I move to stand up.

"Don't worry about it," I murmur back as I cut across the creaky wooden floor of this run-down pub.

In three long strides, I'm standing directly behind Everly and the tall, scrawny guy, who looks like he pisses sittin' down, with no idea what I'm doing. This is not what I usually do when it comes to Everly Fletcher.

"Want to introduce me, Stretch?" I ask, my tone harsh and unapologetic.

Everly turns, and her blue eyes blink back at me in confusion as she hooks her thumb to the guy next to her. "Oh, sure. This is Hilow."

"Interesting name," I reply, reaching out and giving him a firm handshake that he winces through. *Good.*

"It's a family name." He smiles at me as his eyes look me up and down. "And you are?"

"Wolf," I answer with zero emotion on my face.

Hilow's brows lift. "A family name as well?"

"Nickname." I lean in close and bare my teeth. "Because I can rip the face off a person for looking at me sideways."

Hilow blanches, and then his brows pinch together curiously. "Does Ireland have wolves?"

"No."

"So then . . ."

"It's a nickname, Hilow. It's not that deep," I bite and take a step closer to him. He's a tall fucker, but I have at least sixty more pounds on him.

He shoots an apologetic look to Everly, who seems super confused by this entire interaction. I kind of am too, I guess. I'm not used to strong-arming guys in front of her. *Just behind her back when she doesn't know it.*

"Wolf is working at the rescue center for the summer. He's living above the barn too."

"Oh, yes, your aunt mentioned having an exchange student or something. Welcome to Colorado."

"Thanks," I grit, sick of the small talk. "So, were you two an item or what?" I ask, my eyes flicking to Everly for a moment, lingering on the blush in her cheeks before snapping back to

Hilow. I'm trying to determine if this guy is a friend or foe. Stretch here isn't making it very obvious.

"We were together for two years," he answers cheerily, like she was a prize he won at a village fair. He once again moves as though to put an arm around her, and I glare at the motion, tensing every muscle. His arm drops to his side.

I nod slowly, my eyes turning to slits. "So, what happened? Honeymoon phase end when the pints ran dry?" *Did you cheat on her? Hurt her? Make her feel like she didn't deserve love for herself?*

Everly turns horrified eyes to me. "Can we not do . . . whatever this is?" I hate how she's looking at me. But fuck, what am I doing? I let out a breath, trying to relax the stiffness of my body, and slap a fake smile on my face that feels like a sneer.

"I was just trying to get to know one of your mates here, Stretch. You don't mind, do you, Heelow?"

"It's Hilow. Like Hi and Low."

"Hiya!" I bark and give him a matey pat on the back before glancing to the bar. "Should we get some drinks? I think we should have drinks."

"I'm afraid I can't stay. I'm on call. But, um . . . Everly, I'm having a party at my new place in Boulder in a couple weeks. It's sort of a housewarming party. I'd love if you could come."

Everly sucks a breath in through her teeth. "Oh, I'll probably be working."

"On the weekend?"

"Yeah, lots to do. I have big goals for this summer."

"Can you come after? There will be people from school there who would love to see you after your travels. So many are home for the summer and taking a bit of time before starting the real world, you know? Unlike me. I won't be done with school for quite some time, I'm afraid. Vet school. Blegh."

Hilow smiles over at me, and I narrow my eyes to inspect

him more. I can't tell if his niceness is an act or if he's putting on a front. I have a hard time trusting openly nice people.

However, I *am* curious about why Everly seems so determined *not* to go to this party. She's just returned from Dublin. Surely, our resident matchmaker has mates she'd like to reconnect with. Maybe not this Hiya goofball, but others, I'd think.

"Please feel free to come as well, Wolf," Hilow says, turning to me with a smile.

"We're probably going to be busy," Everly says, and my chest contracts at the way she lumped me into her *we*. I watch her inquisitively, noticing that she seems to be refusing to make eye contact with me, like she's embarrassed about this guy. *Interesting.*

"Well, I'll text you the address just in case. I really hope you'll change your mind." Hilow takes a step between us, and I move to stand beside Everly. "It was nice to meet you, Wolf," Hilow offers.

"Grrr," I growl and jump forward as I make a biting motion at him. He shuffles back and laughs nervously. I wave my hand and force a smile. "Relax, Hiya. I'm just taking the piss."

Everly rolls her eyes at her ex's confused expression. "That means he's joking."

"Right. Sure. Irish." Hilow swallows thickly. "Okay then. I hope to see you both in a couple weeks."

He waves goodbye, and I turn to Everly with a dark look. "Now who has secrets?"

Chapter 10

Scrambled: *A defense or attack that's disorganized, could hint at being thrown off-balance socially or emotionally.*

Translation: *Fish out of water.*

Wolf

"I hope you're ready to see Mount Millie Rescue Center in all its glory," Trista exclaims as she drives me, Everly, and Stevie down the gravel road in her ATV.

I'm crammed in the back seat with the child who won't stop calling me Nana. It's weird as shite, but I don't know how to make it stop.

But it's probably better than being seated next to the girl who occupied way too many of my thoughts yesterday.

Saturday with Everly's family was a lot. Maybe too much too soon and part of the reason why I got my nose all bent out of shape with the presence of that guy from Everly's past. But it doesn't mean anything. I worry over Everly the same way I worry over my sister. It's innocent in nature. At least that's what I tell myself. I just need to keep my distance and focus on my job and not Everly's life.

But my curiosity about why she was so weird around her ex is piqued. I'm fighting the urge to pry but know I shouldn't because I don't like when she pries into my shit. So instead, I'm fighting a war within myself to back off or dig deeper. At least if I'm friends with her, I can be everywhere she is.

Fuck. That sounds creepy as shite.

I'm overthinking all of this. But it's strange to be trapped on a mountain with the girl I've been avoiding for the better part of four years. Especially when I've suddenly found myself immersed in her world, her family, her work, her friends. How the hell did I get here?

As I stare at the back of her head in the ATV, a memory from first year at Trinity floods my mind. A memory I try not to think about when it comes to Everly Fletcher.

Trinity College | Dublin, Ireland
Four Years Ago

There's the American, Everly Fletcher, again, I think to myself as I down half my pint in one big gulp and shift on the pub stool at Mulligans.

It's my first year at Trinity, and my teammates and I finished training an hour ago and decided to stop at our favorite pub for a quick team meal. Most have buggered off back to the rugby house to ice their knees because we have lifting early, but I'm staying exactly where I am because of one girl.

Everly Fletcher.

She's always fucking here. I'd hoped after we finished our class together, maybe I'd forget about her. She's occupied more of my thoughts than I care to admit, considering I only had a handful of classes with the girl. But I swear, every time I see long blonde hair on campus, my neck snaps, trying to see if it's her.

Something about this girl draws me in like a sunset that's impossible to look away from.

Tonight, Everly is running another one of her dating clinics that have quickly become somewhat infamous amongst the student body.

How she got the pub owners to agree to this event is beyond my comprehension. The girl is determined.

She stands in the middle of the pub like she owns the place, dressed in her usual Trinity tee and baggy jeans as she clutches a furry notebook to her chest and passes out notecards to each of the couples positioned on various pub tables. It looks miserable, but her clients, if that's even what she calls them, seem to be enjoying themselves.

I, on the other hand, am not enjoying myself because there's a fucking arsehole who won't stop pestering Everly, and it's getting right up my shirt. He looks like a finance lad trolling the campus pub for young college girls. His shirt likely costs more than I make a week working my parents' shop, but the faded black eye he's sporting makes it clear as day he's a wanker.

He keeps offering Everly a drink that she refuses, and when his hands reach out and graze her hip, I clench my fists and fight the urge to walk over there and grab him by the throat.

Everly laughs at him, and that reaction stirs something low in my gut. Possessive. Primal. And completely irrational. I don't know if I'm concerned for her because I know her or concerned on behalf of all womankind.

All I know is I sip my pint and don't taste any of it because I'm too busy watching this interaction play out.

When she finally pushes him back, making it clear she's not interested, he laughs and leans in to whisper something in her ear.

"Take a fucking hint, pal," I growl under my breath as I set my pint down and crack my neck. I lean back on the bar like I'm a hired bodyguard for the annoying American.

Out of the corner of my eyes, I see my teammates get up from their stools, and one of them calls out, "We have curfew, Wolf."

"Go on without me," I say, still watching Everly and the finance prat.

"Coach will have your arse if you're late."

"I said go without me," I snarl, breaking my eye contact for a moment to tell my team captain to kindly fuck off.

He gives me a pointed look, and I sigh heavily, knowing this will get the guys talking about me again in the locker room. I was already top news after my yellow card last week for fighting with the ref. My temper has been on another level these days, and I'm on thin ice with the team.

But tonight, I don't have time to worry about what they all think of me, so I wave them off and turn back to see that Everly is on the move, heading toward the toilets. The guy sits down at her table, making himself at home near her coat, so I take this as my chance to give him a stronger hint than she did.

I cross the room in as few steps as possible, weaving through the crowded pub full of students out on a Thursday night. Mulligans is always packed on Thursdays.

I stop behind his seat, close enough to smell his overpriced cologne, and he must sense my presence because he turns around and stands up when he sees me glaring at him.

"Leave her the fuck alone," I grit, my nostrils flaring with barely concealed anger as I clench my jaw. The one perk of my height is moments like these, when I can put pricks in their place just by looming over them.

"Who the fuck are you?" the prat asks, poking me in the chest. "Her big brother?"

My fingers flex at my sides. I know this kind of guy. This is the kind of guy that would call a kid gay in secondary school for wearing pink. Like casual homophobia is just acceptable. Or he'd be the prat who'd toss a smaller kid's schoolbag on top of the lockers where he couldn't reach it and threaten anyone who dared help him.

Those arseholes were a dime a dozen in my school.

But what they don't realize is that sometimes, the little guys grow up.

I take a step closer to him, and his chin juts up to look at me. "If you don't piss off, I'm going to give you a matching set."

It takes him a moment to realize what I'm talking about, and then his fingers touch his black eye anxiously. He ponders it for a moment, and then he buzzes his lips. "She's not hot enough for this bullshit," he scoffs and turns to walk away, but not before I pull him back by his collar.

"What the fuck did you say?" I give him a shove on his back.

"Nothing," he stammers.

"Exactly."

Arsehole.

He stumbles into a group of lads, his eyes narrowing on me. "You're fucking crazy, man."

"You have five seconds," I grind out, and then he hurries over to a booth and grabs his suit coat before hauling arse out of the pub.

Present Day

I shift nervously as that haunting memory floods my mind. I ended up missing curfew that night and had to do a solo bronco test at training the next day as punishment from my coach. But I didn't give a fuck because I couldn't leave until I knew Everly got home safe. I didn't want to outright tell her I was worried about her because the less I talk to Everly Fletcher, the better.

But it was that night that started something much bigger than running sprints for my coach. It started something I've never said out loud. Not to my teammates, my sister, not even to myself.

For the past four years at Trinity College, I would sometimes stalk Everly Fletcher.

I didn't really know I was doing it until I started noticing a pattern. That first night I just followed her home to make sure she was safe from that prat who looked like the type of bloke that would wait for her in an alley.

And if anything happened to Everly—to any girl—I could never forgive myself.

It felt like a noble quest.

But then I worried about her on other nights too. I wondered how often clients messed with her. I wondered if she was good at sticking up for herself. Eventually I found myself back at Mulligans, looking up the schedule for her matchmaking events so I could be there to keep an eye out from the back of the pub. At first, I tried to leave early when it was clear that guy from before didn't return. But I couldn't get the image of him out of my head, the way he leered at her like a creep.

So, at some point, I decided to follow her home again to ensure she was safe.

It was easy to watch from a distance, in the shadows, tucked into the darkness a half block behind so she didn't see me. And yeah, the way I learned the rhythm of her walk and matched her quiet, careful steps was a tad odd. Honestly, I could see how some might interpret that as creepy behavior too. But I was looking out for her. Someone clearly had to.

Everly Fletcher trots around like she's untouchable. Headphones on, bag bouncing on her hip, eyes glued to her mobile without a care in the world. The girl is a walking advertisement for blokes with bad intentions.

My intentions were pure. I wanted to protect her. Dublin at night is not as safe as it pretends to be. And she always took the same route home, so it made following her pretty simple.

That's always where it ended. She'd reach the Rubrics, and I'd stop at the corner, heart hammering in my chest over the rush of it all. She'd disappear inside, and I'd wait for the light in her room to turn on. It always did. And then I'd turn around, shoulders tight, jaw clenched, and walk back to the rugby house so full of adrenaline from trailing after her that it would take me hours to fall asleep.

I hated that I couldn't stop.

I'd tried not to follow her, but five minutes after she'd leave,

I would find myself rushing out the door to catch up to her and make sure she was okay.

I was obsessed.

Which is why I remind myself that I could never be with a girl who was made for the light when I so clearly belong in the shadows.

"This is the new gravel lane the guys just finished that gives direct access to our center from the main road below," Trista continues with the tour, explaining how the business sits on fifteen acres of land, most of it fenced-in pasture with room to grow if needed.

"The road turned out perfect," Everly says excitedly. "And the parking lot for visitors too."

"Visitors we don't have yet." Trista sighs.

"Don't worry, I have a plan." Everly wiggles her brows.

"Good." Trista smiles back at Stevie. "I'm so sick of planning."

We round a bend, and Trista sings out, "Here we are!"

The center comes into full view, and my brows lift at the grandness of it. I pictured an old, run-down barn with some animals scattered here and there.

This is a proper facility.

The building is a large metal structure, nestled cozily amongst large pine trees. The siding is light gray metal with green trim and a massive sliding bay door down the middle with big black block letters that read Mount Millie above it.

"This was all built with recycled steel and locally sourced timber," Trista says, glancing back at me. "That's Wyatt's brainchild, but I love it now too. We're the only fully sustainable rescue center in all of Colorado."

"I'm going to work on getting that put up on your signage out by the road," Everly says, pulling out yet another notebook and scribbling some notes down.

"Good idea," Trista agrees.

I shift awkwardly in my seat, wondering if I should be taking notes as well. I was a decent student—you have to be to get into Trinity—but I never really knew what I wanted to do with my life, other than rugby. The law path has been pretty much drilled into my head by my parents since I was young. They see a career in law as the ultimate success story they never achieved, and I guess I just accepted that idea until rugby became more of an option.

Now, I'm stuck in this limbo sort of place where I'm not really playing professionally yet, but I'm also not really doing a job fitting of a bloke with a degree from a prestigious Dublin university. And I only have myself to blame.

"The barn is south-facing, so the windows give us good sunlight and heat in the winter, and the green roof keeps it cool in the summer. The solar panels on the roof and that wind turbine in the back pasture provide nearly all the center's energy needs. It heats our water troughs and runs our electric fencing around the paddocks. There's even a composting toilet system in the barn, along the zero-waste recycling station.

"Oh, and of course, we have a rainwater collection system that feeds all our troughs and waters our vegetable and herb garden that's maintained by volunteers. We use all that produce to feed the animals and the staff. I really love that part."

"Me too," Everly says, her eyes marveling at everything. "I'm aroused."

I blink back my shock over Everly's choice of words, and Trista replies, "Girl, same."

"What's aroused?" Stevie asks from beside me.

"Nothing, baby girl," Trista replies absentmindedly, not the least bit embarrassed for talking that way in front of a child. I'm gathering this is where Everly gets her bold honesty from. Her family doesn't hold back at all.

"That's my bike rack." Stevie points to the tiny little row of old horseshoes up by the barn.

"We'll get your bike out and show them in a bit, Stevie." Trista drives past the center to loop around the various outdoor areas. "The pasture fencing is all built from reclaimed wood, and the couple shelters we have out there for the animals to use during inclement weather were all donated by a farmer down the road."

"Epic," Everly says with a smile as she pushes her hair off to one side. The morning sun glitters through her light hair, and I have to force myself to look away.

"That covered paddock area by the center was recently reinforced with rubber flooring built out of recycled tires. It helps prevent the animals from having to walk in mud for too long and get hoof rot. That was Hilow's suggestion."

"Oh, really?" Everly's head spins around to look at her.

"Yeah, he got the tires donated from Tire Depot in Boulder and everything."

"How nice," she replies, and I stare at her curiously to see what she means behind those words. Is it a . . . that's-nice-because-charity-is-nice? Or is it a . . . that's-nice-because-I-want-to-fuck-my-ex-boyfriend-again nice?

A sharp poke on my leg distracts me, and I turn to see Stevie jabbing my thigh tattoo with her little pointy claw again.

"Quit that," I grumble, and she just giggles. Weird fucking kid.

I've been around my fair share of kids with the youth coaching I've done. But the kids I normally interact with come up a lot higher than my kneecaps. And they don't do the poking thing.

Trista parks the ATV in front of the barn, and we all climb out as she points to a large pile of shit located on the backside of the building. "We do manure composting because that's killer fertilizer for the garden, and any manure we don't use, that same farmer comes and takes it out to his fields. So that's where you'll be mucking the stalls out to, Wolf."

I nod and then notice Trista staring down at my legs. "I probably should have told you to wear jeans and boots."

I glance down at my athletic shorts and trainers. "These are old shoes."

"If you say so," Trista replies, and I swear Stevie covers her mouth to snicker at me.

Stevie's wearing a bleedin' dress with cowboy boots, so I don't know how that's any better than what I'm wearing. Everly is, of course, dressed perfectly in jeans, cowboy boots, and a flannel shirt draped over a cropped tank top. If I'd known before coming to Colorado that flannel was such a popular dress code, I'd have done some shopping.

"Come on inside, and I'll show you what we have going on."

Trista pushes the giant sliding door open to reveal the inside of Mount Millie. It smells like fresh cedar chips and steel mixed with whatever animals she has in this place. It's clean and still very new-looking but also manages to be warm and welcoming. Light pours in from the glass roof panels on the ceiling as our feet scrape along the concrete floor.

She guides us over to the right side. "This is the receiving end of Mount Millie. It has our feed room, which is our makeshift office, the vet care area, and a large quarantine pen for new arrivals just outside that gate. Avery is our primary vet on call, but I think we'll be seeing a lot more of Hilow as well this summer."

Everly's eyes move to mine for a moment before snapping back to Trista.

"Every new animal has to be examined by the vet first, then we work to determine if it's a plays-well-with-others friend or a grumpy, need-my-own-mountain-to-function friend."

"Like Daddy," Stevie adds, kicking her little cowboy boots onto the gate beside her.

Everly laughs, and Trista winks at her daughter. "Currently, we have ten calves, five goats, one donkey, one big old Clydesdale horse, two alpacas, and a rogue goose that wanders around Fletcher Mountain freely. There's a binder of all the animals and their backgrounds over by the pens. Wolf, that will pretty much be your bible this summer. Take the first hour today and really look over that so you can learn about everyone's quirks."

"Oh, um . . . will I be . . . handling the animals a lot?" I ask, my body tense with anxiety.

"Definitely. And it's going to be baptism by fire today because we're receiving a new alpaca, so we'll want to prep a fresh pen for him. When you're done with the binder, you can grab a couple fresh bags of cedar chips off the shelves in the back and distribute them in that pen next to the other alpacas. Then you can start mucking out all the other pens. Stevie can show you where the wheelbarrow and pitchfork are. Watch out for Clyde. He kicks if you spook him."

"Are there photos in the binder? I'm not sure I know what an alpaca looks like."

Trista blinks back at me and then bursts out laughing, clutching her belly and bending over as she fights to recover. "Good one, Wolf. That was really funny!"

Everly joins her in the laughter and then grasps her arm to refocus Trista. "Do you have time to go over my plans? I have all the ideas in my notebook here."

Trista wipes tears from her eyes and nods. "Yeah, let's go into the feed room." She points to the space beyond the vet area. "There's a desk in there we can spread out at."

And with that strange interaction, Trista and Everly turn and walk away, leaving me standing there with a confused frown on my face beside a curly-haired little kid who I think I've just discovered may be my boss for the summer.

Everly

The feed room looks like the command center for Mount Millie. It smells sweet and nutty, and there's a mini fridge in the corner with human snacks on top—Stevie-friendly foods like fruit snacks and chips. The wooden shelves on the wall sag under the weight of feed bags that look like they were dragged here by a donkey. There's a bucket of fresh carrots in the corner and a bin labeled "For Goats Only." Someone has scribbled on one pail, "Do NOT Let Stevie Near This Again," in black Sharpie.

There's a sense of barely controlled chaos, and it's here that I get a sense for just how overwhelmed Trista has been the past year. Mount Millie has only been open about six months, and it's clearly too much for Trista to manage the business side of the rescue and take care of the animals.

That's where I step in.

"I worked on this plan in one of my business classes, so I got lots of great advice from my professor."

"Amazing," Trista says, looking over everything.

"I want to eventually open up for visitors on Sundays," I say, spreading out my business plan for Trista on the wooden workbench that was covered in corn scoops and buckets just moments ago. "We can invite local vendors up here and allow them to set up booths and sell their products. Thinking ice-cream trucks, jewelry stands, local honey, that kind of thing. I talked to Judy on Saturday, and she's on board for doing a food truck as well. Basically, Sundays are going to be like a bougie farmer's market up in here. We'll do live music anytime I can get a guitarist or someone to do it for free . . . and don't worry, I'll be able to find someone to do it for free."

I exhale heavily as I continue thumbing through my notes, excited by all my ideas. This is like matchmaking for a business in many ways. Only instead of obsessing about finding the perfect two types to go together, I get to obsess over graphics and slogans, vibes and outreach ideas. Something that makes Mount Millie tangible and long-lasting, not a place someone posts a one-star review on social media about after one bad experience. This kind of helping fills my cup almost as much as matchmaking, and it's high time I find my identity outside of that skill.

"And I'm going to work on your website and take that binder of yours and add all that animal info to the site. It'll be like a cute Meet the Residents of Mount Millie page where we share the backstory of how each animal came to live with us. But the stories will be works of art. Stuff that can go viral because it's so cute and wholesome you can't help but share it.

"Also, I'm thinking eventually we could launch a Patreon account for you where we make exclusive video content to our subscribers, which will be a new income source. Match that with extra foot traffic up here and donation stations all over this facility, and hopefully, you'll soon have the funds to hire actual staff and not just delinquent rugby players."

"Breathe, Everly," Trista says, touching my arm with a worried expression.

"I haven't even got to my big launch idea!" I exclaim and flip to another section of my notebook. "I want to do a matchmaking auction to introduce Mount Millie to society. Basically, win a day with a mountain man. Obviously, all my uncles are romantically taken, but it doesn't have to be a romantic sort of date. You're bidding on a day of free labor. I mean, Fletcher Brothers Construction is well-known. The community would be crazy to not jump at the chance to have them for a day to do some handyman work."

"Holy shit, Wyatt will hate that idea," Trista replies, her eyes twinkling with mirth. "So of course we have to do it."

I bite my lip and wrinkle my nose. "They'll do it for a good cause, don't you think?"

"They'll do it because their favorite niece asks them to." She winks knowingly at me.

"I can't wait to get started." I beam as I drum my fingers on the desk. "I also have some ideas around the facility to make them more visitor-friendly. Adding a couple benches, things like that. I'll see if Calder has any reject pieces lying around."

"Sounds amazing." She sighs and smiles as she glances around the enclosed space. "This place needs to thrive. We've invested so much money into the sustainability. It can't fail now."

"It won't," I state firmly, gripping my aunt's arm. "We won't let it. It just needs publicity to become an institution everyone wants to help with. This is just the beginning, Trista. Once they see the magic up here, they'll be so inspired to come back and help out. I have a meeting later this week with Dakota to discuss merch. Selling T-shirts is a no-brainer."

"You're a wonder, Everly Fletcher. A true wonder." She smiles at me. "To think none of this would have been possible if I hadn't smacked you in the face with a surrogacy clinic door."

I burst out laughing and shake my head. "You would have found a way, I'm sure of it."

"Naw. Strong women build up strong women." She pins me with a meaningful look. "I'm excited to get to spend some time with you this summer."

"Ditto." I push my hair out of my face to jot down a few notes, fighting the niggling words from Wolf on the plane and how I'm just working for my family, using my connections because it's safe and easy. It's not safe or easy. This is work. Will it be my forever future? No. But it feels right, and I'm not going to let that Irish rugby player get in my head.

I can feel Trista watching me curiously.

"So did you enjoy seeing Hilow Saturday night?" she asks, her voice pitched in a funny sort of way.

"Um . . . not really," I reply with a cringe and look up to see her face fall. "Sorry, he's fine. I'm just really and truly over him."

"Oh, that's a shame because he's totally still hung up on you. Asks about you every time he's here. I felt sorry for the poor guy. He's really very sweet."

I resist the urge to roll my eyes. I know what she was trying to do, hooking me up with my ex. And even though Hilow is a nice guy . . . that's all he is. I've barely thought of him over the last four years. And seeing him next to Wolf, who makes my body feel all sorts of things I barely understand . . . made me realize I'm not even attracted to him anymore. I wonder if I ever was.

"I know, he's great. But I'm not looking to date anyone right now."

Trista chuckles. "Why not? I'm no matchmaker, but even I know you're in the prime of your life. Surely you met some cute guys in Ireland?"

I groan and cover my eyes with my hand as I wonder if I should confess my woes to my aunt. She's only been in our family for four years, and I lived in Dublin a lot of that time. We haven't had a ton of quality time together. But there's something about Trista that feels safer than even my stepmom, Cozy. Like she's unbiased Switzerland.

"Can I do some real talk with you, Trista?"

"Of course! I'm a sealed vault over here."

My jaw tenses as I glance at the door, ensuring it's still closed. "I thought I would have so much fun in Ireland. Like somehow, Irish guys would be cool with my oversharing awkwardness that I can't seem to stop myself from doing. I'd be the quirky

American girl or something. But that never happened. I tried dating and was a disaster over there. One guy literally gave me a one-star review on Instagram for being so awful right before I graduated."

"What a fucker," Trista snaps back with zero humor on her face.

"I know. So, I'm not going to worry about my dating life. I had so much fun traveling with Cliona. She's a great friend. That was really the best gift I could have ever found at university, and I'm good with that. Who cares about dating?"

Her brows furrow intently. "But you were with Hilow for two years, right? How bad at dating can you really be?"

I tsk knowingly. "I'm afraid Hilow was like a platonic buddy that I felt comfortable with. Maybe too comfortable. And sadly, we were never very romantic." I lean in close and whisper, "And that was painfully clear in the bedroom, if you know what I mean." I can't hold back the way my face scrunches and body shudders in revolt at the memory. Fuck, it was bad. So bad.

"Shit." Trista winces, and that reaction only confirms how destitute I must be.

I growl and scrub my hands over my face. "And it sucks because I'd hoped Ireland would change all that. I thought broadening my horizons would help shake things up. But it's not just that I'm awkward. It's that I don't ever seem to find that perfect spark—that spark that I look for when I matchmake. Like when I matchmake . . ." I pause and look Trista deep in the eye. "I've never told anybody this before . . ." She nods and leans in close, propping her chin on her hands as she stares back at me with eager interest. "I get like . . . reverse anxiety."

Trista frowns. "What does that mean?"

I inhale deeply through my nose and move my hands around my head to try to illustrate. "Like when I know two people belong together, it's like my brain finally calms down. It goes still. No buzzing, no overthinking. It's like ninety percent of the time, my head is a snow globe being shaken all day long until I find a match for someone. Until I see a little glimpse of a perfect pair who I just know could work together. Like when I saw you and Wyatt together for the first time . . . I knew it was endgame. Same thing for Dakota and Calder and Addison and Luke. When two people are meant to be together, the snowstorm in my head just magically stops." I hold my hands out still for effect. "And I'm left with this amazing sense of calm."

"My goodness," Trista says, her eyes glossy. "And all this time, I thought you were just concussed when you said it'd be a good idea for me to carry your uncle's baby."

I giggle and shrug. "It goes deep. And man, do I love that feeling. It's better than any drug out there."

"Then you can't give up on finding it for yourself," Trista replies, slapping her hand on the counter. "You're way too young to be done with dating."

"I know, I know," I groan haphazardly.

"And not for nothing, but have you laid eyes on that Irish boy you brought back home with you? Good Lord, if that's how the guys in Ireland look, no wonder you struggled . . . I'd struggle too!"

My body inwardly buzzes at just the thought of Wolf. "Yeah, he's something, alright."

She licks her lips and nods. "No calm snow feelings around him, I take it?"

"Absolutely not," I bite back seriously. "Wolf is like a blizzard."

She giggles naughtily. "I thought so."

"Not that it even matters," I reply, steeling myself to come off a bit more aloof. "He's my best friend's brother, and he barely tolerates me."

"Um . . . I beg to differ," Trista says, lifting a finger. "He marched over to that bar within seconds of you leaving the table on Saturday with Hilow. Everyone noticed."

"They did?" I ask, my chest contracting with anxiety over that thought. I try to think back to everything that happened. But all I can recall is trying to be nice to Hilow while mentally trying to figure out how I'd have to squirm out of his touch if it happened. Then Wolf was there, likely doing that overprotective, big-brother thing that was honestly kind of helpful. "Well, it was no big deal."

"Are you sure about that?" Trista asks knowingly.

I shake my head, refusing to believe whatever she's implying. If she thinks Wolf was jealous of Hilow, her head is a snow globe too. If anything, Wolf was just trying to irritate me. Or maybe he was just trying to get away from my family. They can be a lot. Maybe he'd been poked in the thigh one too many times by Stevie. My cousin is a cutie, but given Wolf isn't really a people person, a little person might have tested his limits too far.

But romantically? Me and Wolf? Never in a million years.

"For the past four years on campus, he ignored me, even when we were regularly in each other's orbit. The FESS program isn't that big at Trinity. We had some classes together, and he was always at the pub I hosted my dating clinics at. Like, clearly, if he wanted to, he would, y'know? He was only forced to acknowledge my existence when I randomly became roommates with his sister, and even then, he acted like we were strangers."

"Huh, that's weird," Trista replies and taps her fingers on the table. "I thought I was picking something up Saturday night."

I shake my head. "He's just being decent to me because he's alone in a new country and his sister probably told him to be nice."

Trista gets a defeated look on her face. "Well, hopefully you two become friends at the very least."

"It's possible," I reply with a smile. "I mean, I love his sister, and she loves him, so he must have a nice side to him somewhere in that gruff rugby exterior. I just hope no one gets the wrong idea about us because, well . . . you know my uncles."

"Yes, I do. They're animals. Fucking animals," Trista replies with an exasperated sigh. "But you gotta not worry about what they think. They're living their lives. You need to live yours. If they get in your way, you let me know. I can handle them. Or Dakota. Or Addison. Or Cozy. Or your grandmother! Especially your grandmother." Trista laughs and shakes her head. "My point is, you cannot let some pushy Fletcher brothers make you feel like you have to be celibate all summer just because you're living on the same compound as them. You deserve to find your calm snow globe, Everly. And the ladies of Fletcher Mountain got your back always."

The warmth that spreads in my chest over that sense of solidarity feels incredible. This is what I've been missing. That deep sense of family. Of belonging. Of loving someone despite their flaws and trusting that love is true and won't turn on you when you least expect it.

It may not calm my snow globe, but it warms my heart.

"Thank you, Trista. I love seeing you all together," I say, pressing my hand to my chest. "So much has changed, and yet . . . it feels like this was always how Fletcher Mountain was supposed to be. A real family unit."

"Don't get all mushy on me," Trista snaps, waving a hand in front of her face. "Your grandma Johanna already makes me cry every time she hugs me. I've gone soft now that I'm a mother and am seriously always a hair trigger away from blubbering." We smile quietly at one another before she adds, "You know, you little mastermind, Fletcher Mountain feels complete now that you're here. Like a little missing puzzle piece your uncles needed."

I nod and smile. "I couldn't agree with you more."

Chapter 11

Goose Step: *A running technique when the player slows down and takes a small hop before sprinting in a different direction.*

Translation: *A wonky sidestep that works well against alpacas.*

Wolf

So, we have Trumpet and Manwich, the alpacas that live here permanently, as the welcome committee for Mount Millie. We have a small ten-cow herd of no-name cattle, Clyde the Clydesdale, Diego the donkey, and the goats are all named after the Spice Girls. But I cannot remember the damn goose's name.

I set my pitchfork down after mucking out the last of the stalls and walk over to open the binder again. "What was the name of the damn goose?" I murmur to myself.

"Fowl Pacino," a voice utters from down the alley, and I turn to see Everly walking toward me with two bottles of water. She hands one over, and I accept it gratefully, my body drenched in sweat from the day.

I take the bottom of my shirt and scrub away at my face to wipe the sweat off. When I lower it, I find Everly staring at my abs. I can't help but flex a little before dropping it, breaking her eye contact.

"Trista loves a good pun," Everly says as a flush creeps up her neck. She takes a dainty sip of her water, trying to look casual. "How's it going out here?"

"Alright," I say as I point to the pens. "I think I've got them all cleaned out, but I don't exactly have a frame of reference for what's good cleaning and what's bad, so if it's not good enough, someone will have to tell me."

Everly tips her head and eyes Stevie sitting on the floor outside the pen I just vacated. "What's she doing?"

I shrug. "Coloring."

She laughs. "Why there?"

"I don't know. She sits outside every pen I'm working in. I almost tossed a shovel full of shit in her face once by accident. Can't seem to get rid of her. Is her mam okay with her being out here alone?"

Everly smiles and shrugs. "She's got you."

I huff out a noise of discontent. "I don't have a lot of experience babysitting."

"Maybe it's Stevie doing the babysitting," Everly replies with a waggle of her eyebrows. "Hey, Stevie? You want to come back up the mountain with me in a little bit? After we input this new alpaca that's on his way up, I'm going to work from my cabin for the rest of the day. You can color there with me."

"I'll stick with Nana," she sings, barely looking up from her coloring book.

Everly frowns, and I just roll my eyes.

After a moment, she locks eyes with me, a peculiar look on her face, and then shakes her head like she's changed her mind. She makes a move to leave before my words halt her in her tracks.

"You planning a matchmaking event for the animals in there with your aunt or what?" I bite the inside of my cheek to stop my smile.

Everly's eyes fly wide. "No . . . but I am planning a matchmaking event. Maybe we can throw an animal in with it."

"It was just a joke."

"I know, but how cute could that be? I'm totally writing that down."

She hums to herself as she tucks her water bottle under her arm and opens her furry notebook to take a note. She always has furry fucking notebooks. This one is white fur with pink polka dots. Her tongue darts out and slides over her peach-toned upper lip, and I have to clench my jaw and look away. Being this close to her is a strange thing to get used to. However, I can't help but admire her passion for something as simple as matchmaking animals and people. I'm trying to remember the last time I was excited about anything as much as Everly is about her crazy matchmaking. Rugby maybe?

She recaps her pen and taps it on her notebook as she hits me with an odd look. "Hey, can I ask you something?"

I frown and prop an elbow on my shovel, eyeing her curiously as her neck starts to turn red and blotchy.

"Did you really want to come to that party with me?" Her eyes fly wide. "I mean, not *with* me, of course . . . not like a date. That's weird. You're my best friend's brother. Ick!" she sputters, and a little spit comes out of her mouth and hits me right in the eye.

I fight the urge to wipe it off because I don't want to make her even more uncomfortable than she clearly already is. Could have done without the *ick* comment at the end of her little sputtering rant.

"But like . . . do you wanna come with and stuff?" she stammers out, that red in her neck crawling all the way to her cheeks. "Like as a companion? Not like a sexual companion. I just mean like . . . a buddy. A pal. A big-brother thing."

"Big brother?" My brows lift.

She shoves her fingers through her hair and shakes her head. "Just forget I asked." She turns around, her shoulders practically pinned under her ears, and I can't help but smile as I watch her shuffle away.

"Hey, Stretch," I call out, my eyes lingering on her ass before she stops in her tracks.

"What?" She sighs and turns back to me, her mouth turned down in an adorable little pout. "Just say it. I'm a moron."

"You're not a moron." I chuckle and prop my hands on my hips. "But sure. If you want me to go, I'll go."

Her lips part. "You will?"

I shoot her a teasing smirk. "Yeah, I need to see for myself if you spit on everyone's faces you talk to or if that was a gift just for me."

She narrows her eyes at me. "You know, one of these days, you're going to embarrass yourself, and I'm going to be super kind and gracious and not point and laugh at you."

"I didn't point."

"You didn't have to," she tuts and then smiles. "But you'll really come with me? 'Cause I don't want to go alone."

And I don't want you to go alone are the words that I want to say back, but don't. Because she'd probably think I'm a loon.

Which clearly, I am.

"Yeah, why not. Not like I've got anything better to do."

She rolls her eyes and smiles before the sound of an engine distracts us. I look out the barn door and see a truck and trailer pulling in. Everly turns her clear blue eyes to me. "Showtime, Wolf."

"Okay, the owner said this alpaca isn't halter broke, so whatever you do, *don't tug on the halter*, or he'll fall down on his side, and you'll never get him back up," Trista says as she pulls open the door to a white livestock trailer, revealing a four-foot-tall ball of white wooliness.

"Oh, he's a cutie," Everly says excitedly as she peers into the trailer from the ground.

"Super cute!" Trista agrees in a weird, growly voice as she climbs up into the trailer. "You're going to get along great with Trumpet and Manwich."

I cringe from my place beside Everly. I wouldn't use the word *cute* to describe this creature standing before me. This one might even look diseased. It's definitely different-looking from the two we already have.

"Come on up here and join me, Wolf," Trista says as she gently grabs the halter rope hanging from the animal's face. She hands it gently over to me. "I'm going to let you bring him into the holding cell while Everly and I go fill out the paperwork with the owner, Mr. Smith. Here at Mount Millie, we let all animals come in how they want to. So just ease your way out with our new wooly friend. Take your time and let him lead you into the holding cell, not the other way around. We'll be back when we're done with the owner. Sound good?"

"Um . . . I guess so." I gape back at Trista. "Are you sure I'm the one who should be doing this?"

"Yeah, this is a good first-day confidence booster. You'll be great." She laughs and pats my arm as she hops out of the trailer and follows Everly into the barn with Mr. Smith.

"You can do it," Stevie says, hanging over top of her bike rack on the side of the barn. Her hair is dangling in the gravel, but she still has a perfect upside-down view of me.

I feel like all she's missing is a bowl of popcorn to enjoy the show.

"You wanna help me out, maybe?" I ask, obviously very desperate if I'm seeking the assistance of a three-year-old.

She shakes her head, and I sigh as I gaze back at the strange-looking animal inside this smelly trailer. He has a tuft of white, wooly hair at the top of his head, and his eyes are dark and glossy like two creepy marbles stuck in its face. His mouth is a weird black line, and his crooked lower teeth stick out above his lower lip.

"You kind of look like a llama and a poodle had a baby, don't you, lad?" I take a deep breath as I take one cautious step toward the alpaca. He jerks his head, eyes wide like I just offended the sorry bastard . . . and then, without warning, the feckin' thing launches at me, slamming its fuzzy head straight into my gut like a rugby player attempting a tackle. He catches me on my heels, and I fly backward, landing hard on my back.

A warm squishiness on my spine has me dry heaving in disgust, but before I can even look at the horror show that is likely the back of my shirt, the animal takes a flying leap out of the trailer, stumbling all over like a baby giraffe who barely knows how to walk.

I scramble up, legs wobbling as he jogs toward the barn entrance. He stops in his tracks before he crosses the threshold, like he got a look at the accommodations and didn't approve.

Jaw clenched, I tear after the animal like we're in a fucking match, and when it swerves left and attempts to run again, I do a rugby goose step and course correct just in time to follow him. I manage to snag a fistful of halter rope and lock my fingers tight as the fucker drags me in my sneakers across the gravel with more strength than it has any business having.

Suddenly, the little bastard stops dead in its tracks, and without thinking, because I've clearly lost all use of my brain after getting my ass tackled by an alpaca, I catapult forward and yank hard on the halter.

Big. Fucking. Mistake.

The animal freezes, chin pointed up to the sky in protest as his whole body goes stiff, legs straight as fence posts, and as if in slow motion, the massive thing collapses sideways into the gravel, neck flopped backward, freaky eyes bugged out of his head, mouth clenched tight like it's having a fucking stroke.

"Jaysus, is it dying?" I shout, wide-eyed and covered in what I now have confirmed is alpaca shite.

"No," Stevie answers casually while climbing on the bike rack.

My heart batters in my chest as I loosen the slack on the halter and wait for the alpaca to jump back up, but it doesn't move. It just lies there like some sort of fuzzy crime scene, foam bubbling out of his weird little mouth. I start to wonder if it has rabies or is possessed by the devil. Maybe both.

I inch closer to give his body a gentle nudge, trying to coax him back onto its feet. He makes a weird, throaty groan that doesn't sound good, so I move back.

Unfortunately, I'm not quick enough.

"Fuck!" I roar and jerk violently as a sticky liquid explodes across my face. "The bloody creature spit on me!"

I grab the hem of my shirt and wipe the horrifying substance off my mouth. The feel of it makes my stomach churn again, and I kick at the gravel in frustration. "What the actual fuck! I didn't know alpacas spit," I roar as the animal remains lying on the ground with zero signs of remorse.

Stevie giggles knowingly.

"How do I get it up?" I ask the likely fresh out of diapers child as I stand there panting for my life, barely holding it together.

She shrugs and continues watching me with a gleeful twinkle in her eye.

Voices echo from inside the barn, sounding like they're coming my way. My breath hitches with worry. The last thing I want to do is look like a fucking idiot on my first day. And I especially cannot be unmanned by a bleedin' alpaca in front of Everly Fletcher. My ego could not survive it.

I need to get this animal inside. *Now.*

So, I decide if the alpaca doesn't want to walk, it's decided exactly how it wants to enter Mount Millie rescue center.

Holding my hand up in case the damn thing wants to spit again, I get close, squat down, and wrap my arms around the wooly beast's neck and arse. With a grunt, I heft the giant shag rug with legs up into the air and clench my jaw as I shuffle over the gravel toward the barn.

The owner, Trista, and Everly appear just as I hit the doorway. Their timing is impeccable. They stop dead in their tracks and blink back at me as sweat pours down my face.

Teeth clenched, I growl, "The alpaca wanted to be carried inside," and muscle the animal straight past them toward the holding pen, where I lower the wriggly bastard back down to its feet, my lungs burning with exhaustion.

The animal immediately springs to life and trots around the pen like nothing happened.

"Magical bleedin' recovery, fucker," I mutter under my breath as I look down at my body, which is covered in shite that I've never seen before. My trainers have a hole in the toe, and I have no idea when or how that happened.

"It's his first day," I overhear Trista whisper loudly.

When I turn around, my eyes lock with Everly, who looks like she's about to lose it as she covers her mouth and fights back a laugh.

I scowl at her, fighting my own smirk, until the owner distracts both of us with, "I'm afraid I have one more animal sitting in the front seat of my truck that I need you guys to take as well."

The owner walks over to his vehicle, opens the door, and lifts out a large, clear tank with a freaky-looking lizard of some sort inside. "This is my daughter's bearded dragon," he says with a regretful look. "I know I should take him to a pet store, but I was hoping you could handle him for me."

"Oh my God." Trista bends over to tap on the glass. "A reptile is a first for us, but I'm sure we can find him a good home."

Chapter 12

Selector: *A person who is delegated with the task of choosing players for a team.*

Translation: *Rugby boy is officially a Dragon Daddy.*

Everly

"Fun facts about bearded dragons," I call out as I follow Wolf up the wooden steps leading into his barn apartment. "They can run standing up. They live longer in captivity. Stress stiffens their spikes. They are poisonous, but not much."

"What is that supposed to mean?" he asks, stepping aside so I can open the door for him.

"It means, if he bites you, it will sting like a bitch but not kill you."

"Oh, how comforting," he murmurs as he walks over to the long table that houses the desktop computer. "Is here good?"

I prop my hand on my chin and frown. "Not much of a view."

"Do lizards need a good view?" Wolf deadpans.

"Over here!" Stevie calls out as she runs through Wolf's apartment like it's hers.

I suppose she's spent more time up here than he has since Trista used this area as an office for a long time while the rescue center was being built. Stevie darts past the living room area and points to the long dresser on the wall opposite the foot of the bed. I'm impressed to see the bed is made.

Wolf and I make eye contact, silently agreeing that it does

look like a decent place for this guy to live. So, we both listen to the three-year-old and take the reptile over there.

I try not to squirm too much at how this entire space smells like Wolf. Like clean laundry and a warm, spicy sort of cologne that clings to the air. I shouldn't notice it. I shouldn't imagine it on his skin or him in the big bed. *I wonder if he sleeps shirtless?*

My stomach flips as I glance back down at my phone to focus back on the bearded dragon intel. I'm here for work, not for peeling back a layer of Wolf Reilly, even if he did surprise me by agreeing to come with me to Hilow's party. This is just business.

Get your shit together, Everly.

"It also says here that bearded dragons can develop strong attachments to their humans and even want to cuddle."

"Cuddling, you say?" Wolf murmurs as he obsessively straightens the large tank on the dresser, and I can't help but smirk at the way that doesn't appear to freak him out in the slightest. My God, is this guy going to cuddle with this lizard? This, I have to see.

Stevie pushes Wolf out of the way and taps on the glass. "Hi, Rugby."

"Rugby?" He directs that question to me.

"The owner said his daughter never named him."

Wolf scowls down at Stevie. "If I have to take care of it, shouldn't I get to name it?"

"No," she replies with a sharp tone.

I laugh as Wolf squats down to argue with the child in the room. I'm impressed with how quickly he volunteered to take home the bearded dragon. Trista brought the tank into the barn after the owner left and said, *"Wolf . . . would you like a new roommate?"*

And that's all it took.

She said we could share the responsibilities of the lizard, but

Wolf seemed like he wanted him all to himself. It made me smile and wonder what he was like as a little child. I wouldn't have pegged him for a reptile lover, but I am gathering there's a lot about Wolf that I don't know. Life at Mount Millie is forcing me to learn all sorts of new things about my best friend's brother.

Wolf stands and looks at me with a flat expression. "His name is Rugby."

"Rugby it is." I cover my lips with my hand as I try to hide my giggle. Mr. Grumpy Rugby gave in to a three-year-old pretty quickly, it would seem. "He eats live mealworms, kingworms, and crickets, or greens like parsley and kale, not lettuce. You can also feed him vegetables like peppers and sweet potatoes. You can give them some fruit, but not much. The previous owner gave us this container of freeze-dried crickets."

"Ewww!" Stevie squeals, wrinkling her nose at the tub I pull out of the bag on my shoulder.

"Stevie!" Trista's voice calls from down in the barn. "Get down here, please. You don't need to be in Wolf's space. Plus, I need help with Reginald."

Stevie makes a growling little noise as she stomps past us to leave, but then she stops and hugs Wolf's leg. "Bye, Nana." She moves to hug my leg next. "Bye, Everly."

"Bye, kiddo," I call back and watch her as she runs through the apartment and out the door to meet her mother on the steps. "She's obsessed with you."

Wolf grumbles his discontent, but I swear I see a twinkle in his eye. He turns around and sets about plugging in the heat lamps connected to the tank, so I continue my education.

"They call 'em beardies."

"I'd rather call him a dragon," Wolf says, eyeing the animal closely. "More manly."

My view drifts to Wolf's back, and I have to cover my mouth

because he's covered in alpaca shit, dirt, and other grime that I don't even know where he picked it up. It's been a big day for Conri the Convict. And I hate to admit that even covered in manure, he's still painfully good-looking.

Did I ever notice how hot he was at Trinity? Admittedly, when we had class together, I couldn't *not* notice him. He towers over most people and has that dark, rugged look down to an exact science.

But I rarely ever look at guys romantically for myself. My brain just instantly starts churning about what type of person he'd match with, and that person is never me.

My one big relationship in high school proved to be a fluke. Hilow lived down the street from me, and we knew each other for years. Then one day, he asked me to go on a date, and I really had no reason to say no. Logistically, we made sense. Similar socioeconomic backgrounds, similar educational and professional goals, supportive families. We were both kind people with similar interests and hobbies. By matchmaking standards, Hilow and I checked all the boxes on my matchmaking manifesto.

But after graduation, I just couldn't stick with him. I felt stir-crazy and bored and guilty for not wanting to hang out with him. I knew I had to end it before I went to Dublin, and I've never regretted it because I never really missed him. We were just better off as friends, simple as that.

Maybe I can develop that friendship with Wolf. He's not nearly as sweet and easygoing as Hilow, but he did agree to come with me to that party. That's a good start.

I just need to stop ogling his ass as he reaches into the tank to pet his lizard.

God, that sounds dirty.

I snort back a laugh at my own thoughts, and Wolf turns around, eyeing me curiously. "Something funny?"

I shake my head. "No, nothing funny at all. I'm just shocked you wanted to take care of this thing so much."

He turns his focus back to the cage, tending to it like a doting father. "It'll be nice going from slaying dragons to feeding one crickets."

"Excuse me?"

He offers me a rueful smile as he stands up and pushes his hair back on his forehead. "I played a lot of D and D as a kid."

I stare back at him, my jaw dropped.

"What?"

"I cannot picture this—" I wave my hand in front of Wolf, gesticulating his whole being "—playing Dungeons and Dragons."

"Don't judge a book by its cover, Stretch," he drawls, his eyes narrowing on me in a way that lights my skin on fire. "That'd be like me expecting you to only ever play with Barbies."

"Oh, you'd be spot-on there," I reply with a nod. "I'm a boring and predictable basic bitch."

He frowns and looks forward, his jaw muscles shifting under his skin. "I don't think moving to a foreign country and managing to get the most popular pub near Trinity to host you and all your dating events is what I would call basic bitch behavior."

"More like crazy bitch behavior," I retort with another weird snorty laugh. *I have got to stop doing that. Even Rugby is judging me.* I frown as I process what Wolf just said a bit more. "Which is probably why you rejected my matchmaking offer all those years ago now. Any regrets?" I waggle my brows knowingly at him as our eyes connect.

For a beat, he doesn't answer. Doesn't even blink. His gaze drags over my body like he's seeing the memory play out between us. And when his tongue sweeps out over that lush lower lip of his, my insides squeeze, and my face flames with heat.

What is this?

What is he thinking?

He's never looked at me like this before . . .

Has he?

His voice is rough when he answers with, "I have regrets."

And I swear you could knock me over with a feather because I get the impression those three simple words are anything but simple. I cough loudly and turn my focus away from him before I spontaneously combust and become food for the beardie. I survey the space, my eyes blatantly avoiding his bed as I try to turn the conversation to a safer category. "How do you like it up here?"

"It's brilliant," Wolf replies easily, like that charged moment between us never happened. He reaches into the tank and pets Rugby with his finger. "Nicer than what I had in Dublin."

"I guess I never saw your place there." I can't help but frown as I wonder how many girls he brought back to his flat. Why is my brain being such an asshole right now?

"I shared with a few other rugby guys. They were disgusting."

I force a smile. "Did you host all those rugby parties I always heard about?"

"A few," he confirms casually, but his eyes feel very noncasual. "Why didn't you ever come to any of our parties?"

"I wasn't exactly hanging with the rugby crowd," I reply honestly and feel my cheeks flush. "Even after Cliona and I became roommates, we didn't really socialize much with her teammates. We just kind of did our own thing. Though I'm not sure I would have come anyways. Big parties stress me out. They're so chaotic. Not my thing."

"You were good for Cliona," Wolf says, his eyes tender on mine.

"What do you mean?"

"I mean, after all that shite with her teammate and her ex

fucking behind her back, she needed a friend outside of rugby. Glad she had you."

My brows lift. "Are you . . . complimenting me right now? Hang on, I need to sit down. I'm feeling lightheaded."

"Sod off," Wolf murmurs, rolling his eyes.

I can't help but marvel though. Wolf always made me feel like a nuisance. Like he couldn't get far enough away from me. I never would have suspected he actually appreciated my friendship with his sister. "Her ex and her teammate are both assholes."

"You can say that again."

"They're assholes."

Wolf tilts his mouth in a sly curve. "You still could have come to our rugby parties. Who knows, you might have enjoyed yourself."

I smile and nod. "That's why I'm committing early to Hilow's party. I need to start saying yes more. Put myself out there a bit."

"Like your mate's party," he confirms, his face scrunching up with thought. "Do you ever say yes to something that makes you feel unsafe? I suspect you're a bit of a good girl, aren't you, Everly?"

Heat sparks low in my belly at the way he says my name. My actual name. Not Stretch. Not pain in the arse. Not my sister's friend. He called me *Everly*, with that accent of his that rises and falls in a way that makes the most ordinary sentence sound like a naughty secret. Like a gentle caress on my belly. I feel nearly woozy at the sound of it.

"You think I'm a good girl?" I pant and cringe because I sound like a total simp.

His lips curl up into a sly grin as he leans closer to me. "Definitely."

A noise from downstairs pops the bubble that formed between us, and I jerk back, shaking myself out of whatever stupor I was just in. *Pull yourself together, Everly. Good girls don't lust after the mountain farmhand.*

But his words stir some curiosity inside of me. I don't really do anything unsafe. Even at Trinity, I never so much as considered a one-night stand with anyone. No one ever made me want to take the risk. Not that I got too many propositions. After I started my matchmaking business, most guys I talked to were interested in being set up with anyone but me.

I bet Wolf has had tons of one-night stands. In a way, I admire it. I admire people who do something for themselves because they feel like it and don't overthink it. How freeing.

I glance down at the bearded dragon. "I should get out of your space. It looks like you have our dragon well taken care of."

"Our dragon?" Wolf frowns back at me.

"We're co-parenting Rugby, obviously," I state primly. "I'll expect daily updates on how our little guy is doing. And anytime you need a break, he can come spend the weekend with me at my place."

"I had no idea I was agreeing to shared custody." Wolf fights back a smile that looks really good on him.

I shrug. "Does it make you feel a bit . . . unsafe?"

He narrows his eyes. It's that dark, wicked look of his I will allow myself to have very unsafe thoughts about well into the night.

Chapter 13

Turnover: *When the possession of a ball switches from one team to the other unexpectedly.*

Translation: *Rugby boy is caught on his heels.*

Wolf

"Oh my God, I am pissin' myself," Cliona cackles on the other end of my phone where I have her propped up on the gate of the mini horse's empty stall in the red barn. We're on a FaceTime call, so she's getting a full view of me after working two weeks at Mount Millie. I've now completed my afternoon job of mucking out the barn before bringing all the livestock in for the night.

I have no idea who I am anymore.

I have blisters all over my hands, my body feels sorer than it does after rugby training, and I've shoveled more animal shite than I ever wanted to see in my lifetime. Not to mention, I smell like a mixture of hay, sweat, and alpaca piss.

Every day.

This is my scent every day.

I've taken to rinsing off in my boxers in the shower outside the barn in hopes of not bringing my stench up into my apartment.

And I'm pretty sure there's a piece of straw permanently embedded in my sock that's driving me absolutely mental.

"So, just to recap your first couple weeks," Cliona says, her eyes wet with tears from laughter. "You now sleep next to a pet lizard. You also manhandled an alpaca, got chased by a goose, tripped over your boss's daughter three times, and accidentally let out all the cattle because you didn't get the pasture gate closed properly?"

I sigh heavily and nod, which just makes her laugh harder. The cattle fiasco was a proper mess. All the Fletcher lads had to come down in their quads and help round them all up. The oldest one, Wyatt, looked like he wanted to throttle me. The second one with the tattoos yee-hawed and yelled, "Yippy ki-yay, motherfuckers," and the youngest one—Luke, I think his name is—handed me a six-pack of beer afterward like I'd earned a medal.

The only saving grace of a mostly awful day was that Everly wasn't around to witness that epic failure. Thank feck for that.

"I'm lucky I haven't got sacked yet," I grumble and pause as I lean against the gate and wipe my damp forehead off with the hem of my shirt.

"Ah, go on. I'm sure you're doing great otherwise. You did a nice thing for them by taking the lizard too. Is that little Stevie girl still following you around everywhere?"

"Yes," I reply instantly. "And she won't stop calling me Nana. I had to explain it to her dad, who looked at me like I was a weirdo."

Cliona erupts into another fit of giggles while I pull my gloves off and scowl back at her. "Are you about done yet?"

"I'm done, I swear." She settles after a moment and sighs heavily while her smile turns more thoughtful. "Have I thanked you lately for doing all this?"

I roll my eyes. "You've only texted me thanks three times a day every day since I left."

"Well, I mean it." She licks her lips and gets a pensive look in her eye. "I know you wanted to give up on rugby after your last match, but we've both worked too bleedin' hard to give up now. You remember our shared birthday wish when we were sixteen?"

My jaw tightens as I nod. "To be the first boy-girl twins to both play for Ireland in the Rugby World Cup someday."

"Exactly. And we can still do it. We can still take the rugby world by storm, Wolf. You just need to turn your image around, and I'm certain you'll get called back to Ireland soon enough. Leinster even. I'm talking you up to my coaches all the time, and they talk to the men's coaches. And heck, maybe all this mountain farmyard work will be good for your rugby game if you're out there wrestling alpacas."

I shake my head and try to hide the fact that playing the game doesn't appeal to me as much as it once did. So much has happened in the past several years. Heavy things. And I hate that it changed my relationship to the sport that once saved my life.

"How's Everly doing?" Cliona asks, thankfully not noticing any of my inner musings.

"Alright, I think," I reply, my body stirring to life at the mention of her name. "Why are you asking me?"

"Um . . . because you work with her."

I eye my sister harshly. "It's funny that you failed to ever mention that when you told me about this job. Almost like you wanted me to be surprised by it."

"I did not," Cliona retorts defensively, guilt written all over her face. "It just never occurred to me to tell you."

I roll my eyes at that. Cliona was always begging me to be nicer to Everly. I was as nice as I could be, especially since nice isn't exactly my forte. And being nice to her these past couple of weeks has made my thoughts about her get even more muddled than they already were.

I refocus and attempt to answer my sister's question. "I think she's alright, but I don't see her every day. She does admin work from her cabin a lot, or at least that's what her aunt said." I shudder when I wonder how nosy I must have seemed when I asked Trista about Everly the other day. I tried to get Stevie to ask her, but the little shite just wants to poke me in the leg and ask annoying questions every chance she gets. "I text her photos of Rugby whenever she asks."

Cliona makes a noise into the phone.

"What?" I stop my work to look back at my sister.

"Nothing. I just worry about Everly. The girl doesn't know when to stop working."

"You can say that again," I murmur under my breath, my mind flashing back to the notebook of information she brought on her first day of work. It reminded me of her at Mulligans during her matchmaking events. The way she'd pore over that notebook like she was on the brink of solving some difficult puzzle. She doesn't do anything by halves, that one.

"You know you could work on having a bit of fun while you're there too." My sister narrows her eyes at me. "It's not all just about work and rugby."

"I haven't even started the rugby bit yet. And I am having fun."

"Are you? 'Cause as far as I can tell, you look like you're being punished instead of having a potentially life-changing experience."

"Aren't I being punished?" I ask, my tone grave.

Cliona sucks in a sharp breath. "Is that really how you feel?"

"A little." I offer a small shrug, and my sister's face bends with guilt.

"Moon, no. I hate that. I don't want this to feel like that at all. Please tell me you're joking. I would hate myself if you're only doing this for me."

I flinch and force a smile I don't feel. "I'm just joking with you, Sunny. I'm fine." I swallow the knot in my throat and add, "I'm even going with Everly to one of her . . . *friends'* . . .

houses tomorrow night for a party," I mention, refusing to call that Hilow lad her ex. He didn't give ex-boyfriend energy. He gave . . . I'm-desperate-for-anything energy.

"Really?" She clasps her hands in front of her face. "Oh, go on, that sounds lovely. I'm wild with jealousy."

"Yeah, we'll see how fun it really is," I reply knowingly as I turn to look out the window of the barn, up toward Everly's cabin.

I find myself looking up the mountain toward her cabin at night quite often, imagining what she does in the evening. I've half wondered if I'd see a strange car outside her place because that Hilow bloke weaseled his way over, but it's been pretty quiet over there.

Been pretty quiet everywhere, really.

I like Fletcher Mountain and all. The views and the nature are grand, but I've always been a city lad surrounded by people. Grew up with my sister right next door to me. Then at uni, I lived with my teammates. We went from training—to studying at pubs—and then back to training. I miss that. Even the lack of traffic noise up here has me out of sorts.

"The party is in Boulder, so I'll get to see some signs of civilization, at least," I add with a rueful laugh.

"That's the spirit," Cliona cheers excitedly. "Oh, I can't forget to tell you—you'll never guess who I ran into at the pub this week."

I frown as I glance up from what I'm doing.

Her eyes look grave when she answers, "Finn."

"Finn Murphy?" I ask, my chest instantly tightening as she name-drops a blast from my past. I drop the pitchfork and walk over to grab the phone. "Did you talk to him? How is he?" I ask, blinking back at her.

"He looked good. Well. Healthy."

I nod and exhale heavily. "That's good."

"Said he was getting married."

"What?" I ask, my jaw dropped. "Married?"

Cliona shrugs. "That's what he said."

"Christ," I murmur, blinking back my shock. "Bit young for that, aren't we?"

Finn Murphy was my best friend for over a decade. Growing up, we were thick as thieves until secondary school, when I started playing rugby and we sort of grew apart.

Cliona shrugs. "I passed on a congratulations from both of us. He asked for your address to send an invitation."

"Did he? That surprises me. We haven't spoken in years."

"Well, you two were close at one point in your life, and I'm sure he wants you to see him happy."

"That's great. I'm happy he's happy," I reply, putting the phone back in place so I can get back to work.

"You should try to be happy too," she says firmly. "Let yourself have a bit of fun this weekend. Everly too. Anyways, it's late here, so I must crash. Keep up the good work. I'll call next week to hear how your weekend went. Night, Moon."

"Night, Sunny."

I hang up, feeling grateful for that little life update on my childhood friend. I always worried about Finn and how he got on in life after we stopped being mates. It brings me a bit of comfort to know he's doing well.

Feeling lighter, I step out of Handsome's stall and bend to grab the handles of the wheelbarrow when the scrape of footsteps stops me in my tracks.

I look up to find Wyatt Fletcher standing in the dutch doorway of the barn, blinking back curiously at me.

"Oh . . . you're down here," he says, glancing at the bag in his hand.

"Yeah, sorry," I reply, gesturing to what I'm doing. "I was just about to bring the animals back in after I empty this."

"No need to be sorry." He frowns and hesitates for a moment. "I was just going to leave these on your steps after I took care of Millie, but since you're here . . ." His voice trails off as he walks over and hands me a large white shopping bag.

I look inside and frown. "Work boots?"

He nods. "Those sneakers you were wearing chasing the cattle around Wednesday are not going to last another week. These should hold up better."

I pull the boots out and note that they're steel-toed and expensive-looking. And thankfully not cowboy boots like what Everly, Trista, and Stevie wear. I'd look like a proper fool in a pair of those.

But these? These are decent. And they're something I know I needed. I was even planning on purchasing something similar when I got to town next because this job is a bit more labor-intensive than I originally expected. Only problem is, I'm not really used to shopping for myself. Cliona would always do that, often forcing things I didn't need upon me. Dressing me up like she could fix me in one of those ridiculous makeover films.

I could use a bit of that now. Transform me from looking like a foreign rugby player into a proper farmhand who picks up giant alpacas like it's his job . . . because it is now. But I don't want that from the husband of my boss. It feels wrong. Like I'm imposing when it's something I should do for myself. I take pride in doing shite for myself.

"I appreciate the gesture, but I can't accept these," I state, my brows furrowed as I hand the bag back over to Wyatt.

He frowns. "I could exchange the size if we guessed wrong."

"It's not about the size. I'd just prefer to buy my own boots if you don't mind."

Wyatt's eyes narrow. "What if I insist?"

My brows lift, but I straighten, refusing to let this man intimidate me into accepting a gift that I know cost a decent amount of money, no matter how nice he's trying to be. "The same way you insist on being the only one to muck out Millie's pen?"

This causes Wyatt to pause, and the corner of his mouth tugs up. "Very well, then, Wolf."

"Thank you though, Mr. Fletcher. Truly."

"Call me Wyatt . . . please. That, I will insist on."

I smile and nod. "I appreciate the gesture, Wyatt. I just like to make my own way in life."

"Fair enough." He huffs a soft laugh and hooks his thumb down toward the pens. "I'm going to go tend to my favorite girl." He presses a finger to his lips in a shushing motion. "Don't tell my other favorite girls."

I smile and nod. "Your secret is safe with me."

And I finish my work for the day, leaving the grumpy mountain man to his goat and me to head upstairs to take care of my bearded dragon and prepare for a night out with Everly Fletcher tomorrow. If someone had told me this would be my life a year ago, I never would have believed them. But if I'm being honest with myself, I'm enjoying this fresh start in Colorado. It feels almost as though I can be the person I want to be and let go of my past and the things that haunt me still. Now if only I could let go of my fixation on Everly Fletcher.

Chapter 14

Selling the Dummy: *When you really commit to the fake, and the opponent completely buys it.*

Translation: *Faking it with a hot Irish rugby player is risky business.*

Everly

Okay, Everly Fletcher. You're going to go to this party, and you're going to like it, I tell myself as I stand in my bathroom, applying my last coat of mascara. *You're a different person than you were in high school. Everyone is different. It's going to be fun to see some old friends. You can tell them all about Ireland. You saw a bit of the world with Cliona. Just tell them about that. But don't tell them too much. Avoid the "too much" part of your brain. Plus, you have a hot Irish guy as your plus-one . . . Lean on that.*

My phone pings with an incoming photo from Wolf. When I open it, I can't help but burst out laughing.

It's a photo of Rugby in his enclosure with a little bow tie around his neck and the caption that says: Let's party.

I scroll back through the endless text messages I've had with Wolf the past couple of weeks. They're 90 percent about *our* boy, Rugby, 5 percent work-related tasks, but that last 5 percent . . . dare I say, we're verging on flirting. It's always on the days I don't make it down to Mount Millie. Wolf sends me simple messages like: How was your day? And I find myself grinning like a dork as I try to text him back something clever and not embarrassing.

I usually fail.

I epically failed when my uncle Calder caught me texting Wolf back the other night. He and Dakota invited me over for dinner and to hang with their cats, to which I said, of course. In fact, between my uncles and aunts and parents, I rarely go a night without a dinner invite. Which makes my co-parenting of Rugby a bit difficult.

However, Wolf and I have been getting along pretty well as coworkers, if I do say so myself. Earlier this week, we had to work together to haul furniture from Calder's workshop behind his cabin down to the rescue center, and Wolf was basically my muscle as I arranged benches and chairs around the property with potted plants that I purchased from Costco.

We planted some greenery along the pathways and turned mismatched chairs into cozy nooks. I added flower boxes to the windows of the barn and filled them with lavender and rosemary so the whole place smells like summer. In just a few days, we transformed Mount Millie from a top-of-the-line, self-sustaining rescue center to an adorable visitor destination. And we didn't kill each other! It gives me hope that maybe tonight, we'll actually be able to have some fun together.

I give myself one last look in the mirror. I'm dressed in jeans and a lacey black bodysuit that's a little revealing, but if I'm going to be reconnecting with people I never really connected with in high school, I'd better look hot while doing it. I drape my motorcycle leather jacket over my arm and slide my feet into some black strappy heels to make my way out to my SUV to go pick up Wolf down at the barn.

I'm grateful he agreed to come with me. After my chat with Trista and getting text messages from Hilow and my childhood bestie, Claire, I know I need to go to this freaking party to prove to everyone, as well as myself, that I'm not hiding anymore. And the idea of going alone feels just too pathetic. Like it's openly telling them I'm still the same weird, oversharing head case that I was in high school.

I clomp down the steps of my cabin deck, digging in my purse for my keys, when I hear a throat-clearing so intense it has me looking up to find that Wolf is standing by my vehicle, waiting for me.

"You didn't have to walk up here," I say, making my way down toward him. "I was going to drive down and get you."

"I was ready early, so . . ." His throat contracts as he looks me up and down before he shakes his head and looks away.

My eyes can't help but do a sweep of him as well. The sun is setting, so it's casting that perfect summer glow over his creamy Irish skin. He's dressed in jeans and a black T-shirt that hugs his insane muscles. His gold cross chain shimmers, giving him that iconic rebel look he wears so well with his rumpled dark hair and narrow, pensive eyes. But there's something softer in him now. A lightness in him that I never saw in all my years of orbiting him at Trinity. Maybe being a pet owner has tempered this bad boy.

We look like a couple who should be climbing onto a motorcycle, not jumping into my "Ostuni Pearl White" Range Rover. But I think we'll look pretty good climbing into my new ride anyway.

An errant thought about how people might think we're a couple hits me, and I wince and stare at the ground to scrape that fantasy from my mind. I can't just casually date my best friend's brother. I can't just casually date the guy living on the same mountain compound as me. Just because he's stopped ignoring me doesn't change the fact that he's never looked at me twice. Wolf and I are not a thing and never will be. We're far too different.

We make our way down the mountain and out of Jamestown, and the silence in my car feels deafening. Wolf's cologne is mixing with the smell of my new car, and the combination is causing my body to hum to life. I'd notice his scent when he would come to me and Cliona's dorm room on occasion. Like the first snap of cold air after a heavy rain. It always made me want to purr like a cat.

Jesus, I'm a freak.

"Is our baby mad about not coming to the party?" I ask, finally breaking the silence after we've passed through the winding mountain roads and are on the main highway to Boulder. "How has he been this week?"

"He's good." Wolf turns to look at me with an arched brow as he holds his phone up to reveal that our little bow tie beardie is now his background.

Dammit, that's adorable.

"I love it."

He shrugs and offers me a wink. "I was just relieved to discover Amazon delivers to Fletcher Mountain. I have a hoodie saved in my cart for him next."

"You are obsessed."

He smiles down at his phone. "I always wanted a pet growing up, but my parents would never allow it."

"So should I hold off putting Rugby on the Mount Millie website?"

Wolf's head snaps back to me. "Why would he go on the website?"

"To be adopted, of course." I glance over and can't help but notice the anxiety in his eyes.

He clears his throat and struggles a bit with his words. "I don't mind watching him while I'm here. It's kind of decent having something to come home to at night. I've never properly lived alone."

"You're not really alone," I reply with a grin. "You've got Handsome and Millie and Reggie and Butterscotch . . ."

He rolls his eyes.

"Okay, fine. I'll delay listing Rugby."

"Thank you," he murmurs, fingering the denim of his jeans.

I eye him carefully, trying to tread lightly when I ask, "Your parents were pretty strict, huh?"

Wolf looks curiously at me as I dig deeper than we've ever really gone before.

I offer a sympathetic smile. "Cliona doesn't say much, but it was just an impression I got. I know it always bothered her that they never came to any of her rugby matches."

Wolf exhales heavily. "It always bothered her more than me. Our parents are good people. They just have to work a lot to keep their shop afloat. Our nana lived with us growing up, so it really wasn't all bad."

I nod slowly. "My dad worked a lot when I was younger too. His thing was always quality time over quantity. When I had my weekends with him, he made sure to give me his full attention. But it was almost stressful in a way. Like we couldn't ever just do nothing together."

Wolf eyes me curiously. "Does he still work a lot?"

"He's still a busy guy, yeah. But he's better since Cozy. She really helped him see that life doesn't always have to be so black-and-white."

I feel Wolf's eyes on me still when he asks, "Is it weird having two mams? Or three, I guess, with your stepmam?"

"It feels normal to me," I reply with a soft smile. "It feels like I have three extra dads with my uncles, so I guess we're all used to the more, the merrier. Even my mom and her wife, Kailey, parent my brother, Ethan, a bit. Boundaries really aren't a thing in the Fletcher family."

"I've picked up on that," Wolf says, staring forward. "Trista keeps inviting me to their house for dinners."

"You should say yes sometimes," I say, fighting back the

swirling feeling in my gut over the thought of spending more time with him. For some strange reason, I like the idea of him infiltrating more of the mountain life. He's starting to fit in, even when he stands out.

"I don't want to be a bother."

"You wouldn't be a bother," I state seriously, turning to look at him. "You're a huge help to Trista down at the center. I'm sure she'd love to get to know you a bit more."

Wolf's eyes are pensive as he watches the road, but I can't help but continue prying. "So, your plan is to be a lawyer someday?"

He expels a deep noise in his throat. "I guess so."

"You guess?" I laugh. "Isn't that kind of a hard job to just stumble into?"

He sighs. "Yeah, it's just always been the plan for us with my parents."

"What would your plan be if your parents weren't a factor?"

Wolf buzzes his lip. "Christ, I haven't given that much thought, I guess."

"Oh, come on. I'm guessing there's something that's crossed your mind. No one goes to Trinity and doesn't get inspired by something."

Wolf's large hands splay out wide on his thighs. "Social work of some sort, maybe, if my parents weren't so worried about money. I like the idea of doing something that makes a difference in someone's life the way rugby did for me."

My lips part at this rare moment of vulnerability from a guy who never had much to say to me while we were at college. This career path is unexpected from Wolf, but strangely, I can see it perfectly. He always was a really hard worker and seemed to take his classes very seriously.

"You'd probably make a great teacher."

Wolf frowns and shakes his head.

"No, I mean it. I've watched you and Stevie these past couple weeks. You treat her like an adult, and it just works."

He shrugs. "I just pick my battles with that one."

I laugh.

"What about you?" he asks, and I get a swirling feeling in my stomach when I feel his eyes on me again. "What would your plan be if you didn't have all the family businesses to keep you occupied?"

I rub my lips together and think. "Honestly, as much as I love my family, I think eventually I want something for myself. Something that none of them know anything about. No connections, no pressure. Just . . . my own thing."

"Good luck with that," Wolf says with a laugh. "Your family seems well-connected."

"You're telling me," I grumble knowingly. "Eventually, we have to grow up and forge our own paths, don't we?"

He nods thoughtfully before clearing his throat. "So will you know a lot of the people at this party tonight?"

"I'm not sure who all is coming," I reply, grateful for the change in subject. "Obviously, I'll know Hilow. And I got a text from a family friend I know named Claire that's going to be there. She was a year younger than me and didn't go to my school, but she's great. Her uncle is a doctor in Boulder and close friends with my dad, so we grew up together."

Wolf nods, his jaw tight. "What made you change your mind about wanting to go? When he first invited you, you didn't seem too keen."

I rub my lips tighter, tasting my sheer gloss. "Just trying to say yes more . . . remember?"

I feel his eyes on me, pensive, probing, and curious. Wolf has this way of looking right through me. And it's weird how much I like it. It makes me feel seen somehow. And even when he doesn't say anything, I feel like we're still talking.

This is a very different person from the one I saw around campus at Trinity. Back there, he'd always seemed determined *not* to look at me, like I was invisible by choice. But the moments when our eyes caught felt intentional somehow. Like he'd been waiting for it. Maybe it was just because I was best friends with his sister, but it felt like he was always there. Background noise that wouldn't go away. Comforting in a strange way, like the sound of lapping ocean waves or birds singing in the forest.

Now being near him so often, I feel the opposite of comfort. Like I want to crawl out of my skin if I don't do something with him. What I want to do, I still don't know.

"What made you decide you wanted to come?" I rebound the question back to him with a hopeful look.

"My sister made me," he murmurs and looks out the window.

I sigh and roll my eyes. "Okay, Wolf."

"Don't believe me?"

"No," I retort, ignoring how square his jaw is. "I think you want to come because you don't dislike me as much as you act like you do, and it'd be easier if you just admitted to being my friend. I mean, we are working together and co-parenting a bearded dragon."

"Oh, is that right?" he asks, his voice holding back a laugh. "I guess I missed the part where you helped me hand-feed the crickets to him every night."

"I'm ready to take my turn anytime. You just have to admit you want to be my friend and invite me up." I swallow the knot in my throat because that sounded more erotic than I intended. Like I want to be invited up.

Maybe I do.

"You think you're good at reading people, don't you?" he asks, his jaw taut as he watches me from the passenger seat. "Is that why you like to set people up so much?"

I shrug. "Matchmaking really is just the art of reading people, and whether you'll admit it or not, I can see right through you, Conri. You like me."

He makes a grumbly noise in his throat, and my cheeks heat at the feral sound of it. His large hands twitch over his thick thighs, and that causes my body to heat as well.

With a sharp inhale, I decide to lay it all out there. "Being real? I'm going to this party because I don't want to repeat Trinity." I pause when I feel his eyes on me again. "I may be good at reading people, but I'm not great at reading myself, and I think you already kind of know that I didn't have the best social life at Trinity. Or dating history, for that matter."

"Is this about that guy you went to the Trinity Ball with who posted all that shite about you?"

My jaw falls open. "You know about that?"

"The whole campus knew about that," he replies darkly.

My face flames with mortification. "Well, great. Then you have a perfect example of how much I struggle. Before I lived with your sister, there was no one I wanted to keep in touch with after graduation." I throw a cautious look at Wolf and notice he's frowning pensively, so I try to elaborate more. "I'm sure you have loads of friends from rugby and growing up in Dublin. But making friends isn't easy for me, especially as an international student. Your sister all but forced our friendship. She's kind of amazing like that."

My hands tighten on the wheel as I say the next bit. "But she's not here, so I'm trying to rebuild my social life here at home. My family is all busy with kids and their partners. I can't rely on them for everything like I did when I was younger. I need to find my own life and say yes to invites that come my way—like Hilow's party."

Wolf clears his throat. "I don't think that bloke is looking at you for friendship."

I roll my eyes. "He's harmless, and I could use all the friends I can get."

Wolf makes another growling noise, and my stomach swirls. He's a hard one to read, this guy. In one breath, he makes me feel like he doesn't care about me at all. And in the next, he's acting like he wants to rip the head off a guy from my past while sending me adorable pictures of his pet. If this truly is just the big-brother treatment, I seriously need to stop checking out his ass, because the feelings he's igniting in me are far from familial.

My blood pressure is still high by the time we reach Hilow's place. He's in a house on University Hill, which is historically a bit of a party neighborhood, as is evident by the people pouring outside various front porches, drinking and smoking. I manage to find a parking spot on the street a block away, and as we walk toward his house, I exhale heavily, trying to calm down before we go inside.

Wolf stops in front of the house, so I turn to look at him curiously. "Did you forget something?"

"I'm not very good at friendships either." He grips the back of his neck and adds, "But you can do loads better than me for a friend."

I laugh and cross my arms over my chest. "More like *you* can do better than me."

"Impossible," he murmurs under his breath, and I jerk my head back in disbelief. Surely, he didn't mean that the way it sounded. He's just being self-deprecating. Maybe we're both too critical of ourselves. We might have more in common than we realize.

"Tell you what," I state, taking a step closer to him. "Why don't we both go in there and just do our best to have fun." I tilt my head to offer him a coy smile. "We can try to be cool and see if anyone notices."

The corner of Wolf's mouth twitches as he fights back a smile. "You're not even close to cool."

"I can be cool." I hold my jacket up to him. "A motorcycle jacket is like . . . really cool."

He chuckles softly, and his smile falls as his gaze sweeps over my body. "You're stunning tonight, Stretch."

Goose bumps erupt over my skin as I fight the outward reaction attempting to break free from my body. He's right. I'm not close to cool. Because cool people don't want to squeal and skip down the street the minute a hot boy compliments them.

I shrug casually. "That's nice to hear because I usually veer on the side of cringe over cool, even with my hot jacket."

My breath hitches when I realize he's taken a step closer to me, his eyes glittering in the darkness. "Cringe is sexier than cool because at least you're trying."

I force myself to take in oxygen. Deep breaths. Deep breaths are required when you're making word mountains out of word molehills. Those were just words. Silly words coming out of his mouth. They don't mean anything. Even if they are quite possibly the nicest thing anyone has ever said to me.

His smile is faint, but it's there, so I force a wobbly smile back. "Well, let's go into this party and both be cringe together, then."

I turn on my heel and drape my jacket over my shoulders as I struggle to walk straight and show no signs of the girlie party going on between my legs.

Cringe is sexier than cool.

Weirdest hot words I've ever heard, but said in that Irish accent of his, damn, they were effective.

We climb the front porch and make our way inside, the base of the music thudding loudly as we let ourselves in the front door and stand in the entryway, taking in our surroundings. The house smells like booze and weed, and I'm shocked by the sheer number of people crammed in here.

Hilow wasn't this popular in high school. He was kind of a quiet, generic guy who got along with everyone. He certainly wasn't a party boy throwing ragers like this. Since I don't recognize most people, I can only assume it's his new college connections, which means he fared better than I did at the socializing after high school.

"Everly," Hilow shouts from across the living room, where he's seated on a leather couch with a few people. He pushes his long frame up out of the low sofa and strides over to us, beer bottle in hand, with a wide smile and slightly red eyes. "I'm so glad you made it," he murmurs and pulls me in for a hug, his hands dipping low on my back. He releases me and shifts his gaze. "And you brought Wolf. Good."

Wolf gives no outward response to Hilow. Just a flat look that I know all too well.

"Come on into the kitchen for a drink. I have everything." He grabs my hand and pulls me through the throng of people, and I can't help but look back to make sure Wolf is following. His eyes are surveying the room like he's a bodyguard, not a twenty-two-year-old at a party, but thankfully, he is trailing us into the kitchen.

"I'm just having one since I'm driving," I say, accepting the seltzer Hilow hands me.

"Wolf?" he asks, his eyes blinking. "What do the Irish like? Guinness? Whiskey?"

"Nothing for me, thanks," he replies stiffly. "I start training Monday, so I'll take it easy tonight."

Hilow nods and turns all his focus back to me, edging Wolf back behind him a bit. He touches my arm and leans in to whisper in my ear. "Do you want to see my bedroom?"

My eyes widen, and I feel Wolf's attention turn from the party to me, clearly hearing this strange request. "No, that's okay. I'm just going to stand here and have my drink."

"Okay." Hilow takes a drink of his beer, looking disappointed for a moment, which is crazy. I know we were together for two years, but the bedroom thing is a weird ask, considering I haven't been in the house for more than a minute.

"These are a lot of my vet school friends," Hilow says, gesturing to the crowd.

I nod and smile. "That's nice."

He smiles back. "Vet school students know how to party."

"I guess." I sip my drink, hating how awkward this is.

Someone comes in the front door, and Hilow touches me on the arm again. "I need to go greet them. I'll find you in a few."

"No rush," I call back as he makes his way through the crowd to the entryway, where more people I don't know are standing.

The moment he's gone, I drop my shoulders and take a fortifying sip of my drink, rubbing the area he touched me. "This is miserable."

Wolf huffs out a noise of agreement.

"I don't think I like meeting new people like this." I wrinkle my nose and glance over at him. "I prefer more controlled settings. This just feels too unpredictable." I survey the room and see everyone having fun, talking, conversing. It looks so easy for them, but I still feel like an outsider looking in. "I wonder what a matchmaking clinic for friends would look like?"

Wolf shrugs dismissively, and I can't help but notice all the girls in the room glancing over at him, whispering in packs to each other. He sticks out like a sore thumb here. Tall, rugged, with dark unkempt hair and simple but sexy clothing that gives the air of "just randomly deciding to show up." A far cry from the frat boy Patagonia pastel quarter zip that Hilow was rocking. Definitely more effortless than my look.

Wolf also has this quiet, focused energy about him that just exudes sex. How does he do that?

A blonde walks over and reaches behind me to grab a drink. I have to move out of her way, and when she gets what she's after, her eyes move up and down Wolf, who looks back at her with a flat, unimpressed stare. That's probably his move. Act like you don't care, and they will want you more. "Hard to get" is a solid strategy for many. Wish I knew how to master it myself.

"Don't feel like you have to stick beside me," I murmur, elbowing Wolf gently as the girl saunters away, swaying her hips.

"What is that supposed to mean?" His brows pull together.

I pull my jacket up tighter around my shoulders so it doesn't slip off. "I mean . . . if you want to mingle, you should. I'm sure there's some ladies here who would love to hear your sexy accent."

Wolf's head snaps toward me, and just like that, the air between us tightens as heat crawls up my face.

"What's that you just said?" he asks, his voice deep and husky, almost intimate-sounding. He turns so he's fully facing me, blocking out the noise of the party going on behind him like we're suddenly in our own little bubble.

I struggle to make eye contact with his probing whiskey eyes, which are currently trying to burrow a hole right through me. I squeeze my arms over my chest and take another big drink while murmuring, "I didn't mean—"

"Oh, I expect you did mean." He licks his lips and eyes me thoughtfully.

"I just mean . . . some people might think it's sexy."

"Some people," he repeats slowly, like he's taste-testing that answer and not accepting it. His dark lashes dip as he stares at my mouth before lifting his gaze back up to my eyes. "But you're not one of those people?"

"I don't . . . I've never—" my voice cracks "—thought about your accent," I reply with a bouncy, careless tone. "Like I've never noticed the musical quality to it."

"Musical?" His brows pop, his face the picture of delight, a rare look on him. "Tell me more, Stretch."

"Some people have said that!" I retort, holding my hand up defensively. "Not *me* people. Like I'm just repeating what others say."

"Not you." He leans in close, pressing his hand against the counter next to my ass. I can smell his cologne again. Clean and earthy with a hint of something dark and spicy. His brows pinch together in a serious furrow that I mirror as he looks down at me.

"No . . . not me," I repeat weakly, feeling so utterly small as he half cages me in.

The corner of his mouth tugs up, and so does mine, and before I know it, we're both laughing, me even buckling over as I realize what an idiot I sound like. My jacket slips off my shoulders onto the floor, and when we both lean down to reach for it, our fingers brush, causing a roll of energy to shimmy up my arm.

I jerk back at that bizarre sensation, leaving the jacket for Wolf to grab. He lifts it up and hands it to me, his eyes alive with humor that is so rare on his face, transforming him from broodingly attractive to drop-dead gorgeous.

I grip the leather tightly in my fingers, my palms sweating at the way he's looking at me right now.

"Stretch, I think you're blushing."

"I'm not."

"You are."

I drape my coat between my crossed arms and scowl at the

floor, hating how good he looks with a smirk. Hating how he can probably see the goose bumps all over my bare arms.

The truth is, I *love* the Irish accent. I chose Trinity College because of my obsession with the book *Normal People* by Sally Rooney. I bought it in every format, and the audiobook would put me to sleep so many nights when my brain wouldn't shut off.

Cliona served as my own real-life *Normal People* audiobook at Trinity. I'd often fall asleep to her complaining about her rugby team drama. Best sleep of my life was in that Rubrics dorm room, talking to her in the wee hours of the night.

God, I miss her.

My uncles have done a good job making me feel at home, inviting me over for dinner nearly every night of the week. I have a hot meal and a laugh at any of their houses any night I want. But going to bed in my cabin all on my own? It's often when I want to call Cliona . . . if only to hear her soft lilt.

But that's what brings me out tonight. I can't escape in a book fantasy forever. I need real-life friendships. I need to matchmake myself a best friend. And not whatever this is I'm doing with Wolf. We can't possibly be flirting, can we? I can't flirt with my best friend's brother. Absolutely not.

"Everly!" a voice squeals from behind Wolf, and I look up to see Claire barreling right toward me.

She shoves past Wolf without a second look as she wraps me in her arms, and I squeeze her lush, full figure back, not realizing how much I missed my childhood bestie.

"Claire Bear, I'm so happy to see you!" I exclaim, my eyes stinging with emotion overload.

"You can say that again." She pulls back and hits me with a big smile, her round, freckled cheeks just as adorable as always. "I can't believe you're finally home for good! I want to hear all about your last year at Trinity. Tell me everything."

Wolf's warm hand touches me on the side, and he head

nods, indicating he's going to give me some space. It feels intimate and sweet. He walks away with a forlorn expression, my eyes drinking in his backside in those jeans.

"Um . . . who the hell is that?" Claire asks as she ogles his backside as well.

I swallow the knot in my throat. "That is Wolf. He's working at Trista's rescue center this summer and living up on the mountain."

"With you?" she squeals and covers her mouth.

"Not with me exactly, no. He's in the barn apartment. He's actually my Irish friend's brother. He's playing rugby in Denver."

"He's Irish and plays rugby?" she squeals again, and we both giggle like we're twelve and have a big crush on the new boy in school.

"Stop, okay? Please be cool." I swipe my hair back off my face. "He already thinks I'm the uncoolest, and I don't need to give him any more ammunition."

Claire rolls her eyes. "You're the coolest friend I have."

I can't help but smile at that lie she tells so well.

Claire was my first real friend I ever made. It was hard maintaining friendships when I was younger, being shuttled between my mom and my dad's house and enrolled in so many friggin' activities I could barely see straight. It wasn't until the summer my dad hired Cozy to be my nanny that she convinced him to let me give up some of my extracurriculars.

And with that free time came Claire. We'd have sleepovers in the guesthouse at my dad's place when we were ten and eleven. She was just this perfect piece of easy. I always felt like my social life would have been so much better if we'd gone to the same school.

Claire had all these self-proclaimed musical nerd friends she was always with, and they all seemed so confident in their own skin. I admire Claire and her curves and have always been jealous of how she never seems to have moments of insecurity. She and her friends just seem so easily themselves.

"Tell me about your life," I say, giving her arm a squeeze. "How's school?"

"Oh my God, where do I begin?" she groans and throws her head back. "I just changed my major for the third time . . ."

She downloads all her college drama on me, and while I listen, I can't help but watch Wolf across the room, talking quietly to another girl. A pit forms in my stomach, and I feel silly because of course he's going to talk to other girls. I was just trying to matchmake him a second ago. He's probably trying to show me he doesn't need me to matchmake him. *The ass.*

Not that it would be a good idea to set him up anyways. He says he's not planning to be in America long term, and he's not a relationship guy. Those are two ticks that would get him booted off my list of matchmaking hopefuls real quick.

Claire excuses herself when she gets a call, telling me that her girlfriends are lost and she needs to guide them to Hilow's place. She's still super-close to her friends from band and choir, so I wave her off and maintain my spot in the kitchen to do some people-watching.

After finishing my drink, I realize I'm being antisocial, so I push off the counter and make my way over to join Wolf in the corner when I see a familiar face walk in the front door that causes my stomach to drop. It's not Claire and her sweet band friends. It's Taya Donalson, the girl from my high school who crushed me with very little effort.

And she's walking in like she owns the place. So very on-brand of her.

My pulse quickens, thrumming in my ears, my neck, and my fingertips, so I beeline across the room right over to Hilow, who's in the middle of a conversation. I yank his arm so he's forced to look at me. "Did you invite Taya here tonight?"

Hilow's eyes widen. "Oh, yes. Is she here?" He stands up tall to look over the mob of people currently separating me and her.

"What the hell, Hilow? You know I can't handle her," I hiss, my tone acidic as my shoulders tense.

Hilow looks down at me in confusion. "Isn't that old high school stuff? Surely things have changed now, haven't they?"

"No, nothing has changed." I seethe and turn on my heel to walk away from him, ignoring his pleas behind me. Hilow is one of the only people who knows the horrors that girl bestowed on me, aside from Taya, who I'm sure remembers things very differently.

I head back to the kitchen, my eyes landing on the counter of booze in front of me. Booze is what I need to be in the same room as fucking Taya. I'll figure out how to get home later. I'll call my dad for a ride if I have to.

I grab a bottle of Fireball and pour myself a double shot and down it in one fell swoop, relishing in the burn of cinnamon. I pour another and take it, sniffing loudly as the flavor blasts through all my senses.

"What the fuck are you doing?" a deep voice booms behind me.

"What does it look like?" I reply, not looking back.

"I thought you were only having one. We have to get back up the mountain."

"Things change, Wolfy. Keep up." I prepare to pour myself another shot, but Wolf's warm hand grips my arm and halts me in my tracks.

My shoulders drop as I sigh heavily and shake my head, my eyes swimming with rage. I turn around and lean back on the counter, my lips taut as I look past Wolf to the familiar brunette across the room, slowly making her way inside.

"What the fuck is going on?" he asks, his tone harsh.

My throat tightens as I notice Taya's with the other two

mean girls from my high school days. Three girls who made my life miserable. Girls who I thought were my friends but . . .

Wolf's fingers clutch my chin as he forces me to look up at him. "Start doing that babbling thing you do because I need to know why I'll be fucking punching a guy out."

"Who would you punch out?" I ask, my voice rising in pitch.

"I'll start with Hilow." He shrugs like it's the most obvious answer.

"What did he do?"

"I don't know, but he fucking irritates me. And I hate his shirt."

I balk at that. "He didn't do anything. Not really. Some girls just showed up that I didn't know were going to be here. I can't believe Hilow didn't tell me. He should have told me." I blow out a long breath and feel my chin quiver with emotion. "Maybe you can punch him."

"What did they do to you?" Wolf asks, his voice low and threatening. His brown eyes lock on me with concern and anger. Anger that I don't fully understand because he still doesn't know me all that well to be this protective.

Then again, he has a sister. This is probably the big-scary-brother bit he must be doing. Maybe as her best friend, I get adjacent big-brother privileges. The alternative is just too ridiculous to imagine . . . right?

"They made my life hell."

"How?"

"By making me feel pathetic." I sigh heavily. "I am pathetic."

"No, you're fucking not," Wolf growls. "Don't talk about my sister's best friend like that."

My eyes snap up to his, and the concern I see is so touching it brings tears to my eyes. "I don't want to look like a failure to them."

"What do you need from me? What can I do?"

"I don't know." I inhale a trembling breath as they begin moving toward us, my heart hammering in my chest. "I just . . . I went to Dublin to get away from them, from everything. From feeling like a pathetic loser. And now I'm back, and literally nothing has changed. I cut my hair, like that was somehow going to make me look like a new person. But I'm not. I'm not. I'm still just me. This over-the-top nuisance who all of them only pretended to like."

"Let's fucking bugger off, then," Wolf grumbles under his breath.

"No, I'm not leaving," I snap, my chin jutting out defiantly. "I'm going to face those fucking assholes and not let them think they still have power over me." An idea strikes me, and I reach up to grab Wolf by the shoulders. "I know what you can do!"

"Anything," he whispers, and I can't help but jerk my head back at the desperate look on his face.

I blink and refocus when I ask straight up, "Will you be my boyfriend?"

"What?" Wolf's eyes flare with horror that makes me want to cry or laugh. *See? Pathetic.*

"Just for pretend so I don't look like the same old Everly they fucked with," I add with urgency. "Will you do that, Conri? Just for an hour. Then we can get out of here, and I will owe you the most massive favor ever. Please, please, please?"

A deep grumble vibrates in his chest, but he nods stiffly.

"Thank you, I love you, thank you." I grab his arm and yank him around to stand beside me just as Taya closes in.

Wolf

"Everly Fletcher?" a brunette girl calls out from across the room as her eyes slide up and down me and then right over to

Everly, who's currently shaking with anxiety and wriggling to wrap my arm around her.

I feel bad she's struggling with my embrace, but I can't exactly make my limbs work on command at the moment. A lot has transpired in the last sixty seconds. More than I was prepared for. I guess I need a few more seconds to absorb the fact that I'm going to be Everly Fletcher's fake boyfriend for a moment.

Never mind that I've never been anyone's real boyfriend, but sure, let's start here as a fake one at some random party house in America. *Sink or swim time, Wolfy.*

Wolfy. I can't help but mentally repeat what Everly fucking called me. I would have her arse for it if she didn't look so despondent.

It's shocking, really.

Sure, Everly Fletcher isn't exactly known to be Miss Social, but she always carried herself with so much confidence in Dublin. She walked around like the world was made just for her.

This Everly that's being revealed tonight is the exact opposite of that. She's nervous and withdrawn and fighting back so many emotions I'm not sure which one to react to.

Then again, if I had to go back and face all my past classmates from secondary school, I'm not sure I'd fare much better.

I blow out a long breath and relax my hand around her waist, allowing my fingers to clutch her outer hip in the possessive sort of way a boyfriend might hold his girl. I loop a finger through one of the belt loops on her jeans and drop my shoulders a bit, my jaw brushing against her hair. I can do this. *I can pretend to want Everly Fletcher.*

"Great to see you, Everly. Your hair looks amazing," the brunette with a high, slicked-back ponytail says as she walks over to us like she's floating. The words she said sure sounded like a compliment, but the look in her eyes make me think it's all bullshit.

"Hi, Taya, it's been a while," Everly says, her voice sounding weak and unsure. I hate it.

I turn my head and bend my neck to kiss her bare shoulder, willing her to do better. Her skin is warm and salty, and I fight the urge to run my tongue along her flesh just for a better taste.

She sucks in a sharp breath at my touch, and I feel a shiver run through her body. My own shudders in response. Maybe the kiss was a bit much, but I'm just going on instinct here.

"Who's this?" the annoying girl asks in a smacking tone that grates on my fucking nerves.

"This is Wolf," Everly replies, holding her chin up a bit higher as I pull her in closer, setting my body on fire like I do it all the time. Our bodies are flush next to each other, my cock pressed against the side of her waist, and I hate how much I enjoy this kind of touch.

"Her boyfriend," I add, the word strange and unfamiliar on my lips, but I think I pull it off.

"Wolf?" Taya laughs, looking back at the two girls behind her who look just as evil as their ringleader. She licks her lips and steps closer to me, her eyes full of sex as she adds, "Why do they call you Wolf?"

I blink slowly at her, shocked that I've somehow been plunked into the middle of an American film where the cliché mean girls go after the awkward, unfortunate girl. It's a tired fucking story and one that sadly happens in Ireland as well.

But little does this girl know, I've been on the receiving end of far too many of these moments myself, and I've well and properly outgrown them.

I force a smile and answer, "Because my name is Conri, and it means King of the Wolves . . . and also because I bark like a dog."

She jumps back when I aggressively bark.

"Fucking asshole," she snaps, her eyes turning lethal on me and then sliding to Everly.

I feel Everly shake as she covers her laugh and turns bright red. The kind that crawls up her neck and into the apples of her cheeks. Gorgeous.

"Sorry about my boyfriend," Everly says, her tone more confident than before. "He just can't help but bark at bitches."

All three girls' mouths gape as they glare back at us, and I can't help but smile with pride. Ruthless. Cutthroat. And completely unapologetic. It's a nice change of pace from the sweet people-pleaser who was panicking only moments ago.

"Did you have to buy this guy like you tried to buy us?" the Taya girl asks, and Everly inhales sharply, her body hard as stone beneath my arms.

"I never tried to buy you."

"Mm'kay, girl." Her eyes flash over to me, dark and full of hate. "My guess is he's just with you for your money too."

Everly pushes off me and steps forward to snap back at her, but I grip her by the wrist, stopping her from getting too far away from me. "You're the one with a history for transactional relationships."

The girl's lips curl in disgust, and to prove Everly's point, I pull her back into me and spin her around with a force that knocks the air out of both of us. Her breasts crush against my chest as her delicate hand braces on my pec.

"Besides, the truth of it all is I'm really just with her for her sexy arse," I say cheekily. Before Everly can argue, I slide my hand down her lower back until it curves over the swell of her round bottom. With a grunt, I massage her through the tight denim, and she lets out a warm exhale of shock on my lips as the pressure brings our two groins together in a way that's positively indecent.

Her eyes half close, giving me the impression that she likes me claiming her like this.

I'm afraid I like it too.

Her peach lips part, and I catch sight of her tongue, and like a starved animal who hasn't eaten in weeks, I grab her by the neck and tilt her chin up to crush my mouth to hers.

It's a hard, hungry scorcher of a kiss. One I didn't even remotely think through.

At first, this was just going to be a cheeky bottom squeeze. Something to send the bitchy girl on her merry fucking way.

But Everly's full, lush lips were just too tempting, and my primal instincts took over. I descended upon her like a madman, and the moan she utters against my lips makes me think this was a good risk to take.

Everly's fingers curl around the front of my T-shirt as she pulls me closer, arching into me as her tongue meets mine with a desperation that I feel all the way down to my balls.

She tastes like cinnamon and peaches. Like a sweet, delectable fruit I should have never taken a bite of. Because now that I have, I might not ever want to stop biting, stop devouring, stop feasting on this person. This maddening woman that I've circled around for years and managed to never touch.

All because she said please.

Christ, this girl makes me weak.

Our mouths finally break apart for air, but we don't move, both of us frozen as we pant into each other's mouths like we just ran bronco sprints on the rugby pitch at six-thousand-foot elevation.

Everly breaks free from me first and looks around to find that our audience is gone—who knows for how long. Did we even need to kiss that long? We'll never know.

"Are you going to slap me?" I croak, knowing that I very well may have fucked things up properly here.

She inhales deeply through her nose as she backs away. "I haven't decided yet."

"Fair enough." I push off the counter, willing my cock to settle down. "Let's get out of here."

She nods and takes my arm, hanging on to me for balance, and to possibly maintain the illusion that we're together as we make our way through the party and out the door. Hilow's devastated eyes follow us the entire way out, and I can't help but tip a smug grin his direction. *I'm not proud.*

The summer air does little to calm the pulsing in my body, and as I usher Everly into the passenger side of her vehicle and close the door, I stab my fingers through my hair and murmur under my breath, "What the fuck have I done?"

Everly

"Can you drive?" I ask Wolf as he slides into the driver's side of my vehicle.

"Of course I can drive. What do you mean?" he asks, his eyes avoiding mine and causing a pit to form in my stomach.

"I just . . . didn't know if you knew how. You're planning to take the bus to Denver for training."

"I know how to drive. I just don't have a car here, and a rental costs too much." His tone is sharp and dismissive as he mutters, "So American," under his breath.

"Okay, sorry," I murmur as I hand him over the keys, careful not to let our fingers touch. How did things go south so quickly? I really managed to fuck this up.

He presses the start button on my SUV and pauses. "But it would help if you stay quiet while I drive because navigating this bloody expensive car on the opposite side of the road is going to take all my concentration."

I nod and press my lips together, my face burning with mortification because whatever flirty vibes he was giving me inside are well and truly gone now.

As Wolf drives out of the neighborhood, I can't help but chew my lower lip. *I can still taste him.* Salt, heat, cinnamon, and something sharp and wicked.

What the hell happened in there? Conri the Convict, six-foot-five behemoth of a man, pressed his mouth to mine in front of Taya and a good chunk of the city of Boulder. And he seemed to like it.

Right?

I didn't dream that?

I'm not on an Ambien trip right now?

This wildly validating feeling of kissing a hot boy in front of my nemesis certainly feels very real.

I turn away from Wolf so he hopefully can't see how red my cheeks are or how much my hands are still trembling. I've kissed a few boys. Not many. *But none felt like that.*

It wasn't real.

It wasn't real.

It wasn't real.

Except whatever was happening in his jeans felt real. I swear something manifested between us that didn't exist at the beginning of that kiss. How long did we even kiss for? Felt like hours and seconds all at the same time.

I wanted it to go on forever. I wanted to commit it all to memory because I'm not sure I'll ever experience something like that again.

But it was fake. It was performative. Wolf read Taya like a book, and a kiss was the only way to shut her up. And he was right because she scurried away without another snide remark.

Although if she did say something, I wouldn't have caught it. All I could hear was my own heartbeat thumping in my ears as he lit my whole body on fire. I swear I could even hear my vagina calling out for Ireland.

But it was all an act. An act I should be grateful for. I should tell Wolf thank you and tell him I owe him big. Keep it light and easy breezy. Cool, not cringe.

But as we traverse the winding roads toward Jamestown, my stomach starts to churn with disappointment.

Because it wasn't just a spiteful revenge kiss . . . It was a pity kiss.

Of course, Wolf pitied me. I was downing double shots of Fireball one after another as I was losing my mind over high school bullshit. After I confessed how pathetic I am to him in the car earlier tonight.

To him, I was a stray dog he offered a scrap to. A sad girl he had to rescue.

The most humiliating part is that I wanted it to be real. I wanted him to want me. For those few seconds our lips touched, I let myself fantasize that Conri Reilly could want me. *What a joke.*

I can't even stand up to my high school nemesis, so what must someone like Wolf, who I had to beg to be my momentary boyfriend, think of me now?

Will you be my boyfriend? Just for pretend so I don't look like the same old Everly they fucked with. Will you do that, Conri? Just for an hour. Then we can get out of here, and I will owe you the most massive favor ever. Please, please, please?

I seriously begged. Now he's angry at me—repulsed by me—which I'm not surprised about. Obviously.

And then there's Taya's words.

Did you have to buy this guy like you tried to buy us? . . . My guess is he's just with you for your money too.

God, her words are so mortifying. Memories of high school flood me. Stupid memories. Memories that don't deserve my emotions. I lived a good life. I'm a privileged kid. I don't deserve pity.

My throat tightens as we turn on the road that leads up to Fletcher Mountain. I dig my nails into my palms, staring hard out the passenger window as I focus on the trees, the gravel road, the signs of nocturnal wildlife. Every breath I take burns in my throat as I fight back what I feel coming.

Don't cry.

Don't cry.

Don't cry.

Wolf drives past the red barn, and I can feel his eyes on me, but I refuse to look at him. If I show him what a mess I am, he's just going to pity me more. I can't take any more pity. I'm sick of feeling pathetic.

Before he even fully stops the car, I unbuckle my seat belt and fling the door open, sucking in a huge breath of mountain air as my vision blurs with tears. I slam the car door harder than I intended as I beeline for my front steps, my sandals crunching over the gravel as I squeeze myself inside my leather jacket.

"Thanks for the ride," I exclaim cheerily without looking back, my garbled voice likely giving me away.

If he says anything back, I don't hear it.

I close my front door behind me and rush into my bedroom to hide as tears fall freely down my face, my nose running, heart racing, head spinning like a snow globe blizzard.

Four words come to mind: *Poor little rich girl.*

Chapter 15

Penalty: *Given to players for serious infringements like dangerous play, offside, and handling the ball on the ground in a ruck.*

Translation: *Tonguing my sister's best friend is a definite penalty.*

Wolf

I'm seated in the back seat of Wyatt's truck early Monday morning. Luke is in the passenger seat, and Calder is right beside me. They all have coffee mugs in hand, ready to start their day at their construction company, and I'm holding my protein drink, mentally prepping for my first day of rugby training camp with a new team.

As the sun continues to rise, I shift nervously in the truck, worried that the daylight is going to somehow reveal to these three uncles what I did to their niece on Saturday night.

What the fuck did I do?

Flirted with her, groped her, and snogged her senseless. Then I considered asking her to fuck when I dropped her back off later that night—because I was horny as fuck after that kiss—except she hightailed her arse into her cabin like she was going to catch a disease if she stayed in that car with me for a second longer.

I don't even think the kiss was my worst offense of the night. I think it was the flirting. I was supposed to keep Everly Fletcher at a distance this summer. Maintain my hardened demeanor around her. But she gave me that big speech about being friends, and I found myself softening to her like a fucking simp.

She's funny. And sharp. And more generous than the world deserves. All things I expected about her, but now I have them confirmed more up close and personal.

And I want to know more.

I want to know exactly what those fucking girls did to her. I want to know why she struggled to make friends or why she dated a fuckhead guy who would let someone who hurt his ex-girlfriend darken his doorstep. I want to know what her belly, her neck, her breasts . . . all of her . . . tastes like. I want too many fucking things.

I've lived my life in extremes for as long as I can remember. I become obsessed with things until I master them.

When I was young and mates with Finn . . . we obsessed over Dungeons and Dragons. It was our fantasy world we played in constantly. When I hit puberty, I became obsessed with bulking up and growing muscle on my tall, slender frame. Then rugby came at me via my sister, and I obsessed over that until I mastered that too. It's why school was always easy for me. When I commit to something, I'm all fucking in.

I'm sure it's not proper of me to want to conquer a person, but if I could, I would conquer the fuck out of Everly Fletcher. My cock twitches at just the fantasy of it.

Only she had not a single fucking word to say to me after we got back.

Sunday, I stewed over it for hours, worrying myself sick that what I did to her was assault because I didn't get her consent to kiss her. I texted her to check in, and she kept telling me all was well. She asked for pictures of Rugby like it was a normal bloody Sunday.

But she kissed me back. I know I'm not making that bit up.

So why the fuck is she making me feel like I'm some kind of deviant?

I half expected her uncles to show up on my doorstep this morning and walk me to the edge of their mountain to jump because this was the end of my journey here on Fletcher Mountain.

All a bit dramatic, but I had a lot of time to stew over it. I even called Cliona to see if she'd spoken to Everly, and she hadn't, so I know nothing except that I'm now to ride three days a week with these uncles of hers, who can probably read all my dirty, fucked-up thoughts.

Fuck me, I screwed things up good and proper.

"So, what is rugby training camp like, exactly?" Calder asks, breaking through my inner freak-out as we make our way through the winding roads outside of Jamestown.

I wipe my sweaty palms off on my shorts, my fingers toying with the hem as I reply. "Um . . . I guess I'm not sure how this team runs their summer camps, but Trinity and the club I played for in secondary school ran theirs pretty similarly. So usually there's stretching and warm-ups, then a gym session—like weight lifting. After that, we have to run. Sprinting drills and-or explosive power exercises like sled pushes and plyos. Then they'll likely split the forwards and backs to work on their own things for a bit—passing drills, rucking, positional plays, and stuff. Then after lunch, there's typically a meeting where we'll review footage or discuss formations."

"Jesus, that's all before lunch?" Luke asks, turning around to watch me curiously.

"Yeah, it's a long day," I reply with a shrug. "Afternoon is often scrimmages on the pitch to apply everything we learned for the day. Then recovery. Ice baths, stretching, foam rolling. Any kind of physio treatments we might need."

"You get your ass beat in rugby, don't you?" Calder asks, pinning me with a knowing look.

I nod woodenly. "It's physical."

"Addison played rugby some," Luke offers over his shoulder as he takes a drink of his travel mug. "She's tried to explain the rules to me, but I can't make heads or tails of it."

"It definitely takes some time to get it all sorted," I reply with a wry grin. "My sister knows it all even better than I do."

"Oh, yeah, you have a twin, Everly said?" Luke turns around to give me his full attention now.

I nod. "Yeah, Cliona is in Dublin with Leinster, which is like . . . top-level rugby. Very competitive. Much bigger than what I'm doing here. She's brilliant. Ten times better than me at the sport."

Wyatt nods knowingly from the driver's seat, his eyes remaining on the road as he asks, "So what exactly did you do to get exiled to America for rugby?"

I frown as I meet his eyes in the rearview mirror.

His brows lift. "From what I can tell, this rugby program is new in Denver. And Trista said you needed a job at a nonprofit to log community service hours for bad behavior. She has to report your hours to your coach. What happened back at Trinity to create all of this?"

My jaw clenches as my hands turn to fists on my lap. I glance over at Calder, who looks a lot less friendly now than he did five minutes ago. Even Luke seems pensive and cautious.

I suppose this is the interrogation I should have expected from overprotective uncles. I'm living on their mountain, eating food Wyatt's wife bought for me, hanging out with their niece, having his wee daughter follow me all over the rescue center. It's no shock they want to size me up. I'd do the same if Cliona were in this situation.

I clear my throat and decide to give them the honest truth of it all because lying clearly isn't going to earn me any respect.

"I got in a fight with a bloke on the pitch who fucked over

my sister. He was a player for the other team that my sister was in a relationship with for a year before he cheated on her. Toward the end of the game, when they were about to lose, he said some fucked-up shite that he knew would set me off."

"What did he say?" Calder asks, his eyes tight.

My head twitches as I turn to look out the window, willing my temper to remain in check as I replay that day on the pitch. I've had fights on the pitch before. I've gotten red cards plenty of times. But that day . . . that day, I wanted blood.

Trinity College
A Few Months Ago

The whistle trills, and we're lining up for the extra two points. My jaw's clenched so hard on my mouth guard it's a wonder I haven't gnawed right through it.

I'm playing the game of my life. Everything is going my way. I'm seeing the pitch in ways I've never seen it before. Anticipating movements. Seeing holes, finding space. Scoring fucking tries like it's my job.

The timing couldn't be more perfect. This is my moment to be discovered. This kind of comeback is how I prove myself to the scouts here today. We just need this two-point conversion, and we've made it.

Then I hear him.

That bastard in the opposite jersey—the flanker that's my sister's fucking ex. "You moan when you score just like your sister does with my cock in her mouth."

A beat passes. Just one.

"What the fuck did you just say?" I spit, turning my head in his direction.

He grins around his mouth guard, his eyes beady and full of pure evil. "Ask my teammates. They've all seen the video of how she . . ."

I don't hear the rest. My vision goes white.

I launch, slamming into him with full force, my teeth bared. I drive him straight back. And when he recovers and walks toward me with a cocky smirk on his face, I swing, my fist exploding in pain as my knuckles connect with his jaw, creating a satisfying crunching sound.

The air splits with the shriek of the ref's whistle, but it's drowned out by my pulse rushing in my ears as arms try to drag me away from him. Someone is screaming my name, but I'm gone.

Gone.

It takes four teammates to haul me backward, boots scraping against the turf, blood on my knuckles, breath ragged. My eyebrow leaks blood, but I don't even remember getting hit.

My chest heaves, and when I can finally see straight again, I see my sister's ex grinning at me.

Grinning.

My teammates release me, so I lunge again. Right at that exact moment, the ref appears, and my hands barrel into his chest instead of my sister's ex. Unable to stop the momentum, I push him hard, sending him flying onto the ground like a heap.

A collective groan from the crowd breaks through my rage as more gloved hands grab me, trying to trap the fury eating me alive.

An assistant's voice cries, "Number eight—off! Red card! You're out of here."

And I turn my face to the stands, eyes connecting with my sister and her knowing look that confirms the fact that I just fucked my last chance.

"I'd have punched him the fuck out too," Calder confirms, and I blink in shock, looking at three grave, bearded faces all around me in the cab of the truck. There's a heaviness in the air as they all process what I've just shared.

"Your sister needs to press charges," Luke says, his fist clenching on the back of the seat.

Wyatt's knuckles are white on the wheel of his truck. "You should have killed him."

"I wanted to." I swallow the knot in my throat, not realizing how intense this has all felt for me. I couldn't even bring myself to tell my sister what her ex even said. Though I expect she already knew. She knew about the video. She knew it was passed around to teammates. I begged her to report him to the police, the university, anyone. But she refused. Said she consented to the video and deserved what she got.

I hate that a world exists where she thinks she deserves that kind of treatment.

"I've struggled with my temper on the pitch ever since my last year in secondary school. I'm working on it."

"So are we," Calder says with a laugh. "Some problems are just easier solved with a little violence, if you ask me."

The corner of my mouth tips up at that response. It's unexpected. I've gotten used to feeling like a thug the last several years. No one has ever made me feel . . . understood.

Until now.

We pull up to the bus stop, and I slide out of the truck, my rugby bag on my shoulder, my head hanging low.

"Someone will be here at six to pick you up," Wyatt says from his open window.

"Thanks for the ride . . . and for . . . not judging me too harshly."

Wyatt nods. "If fighting for your sister is the worst you got, you're alright by me, Reilly." He taps the side of his truck and then pulls away, leaving me winded and morbidly curious if what I did to his niece would be considered worse.

"I'm going to fucking die," I groan as I drop myself into an ice bath in the recovery room after training. "This is the end."

Laughter echoes from the tub beside me. "You need more than a week to get your lungs straight, Wolf," a Scottish voice utters.

I glance over at Jacob Fergus Maclay, aka Fergie as the team calls him. He's a few years older than me and just finished as a star player for the Grizzlies on their debut season this past year. He transferred from a team in London that he played for previously, and as a couple of the only internationals here, we connected relatively easily today out on the pitch.

When I wasn't fighting for my life, that is.

"I've been doing runs on the mountain I'm living at to prep, but this was next-level."

"Coach Harper had it out for you, I suspect," Fergie chortles with a laugh.

"Reilly," a gruff voice yells, and I stand up in the ice bath, my body shivering in my compression shorts as my new coach comes stomping into the room to face me.

He's a short, stocky guy with frown lines that have frown lines. "Have you started work at that rescue center yet?"

"Yes, Coach, I started last week."

"Confirm your hours with administration. You have to log twenty every week to be eligible to train with us."

"Yes, sir. I remember." I shiver, my abs clenching in the cold as I look down at him.

"And stop in my office after you're done here for your youth team information as well, okay? Season starts in a month."

"Y-y-yes, sir," I stammer as ice-cold water sluices down my body.

He slides a grumpy gaze over to Fergie, who smiles like a cat that got the cream. "He's with you on your team, Fergie, so keep him in line, or it's your ass."

"Aye, aye, Captain." Fergie salutes cheerily, and Coach glares at him before turning to walk away.

I drop back into the ice water, the frigid temp sweltering compared to the icy, militant communication style from my new coach. "He fucking hates me."

"He hates everyone," Fergie says with a laugh as he hops out of his tub and begins toweling off. "You just have to prove yourself to him."

"Throwing up in the bin today probably wasn't a good first impression."

"Aye, you may have screwed the pooch on that one, lad." He laughs and wipes down his chest. "But everyone is shite on their first day. Just stay the course."

I nod and offer him a grateful look. "Thanks for having my back today."

"No problem," he says, bunching his towel. "As long as you have mine with this youth team. These kids are rough, lad."

I frown and shrug dismissively. "I coached a lot of youth teams back in my neighborhood. It's no bother."

He huffs out a disbelieving sound and changes the subject when he asks, "So what mountain are you staying at?"

"It's a private residence outside a small village called Jamestown."

"That's near Boulder, aye?"

"Aye, there's a rescue center up there that I'm working at, and I'm living in the apartment above the barn."

"How did you score that setup?"

"My sister's roommate at Trinity is from there. She hooked me up."

"I'd say," Fergie says, his lips turning down. "So, is this friend of your sister's hooking you up in other ways as well?"

He waggles his brows at me and jumps back when I lurch out of the tub and take a large step closer to him. "Don't speak about her like that," I growl as water drips down on the floor around me.

His eyes widen as he holds his hands up in surrender. "Okay, lad, okay. No harm meant. Just trying to get to know your situation a bit."

"What's your situation?" I jut my chin up defiantly as I reach for a towel to dry off. I know I'm the new kid on the team, but that doesn't mean I'm just here for his amusement. "Wanna share your life story?"

Fergie laughs and hoists himself up onto a stretching bench, kicking his feet casually. "Aye, sure. I'm an open book, pal. My dad was a pro footballer in the UK for years. Maclay Logan, if you follow European football, not the American shite. Anyways, I broke his bloody heart the day I fell in love with rugby, but he's gotten over it for the most part because he and my mum show up to as many matches as they can. Or they did until I came over here." He winces and shakes his head as he looks down at the long scar on his knee. "I was in my prime until I buggered my knee up a couple years ago and can't seem to get my speed back, no matter how hard I try. So here I am . . . in Colorado, bottom-barrel feeding for a shite team just like you. So don't get defensive, lad. You and me . . . we're in the same boat."

I nod and exhale heavily, my eyes doing a sweep of the guy who has been nothing but kind to me since I arrived at camp early this morning. I push my damp hair off my face and grip my towel around my neck. "I'm sorry, mate. I'm still just . . . adjusting to all of this. It's been a stressful few months."

And I only made things more stressful when I decided to lock lips with my sister's best friend.

Fucking hell, what was I thinking? And the fact that Everly hasn't spoken to me since is not a good sign. Not a good sign at all.

"Let's go grab a pint, aye? I can prepare you for the little monsters we have to coach on Thursday after training. Then I can drop you to your bus stop if you like."

"Sounds good. Thanks, mate." And I head to the showers to clean myself up and work on pushing down my wall so I can help build up a new team.

Chapter 16

Hospital Pass: *A poorly executed pass that puts the receiver in a vulnerable position, making them likely to be tackled heavily by an opposing player.*

Translation: *Mountain men aren't good at passing new babies.*

Everly

"Everly, it's Wyatt. I'm going to need you to pick up Wolf from the bus stop in Boulder today," my uncle says into the phone line, and my heart lurches up into my chest.

"What? Why me?" I ask, my chest contracting with instant anxiety.

"Because I'm on my way to the hospital."

And now my anxiety ratchets up to a whole new level. "What? Why? What happened? Are you okay?"

"Addison is in labor!" I hear Luke's voice call out, and then the phone shuffles noisily as Wyatt passes it over. "Her water broke at the lumberyard, and Bullhead is driving her to the hospital now."

"Oh my God! Oh my God!" *Also, who the fuck is Bullhead?* "This is scary as shit."

"She's going to be great. What else can I do?"

"Can you run to my cabin and get our hospital bag?" Luke asks, his voice sounding more stressed than I've ever heard it. "She was supposed to leave it in her vehicle but said she forgot. Oh, and she needs someone to put Mildred in the fridge."

"Who is Mildred?"

"Her sourdough."

"Oh, that's right. Yes, I'm on it," I exclaim and slam my laptop closed.

"Trista is coming up from Mount Millie. Bring her and Stevie down the mountain with you. Don't drive separate."

I hear Calder's voice in the background. "Papa Bear, if ever there was a time to not worry about the fucking environment, it's now."

"Carpool, Everly. I mean it," Wyatt exclaims again, and I hear Calder grumbling in the back seat.

"Okay, no problem," I exclaim, running into my room to grab the present I had wrapped and ready for this exact day.

"I texted Wolf to let him know you're going to be late," Wyatt says, grabbing the phone back. "I'd ask Grandma to get him, but Addison wants her in the delivery room when the baby comes, and she's already at the hospital waiting. Dakota is alone at her T-shirt shop, so she can't leave, and Max and Cozy are dropping Ethan at camp today. Luke is a fucking mess. We're all falling apart, kid."

"Put me on speakerphone," I demand, my voice firm.

When the hum of the car grows louder, I call out, "Uncle Luke?"

"Yeah, Evs?" Luke replies, his voice trembling.

"Everything is going to be okay. I'm getting your bag now, and we will all be there soon."

He inhales sharply, and I can hear the tremor in his voice as he says, "Addison acts tough, but I know she's so scared."

My heart lurches as I picture him in the truck, running his hands nervously through his hair. Calder is probably squeezing his shoulder, and Wyatt is most likely gripping the wheel so hard it's going to fall off. Luke and Addison lost their first baby early in the pregnancy, so I know their anxiety must be high. Who wouldn't be nervous?

"It's normal to be scared," I say calmly, feeling the essence of my grandpa move around me. "Grandpa always said being scared just means you're about to do something really brave. You're about to become a dad, Luke. Nothing braver than that."

A gruff noise echoes in my phone, and I think it might be Luke crying. Or Calder. Or Wyatt. Or all of them. They all get equally choked up with one of Grandpa's infamous life lesson quotes. He was full of them.

We're not here for a long time, we're here for a good time.

Rejection just means you're one step closer to finding your solution.

And now this one. *Being scared just means you're about to do something really brave.*

My grandpa left his mark, that's for sure.

"But we're all going to be there for you guys, okay? We're all going to be waiting and brave and ready to celebrate with you the minute that baby boy is born."

Luke sighs and murmurs, "Thanks, Everly."

"I love you, Uncle Luke. See you all soon."

"I love you too, kid," he croaks and then hangs up.

I blow out a calming breath as I stand in my cabin and glance down at the mountain compound. That's the terrifying thing about love—it just raises the stakes for heartbreak. And the stakes are mountain high for all the Fletcher brothers.

It's six thirty when I pull up to the bus stop in Boulder and see Wolf sitting on the bench, dressed in a pair of jersey shorts and a T-shirt. He stands up and walks toward my car, his eyes cast downward as he throws his duffel bag into my back seat. When he slides into the passenger seat, my eyes land on his groin and instantly flash back to that night he kissed me and what that groin felt like pressed up against me.

Fuck, this is awkward.

And now I have to speak to him. There's no avoiding it.

"Hi, how's it going?" I ask cheerily as I put the car into Drive. He turns to gape at me like I'm speaking a foreign language. "Did you have a good training? Like your new team? How's the coach?" I ramble as I pull out onto the street and head back toward the hospital.

"Are you okay?" Wolf asks, and my cheeks flame as I feel him staring at me.

"I'm great. You've heard the news about the baby coming, right?"

"Yes, Wyatt told me," he grinds out.

"Great! I've dropped off Trista, Stevie, and the hospital bag already and am making my way back there to join the family. So, I'm thinking you can take my car back up to Fletcher Mountain, and I'll just catch a ride with Wyatt or Dakota if she sticks around. Or I'll just spend the night at my dad's. Lots of options."

Wolf releases a low, guttural noise as he rubs his hands along his muscular thighs. "I could have just taken a cab up the mountain."

"This is no trouble. I'm happy to help!"

"Can we just speak normally?" he bites, his tone acidic.

"What do you mean, normally?" I ask, my voice hitting a new octave. "Everything is fine."

"Everything is not fine," he argues as I pull into the hospital parking ramp. "You've been weird since Saturday night, and I just want to have it out already and be done with it."

"Well, now isn't a great time. Luke and Addison are having their baby." I pull into the first open spot I find, my hands trembling as I shut off the car. I'm not even close to the entrance to the hospital, but my brain isn't exactly braining right now, and it's just better for me to be done driving.

"Bloody hell, Fletcher, just tell me if I need to pack my bags, at least."

My head snaps over to look Wolf in the eye. It's dark in the ramp, but a yellow security light casts a glow through the sunroof, enough for me to see him. The expression on his face cuts right through me. He looks tortured. Stressed. Depressed. His brown eyes reveal the most emotion I think I've ever seen on Wolf.

"Why would you need to pack your bags?" I ask, my voice timid and unsure.

His jaw muscle shifts under his skin. "Because I expect you're about to turn me in for fucking sexual assault, which I deserve."

I inhale sharply. "You think that kiss Saturday night was assault?"

"Of course I do," he exclaims, his voice fraught with worry. "Why else would you be acting so weird toward me?"

"I've been acting polite!" I squeal defensively.

"That's weird," he roars back.

"I was just . . . trying to be cool about it all."

He rakes a stressed hand through his hair. "We've been over this . . . You're not cool."

"I know. I'm cringe." I spit his words back in his face. "And you said it was better than cool. And then you kissed me out of *pity*, and now I'm having a fucking identity crisis because I don't know how I am to behave after all of that."

Silence squeezes us into the car, and all I hear is the heavy breath of Wolf and the racing pulse of my heartbeat in my ears.

His voice is quiet and resigned as he looks forward and asks, "You think I kissed you out of pity?"

"Obviously," I sputter, wiping at some spit that just came out of my mouth. "Because I am pathetic, and you were trying to help me, but that help just made me feel even more pathetic."

He shakes his head, his eyes glassy in the dark car. "I didn't kiss you out of pity."

"Then why did you?"

His jaw ticks angrily. "I kissed you because I know what it's like to be looked at like you're less than. Like you're not worth someone's time."

"Okay, sure." I bark out a disbelieving laugh. "No offense, Wolf, but the six-foot-five rugby bad boy with anger issues is usually the asshole *doing* the bullying, not *being* bullied."

Wolf's whiskey eyes snap to mine. They're dark and punishing, and his tone is acidic when he replies, "And the rich, blonde, white girl people-pleaser is the classic blueprint for being a mean girl cunt."

Our harsh words hang between us, thick and heavy, as fear builds in my chest. But I'm not afraid of Wolf. In fact, I feel safe with him always. What I'm afraid of is what I don't know. What he carries with him. I think perhaps I've always known there's something darker going on with him . . . even before I became close to his sister.

"I'm not a cunt," I reply firmly.

"And I'm not a bully," he bites back.

I sigh heavily. "Forgive me, but for years, all you've ever sent my way has been snarls and silence. It's like you're always ready for a fight, no matter who it is." I hate saying that, but it's true.

His lip curls. "You think I wanted to learn how to fight? You think one day I woke up and decided it would be fun to be the scary bastard the whole uni calls a convict?" He leans in, his voice low and strained. "The only person who ever stood up for me my whole life was the girl I shared a womb with. Why should I talk when I don't want to? Why shouldn't I snarl if all I get from others is judgment?"

I open my mouth to argue, but then close it because what can I say? I started this. I made an assumption about him. People do it to me all the time, and I should have known better.

He grumbles under his breath and turns away, refusing to look at me. "The truth of the matter is, I was wee most of my life. Too soft, too skinny, too quiet. Easy target." He releases a bitter laugh. "Kids in school called me a lamppost. I had a broken nose at age nine and a chipped tooth at age eleven. And I wasn't even playing rugby at the time."

I inhale a trembling breath, picturing Wolf like that. It breaks my heart. "I'm sorry, Conri."

"Don't be," he bites, shaking his head. "My best mate, Finn, got it far worse than me, if you can believe it." He looks down at his hands, which have formed fists on his lap. The air sizzles with anger and sadness and something I can't quite wrap my head around.

"Childhood can be such a bitch," I offer, my words small and trite, but true nonetheless.

Wolf flattens his hands over his legs, his finger tracing the GPS coordinates on his thigh. I wonder if it has something to do with his experience. Or maybe his friend. I want to know more, but he's shared more with me in these past five minutes than he has the whole four years I've known him. I don't want to push him too far.

"Those girls from my school made a bet with a boy they knew I liked to take me out on a date," I confess, my voice rushed and nervous because I've never told anyone this story, not even my family. "It was revealed next week at school that it was all a lie, and he was paid to do it." I exhale a trembling breath and tell the last part. "He was my first kiss too. So now it's all I think of when I think of my first kiss. It was mortifying and messy. And I've hated dating ever since. I was with Hilow for those two years in high school because he felt safe at the time. Like a little shield from the world when I was lonely."

Wolf turns to look at me, his eyes full of sympathy and understanding. An understanding that perceptions aren't often reality.

But what I'm not saying, what I'll never be able to say, is that even after Wolf kissed me, I somehow still felt like I was being duped. Those girls triggered that old paranoia in me, that the kiss Wolf and I shared was all a lie. And it *was* a lie . . . I know it was fake. But in my delusional mind, I worried that even those girls were in on it with him. That everyone around me knew I was pathetic, and I was just naive and grinning my way through it to avoid the truth.

"They're being cunts," Wolf says, his voice resigned as if he can hear my racing anxious thoughts and he's trying to quiet them with two simple but effective words.

"Your bullies were being cunts too," I reply softly, the corner of my mouth lifting with a soft smile. "Can boy bullies be cunts? Is that like a universal insult, or should it only be applied to women? I'm not sure I've ever said that word out loud before. It's pretty harsh when used here in the States, but I heard it a lot in Dublin, so maybe I can appropriate it here more . . ."

"Everly." He says my name like a plea, his hard expression softening. He looks exhausted. Like confessing all of that wore him out more than his full day of rugby training. "I kissed you because I wanted to kiss you. I kissed you because you're fucking gorgeous and kind and nothing like those girls or the cunts who bullied me. I kissed you because if I didn't kiss you, I knew I'd regret it for quite possibly the rest of my life."

His voice is low and certain, slicing through the haze of my anxiety as every nerve in my body pulsates like it just heard the world is going to end. Maybe it will.

"You . . . wanted to kiss me?" I whisper, my head still catching up with what my ears heard.

"Fuck yes," he bites back with a dry huff. "I want to kiss you now too."

"Even after you called me a cunt?"

He inhales through his nose. "I did not call you a cunt."

"You called me cunt adjacent."

"That is not a thing."

"Feels like a thing."

"You know what I meant," he growls, and that familiar little sound of his weirdly soothes whatever tension was between us. "But I'll never kiss you again," he says, his brows furrowed. "Not until you ask me to. Properly."

I swallow hard, my vision clouding with information overload. My head is a snow globe, a blizzard of everything that was just revealed in the quiet of this hospital parking garage. But the weight of his words wraps around me like a thick, warm, comforting Wolf-sized blanket that I want to curl into.

This Irish boy shared a lot with me tonight. The least I could do is ask him properly to kiss me.

"Then," I whisper, my chest heaving inside my car that suddenly feels ten times smaller than it did when I got it. "Will you kiss me now?"

I turn to meet his eyes. They're full of fire and yearning, and they cause an ache to bloom between my legs that I'm not sure I've ever felt.

"Ask me properly." He says it like a warning. Like once I say it, I'll never be able to take it back. I don't want to.

"Conri . . ." I pant out a breath. "Kiss me."

And like a flash, we come together in the narrow space between us, his hand threading through my hair with a rough, greedy sort of tenderness as his other grips my waist. Like he's anchoring himself to me. I fist the front of his hoodie, anchoring myself to him as well as I pull him close, our lips crashing together in a feverish, hungry rhythm. It's familiar and prepared, so different from our first kiss.

Our first kiss blindsided me. It was unexpected, and I barely had time to process what was happening before it was over.

This one. This one is all too real. Deliberate. Chosen. Raw, wet, and vulnerable, like every wall he had built up against me has crumbled under the press of our lips.

I gasp into him as his tongue sweeps in, coaxing and demanding all at once. He tastes dark and hot, like fresh toothpaste and *him*. His scent is different today than other days. Similar to that Icy Hot cream that Cliona would wear after her rugby matches. I can't help but taste and explore him, committing all the sensations to memory. He groans, deep and throaty, dragging me closer over the center console as he devours me with so much purpose I feel my insides melt.

I gasp for breath in shallow fragments as I slide one hand down, fingertips grazing the powerful lines of his thigh. He burns through the fabric, and when I slip my hand lower, I gasp at the skin-on-skin contact. He's firm and pliable yet still quivering under my touch. His lack of control makes me want to feel more. So much more. All of him, even what's inside—

A thunderous bang rattles the window of my car, jolting us apart like a hose was turned on us. I look toward the passenger window and see Trista on the other side, waving with a big smile on her face. She bends over and picks up Stevie, resting her on her hip as she points to something in my back seat.

"I need Stevie's car seat," Trista's muted voice says through the closed window.

I shove a hand through my tousled hair and fumble like a maniac as I try to put the window down so I can talk to her, but then realize I shut my car off, so I have to start it up. I accidentally turn the wipers on somehow and bump the horn with my elbow, causing Stevie to scream before finally Wolf reaches over and slides the window down with a gentle, calm push of a button.

"Nana!" Stevie sings first, and I see Wolf offer a weak smile to my little cousin.

Trista props her elbow on the frame. "Hey, guys, whatcha doing?" she sings merrily.

"Um . . . I was just about ready to come inside," I reply, covering my lips, which feel swollen.

Trista's brows lift. "Oh, were you now? Because it looked like you were sucking face."

"What's sucking face?" Stevie asks, clearly not privy to the little show we were just putting on in the front seat of my SUV.

"It means popping zits," I sing back, my eyes begging my aunt to please not rat me out to sweet little Stevie, the namesake of my departed grandfather.

"Yes, popping zits. Wolf has a lot of zits, it seems like," Trista says with a pat on the open window. "Do you mind opening the back seat so I can grab Stevie's booster? Wyatt took his out of his truck this morning so he could make room for zit face here."

Wolf bows his head in shame.

I don't blame him.

This is hell.

We're in hell.

Trista bustles into the back and grabs the car seat before tucking her head inside the car one more time. "Anyways . . . as you were, young ones. But, Everly, I do want to let you know that Addison is already ten centimeters, and they're getting ready to push soon."

"Oh my God," I exclaim, reaching back to grab my purse. "I need to get in there."

"Mom, I wanna stay with Nana."

Trista smiles down at Wolf, who adjusts himself in the passenger seat. "I think Nana is a little busy right now, sweetie."

They walk back toward the hospital, leaving me and Wolf in

the quiet of my car with more unanswered questions than we ever had before.

"You have to sit down, or I'm not passing him to you," Luke says to Calder, who stands beside Addison's hospital bed.

"I hold Milkshake and Malt all the time. I can handle this little guy." Calder holds his grabby hands out to his brother.

"I won't pass him unless you sit down."

"Addison," Calder complains to Luke's wife, who laughs and shakes her head.

"I'm on my husband's side. Sorry, Calder."

Calder grumbles as he goes over to sit down on the small sofa under the window. He holds his hands up. "Now, pass me my new nephew, please."

"Okay, Levi Aaron . . . you're going to go to your Uncle Calder, but don't judge him too harshly. He's the middle child and can't help how he is. He apparently was deprived of attention his whole life, which he will tell you all about ad nauseam."

Calder hits Luke with a flat look, and I cover my snicker from my place on the other side of the room, where I stand with Cozy, Dakota, and Trista.

Wyatt comes over and growls at both of them. "Let me show you how to pass a baby."

The three of them begin arguing until my dad steps in to try to boss them all around. The Fletcher Brothers are a mess. A complete and total mess.

My eyes slide over to my grandma, who is coming back into the room with a fresh cup of ice water. She goes right to Addison's side, handing it over to her and brushing back a stray piece of black hair on her forehead. Grandma has barely left Addison's side since we've all been allowed to pile into this room. Levi's middle name, Aaron, is after Addison's little brother, who passed away many years ago when they were children. It's a special day for Addison. And I know she's breathing so much easier now that he's out and safe and being loved by so, so many mountain men.

Addison's dad sits in the chair next to her bed, smiling at the action of the Fletcher family piled into a way-too-small postpartum room. He sat in the waiting room with all of us earlier, and I could tell he was a nervous wreck. Losing one child at a young age has to make anyone a little gun-shy when it comes to their kids. But he seems to have calmed down now that he sees his daughter recovering well.

"I'd like to think that my Steven has found your Aaron up in Heaven," Grandma says, drawing everyone's eyes to her as she speaks to Addison and her dad. "I bet they're both enjoying this show."

Addison's face contorts as she covers her mouth, overwhelmed with emotion.

"Oh, I'm sorry, sweetie." Grandma bends to hug Addison. "I said too much."

"No . . . you said just enough," Addison's father croaks, handing his handkerchief over to his daughter. "It's a real nice thought."

The entire room goes quiet, all eyes wet and teary as we reflect on those who aren't here with us anymore and how lucky we all are to be experiencing this together. This is what dreams are made of. Love in abundance. And I played a small part in making a lot of this happen.

"Right in here," a nurse says, and our entire family looks back at the door to see who else is coming in. Everyone but my brother, Ethan, is here. Dad and Cozy made it back from dropping him off at camp just in time for the delivery.

My throat goes dry when I see that it's Wolf walking into the room with two brown bags in his hands. Trista nudges me with her elbow, and I turn to frown back at her, totally confused about why he's here. It was hours ago that I told him he didn't need to wait for me. I sincerely hope he hasn't been in the parking garage this whole time.

"Nana!" Stevie squeals and runs over to grab Wolf by the leg.

He clears his throat and offers a wobbly smile. "I'm sorry to interrupt. I asked the nurse to bring this in, but she yelled at me and said she wasn't Uber Eats. I'm afraid I offended her."

"What do you have here?" Cozy asks, stepping forward to peer into Wolf's bags.

"Oh, I just brought some sandwiches for everyone. Stevie makes me get her snacks in the center every hour or so . . . so . . ." His voice trails off as an entire room full of people stares open-mouthed at him. "You hungry, Steve?"

"Yes!" she squeals, and I hurry over to help Wolf with his full hands.

"If you already ate, I can take the rest and just bugger off."

"We'll take the sandwiches," Calder calls from the far side of the room, still holding the baby. He eyes Dakota. "Ace, you know what Cat Daddy likes."

Dakota rolls her eyes.

Wyatt walks over and frowns at Wolf. "Did you drive up to the mountain and come back?"

Wolf blinks back at him. "Um . . . yes."

Wyatt shakes his head. "That's really wasteful, Wolf."

"Everly's car is fully electric," Wolf says, gripping the back of his neck. "And your truck is hybrid?"

"What's your point?"

"My point is, I expect I used less energy driving Everly's car here and back than you did in one trip today."

"Oh . . . shit. He got you there, Papa Bear," Calder calls out, and Luke covers his mouth with a laugh.

Wyatt frowns over at Wolf. "Hauling trailers of construction materials on a fully electric truck isn't sustainable yet. The battery drains too quick. You know what, just give me a sandwich, Rugby Boy. You have a lot to learn about mountain life still."

The entire family chuckles and teases Wyatt as they dig into the food, Stevie going to town on her sandwich. Wolf offers a subtle wave and turns to leave, but I walk over to him.

"You don't have to go."

"This is a family thing. I just wanted to drop off some food."

"Come meet Levi, at least," Addison says from the bed.

"No, my Nana." Stevie drops her sandwich on the floor to grab Wolf's leg.

"Why does she keep calling you Nana?" my grandma asks with an amused grin on her face.

Wolf shakes his head. "She asked why people call me Wolf, and I told her my nana started it, and I guess she misunderstood, but I can't get her to stop. I've tried. Steve. Call me Wolf."

"No, Nana."

Everyone laughs, and I watch my grandma's reaction to Wolf calling Stevie Steve. I'm sure she loves hearing my grandfather's name said aloud. Everyone seems to, and Wolf and Stevie don't even notice the little moment they've given all of us as she pokes his leg tattoo and he swats her away, barely paying her any attention.

We all snap out of our fixation as Calder manages to pass Levi back to Luke, and Luke brings the baby over to Wolf. "This is your new compound neighbor, Wolf."

"Massive congrats to you both," he says, looking to Addison and then to Luke. Levi's shock of dark black hair peeks out around the beanie the hospital put him in.

"Thanks," Luke says with a proud, fatherly smile that brings tears to my eyes. "And thanks for the food. Nice play, Rugby."

"You can't call him that," I reply with a laugh. "That's the name of our bearded dragon."

"Your what?" Grandma asks, her smile dropping.

Trista steps forward, wiping her mouth with a napkin. "Our alpaca rescue had a bearded dragon sibling, and Wolf is taking care of it."

"I'm helping," I add defensively.

"Stevie named him," Wolf says, shooting a glare down to my cousin.

Everyone laughs knowingly, and Wolf hooks his thumb toward the door. "I'm going to head out. Let me know if I can do anything else. I did get all the animals penned up for the night, so we're set for tomorrow."

"Wolf, you're the best," Trista groans and pats him on the back. "I'll see you at work tomorrow."

"See you tomorrow."

My eyes follow the boy who just kissed me senseless a few hours ago, and just as he turns to walk out the door, he looks back at me and shoots me an imperceptible wink that I feel squarely in my gut.

A second later, he disappears, leaving me with my family. But for once, I wish I could walk out that door with that bad boy.

Chapter 17

Chancing Your Arm: *Irish rugby slang for taking a wild gamble instead of playing it safe.*

Translation: *Fuck it.*

Everly

The clock reads 11:11 p.m. as I pace in front of the floor-to-ceiling windows of my cabin, staring out at the Fletcher Mountain compound. It was just after ten when we all got home from the hospital. Stevie went for a sleepover with Grandma, so it was just Dakota, Calder, Trista, Wyatt, and me who came back up the mountain together in two vehicles. All the lights have been out in the cabins for almost thirty minutes, so everyone is probably fast asleep.

Must be nice to just fall asleep without a care in the world. What would that kind of peace even feel like?

I check my phone to see if Wolf has texted me back, and still nothing. The fucking asshole. The audacity he has to open up to me like that, kiss me like the world was burning, and then bring sandwiches to the hospital, and *then* not text me back when I ask him if he is still up is *infuriating*.

I kissed you because I wanted to kiss you. I kissed you because you're fucking gorgeous and kind and nothing like those girls or the cunts who bullied me. I kissed you because if I didn't kiss you, I knew I'd regret it for quite possibly the rest of my life.

Does he just say shit and kiss girls like that all the time, so it's no big deal to him? He probably does. He probably kissed a new girl at Trinity every weekend. Maybe even on weekdays. I bet he kisses girls on a random Tuesday, even. Just gives them that dark, smoldering look of his, shares a little about his childhood trauma, and they just pucker up and play tonsil hockey all night long with him. Tonsil rugby? Is that a thing?

The red barn sits at the bottom of the hill like a large, ominous shadow taunting me in the night sky. The yellow security light out front casts a warm glow on the dutch double doors, practically demanding I go down there and give that boy a piece of my mind.

"Fuck this," I growl and open my front door. If Wolf can't text a girl back, he deserves to have me banging down his door after eleven at night.

My breath hitches when a light flicks on inside Wyatt and Trista's cabin, so I beeline off the deck to duck into the forest on the mountainside. Wyatt's cabin has these huge, angular windows, basically making it like a snow globe. He can see everything on Fletcher Mountain, and I do not want to get busted skulking down toward the barn at this time of night. I'd never hear the end of it.

I survey the sloped landscape that overlooks Jamestown and note that it's not too steep if I stay up here, close to the top, but far enough down that I'm out of the eyeline of Wyatt's cabin. I could probably manage to walk this tree line and make it to the barn with very little exposure to any lurkers.

Determined to accomplish my mission, I flip on my phone flashlight and crouch down to navigate the treacherous terrain through the darkness, as that sliver of a moon above me isn't providing nearly enough light to make me comfortable. Although turning a flashlight on the nature freaks me out even more. Maybe what I don't know can't hurt me.

The pine needles crunch under my Birkenstock sandals as I walk with all the stealthiness of a rabid raccoon. I have to crawl over a huge fallen tree and murmur, "God, this is so pathetic," as I cross below the lookout point bench that my uncles installed years ago. It's a gorgeous, civilized little area with a pergola and flowers all around it. It has our grandpa's favorite catchphrase engraved on it.

We're not here for a long time, we're here for a good time.

There is nothing *good* about the number of branches scraping my ankles and arms and snagging into my hair as I traverse this hilly area. But I am a woman on a mission. A mission to chew the ass out of an Irish rugby player who thinks it's okay not to text back the girl he tongue-fucked mere hours ago. If he were one of my matchmaking clients, this never would have happened. He would have seen my rules and known better.

A rustle of leaves has me freezing mid-step, heart lurching up in my throat as I glance behind me. A loud snap of a twig echoes in the canyon, and I can't help but expel a weird, inhuman sound as I scurry away in search of shelter behind the large oak tree ten feet away.

I think it's oak, but I really don't know. I'm not exactly an outdoorsy girl. I enjoy the idea of nature but in the sense that I like to go for leisurely walks on flat surfaces that end in an overpriced coffee. Not nature hikes where I need to pack my own water or survival tools. Any kind of hike where I have to wear my water on my back and drink from those long fluid straws? Absolutely not. I'd rather die. If I can't wear my Birkenstocks on the hike, I'm not going.

Bug spray? Sure.

Bear spray? Fuck no.

I like to be *next* to nature, not *inside* nature.

And as my heart thrashes in my chest and I hug an oak tree for dear life while mentally telling myself that Bigfoot isn't real, I realize that I am very much *inside* nature right now, and I do not belong! Why did my uncles have to build their compound so far from civilization?

Another crunch of leaves, followed by a strange hissing sound, has me shrieking in a very undignified manner, and like a shot, I turn on my heel and tear through the forestry to get the hell away from whatever bit of nature is trying to end my life.

A fluttering noise echoes behind me, and I look back to see what it is, only to stub my toe on a stump that sends me toppling down into the brush. My shoulder connects hard with a boulder, and I groan as I roll onto my back, my hair dragging through the dirt as I rub my aching arm.

Heart racing, I shine my flashlight into the darkness, expecting to see evil glowing eyes emerge from the darkness. Bared fangs. Raised hackles. Whatever a mountain lion does before it attacks. And I'm not proud to admit I'm even concerned that Bigfoot could be coming for me because my mind is dark and full of irrational terrors.

Why am I too prissy to carry bear spray? If I were outdoorsy, I would be prepared for this kind of danger.

A bush trembles in the darkness, and I crab-walk backward on my hands and feet. I open my mouth to scream for help when a white beastlike creature emerges. It opens its mouth and releases a deep, bellowy honk that reverberates down the canyon, and I drop my arms when I register the animal in front of me.

"Fowl Pacino!" I hiss, my voice just above a whisper. "You scared the shit out of me!"

He flutters his wings and shakes his head, staring at me with a look of undiluted judgment before he turns and marches his way back down the mountain, his ass waddling side to side. I wipe my filthy hands off on my hoodie, noticing my bare legs are covered in dirt as I attempt to slow my racing heart from the adrenaline rush of almost being murdered . . . by a goose.

"I suddenly understand why Dakota hates birds so much," I grumble as I stand and turn around to see I'm just twenty yards from the barn.

My shoulder aches, my lungs are burning, I have dirt all over my hands . . . But all that pales in comparison to the fire in my belly over the fact that I'm about to give Conri Reilly a piece of my mind.

In seconds, I'm marching through the barn, ignoring the stirring of all the animals as I disrupt their peaceful slumber. I stomp up the long wooden staircase and pound hard on the door, not even attempting to be quiet anymore. My rage doesn't give a shit who hears me now. I just merely avoided death, and it's all Wolf's fault.

The door swings open during my third pounding session, and there he is, dark rumpled hair, bare chest, and sweatpants hanging indecently low on his hips.

His eyes are heavy with sleep as he rasps, "Everly? What's going on?"

"Sandwiches is skipping some valuable steps," I exclaim, my voice sputtering as my brain short-circuits over his pecs, his abs, his shoulders, and those hip bones. *Focus, Fletcher. You're big mad right now.*

"What?" Wolf's voice is gravelly as he runs his hand over his hair, tousling it and somehow managing to make it look even better. He's one of those assholes whose hair looks better the messier it is, not worse. He can roll out of bed and be photo-ready. Not me. My hair turns into a nest in my sleep. Probably because I toss and turn as I rethink the day, so by the time I knock out, it's already a disaster.

Yet another thing that irritates me about the tortured boy before me.

"Sandwiches," I repeat, my eyes roving over the ink on his sinewy arm before snapping back to his. "You brought sandwiches tonight. Are you fucking crazy?"

He blinks. "What's wrong with sandwiches?"

I jab a finger into his soft, meaty chest. Only it's not soft. It's hard. The skin is soft though. Incredibly so. So soft I get this weird, intrusive urge to rub my cheek along it.

I push my way into his dark apartment, noticing he smells like soap and sleep. Apparently, he had time for a leisurely shower when I was a sleepless ball of anxiety. A light is on over the stove, and it only further adds a sultry, sexy appeal to this ridiculous godlike figure in front of me.

"Sandwiches is arguably a soft-launch boyfriend move, Wolf. Are you my boyfriend?"

His face instantly turns into the bug-eyed emoji.

I roll my eyes. "Relax, I know you're not my boyfriend, and I hate to be *that* girl, but like . . . what are we? Are we dating? A situationship? Friends with benefits? Sum this up for me because I like my rules, and I don't know what kind of guidebook to go off for all this."

I gesture to his whole body because it's a lot. He's six foot five, half-naked, and standing there like a fantasy brought to life. And he told me mere hours ago he wanted to kiss me. Like for real-real. And then we did kiss. Like for real-real. I need to know what this is.

"Okay . . ." Wolf replies, his brows furrowed in confusion as his eyes drift from my face to my hair. "Did you lose a fight with a Christmas tree?"

"What?"

He reaches forward, radiating his body heat on me as he plucks a twig out of my tangled hair. Great. I've stormed in here asking the cliché question "what are we?" while looking like Bigfoot's dick.

Meanwhile, he is fresh out of bed and looking like one of those pornographic Calvin Klein ads.

"I hiked over here through the woods so no one would see me," I grumble petulantly, still bitter about how hot he looks.

Wolf's lips twitch like he's fighting back a smile. "God, you're a lot." And then he loses all humor on his face as he stares at my shoulder. "You're fucking bleeding, Everly."

Oh, I love the way he says my name.

Before I can object, he grabs me by the arms and angrily manhandles me through his apartment, grumbling curses under his breath the whole way toward his bathroom.

Bathed in the warm yellow vanity lighting, he grips me by the waist and hauls me up onto his small bathroom counter before I have a chance to catch my breath. It smells like boy in here. Like manly bodywash and toothpaste. I immediately feel like I'm getting a glimpse behind the curtains of Conri Reilly's personal hygiene.

"How did this happen?" he growls, his jaw muscle twitching under his five-o'clock shadow. Damn, his mood changed quickly. One second, he's smiling at me like I was a cute, lost puppy he wants to rescue, and the next, he's scowling at me like I'm a rabid racoon he wants to call animal control on.

Honestly, I've been both tonight, so I guess I'm grateful he noticed.

My eyes snag on the loofah inside his shower, and I quickly shake myself out of this stupor to answer his question. "Fowl Pacino got me."

"Excuse me?" I feel his eyes blaze on mine.

I shrug and look down. "I thought he was Bigfoot."

"That makes perfect sense," he deadpans. I think he's being funny, but for some bizarre reason, I feel a tiny urge to cry over how pathetic I must seem to him.

I hook my finger through the four-inch tear on my sleeve

and hiss when I accidentally graze my injury. "Dammit, I love this sweatshirt."

Wolf makes an irritated noise in his throat. "Don't touch it."

He reaches under the sink and sets a first aid kit beside me. With deft precision, he opens the container and pulls out a rubbing alcohol pad. "Are you wearing anything under this?" He grimaces as he struggles to access the wound through the tear.

I nod and peel my hoodie off over my head, now sitting before him in a white athletic tank top and shorts that feel scandalously small without my giant hoodie hanging over my hips. His sour mood lightens for a fleeting moment as his gaze drags over me, slow and unhurried. When his eyes linger on my braless chest, I inhale sharply as my nipples pebble under the thin fabric, acutely aware of his whiskey-brown stare.

And judging by the way Wolf's jaw flexes, he notices.

"Hold still," he mutters, voice low and rough as he steps in close, pushing my legs apart to give him better access. His fingers brush my bare shoulder gently, and the tender contact, coupled with the heat of his close, *shirtless* proximity and my nearly shirtless body, has my heart hammering in my chest. "Doesn't look too deep, but I need to clean it."

I nod and struggle to breathe normally as he bites the corner of the alcohol pad packet with his teeth to open it. Awareness floods my skin as I get a flash of how he would look opening a condom as well. With how naked both of us are and how thick the air is in this bathroom, an aching need blooms between my legs, making it hard for me to breathe normally.

I swallow thickly, trying to make sense of this because I don't often get "turned on." I'm not one of those girls who even finds the need to masturbate. I just don't ever seem to desire that kind of maintenance, I guess. But whatever is happening in my body every time I'm near Wolf lately is definitely something I want to explore, even though I know I shouldn't.

I look away, trying to hide my lustful thoughts, and then hiss loudly when he presses the pad to my scratch.

"Ouch," I exclaim, reaching up to grab his arm as I brace myself against whatever he's doing.

He frowns down at me, all tall and towery and grumpy. His brows furrow as he says to my lips, "Stop squirming."

"I can't help it."

"I think you can."

"Maybe it's not the wipe that has me squirming," I blurt, my breath hitching in my throat. "You're just . . . *looming* over me so much, it's hard to sit still."

"Looming?" The corner of his mouth tugs up like he's trying not to smile. "I wouldn't have to *loom* if you'd take better care of yourself."

"And I wouldn't have to hike through nature if you'd answer your texts. Why on earth do you think it's okay to not reply to text messages after you kiss someone? That is like common human decency." I glare up at him, trying to hold my own.

He shrugs and glances out toward his apartment. "I went to bed at nine. I didn't see any text."

"Nine?" I balk and shake my head. "What are you? Ninety years old?"

His eyes dance with mirth, like he enjoys the fact that he's irritating me. "I like my sleep."

"Must be nice," I mutter, and then realize I'm still gripping his arm.

I release it quickly, and he takes his newfound freedom to fish a Band-Aid out and apply it to my cut. When he's done, his eyes move upward as he reaches out and plucks something out of my hair. "You have a whole ecosystem in your hair."

"Ugh." I push him back and comb my fingers through my strands, catching on various dried leaves and twigs. Fucking nature. I drop my head and avoid eye contact, only to have his finger crook under my chin as he forces me to look up at him.

"What did your text say?" he asks, his touch lingering on my face as he hits me with a tender, thoughtful look.

I lick my lips nervously. "I was texting to see if you were awake still so we could discuss what happened earlier."

"And Saturday," he adds, dropping his hand from my face and taking a step away from me to lean on the opposite wall. Like he feels the need to create some space between us for this discussion. It's probably a fair assessment, but I instantly miss the heat of him. He crosses his arms like he's bracing for impact.

"I really don't think we should do that again," I utter robotically, my tone flat and uninspired. These were the words I was saying in my head all night in my cabin, and I need to say them now. "And just because you open your door all sexy and shirtless, doesn't change anything."

His brows twitch. "That's the second time you've called me sexy."

"When was the first?" I ask, my lips parting in shock.

He hits me with a deliciously provocative smirk. "You said my accent was sexy at that party."

I roll my eyes. "Whatever. It's not like you don't know you're sexy."

"I didn't know *you* think I'm sexy." He pins me with an inscrutable look that I can't quite decipher.

My nostrils flare as I grip the edge of the counter, forcing myself to stay seated right here and not move closer to his heat. "It doesn't matter what I think. We can't do that again. For so many reasons."

He eliminates the space between us and plucks a pine needle out of my hair. "What were those reasons again?"

My throat tightens as I inhale his fresh shower scent again. "We work together."

"Yeah, that could definitely be awkward." He nods in agreement.

I nod too, my breath coming in short bursts. "And my family is like . . . everywhere. Those sandwiches were probably a dead giveaway."

"A dead giveaway that I stuck my tongue down your throat earlier?" His tone is wicked and causes a stirring low in my belly, because all I can think about right now is having his tongue down somewhere else doing indecent things. I know his tongue would feel amazing in other areas.

I'd squeeze my thighs together, but he's sort of standing in between them at the moment.

I clear my throat, my voice weak as I add, "I feel like we were finally starting to become friends. We trauma-bonded."

"Yeah . . . I like you well enough now that it's confirmed you're not a mean girl—"

I reach up and cover his mouth. "Don't say the last part."

I feel him smile under my hand and lower it so I can drink in the rare sighting. Although arguably, he smiles a lot more around me than he ever used to. His eyes zero in on my lips when he adds, "And for the record . . . I think you're sexy too, Stretch."

His Irish accent is thick and sultry as he utters my nickname to lighten the whopper of a comment he just made. This boy doesn't pass out compliments freely. To know he isn't "just tolerating" me anymore and that he likes me *and* thinks I'm sexy feels like I've just won the Rugby World Cup. That's a thing, right? I think I heard Cliona talk about it.

"You think I'm sexy?" *I am so weak.*

"Fuck yes," he growls, taking a step closer so his legs are now brushing against the insides of my thighs, causing my whole body to light on fire.

He braces a hand on the counter beside me, his whole body caging me in as our lips come dangerously close together again.

"Your sister is my best friend," I whisper, my voice choked.

He nods slowly. "My sister is really fucking far away right now. And the very last thing on my mind."

Goose bumps race over my body in a hot-cold rush, like every nerve ending has woken up for the first time in my entire life. My sex clenches so sharply I fight the urge to grind myself against the marble counter below me.

But everything hurts. Everything aches. Everything yearns for what is right in front of me, blanketing me in its heat.

I bite hard on my lower lip, fighting this desire coursing through me. I shouldn't do this. I shouldn't even think of this. Wolf is dangerous in a way that has nothing to do with his temper or his trauma or his relation to my best friend or the fact that we work together.

He's dangerous in the way he makes me want to be dangerous myself. Throw out my own manifesto and just . . . *fuck his brains out.*

God.

Could I even do that?

Could I stick my tongue down his throat and ride him right here in his apartment, under the mountain moon, next to our bearded dragon? Is there a reality where that's a good idea and no one gets hurt?

"Christ Almighty, Stretch," Wolf growls low and feral, his minty breath so hot on my lips I want to drag my tongue over his mouth to taste it. "If you keep looking at me like that, I'll have ya pinned up against this mirror before either of us can stop pretending we're going to talk ourselves out of this."

And it's his wicked Irish-lilted words that tip me over the edge.

"Fuck it," I pant, grabbing him by the neck and hauling him down to my lips.

Wolf

I grunt my shock into Everly's mouth as her lips crash into mine, hot and wild, like she's been waiting all day to finish what we started earlier. There's nothing tentative about her movements. No testing, no second-guessing. Just teeth and heat and the kind of kiss that has my cock instantly thickening in my sweats.

Fuck, it's a strange feeling to go from dreaming about someone to seeing them in real life. My mind is still struggling with the notion that this is actually happening because when I opened the door and saw her there in her baggy Trinity hoodie, thin cotton shorts, battered Birks, and wide, haunting blue eyes, I was certain I was dreaming. I thought my fantasy of fucking her brains out tonight was happening in my REM cycle, and I was about ready to grab her and kiss the ever-loving shite out of her for the third time.

But I'm not dreaming. This is reality. And the reality is, it took every ounce of my strength not to kiss her when she was sitting on my bathroom counter, looking sad.

She's a mess tonight. She's an overwhelmed, stressed-out, exhausted mess. She blew into my apartment like a hurricane, complete with branches in her hair and cuts on her skin, which did not sit well with me. The way I want to take care of her and fuck her until she feels better is concerning. I want to put her in my shower and scrub every inch of her clean, checking for other injuries while kissing every inch of her flesh.

I should probably be arrested for these indecent thoughts.

But the tightness of her legs around my waist makes me think she'd welcome my barbaric thinking.

Her tongue thrusts deep into my mouth, and I growl in response. She is way too fucking much. *And yet . . . I can't get enough of her.*

Sharing a small part of my past with her unlocked something in me. I started to see her as a person, not just Everly Fletcher—the girl I secretly followed home after her matchmaking events for four years because I was concerned for her safety.

For years, I told myself I couldn't have her like this. I couldn't be with her like this. I was too fucked-up, too dark, too dangerous. And I was well on my way to convincing myself of that tonight. It was true, I didn't see her text, but even if I had, I'm not sure I would have been ready to see her. But she made the first move here. And now I'm about to make the second.

My hands find her waist, my fingers slipping under her thin tank top to brush along the side of her bare breast. I push her back against the cold mirror, causing it to rattle, as my fingers dig into her soft-as-butter curves. She tastes faintly of mint as her tongue tangles with mine like she's trying to prove a point I already understand.

There's no walking this back now. We're not putting on a show for a party, or in a parking garage, sharing our truths before making an impulsive decision to kiss.

It's just the two of us in my rustic barn flat, and there is nothing to stop us now.

"Everly," I rasp against her lips, needing to be fully certain she wants what I want.

"What?" she murmurs, nipping at my bottom lip before grabbing my neck and kissing me even harder.

Something primal thrums in my chest, loud enough to drown out the voice telling me this is a bad idea. I yank her hips forward, and she gasps against my mouth, causing my heart to hammer in my chest. I slide my hand up her bare thigh, my fingers digging into the meat of her bottom, growling as she shivers under my touch. Her breath hitches when she feels the ridge of my cock on her core, but she doesn't stop. If anything, she pulls me closer, her legs gripping me tighter.

I break our kiss and press my forehead to hers, breathing her in, letting her see the barely restrained hunger I usually keep locked down tight. "Are you sure about this? 'Cause you're playing with fire right now," I growl, my voice low and gravelly.

Her raw lips glisten in the warm bathroom lighting before she utters, "I want to burn."

And God help me, that's just what I needed to hear.

With a grunt, I lift her off the counter, my hands gripping under her bottom as I carry her out of my bathroom and over to my bed. Her lips drag down my throat as she licks and nips with fiery passion that I honestly didn't know she was capable of.

I drop her down onto my navy duvet cover, and her eyes instantly zero in on my groin, noting the obvious erection inside my sweatpants. I fight the urge to fist myself when reality prickles into my mind, causing me to stop everything.

"I don't have a condom," I state regretfully, swallowing the knot in my throat as her short blonde hair fans out on my bed. *God, my bed will smell like her for days, and I fucking relish that thought.*

"Oh . . . um . . . that's okay," she says, sitting up on her elbows and looking suddenly insecure. "We can just . . . I can go."

I drop to my knees in front of her. "I don't want you to go."

She offers me a wobbly smile like I soothed her self-doubt. "What did you have in mind?"

My fingers move forward and trace the outline of her nipple, and she sucks in a sharp breath when I dip lower, toying with the waistband of her shorts. "I want to taste you. Would you be alright with that?"

She releases a shuddered breath and instantly tenses up. "Oh . . . um . . . I've never . . . had anyone do that before."

My fingers freeze on her waist. "Christ, are you a virgin?"

"No," she blurts out, pushing away from me. She backs up toward the middle of the bed and pulls her knees up under her chin, squeezing herself for comfort. "I just . . . never had anyone who ever wanted to do that."

"What? Oral sex?" I ask, needing her to be perfectly clear.

She shrugs. "I mean . . . I've done it to him. But he just never did it to me. It's different for guys, I'm sure."

She said *him* as if she's speaking of one person. And if it's that Hilow prick, every marginally generous thought I had about him is now gone forever, and he deserves to be punched in the fucking nuts.

My chest heaves when I ask Everly, "Have you only ever been with one guy?"

She nods and rolls her eyes. "Shocking, I know. I clearly have amazing game."

Her tone is self-deprecating as she forces a laugh, and I fucking hate it. Those fucking girls really did a number on her because, somehow, she went through four years at Trinity having no idea how alluring she is without even trying. The way she always has a smile for strangers or meets people where they are, while also pushing them to be better. I saw it best when she and my sister became close. It's a gift, really. I don't think Everly even realizes all that she did for Cliona in the aftermath of her ex. She brought her back to life.

But from the day I met Everly Fletcher in first year, I could see something unique in her. Her need to help people infuriated me back then, but if I were real with myself, I could admit that it also soothed an ache in me that I'd harbored since my childhood experiences. Her genuine kindness gave me hope in humanity that I'd damn near lost completely before I met her.

And the fact that she doesn't see herself for all that she is makes me irrationally angry.

"Listen, Everly . . . I'm going to say this to you only once, but I want you to remember it for the rest of your life." My voice is low and threatening as my eyes focus on hers and not her body or legs or lips. This is for her soul to hear. "Any bloke who lets you suck him off and doesn't want to do the same to you isn't worth the sweat on his fucking undeserving nut sack."

The corners of her mouth curl into a sexy smirk that I would really like to fucking kiss.

"And if it's alright with you . . . I'd like to make up for all mankind by using my undeserving tongue to give you the orgasm of your life."

Her smile falters for a moment, and she gets a peculiar look in her big blue eyes that I can't quite discern, but then she bites her lip and nods.

"Come here," I murmur before grabbing her by the ankles and yanking her toward the edge of the bed.

She squeals with laughter, her short blonde strands falling into her face as she sits on the edge of the bed, her legs spread around where I'm kneeling between them. I reach up and delicately brush a strand out of her face, drinking in her creamy complexion and that stunning blush in her cheeks before slicing my fingers into her hair and crushing my lips to hers.

I grip her hair and angle her head to deepen the kiss, my body needing to consume her breath and her arousal all at once. My other hand grips her bare leg, digging into her smooth skin as I pull her close, erasing every inch of space between us.

I pull away and murmur, "Stand up."

And she does, on somewhat wobbly legs. Her fingers slide through my hair as I lean back and slowly peel her shorts down her legs so I'm eye level with her pale purple lace G-string.

Goose bumps riot over her skin as I stroke my thumb over the damp area on her underwear.

"Christ, you're soaked," I growl and lean in to drag my tongue over the textured fabric covering her slick heat.

She lets out a throaty moan, buckling over top of me as she holds on to my head like she's hanging off a cliff. Her scent drives me fucking feral, and I feel my cock leak inside my sweats but silently will it to simmer down. She needs this more than I do. She needs everything. And I'm all too happy to be the one to give it to her.

I pull back and look up at her, watching her teeter above me like she's in six-inch heels, not barefoot and straddling my face. "Can I take these off?" I ask, giving her a chance to stop me if she's not comfortable.

She nods aggressively, almost comically, the need in her eyes so clear I want to roar with satisfaction, and I have barely tasted her.

I curl my fingers inside the thin waistband and tug them down slowly, savoring the reveal of her perfect pink center. She has a smattering of light hair above it, and I growl with hunger as I lower her back down onto the bed and grip her thighs. The soft give of her skin under my touch has my pulse kicking like I'm in the middle of a mountainside jog.

"Are you sure you want to do this?" she asks, her breaths coming out short and choppy, her nerves getting the best of her. "I might not be able to . . . um . . . orgasm, and I feel bad making you—"

I cut her off with a low growl, propping her long legs on my shoulders and spreading her wide to reveal every delicious bit of her to me.

"You let me worry about your orgasms from now on, got it?" I murmur, my mouth inches from her core.

I slide my rough palm over the sharp edge of her hip bone. Her breath catches as I gently brush my thumb over her clit. She bucks upward, falling back onto her back as she utters out a shocked little moan.

Her back arches off the bed before I've even kissed her, so with a deep breath, I press my mouth to her tender flesh, gently tasting her for the first time.

She gasps, and it snaps something inside of me like throwing petrol on an open flame. I flatten my tongue and run it along the full length of her, over and over. She clutches my hair, holding me like she's afraid I'll stop. It's a baseless fear as I'm relentless and greedy, my tongue switching from her clit to her core, thrusting and sucking and laving like a man possessed.

She tastes like the perfect kind of sin. Like an angel who fell from Heaven and begged for a romp with the devil.

I am the devil compared to her. I'm all trouble and tempers and screwups and last chances. She's clean and sharp and sweet and beloved. Except when she's having one of her meltdowns, maybe. When she's rambling about a project she's passionate about or tearing into me for not meeting expectations I didn't even know she had.

She lights up in those wild moments. Cheeks flushed, hands flying everywhere, that bossy little chin tilted like she's ready to take on the whole world.

That's when she's dangerous.

Not because she's perfect.

But because she's real and messy and unfiltered. Cringe, not cool. And there's an incredible bravery there that makes me fucking desperate to embrace. She is her own person through and through, and I admire the fuck out of that.

I pull my mouth back for a breath and bring my hand around to thrust a finger deep inside her drenched channel. I fucking whimper when I feel how tight she is. "Christ, Everly, how long has it been?" I ask, pumping in and out of her and struggling to get a second finger inside. "How long since you were last touched?"

She rides my hand, her hips gyrating up to meet me with greedy little thrusts. "A long time."

"How long?" I command, needing to know.

"Years," she expels, her stomach contracting as she curls up to watch what I'm doing to her. "Before I came to Trinity."

My body reacts primally to that thought. Like she's been saving herself just for me. Just for my mouth, my fingers, and my cock . . . someday. Maybe. Hopefully. Christ, I hope this isn't a onetime thing. To taste her now and not claim her in all the ways I want to claim her will fucking kill me.

And to know it was just that Hilow prick that had her makes me see red. He doesn't deserve her like this.

I pull my fingers out and bring them to my mouth, sucking her arousal off, tasting her fully as I expel a groan from deep in my chest. He didn't have this. He didn't taste her. He fumbled his chance, and now she's mine.

She shivers as she watches my lips suck around my fingers, and her legs curl tighter around me, pulling me closer, silently begging me for more. So, I give her what she wants and bury my face between her thighs, drinking in every whimper and pulse from her sweet heat while a new coil of hunger for more grows in my gut.

Her gasps turn into tortured moans, and I feel it—her tension melting into me, both in surrender and in a plea. I thrust harder and faster with my tongue, shaking my face between her thighs as I grip her hips aggressively and smother myself in her essence as deep as I can. I want to drown in her. Die in her. Lose myself completely in her.

"Conri." She pants my name, and I think it's the first time a woman has ever done that. Not many girls know my real name.

Many only ever know me as Wolf, which doesn't have the same effect in the bedroom. It sounds more like a dog barking than a woman moaning out my name in pleasure. A bit of a buzzkill, if I'm being honest.

Nothing is killing my buzz with Everly.

"Conri!" she cries out again as her legs clamp around me. I feel her coil beneath my tongue, a vibrational frenzy taking over her groin as she tightens and then snaps, her trembling limbs jittering all over as a flood of liquid enters my mouth and causes me to go absolutely fucking feral. I lap up her climax like it's my most cherished possession. My own personal nectar of divinity.

And I don't even realize that I'm climaxing as well. Blowing it right in my fucking sweats. Christ, when has that ever happened to me? Not since I was a boy and had wet dreams, I suspect. That's what this girl does to me. She makes me lose all control.

Fuck, I could do this forever. See her like this for all time. I know it's the haze of sex talking right now, but the fact that I've climaxed without her even touching me says something. Something really fucking scary.

After an undisclosed amount of time, her legs relax, and I miraculously regain full hearing. I pull back, my face covered in her release, and gaze in amazement at her red, swollen sex, glistening and shuddering like it went through hell and back and is all the better for it. My heart hammers in my chest, pulse still racing with the reality that no other man has had her like this, so in this way only . . . she is mine and mine alone.

The primal satisfaction that stirs in my gut over that reality is fucking terrifying.

Her eyes flick down to me, wide, vulnerable, and I feel something fierce twist inside of me. I misjudged Everly Fletcher. She might be a lot, but she's a lot I'm willing to handle.

Chapter 18

Going Solo: *Ignoring teammates and making a selfish run.*

Translation: *Being selfish feels wrong . . . but sometimes, it's exactly right.*

Everly

"Top of the morning!" Trista exclaims as she slams the brakes of her ATV in front of my cabin, sending a spray of gravel and dust all around her. "Looks like someone has been struck by the luck of the Irish!"

I nearly trip down the flight of steps off my deck as I gape at my aunt. "Excuse me?"

"I mean, lucky for you, I just *happened* to be driving by and can give you a ride down to Mount Millie for our big meeting with Wyatt and Calder this morning."

"Oh . . . um . . ." My eyes instantly move to the red barn. The red barn where Wolf is currently located. The red barn where I had my first orgasm of my life last night and then awkwardly skuttled out of while my other luck of the Irish was in the shower.

I cringe as I flash back to our text exchanges Wolf and I had after he got out of the shower to discover that I'd left.

Me: Thanks for the [tongue emoji]. Let me know when I can return the favor! [Dancing emoji, eggplant emoji, water droplet emoji]

Him: Where the fuck are you?

Me: Back at my cabin. Figured you needed some sleep after all that effort. Big day of work tomorrow.

Him: You walked back alone at midnight?

Me: Yep! No rogue goose attacks this time, thank goodness. Sorry if your bed looks like a Christmas tree wreath exploded on it. I'm still picking out pine needles!

Him: Nothing about this is okay, Everly.

Me: Our dragon was judging me, so I had to get out of there. Rugby should have never seen his mother like that. I'll pay for his therapy.

Him: We will discuss this in person.

Me: No need! I'm cool, I swear.

"Get in, kid," Trista says, her brows waggling excitedly at me.

With a deep breath, I climb into the side-by-side and gird my loins for the conversation I'm betting we're about to have. The kind where Trista tells me how, on second thought, it's horribly inappropriate for me to kiss her employee. He's too valuable around here to mess with, and she'd appreciate it if I could refrain from acting on my urges in the future.

And I will agree with her and promise it will never ever happen again. And tell myself to never tell a soul about what we did later that night because, clearly, I was drunk on mountain air. Hopped up from the adrenaline of nearly being attacked by a storybook-looking goose. All that fear gave me temporary amnesia, and I just forgot that it was my best friend's brother who confessed his woes to me and then tongue-fucked my pussy like he was trying to win an Olympic gold medal in competitive cunnilingus.

It was a onetime thing, and I deserve the shame I carry for carelessly crossing all those boundaries.

"When is Stevie coming back from Grandma's?" I ask, glancing into the back seat and wishing my tiny, cute cousin were here to serve as a buffer for this awkward chat.

"They're doing pool time at Max's, so not until later. Let's take the scenic way down to the center, shall we?" she asks and heads toward the trails between Luke's cabin and mine. "Calder works so hard on these trails to take his insane cats for walks, and I never use them."

Without waiting for my reply, she takes off like a shot, wind whipping her hair around as the ATV bucks and rattles through the carved trail. Trista grins as she blasts through a shallow area of the stream that runs behind my cabin. Her eyes spark with the kind of wild joy that scares the shit out of me. The trees crowd the path she's driving on, and I duck and cover when the ATV scrapes against some hanging branches.

Finally, she hits a dirt clearing that's at the very peak of the mountain. Just as I think she might fling me over the edge for being such a hot mess, she parks right on the edge, giving me the most stunning view of the backside of Fletcher Mountain, which I've never seen before.

It's steep with dense forest that looks impossible to tame. There are several areas of exposed dirt and stubborn roots, where I suspect some landslides have occurred. Honestly, it's all very raw and shocking back here. Terrifying to think we live next to all this nature.

But as my eyes take in the rough terrain, I can't help but see the beauty in it. It's kind of like my uncles before they found Trista, Dakota, and Addison. They used to be these rough, uncivilized troublemakers the city of Boulder gossiped about. They cursed and drank and got into fights and made highly questionable romantic decisions.

Now, they're cat daddies and new daddies and girl daddies. They've softened and matured. Finding love has helped them morph into incredible men like my dad and grandpa. There's no longer a clear line that distinguishes the brothers, and I love that because it's such a wild transformation that is beautiful.

"So, you're making out with my hired help, eh?" Trista says, cutting right into my family musings that were a welcome distraction from my obsessive thoughts about last night.

I cover my face with my hands. "I am mortified that you saw that."

"Don't be." Trista laughs and gives me a gentle pat. "That moment in the parking garage was hilarious. Stevie asked if she could pop Wyatt's zits last night at the hospital."

"She didn't," I gasp, dropping my hands to look at Trista. "I'm so sorry about that. I swear it will never happen again."

"Oh, gosh, I don't care." Trista looks back toward the compound side of the mountain and smiles. "Have you seen the intense coupling on Fletcher Mountain? You missed cuffing season last year, but I assure you, between Calder and Dakota and Luke and Addison and me and Wyatt, Stevie knows plenty about human affection. Plus, it's good for my daughter to have a little competition with Wolf. She's a touch too obsessed with that boy of yours."

"He's not my boy." I cringe and shake my head. "He's my best friend's brother and your employee. It is so inappropriate, and I swear—"

"Everly . . . I'm not the make-out police," Trista interrupts, her eyes narrowed. "You're a twenty-two-year-old grown woman with a whole adult life to live. Making out with cute boys your age is a God-given right."

"I know, but I'm not really a *randomly-make-out-with-guys* kind of girl."

Trista eyes me curiously. "What kind of girl are you?"

I inhale deeply through my nose, hating that I still don't know how to answer that question. Before last night, I never would have thought I was the type of girl to let some bad-boy rugby player go down on me without having a firm understanding of our relationship. Not that there was anything wrong with hooking up. It just never felt like me.

I certainly would have never thought I was the type of girl to beeline my ass out of there after literally *squirting on his face enough to make his sheets wet.*

This summer is proving to be one for the books.

"I think I'm still figuring out what kind of girl I am," I offer weakly.

"That's okay," Trista says, turning to face me, her eyes full of kindness. "Hell, I was twenty-seven and still figuring my shit out when I met you outside that surrogacy agency. I was certain I never wanted to be a mother, and look at me now."

Her hand touches her belly, and my jaw drops. "Trista. Are you?"

"Pregnant again?" she croaks, her eyes filling with tears. "Yes. But no one even knows. Not even Wyatt. I literally just peed on a stick yesterday."

"Oh my God! Congratulations!" I reach out and pull her in for a hug, and she hugs me back but then quickly pulls away. "Don't tell anyone. I don't want to take any attention away from Luke and Addison. And I need to figure out a fun way to tell Wyatt . . . Something that doesn't involve his damn goat this time."

I laugh and shake my head curiously but assume that's an inside story that's maybe better just for them.

She touches her stomach and shrugs. "I'm living a life I never would have dreamed for myself because I took some chances and let myself live a little. You should do the same."

I nod and smile, feeling so incredibly happy for her. And Wyatt. God, they are so perfect for each other I could scream at the top of this mountain for them.

"But can I be honest with you?" she continues. "My observation of you these past few years is that you're very focused on everyone else's lives more than your own. Helping plan our weddings, running Calder's carpentry social media, now getting my business launched to the public. Cozy told me you were matchmaking in Dublin too. That's a lot of helping for other people."

"I like to help," I reply defensively.

"But if you're this worried about making out with a cute boy, maybe you don't know how to help yourself."

I swallow the knot in my throat as she lays it all out there.

"I'm no life expert. Hell, I'm still figuring a lot of things out. But I know you gotta put yourself first occasionally, or you're going to have no life of your own when it's all said and done."

Her words hit me like a punch to the gut. It's exactly what I've been an anxious mess about since coming back from Dublin, but she said it in such a clear way that cuts right to the quick. "I'm trying to have a life." I stare down at my hands on my lap, my stomach twisting into a knot. "But it doesn't have to be with Wolf. He's got his rugby to focus on, and he's not even a relationship type of guy."

"That sounds great!" Trista flings her hands out to gesticulate her point. "A fling with a hot Irish farmhand rugby player sounds like the perfect summer holiday."

I exhale sharply, half a laugh, half a groan. "I could never."

"Bullshit," she sneers. "Throw your matchmaking happily-ever-after rules out the window and have some fun. Or hell, write yourself some new rules if you must, 'cause I know you love your little furry notebook."

"God, I really do," I groan and pinch the bridge of my nose. "It's no wonder I don't have a life."

"You have a life," Trista corrects, giving my knee a squeeze. "You just need to add a bit more fun to it, and you'll be grand." She mimics Wolf's Irish accent, and I can't help the flush in my cheeks at the thought of his voice.

She sighs and looks off into the distance. "I kissed a lot of frogs before your uncle Wyatt. In fact, I was kind of slutty."

"Um . . . should I be hearing this?"

"Probably not," she snorts and shrugs. "But it's pretty mild in comparison to the Stevie conception story, which I told you about last summer when Cozy got me drunk on Fireball."

"Fair point." I smile warmly and feel my heart lighten at the shift in topic. "But what a good story that one turned out to be."

"A great story." She waggles her eyebrows and starts the ATV back up, turning it around to head back down the mountain. "Time for you to make a story of your own, kid."

I take in the beautiful views with renewed hope as we make our way toward Mount Millie. Is that why I ran last night? Was I so bound by my own rules that I couldn't see past them to what was literally in my face? *Or rather, his face was right in my . . .*

I shake away that intrusive dirty thought to refocus on Trista's advice. Maybe Fletcher Mountain can transform me in my own unique way. Perhaps if I can stop fighting my cringe and embrace that side of me, I can find the self-love that I've been lacking these past few years.

I just need to do a new kind of masterminding.

Chapter 19

Set Piece: *Collective term for the scrum, line-out, and sometimes the restart.*

Translation: *He's just not that into you.*

Everly

"You are cordially invited to Mountain Men for a Mission: A charity auction where brawny mountain men are sold for a day of handyman work to raise funds for Mount Millie Rescue Center. Throw on your cowboy hat and flannel and bid on a mountain man who can clean your gutters, paint your house, or fix your toilet! There will be vendors, inflatables for the kids, and a petting zoo featuring our star resident rescues."

I pause reading from my furry notebook to register the reactions of two of my three uncles, who stand in the middle of Mount Millie's feed room staring at me like I've sprouted two heads. I really wish Luke were here right now. He's always been my biggest cheerleader, so he would probably handle this idea a little bit better than Wyatt and Calder. But he's busy raising a newborn next door to me with Addison. I could have called my grandma in for reinforcements this morning, but she's been sleeping over at Luke and Addison's ever since they got home from the hospital, so she's busy too.

I'm on my own here and need to sell this idea to my uncles because it doesn't work without their participation.

I swallow the knot in my throat as I continue reading from

my flyer. "Stick around for a barn dance later that night. All proceeds go to our furry, feathery, and scaly friends at Mount Millie. Event date and details below. We hope to see you there!"

"You have got to be fucking kidding me," Calder drones, shaking his head. "You want to auction me off to a stranger for manual labor?"

"Yes."

"Dakota will not like this, even if it's just for manual labor and not sex."

"It's for charity," I argue, shooting my uncle a dazzling smile. "And it's not much different than what you guys did for Luke at the lumberjack competition a couple years ago, if I'm not mistaken. Didn't you guys literally offer to do a guy's plumbing if he'd throw an axe-throwing competition?"

Calder frowns back at me.

I lift my brows with determination. "I've analyzed the cost versus impact, and this is a low-cost, high-reward event. And we can advertise the Visitor Sundays to a big audience this way."

I slide my eyes over to Wyatt, who doesn't look much happier, but then he shocks all of us with a nod. "It's a good idea."

"What?" Calder bellows, turning on his brother. "You think it's a good idea for us to be auctioned off like pieces of meat?"

"It's for Trista," Wyatt replies, and the eye contact between him and Trista is *eye-contacting*. If I didn't know any better, I'd swear my uncle knows his wife is pregnant. Though maybe he thinks they're still in the "trying" stage, and that's why he's looking at her like that.

Trista hits him with a knowing look, and I have to look away. I *love* love and all that, but I do not need to see my aunt and uncle doing baby-making eyes at each other.

Yet still? I smile.

"However, I have a better idea . . ." Wyatt says, holding up a finger. "Instead of auctioning off me, Calder, and Luke, what about auctioning off single rugby players for dates instead? Less liability."

My throat instantly goes dry at the mention of the sport the man who spent a fair amount of time between my legs plays.

"Oh, my God, yes!" Trista's eyes practically bug out of her head.

"Wolf has access to a whole team," Wyatt continues, crossing his flannelled arms over his chest. "And we've already been in contact with his coach to register his hours. Surely, we could get a few on board to help with this charitable endeavor."

"Genius, babe!" Trista stands up on her toes to give Wyatt a big kiss on his bearded cheek. "Single rugby players will totally draw a crowd, and they can promote their new team. A win-win."

"Wolf just started that training camp," I reply weakly, my stomach twisting into knots. "I'm not sure he's going to be able to convince his teammates to take part in this."

"Then you can," Wyatt says, smiling proudly at me. "If anyone can convince them, it's you, Eves."

I laugh weakly, staring down at my notebook like it's somehow going to produce a reason for this not to work. "This escalates the size of the event to a level I wasn't prepared for. And it doesn't really match my branding plan."

"Call it Mountain Men and Friends," Calder offers with a big grin. "And bigger is always better. Great idea, Papa Bear."

"Have a meeting with Wolf about it and make a plan to go with him to training later this week," Trista says with a knowing waggle of her brows.

I blow out a long, slow breath. Great idea. Now I just have to talk to the boy who is currently raging pissed at me for leaving last night. No problem. No problem at all.

Wolf

My tasks at Mount Millie aren't too complicated. Help check in new rescues, feed and water the animals, muck out the pens and paddock, and wash the animals when they need it.

I also fix things that need fixing, like broken fence lines, gate latches, water tanks, whatever Trista finds. I'm not the handiest guy out there, but I can manage basic tasks as long as they don't get too mechanical. And so far, most jobs are pretty random. She makes me a to-do list every workday and pins it on the board in the feed room, so I always start my days down here by checking the board to see what weird, random tasks might be on my agenda for the day.

One day, she had me paint stenciled name tags on the outside of every pen . . . an order that apparently came from Everly. This is one of a few tasks that are in preparation for the event she's hosting here in a couple of weeks.

Today, Trista tasked me with unloading a flatbed of fresh hay that was just delivered. It's a miserable fucking job of carrying about fifty bales up a ladder to store in the loft area above the barn that's likely made for hobbits, not my giant six-foot-five arse.

But I relish in the grueling labor today. I need it to calm myself down. It took every ounce of my strength not to go banging on Everly's door last night after I came out of the shower to find her gone.

One second, I was going to take a cold shower to chill out (and clean myself up after blowing it in my trousers like a damn teenager). The next, I come strolling out of my bathroom in my towel to read her insane fucking text messages.

I needed a second cold shower just to not completely explode.

But as I've worked on this mindless job all morning, blasting my grunge rock in my ears, I've decided what Everly did was for the best. What I felt for her last night was way too fucking intense. It was impulsive and reckless and should absolutely never happen again.

I was angry at first when she left. Maybe even hurt. Now, I'm grateful. Grateful that she made the decision to put some much-needed space between us. Nothing about us makes any sense, and I need to remember that.

My temper is mildly calmed by the time I toss the last bale up above my head to drop it on top of the stack of the others. I've built some sort of crooked castle walls up here that I bet Stevie would love to play in.

Weirdly, I miss that little tyke today. I've gotten kind of used to her tagging along while I did all my work, and she'd be a good distraction for me.

But it's good to get some distance from her too. I can't get too attached to any of this Fletcher family. I have a goal of getting the fuck out of here as soon as I can, and my time is better served working out and focusing on rugby.

Final bale in place, I use the hem of my shirt to wipe the sweat pouring off my brow, and when I lower it, I jump at the image of Everly standing up in the tiny hay mound with me.

"You scared the shite out of me," I pant, my chest heaving as I pull my headphones off my ears.

"Sorry, I was calling up to you, but you couldn't hear me," she says, looking sheepish. The space feels ten times smaller with Everly's presence in here now soaking up all the natural light. Her eyes take in the damp shirt clinging to my body. "Looks like you're the one who needs first aid this time," she says, offering me a weak smile.

I glance down at my slick arms, covered in tiny scratches from the hay. My veins bulge angrily from the exertion. This is probably why those mountain brothers wear flannel all the time.

I blink as I struggle to look back at her as sunlight pours in through the skylights, giving her an angelic halo. Dust particles float in the air between us, making me feel like I'm in the middle of another Everly Fletcher dream.

She looks beautiful. So beautiful I almost forget why I'm mad at her.

Almost.

I shake my head and pull my gloves off, stuffing them in the back pocket of my jeans. "I'm just grand," I grumble and make my way over to her, passing her by without another look.

"Do you have a second to talk?" she asks, grabbing my arm and stopping me in my tracks.

I stare at her delicate hand on my arm, and she pulls it back like she knows she shouldn't have touched me. "We don't need to talk."

"Are you sure?" she asks, biting her lower lip. "You seemed pretty mad in your texts. And now."

"I'm not mad. Just surprised."

She rubs her lips together and nods. "I'm sorry I left without saying goodbye. I was just . . ."

"You were just what?" I snap, turning to face her fully as my anger returns with full force. "What were you, Everly? What could have possibly been going through your mind when you left last night?"

Her blue eyes are crystal clear and stunning in this gold lighting. "I was freaked-out, okay?"

My eyes widen as I dip my head forward like I need to be closer to hear her. "What freaked you out, exactly? I need you to be specific."

"Nothing." She jerks her head back, looking shy.

"That is the opposite of specific."

"It's hard to talk about." She blushes and looks away from me.

"The fuck?" I ask, my tone sharp. "You talk about everything else under the sun. You overshare about your family. You yell at me about sandwiches. You want to have a what-are-we talk two seconds after we kiss. But I go down on you, give you a proper fucking orgasm, and you can't be bothered to stick around until I come out of the washroom? If one of your ridiculous matchmaking blokes did that to a girl, you'd go fucking mental, Stretch."

"I know I would," she snaps back defensively.

"So why did you do it?" I bite, my voice loud but muted amongst the sound-absorbing walls of hay.

"You had to shower," she exclaims, covering her face with her hands. "I . . ." Her throat works as she struggles to say the next part against the palms of her hands. "I have never orgasmed like that before."

I frown back at her, registering the shame on her face. I don't like it. In fact, I hate it.

She drops her hands, refusing to meet my eyes. "And I realized last night that I've never orgasmed until . . . until you."

My lips part as I struggle to accept this excuse. "What about with yourself?"

"I don't . . . do that with myself."

"Ever?"

She shakes her head.

"Christ," I murmur, pushing my hand through my hair. I don't think I've ever met anyone who didn't pleasure themselves. It's something I thought everyone figured out at a young age, right?

Leave it to Everly Fletcher to be the outlier, once again.

She clears her throat and crosses her arms over her chest defensively. "And I'm guessing you don't have to shower after you do that to other girls, so you'll excuse me for feeling a bit too mortified to stick around and watch you hose yourself off."

My lips part as everything clicks into place. "You think I showered because of what you did?"

"Obviously," she bites, rolling her eyes.

I sigh heavily, my jaw muscle working overtime as I admit the filthy truth to her. "I showered because of what I did, not because of you."

She frowns, clearly not understanding.

I inhale sharply, wishing I didn't have to share this part because it's not exactly the most masculine admission, but I can't have her sitting here thinking I was disgusted by her. "I came as well last night."

"Came where?"

"In my sweats," I murmur, unable to make eye contact with her. "Your fucking noises and reactions and just . . . *everything*. It was too much."

"Too much?"

I nod and shrug. "I lost control."

"You lost control?" She repeats the words like she's taste-testing them, her eyes shifting from shame to fascination in a matter of seconds. The corner of her mouth tugs up into a small, pleased smile, and I instantly regret not just being honest with her right away. "Has that ever happened to you before?"

"Not without assistance," I reply honestly. "So, I guess it was a first for both of us."

She sputters out a laugh and then covers her mouth, her cheeks blazing with a blush that suits her beautifully. Christ, this girl is hard to stay mad at. She's just so pure and honest and alive . . . at least when she's not running out of my flat without a word.

"For someone who habitually overcommunicates, you could have waited and asked me," I state solemnly. "I would have told you."

She licks her lips and shrugs. "For once, I'm not perfect."

The corner of my mouth curves up at her deadpan tone. She's fucking funny, even when she's trying not to be. And I'm an arse. An insecure manchild who should have talked to her before I buggered off into the loo.

"I'm sorry I was cross at you in my texts," I offer with a shrug.

"I'm sorry I left without just telling you I was embarrassed," she offers with her own shrug.

"In my experience with sex, if it's not messy, you're not doing it right." She looks away, a shy smile tugging at her lips. *Fuck, she's beautiful.* I'd love nothing more than to reach out and grab her by the neck to haul her back to my lips. To kiss away that shame and make her proud of the fact that she came all over me like that.

It was fucking hot.

Too hot.

Way too fucking hot.

Instead, I force myself to say the next bit because I know it's for the best. "Let's just chalk it up to another mistake that won't happen again."

"What won't happen again?" Everly asks, her voice pitched high and soft.

"You and me." I gesture between us. "All those reasons you listed last night are still there. We just got carried away last night. It's better we quit while we're ahead before we end up properly hurting each other. We're just too different to do whatever it is we're doing."

Her brows draw together. "Is different a bad thing? I match people all the time that are very different from each other."

"You're not matchmaking us, Stretch." My jaw flexes as I step away from her to get some distance. Because fucking hell, I can't think straight when she's near me.

There was a reason I avoided Everly Fletcher for four years in college. She makes me weak, and I can't afford to be weak right now. I need to focus on making this move to Colorado worth it, on fulfilling my dream with Cliona to become the Reilly fucking Rugby Twins. On being so good here that I can get back to Ireland and play for a team there. Ireland is my long-term goal and where I have my sights on.

Plus, if I couldn't even maintain a friendship with Finn throughout my childhood while playing rugby, how the fuck would I manage professional rugby and a situationship with a girl like Everly who would take over my whole fucking world?

"Us being too close is a bad idea for so many reasons," I add, my voice firm. "Just do us both a favor and don't get close enough to make it hard for me to remember that."

She chews her lip thoughtfully, her body language clearly irritated, but she steels herself as she says, "Well, I'm afraid we're going to have to muster all your strength to resist me because I need your help with my auction event we're doing here in a few weeks."

"What do you need from me?"

She licks her lips and lifts her chin, putting on her Everly business hat as she asks, "Do you think you could get some of your rugby teammates to volunteer to be auctioned off for a date in exchange for a worthy cause?"

"I have no fucking idea," I reply honestly. "I barely know the team yet."

"Well, I'd like to come to your training on Friday to have a chat with them and your coach," she states, struggling to meet my eyes.

"I don't know if—"

"I'll drive," she replies crisply, her voice curt and dismissive, before turning on her heel and making her way down the ladder, leaving my head spinning with what just happened.

Somehow in my attempt to get more space from Everly Fletcher, I wound up with the exact opposite.

Chapter 20

Bronco Drill: *A fitness test involving a series of shuttle runs at increasing distances designed to assess a player's aerobic capacity.*

Translation: *These youths won't know what hit 'em.*

Wolf

The Denver Grizzlies youth rugby program is dedicated to providing underserved youth in Denver with free access to rugby training, mentorship, and academic support. It uses the sport to build teamwork, confidence, and pathways to education or career opportunities.

Or at least that's what the marketing pamphlet says in our locker room.

The reality of the program is a bloody hell lot messier.

"Coach Wolf! Jamal stole the cones again."

I glance up from my clipboard just in time to see a small, wiry kid sprinting across the field with three bright orange cones stacked on his head like some kind of unicorn horn.

"Oi, bring those back," I call after him, jogging in their direction. My trainers sink into the grass that's still damp from last night's rain, weather that perfectly matched my sour mood the past couple of days. "This is rugby, not Dungeons and Dragons, mate."

Jamal laughs so hard he nearly trips over himself, then deliberately launches the cones into the air and pulls back an imaginary bow and arrow like he's piercing them in the sky. A boy named Marcus tries to catch one and misses, landing flat on his back, causing a chorus of ten-year-old giggles to erupt.

"Right," Fergie mutters, coming to stand beside me. "First rule of coaching kids? Don't turn your back, or they'll start a mutiny." He waves his hands and shouts loudly, "Bring it in, ya gobshites!"

"You talk funny," a boy with a gap-toothed smile deadpans at Fergie before running off.

"I'll show you talking funny," Fergie growls and moves to walk toward them, but I grab his arm to stop him in his tracks.

"I've coached kids before," I state calmly, looking out at the field of chaos in front of us. It's one of the things I knew I'd miss coming to the States, and this opportunity to work with these kids was welcome. "They're like puppies. We just have to tire them out, and then they'll be better-behaved." I blow my whistle and draw all their eyes to me. "We're running broncos!" I call out and then take a moment to explain that they'll run out to the twenty-meter line, then forty, and sixty, and that's just one set of five they need to complete. When they all start complaining, I add, "Last one in has to pick up the practice gear, and if anyone beats me . . . that's five quid in each of your pockets."

"Squid? Gross!" Marcus makes a retching sound.

"Dollars," I correct, rolling my eyes. "Five dollars. Ready? Go!"

And without pause, the full lot of them tear down the pitch like their lives depend on it, legs pumping, arms flailing, greasy hair blowing in the wind. It's a messy, corner-cutting sort of competition that involves me yelling at anyone who doesn't touch the line with their hands. But they're laughing and enjoying themselves instead of terrorizing poor Fergie, so I take it as a win.

My lungs burn as I push myself to impress the lot of them,

and bloody hell, it feels good to run without a crowd judging my every move. I lap Marcus on the twenty-meter line and scoop him up under one arm like a rugby ball.

"Oi! No fair!" he squeals, kicking his legs as I thunder past Jamal and another boy named Ricky.

"Adapt, improvise, overcome," I call back a phrase my Trinity coach used to bark at us during training sessions. I barrel toward the post and drop Marcus over the line like I'm scoring a try.

Fergie is laughing and shaking his head when I finish well ahead of them, even with my Marcus detour. I drop down onto the grass and fight to catch my breath because no matter how many times I've done a bronco test, they still crush me.

But Christ, it felt good to clear my mind a bit. Everly has been occupying way too many of my thoughts, which is the exact opposite of what I hoped for when requesting distance from her.

Working with these kids today is reminding me why I love rugby so much. Rugby saved me in ways I think I'm still unpacking. I was thirteen when I first started, all elbows and bony knees, watching the world from the sidelines and feeling like I didn't belong anywhere. Then Cliona made me start playing with her, and when I stepped onto that muddy pitch for the first time, it was like someone lit a fuse under my skin.

Suddenly, my lanky size wasn't a curse—it was potential. My anger wasn't appalling—it was fuel. On the brown grass at Ballymun fields, the noise in my head went quiet, replaced by the rhythm of boots pounding into the dirt, the crack of bodies hitting one another, and the roar of lads playing beside me. Rugby gave me a place, a purpose. It told me I could be strong when all I'd ever felt before that was weak. It was the first time I ever felt worth a damn.

That's what I want to give these kids. If I can do that, then it will make this whole insane trip to Colorado worth it.

One by one, the kids finish and begin dogpiling on top of me, breathless and laughing and a hell of a lot more ready to listen than they were when they arrived.

"You're fast, Coach Wolf," Ricky says, his face beet-red.

"I wasn't even giving it my all," I say, hoisting myself back onto my feet. "Now that I've proven I'm more athletic than all of you combined, who wants to actually learn how to play rugby?"

Every hand shoots up, and my heart swells with pride. *This is what it's all about.* I clear my throat gruffly and clap my hands. "Good. Pair off. We're learning how to tackle properly so you don't break your necks, and then we'll do a proper scrimmage and see what you're all made of."

I grab a tackling pad and demonstrate how to lead with the shoulder, keep your head out of the way, and wrap your arms around your subject. They mimic me with all the coordination of baby pandas. Ricky forgets which direction he's supposed to drive and ends up spinning in a full circle before falling on his face.

"Nearly there." I crouch down beside him, brushing the grass out of his hair. "Try it again, but this time, look where you're going, yeah?"

The more we practice, the sharper they get. Jamal nails a textbook tackle on the pad and pops up, grinning like he's just scored the winning try in the Six Nations.

"That's it," I shout, giving him a fist bump. "Perfect form. You keep that up, and you'll be breaking through defensive lines like butter in no time."

"Like butter?" Jamal giggles. "That's weird, Coach."

By the end of our scrimmage, everyone's red-faced and filthy, even Fergie, who somehow got flattened by a ten-year-old, much to everyone's delight. I pat the lanky kid who took him down on the back. "Well done, lad. You've just taken out a professional rugby player. You best brag about that to all your mates."

He grins shyly, and I can't help but think he looks just like me at his age. Like he's too tall for his body but trying to make it work for him.

"Good work today," I tell them as a big yellow bus pulls up. "Same time next week. And, Marcus—no more cone hats, yeah? It's giving traffic warden, not future All Blacks."

He frowns, having no clue what I'm referencing. I wave him off, watching all of them load up onto a bus that will take them back to the youth center where they spend their summers.

I watch them go, this pack of rowdy, stubborn kids who remind me so much of myself at that age. And of my friend Finn. Just a couple of young lads still figuring out their place in this world.

"Well, Wolf . . . you're good with little gobshites, I'll give you that," Fergie says, patting me on the back as he wipes the sweat from his brow. "If you want to get out of that Mount Millie gig, you should consider applying for one of the coaching positions the center is hiring for in autumn. Apparently, the youth center received a big grant, and they're expanding their sports outreach division. You'd be great at this, and it'd be a proper job that could work around your rugby schedule when you get an offer from the team."

"*If* I get an offer," I correct, shrugging dismissively. "I don't feel certain about that at all."

"What do you mean, lad? Everyone loves you on the squad, which is saying a lot because we all thought you'd be this big, scary beast when you arrived. But if anything, you're a wee bit soft." He laughs and gives me a playful shove before walking off to retrieve the rest of our gear.

I frown as I wonder why that is. I've been different here in

America. Calmer and less anxious. Lower stakes, maybe? Perhaps I just needed a fresh start? Or perhaps there's a certain someone in my life who's getting in my head a bit. Either way, if I want this Colorado thing to work out, I need to keep my eye on the prize.

Chapter 21

Hold Possession: *Playing slow, safe rugby just to keep the ball.*

Translation: *Stick with what you know. It's safer that way.*

Everly

"I just realized you've been away from me for three whole weeks and still not a single poo update like you promised," Cliona's familiar Irish accent sings into my phone line early the next morning as I sit on my bathroom counter applying my makeup.

"I'm so sorry," I drone, my voice echoing off the tile floor. "I promise I have pooed since arriving home."

"A simple photo is literally the least you can do," she replies with a laugh and then a sigh. "God, I'm missing you."

"Back at you." I turn to kick my feet off the edge of the counter. "How are you, my Irish twin? How's your new rugby team?"

"Oh, not too bad," Cliona sings. "Our rucks look like a drunk game of Twister still, but the girls actually pass the ball instead of hogging it for glory plays. Total culture shock."

I grin. "Go, sports."

She laughs, knowing I have no clue what she's talking about. "It's just camp, so we'll see how the season shapes up, but so far, my teammates seem far better than the ones I had at Trinity."

"Go, team!"

"Alright, Fletcher, I've maxed out your quota for sports talk. Let's hear how your summer is going."

My cheeks instantly heat like she knows what I did with her brother just days ago. "I'm doing great," I reply, my voice rising in pitch. "It's been busy on Fletcher Mountain. Luke and Addison had their baby. Levi is so perfect, I'll have to send you a picture. My grandma is staying with them for their first week back at home, so I get to see her around the mountain this week, which is nice. I've been doing random coffee deliveries in the morning for all of them just to be helpful, but I think it's baby madness over there."

"Oh, wow, I can imagine," Cliona snickers.

"It's fun being close to everyone." I force out the words as I glance at the time on my phone to see it's 6:58 a.m. I hop off the counter to head into my bedroom and pace in front of the window that overlooks the creek behind my cabin. In seconds, my heart lurches when I spot Wolf jogging on the trail out there.

Right on schedule.

He runs that path Trista took me on earlier this week every single morning. At first, when I saw him run it, I thought it was a coincidence, but then after a couple of days of mindful observation, I realized he is a creature of habit.

Wolf runs that path every morning around 7:00 a.m. like he has a personal vendetta against the mountain he's trying to overcome. His T-shirt clings to his chest as every muscle in his arms and legs works overtime to remind me just how horribly I fumbled that gift from God.

"How was that party you took my brother to?" Cliona asks as I snap my gaze away from Wolf's moody scowl. "His text messages have been pathetic these last few days, so I haven't got any good details from him."

"Oh, it was great," I peal and then force myself away from the window. *Mustn't ogle your best friend's brother when your best friend is currently on the other end of the phone.* "I mean, kind of great. Some cunts from my high school showed up, and that wasn't very pleasant, but I made it out of there alive."

"Did you just say cunts?" Cliona laughs into the line. "My brother must be rubbing off on you."

"He's not rubbing on me," I blurt defensively, my voice high and breathy.

"What?" Cliona chortles. "I said rubbing *off* on you. I've never heard you casually use the word *cunt*."

"Oh . . . um . . . yeah, maybe." I shrug, even though she can't see me. "It was just stupid high school drama."

"Well, I'm glad you had Wolf there with you, then," she says knowingly. "He's pretty decent in those kinds of situations."

I nod and frown as I think back to that night. Weirdly, it feels like weeks ago, and it was just days. He was great that night. Perfect, even. And he was great in my car when he opened up about his own bully experiences. I felt seen and understood in a way I've never felt before.

And then I fucked it all up by being a freak and rushing from my car into my cabin without talking to him after our first kiss. And then running out of his apartment after he went down on me.

God, Everly, seeing a pattern here?

"Yeah, he was really kind," I reply honestly, walking out to the kitchen for a coffee. "I'm going with him to his training camp tomorrow to talk to his coach and teammates about being involved in a charity auction we're doing for the rescue center."

"Oh, lovely! I'm so glad he's being open to that."

"I didn't really give him much of a choice," I reply with a dry laugh.

"Of course you didn't. Even my beast of a brother is no match for Everly Fletcher."

I chew my lip before I hear myself say, "He kind of . . . told me he didn't used to always be so big."

"Did he?" Cliona says, her voice softer and more serious. "He doesn't often talk about that."

"Yeah . . . it came up after my high school bullshit."

She clears her throat. "Yeah, he didn't have the best childhood. It wasn't until I forced him to start playing rugby that I think he really came into his own. I just wish his friend could have found something like that."

"Finn?" I ask, recalling the name he mentioned in my car.

"Jesus, he really *did* open up to you." Cliona sounds awestruck. "Finn was a sweet lad, but he really resented Wolf for going the sports route. It was some older rugby boys who used to bully them." Her voice trails off as she clearly struggles with how to finish that sentence. "I shouldn't share all this. It's not my story. But Wolf still carries guilt for falling out with Finn, I think. It's a big reason why he struggles with his temper on the pitch. He just can't seem to let go of the past, I think."

My heart breaks for young Wolf, picturing his big brown eyes on a scrawny frame. I wish I could ask Wolf more about Finn and his childhood, but I've screwed up any chance of that type of relationship with him now.

"If you can get him to open up about it at all, I think it'd be really good for him."

"Oh, I don't think your brother wants to be my friend," I reply with a dismissive laugh.

"Nonsense," she tsks into the phone. "Wolf always speaks so highly of you."

"He does?" I ask, my throat tightening.

"Yeah . . . he told me that he thinks you're the sole reason I didn't go into a massive depressive episode after the mess with my ex."

"What do you mean? We barely ever even spoke about your ex," I say sincerely.

"I know, but that's what I needed in a friend at the time," she replies, her voice soft and reflective. "Wolf says you have this uncanny way of meeting people where they are. You push, but never too much. Just enough."

"That's the first time I've ever heard that," I huff self-deprecatingly.

"Then people don't know you the way I do—we do," she corrects.

And when I realize she's including her brother in that statement, my heart flutters. To know that Wolf spoke of me at all to his sister feels good. *He doesn't hate me. Then why is he working so hard to keep me at arm's length? Maybe he truly doesn't want any distractions while he's in Colorado.*

By the time we end the call, I find myself staring down at the red barn, wondering why he doesn't at least want a friend in me when he clearly doesn't despise me.

But maybe I'm reading too much into it all. Maybe him noticing something about me doesn't mean he cares about me. God, maybe if I'd followed my own matchmaking rules, I wouldn't be in this ridiculous situation to begin with.

But this is typical me. I get in my own way and can't ever figure out how to just be happy. This is why I matchmake. It's easier to fix everyone else's love life than work on my own. Why did I think I could be any different with Wolf?

I shake my head as my aunt Trista's advice percolates in my mind. *You gotta put yourself first occasionally, or you're going to have no life of your own when it's all said and done.*

I wish her words could help me, but the moment I tried putting myself first, I ended up getting dumped in a hay mound before I even figured out what I actually wanted.

This kind of discomfort isn't worth it.

I just need to go back to what I know. Helping others. At least when I'm playing Cupid, I'm not handing anyone a bow to shoot me in the heart.

Chapter 22

Counter-Ruck: *Resisting the opposition's ruck, pushing them back off the ball.*

Translation: *Saying no to Everly Fletcher isn't for the faint of heart.*

Wolf

Watching Everly Fletcher command a room full of sweaty, testosterone-soaked rugby players like some kind of tall, blonde drill sergeant was an out-of-body experience.

She had her laptop balanced on a chair as she projected images of all the animals on Mount Millie one by one onto the white cement block wall. In between were graphics about budgets, vet costs, and adoption rates, and she was throwing in stats and rugby jokes like a pro.

My teammates laughed at all her jokes, which is insane because they're usually bored out of their minds during our team meetings, but Everly had them eating out of the palms of her hands. She even has my coach (who, until today, I swore needed his own anger management counseling) absolutely fucking obsessed with her. At one point, he raised his hand and said he'd like to offer four season tickets up for a raffle.

Everly thanked him in that warm, sunshiny way she has about her as she ended her presentation with a clear, confident voice. "Mount Millie Rescue Center isn't just a bunch of cute farm animals looking for a home. It's a place where every scruffy nose and muddy hoof gets a happily ever after. Or, at the very least, a chaotic, manure-scented tax write-off."

Everyone erupted in laughter and swarmed her, instantly signing up for whatever she needed them for. It was madness. Pure, ridiculous madness.

And me? I'm trying not to care. I'm trying not to put her on a pedestal. But I can't help the swell of pride over how great she was up there. The way she can enrapture a room full of grown men who normally only care about tackles and pints and picking up women at pubs and inspire them to genuinely care about alpacas . . . Christ, she is something else.

Rejecting her is likely the worst idea I've ever had.

But deep down, I know *not* being with her is for the best. Not smelling her is for the best. Not kissing her is for the best. Not tasting her is for the best.

Because as I'm sitting here, bathed in her jasmine scent from our hour-long, silent commute to Denver this morning, I'm trying to remind myself of all the reasons that avoiding Everly Fletcher is for the best.

For starters, Everly just gave a presentation about happily ever afters. She deserves someone who can give her that. Certainly not someone like me who has coach-ordered, biweekly counseling sessions with the Trinity sports psychologist for anger management issues.

Too bad my therapy didn't cover the fact that I fucking followed her for four years and she still has no idea. If she ever found out about that . . . I don't know how she'd react. I'm guessing not well.

I know I did it to look out for her. I couldn't help myself. But I did it without her consent. That's the dark, forbidden part. That's why I don't deserve someone as pure and good-natured as Everly Fletcher. Even if it would be only for a short time until I eventually return to Ireland.

My eyes linger on her long legs on display in a white little tennis outfit. She struts around the locker room like she just came out of a country club but still manages to look perfectly at ease as she talks shit with men who are twice her size. She jots down everyone's contact information, looking thrilled with positive feedback. And they all stare at her the way the guys at Trinity would stare at her during her matchmaking clinics. Like they were only in it for the matchmaker herself.

Fuck.

"Problem, Wolf?" Fergie asks with a smirk as I toss my bag into my locker next to him.

I drop down on the bench in front of my cubby. "I have a six-foot-tall problem."

"Oh, come on. Her auction event sounds brilliant. Lochlan even asked her if offering up sexual services could bring in more money for the donkey." He chuckles heartily.

My jaw tightens. Lochlan is a front-row player I had lunch with during Wednesday's training. He seemed like a decent guy, but I'm side-eying him after making a comment like that to my girl.

My girl.

Fuck.

She isn't my girl. She's no one's girl.

Everly's eyes find mine from across the locker room, so I quickly look away, preparing myself as she saunters over with a warm smile that makes it painfully fucking obvious that I've seen her naked.

"This is going amazing," she says, waggling her brows at me.

"How many signed up, lass?" Fergie asks, pushing his shaggy red hair back as he stands to peek over her shoulder at her furry notebook. He looks extra big and bulky next to her, his eyes dragging over her facial features as she counts the names in her notebook.

"I got fifteen names!"

"That's a lot of rugby players' numbers," Fergie says, eyeing me knowingly. "Good on you."

"I only need five for the auction, but I'll hold on to the other names for a rainy day." She smiles brightly. "Conri didn't think anyone would be interested in helping. Guess he was wrong."

"Oh, naughty Conriiii," Fergie sings, waggling his brows and making it very clear he thinks it's interesting that Everly uses my legal name. She used it this morning when she passed me a fancy coffee she made from her fancy cabin with her fancy fucking travel mugs. Her calling me Conri feels intimate and weird. And I hate how much I like the way it sounds with her American accent. Simple and succinct. Like she's always said it.

"Surely, our boy Wolf is going to be auctioned off for the cause, aye?" Fergie adds.

"I hope so." Everly bites her lip and smiles down at me in a way that makes my cock twitch. "Although he hasn't given me consent yet."

I swallow the knot in my throat at the heated look in her eyes. *What the fuck is she doing?*

With a laugh, she looks away and nudges Fergie. "But if I have you to bid on, then I'll be good either way."

"I like the sound of that." Fergie chortles and tosses his arm around Everly in a matey way that irritates me. I level a look at both of them, but they're too distracted with each other to notice my brooding.

Everly looks down at me and licks her lips. "I'm all done here, so I'm going to head out, but I'm the one picking you up in Boulder later tonight, so I'll see you then, okay?"

I nod woodenly, a heaviness pressing down in my chest. No

matter what I do, I can't escape her. I was so close too. All I needed to do was finish uni and find an Irish rugby team to take me. Let her go back to America and me go play for whoever I was going to play for and forget she ever existed.

This was not a part of my plan.

"Have a good practice, boys," she calls out as she waves goodbye to everyone before shooting me a quick wink. Something that was meant just for me.

I can't help but stare at her arse as she strides out of my locker room, my core heating with the memory of knowing what her body felt like in my hands.

"You are so fucked, lad," Fergie says, dropping down on the bench beside me and shoving me in the shoulder.

"What do you mean?" I grumble, pulling out my socks and boots to get ready for warm-ups. I need a hard workout today to get that leggy blonde out of my head.

"I mean you're fucking smitten over that girl. And she's smitten over you. Tell me something is going on there."

I shake my head, hating the way her scent lingers after she left. "Nothing is going on."

"Well, there's about to be." He barks out a laugh. "The sexual tension between you two is next-level. What are you waiting for?"

I work my jaw back and forth. "It's a bad idea."

"Why? Do you not fancy her?" he asks, rolling white athletic tape around his wrists.

"Of course I fancy her," I bite out, my teeth grinding together. "I'm worried that I fancy her too much."

"Is that a bad thing?"

"Yes," I grind out through clenched teeth as my stomach twists with a flashback to the scared, skinny kid I was for a large part of my life. The ghost of that kid makes it hard for me to feel confident enough to reach out and take what I want, especially when it's someone as kind and generous as Everly.

I only found my confidence with rugby because I could prove myself without words. I could hit harder, run faster, bleed for the team—and no one would laugh at that. But in relationships with real feelings involved? There's no scoreboard, no try line, no clear way to win. Vulnerability feels like stepping back into the schoolyard with those same arseholes who pestered me and Finn. I don't want to set myself up for that kind of failure.

"I'm not good enough for a girl like Everly," I add, my voice resolute. "She is sunshine, and I've only ever known rain."

"That's dark, lad." Fergie sits back against his cubby and shrugs. "And it looks like that sunshine disagrees with you."

"She doesn't know what's best for her."

Fergie's blue eyes widen. "Aye, sure. Most modern girls love to be told what to do with their own consent, don't they?"

I glare over at him, and he just laughs.

"You do what you must, pal, but just think long and hard about how often sunshine follows rain."

Chapter 23

Wet-Weather Rugby: *A style of rugby played during a rainy match that focuses on safer options—short kicks, keeping the ball tight, fewer risky passes.*

Translation: *The calm before the storm.*

Wolf

It's pouring when I get off the bus in Boulder to find Everly's white SUV parked and waiting for me, wipers whipping back and forth at rapid speed. Bracing myself, I sprint across the flooded parking lot and jump into her car, sliding into the passenger seat, out of breath and soaked from that short distance.

"Jeez, it's really coming down out there," Everly says, her eyes moving down over my damp shirt and shorts, her gaze lingering on my thigh where my tattoo is etched. Every time she does it, I'm tempted to get us both naked and show her every last inch of ink on my body.

I push my dripping hair back and can't help but notice her own hair is slightly damp, as if she was caught in the rain earlier as well.

The last thing I need to see is this girl wet in her car.

I look forward and say nothing as she pulls out of the bus station parking lot, unsure what would come out of my mouth if I did. I was distracted at practice. My mind was irritatingly consumed with Everly while doing drills, lunch with my team, icing my shoulder, pretending to listen to Fergie ramble on about his weekend plans. I thought about her so much my fucking head hurts.

The silence that follows is thick and damp as we breathe heavily, our chests rising and falling in unison, both clearly feeling a level of tension that wasn't here this morning.

It's painful sitting here and pretending I don't know the shape of her nipples through a thin white tank top. Or how incredible she tastes when she comes on my tongue.

God, I want to fuck her.

"Hey, do you think any of your teammates would be interested in participating in quarterly matchmaking clinics?" Everly's sunshiny voice interrupts my inner brooding, and I turn to frown at her like she's speaking another language.

"What?"

"Like the ones I used to host at Trinity," she elaborates as if that will answer my question.

"Why would you host matchmaking clinics?"

"Because so many of your teammates wanted to help with the auction, and I can't use them all. This would be a good way to connect them to people. Most aren't from the area, and they seemed interested in the idea when I mentioned it. I'm sure Judy would let me host them at the Mercantile. Claire has some friends that might be up for joining too. Could be really fun."

My eyes blink in disbelief. "You literally can't help yourself, can you?"

"What?"

"Meddling in other people's lives."

"It's not meddling. It's matchmaking." She rolls her eyes like the difference is so obvious.

"Don't you have enough going on in your own life to worry about?" I bite, my tone harsh as I feel like she's regressing back to the childish busybody she was at college.

Her eyes snap to mine. "What do you have against me helping people find love?"

"Why on earth do you care so much about *other people's* love lives?"

"I like to believe that there's a right person out there for everyone. There's a comfort I find in that."

I shake my head dismissively. "Utter shite."

"Says you," she snaps, her voice rising in pitch. "Not me. I *love* love. I need love. I need to believe it's possible for others, or I'll feel hopeless. I'll just . . ." Her voice trails off as she sighs heavily. "If I don't believe in love, then who even am I?"

"Normal? Fuck. What's so bad about just being normal?"

"I don't want to be normal. I want to be extraordinary," she exclaims, her hands tight on the wheel. "Even at the expense of my own love life."

I shake my head and mutter, "You're too much."

She jerks her head to look at me for a moment before turning back to face the road as rain pounds on the windshield and the wipers thrash back and forth.

After a long, heated moment, she says softly, "You don't need to tell me I'm too much. I'm already fully aware." She sniffs loudly, and I look over to see her chin trembling slightly. "I'm too much. Too dramatic. I overwhelm people, and I push them to an uncomfortable place where the only thing they want from me is distance. Like you."

"That's not what—"

"This has nothing to do with you and me," she cuts me off and continues, "but it's a perfect example of why I shouldn't have even tried to be your friend. Friends are expendable. They can distance themselves at a moment's notice. Or they can decide to one-star review me on Instagram. Or betray my trust, like Taya. They can decide when my *too much* becomes insufferable and cut and run. Thank God I have my family, or I'd truly be alone in this world."

I stare back at her, my heart pounding in my chest at the sense of defeat in her voice. It rips right through me, and I hate that she feels expendable. She's not expendable. She's more extraordinary than she realizes.

I open my mouth to say that, but my words are cut off when the car jolts hard to the left and a sickening pop-hiss vibrates under our feet.

"What the hell?" Everly gasps, her eyes moving to the dash of her car to figure out what's wrong with her vehicle.

"Pull over," I exclaim, my voice tense as my head jerks back and forth to look for oncoming vehicles. "Over there. You need to get out of the road."

"I'm trying," Everly argues, turning her wheel with great effort as she moves toward a pull-off area that overlooks a cliff.

"You blew a tire," I state when I see the tire pressure reading on her digital screen light up. I blow out a long breath to calm myself down once we're safe and off the road.

"Shit," she gasps as she puts the car in Park and moves to open her door.

I reach across her lap to pull it shut. "Stay here. And stay buckled up. I'll deal with it."

Her eyes narrow on me. "I know how to change a tire, Wolf."

"Please, Everly, just listen to me for once. It is fucking dangerous out here," I repeat, cutting her a sharp look of warning as I open my side and step out into sheets of rain that soak me almost instantly.

My hands tremble as I glance down at the back tire on my side and discover a shard of metal lodged into the wheelbase. I look around, grateful for the lack of traffic on this road as I hustle around to open the back of her Range Rover to hunt for a spare.

Just as I reach down to grab it under the floorboard, a hazy blonde figure comes running around the bumper. "Everly, get back in the car," I growl as she huddles under the tailgate for shelter. The rain is deafening as it hammers above us in loud, metallic thuds.

She pins me with a challenging look. "My dad and three very overprotective uncles made sure I knew how to change a flat, so I'm changing this flat." She shoves me out of her way and begins to unlatch the jack clamped beside the tire as rain drips down her temples. "I've been waiting my whole life for this moment."

My blood pressure spikes as she stubbornly shivers in the cold and struggles to lift both the tire and the jack. I glance up to see if this rain is going to pass anytime soon, but the clouds are dark and ominous, one stacked on top of another, looking very much like the war going on inside my head.

"Would you please just let me do it?" I grind out, feeling like my head is going to explode if I stand here for one more second. What is she trying to prove by doing this herself?

"I know how to do this," she argues back, deciding to grab the jack first. She moves past me to head over to the afflicted area, and when I reach for the spare, she growls. Literally growls at me as she squats down in the pouring rain to begin lifting the vehicle.

"Please, Everly," I beg, standing in the rain beside her. "I know you know how to do this. But you have to know . . ." My voice trails off, my breath steamy in the summer storm.

"What?" Everly asks, stopping what she's doing to stand up and glower at me. She shoves her hair out of her face, her jean jacket soaked through as she wraps her arms around herself in the rain. "Tell me, Conri. What do I have to know?"

My eyes rove over her whole face—the mascara lines running down her cheeks, her red, runny nose, the way her lush lips drip with rainwater as she shrugs back at me like this is who she is, take it or leave it.

"I like how you're too much," I state, my voice raw and ragged as rain cascades between us. "It's refreshing."

"Refreshingly annoying." She squints back at me.

"No, it's not," I state firmly, my eyes fixed on hers. "It takes a lot of confidence to be so utterly yourself all the time. Don't ever be less. You're exactly enough."

Her mouth falls open, confusion in her eyes as she stares back at me and struggles with how to respond to that.

I'm playing with fire.

But fuck me, she already said she wants to burn, and now *I want to burn with her.*

I don't give her time to collect her thoughts. Instead, I grab her by her jacket and haul her against me to crush my mouth to hers. She gasps, lips soft and warm against the cold slickness of the rain, and I groan in satisfaction when I kiss her like I'm dying of thirst and only the taste of rain on her lips could quench me.

In the few days since I had her in my bed, I haven't stopped thinking about her. Craving her. Wanting her. Walking away from her in the hay mound took every ounce of strength I had.

And I'm done being strong.

She makes me fucking weak.

I know there are a lot of unknown variables here. My lack of permanence in Colorado, the fact that she's my sister's best friend, the fact that I can't think straight when I'm near her and that I'm certain she could ruin me. But Christ help me, in this moment, I don't give a damn anymore.

Her hands wrap around my neck as she arches into me, her tongue gliding against mine with delicious savagery, like we're trying to climb inside each other and never come out. I press her back against the side of her SUV, not caring that the rain is running down our faces, not caring that passing cars could see.

This isn't careful. This isn't friendly. This is everything I swore I'd never do.

She tastes like mint, rain, and every bad decision I ever wanted to make. My hands move up to her face, gripping her by the neck to tip her head back so I can kiss her deeper, harder, until she's trembling against me, and I can't tell if it's from the cold or me.

I break the kiss, my breath ragged against her raw lips, swollen from the pressure of our embrace.

"What are you doing?" she gasps, her body arched into mine, her belly rubbing against the ridge of my cock.

"I'm going to change this fucking tire, take you up the mountain, strip you bare, and fuck you until neither of us can think anymore."

Her lips part.

"Any objections?"

She shakes her head, stunned into rare silence. Without a word, I grab her arm and shuffle her over to the passenger side, open it, and use my hand to protect her head as she slides into the seat.

I reach in and buckle her. "Don't fucking move," I warn, my tone lethal. "And don't help me with the tire."

The corner of her mouth quirks, but thankfully, she lets me shut the door.

When I turn around, I run my hands through my hair, flicking the excess water off as I stare up at the sky and try to get my head on straight to finish the task at hand. "Focus, Wolf. Get the tire changed, and then . . . *and then* . . ."

Chapter 24

Full House: *Scoring a try, conversion, penalty and drop goal in the same match.*

Translation: *Oh, yeah . . . I'm gonna score.*

Everly

Holy shit, this is happening, I nearly squeal out loud when Wolf drives the rest of the way toward Jamestown. I bite my lip to stop myself from speaking. Speaking is bad. Speaking is where I get myself into trouble. Silence is good.

"What are you doing?" I ask when Wolf passes the entrance to Fletcher Mountain.

"Condoms." He spares me a heated glance that I feel right between my legs as he parks in front of the Mercantile general store.

While he's inside, I make the snap decision to hop back into the driver's seat, wincing when I spot Judy through the picture window of the bar. "Nothing to see here, Judy," I say through clenched teeth with a polite smile. "Just stopping for some milk."

I drum my fingers on the steering wheel, Wolf's words still echoing in my head. *Don't ever be less. You're exactly enough.*

It's like we're standing outside Hilow's apartment all over again and he's telling me cringe is better than cool. Conri really has a way with words. And he has no idea how much I needed to hear them.

It's always been a trigger for me when someone tells me I'm

"too much." The girls from my high school would say that to me a lot, even though we were all supposedly friends. Moments where I'd get excited about something—the latest Taylor Swift album, homecoming, a boy I liked. They'd call me "extra" but not in a kind way. They said it in the why-do-we-put-up-with-her sort of way.

When Cliona declared that we were soulmates, I remember feeling as though it were helping soothe that childhood wound. *And now her brother is saying similar things . . .*

"Don't ever be less."

Butterflies race in my belly when his tall frame comes out of the Mercantile. He slides into the passenger seat and shoots me a curious look.

"The hills have eyes," I state seriously, my hands trembling anxiously. "I know I'm a grown adult and can do what I want, but hiding this from my uncles is kind of necessary, don't you think?"

He sits back in his seat and nods as I head up the mountain, past Mount Millie and the red barn. As I venture closer to the cabins, I shake my head in frustration. Compound living is fun, they said. Being neighbors with my uncles will be a blast, they said. I'll get to see my cousins whenever I want, they said. All well and good until I want to fuck the crap out of the one guy I shouldn't be without fear of being seen and roasted by my entire family. I reach out and shove Wolf's head down, and he laughs as he bends in half to duck and cover.

I park in front of my cabin and jerk my head from side to side, trying to look for any forms of life down the hill. "Luke and Addison next door are our biggest threat, and they're busy with my grandma and Baby Levi, so I think we should be fine. Plus, the rain makes it hard to see anything right now, but maybe just to be safe, crouch and stay low and hug the shadows when you come in behind me."

"Should I crawl on the ground just to be safe?" Wolf blinks back at me, his eyes full of mirth.

"Hey, man, I'm trying to save your life," I exclaim, ignoring his teasing look. "You told me not to hold back, and I'm taking that literally. Or is it too much for me to openly admit that I want you to fuck my brains out?"

He closes his eyes as if in pain. "It's just enough, Everly Fletcher."

"Okay then," I reply with a smirk. With one searing final look, we collectively jump out of my SUV and scurry into the cabin, still soaked to the bone from the flat-tire fiasco.

As soon as we're inside, I grab his hand to drag him down the hallway toward my room, away from all the windows and closer to my bed. Before I even get a chance to turn the bedroom light on, Wolf's hands are on me. Big, rough palms sliding over wet clothes, unceremoniously peeling the offensive fabric off my body as we toe off our shoes. My fingers scrape along his sides as I yank his shirt off over his head, his dark hair dripping down his forehead and giving me the urge to run my tongue over the trail it leaves down his cheek.

He grips my waist harshly in his hands as I stand before him in my white bra and panties. We both take a moment to stare at each other in our underwear, something we didn't really do last time. Wolf's chest is smooth and sculpted, and the ink that trails down his shoulder to his forearm is dark and rich from the rain.

"I regret not taking the time to see these the other night," he croaks, dragging his finger over the tip of my puckered nipple.

I release a throaty sound when he pinches me lightly, his lower lip pulling between his teeth as his warm palm cups my breast. His other hand splays out on my lower back as he pulls me into his groin, which is already hard in his thin shorts.

"Let's get rid of this too, shall we?" he asks, his long lashes dark as he stares down at my breasts.

I reach back to undo my bra, dropping it to the floor. He hums in satisfaction as he stares back at me. I've not really thought about the attractiveness of my body. I'm fuller and less bony than I used to be, but being tall helps distribute that gained weight around, so I haven't really felt insecure about it. I've just felt ambivalent about myself. So certain that I'd never find love that I didn't really care how I looked to the opposite sex. It wasn't something Hilow ever really praised me about, so I've never really had the pleasure of seeing my body through someone else's eyes.

However, the way Wolf's gaze drags over me now makes me feel like I've been missing out on a lot. He looks at me like I'm carved from something rarer than flesh and bone. His pupils are dark, his jaw tight, like he's fighting the urge to devour me whole.

"You're staring," I murmur, trying to sound teasing, but it comes out soft and shaky.

"Yeah," he says, voice rough. "Don't rush me."

Heat blooms in my cheeks, down my throat, settling low in my belly. For the first time, I feel . . . wanted. Completely.

With a deep rumble, Wolf bends at the waist and pulls my hardened peak into his mouth. I gasp when his teeth tap on the tender flesh, a rush of wetness pooling in my panties that has nothing to do with the rain.

"Everly, I need to ask you a question, and I want you to be honest with me," he murmurs against my breast as he slides his face to the other one and drags his tongue around the peak, causing me to squeal inside.

He pulls back and stands to his full height, looming over me as his eyes grow serious. "Were you serious when you told me in the hay mound you never had an orgasm before?"

I jerk my head back, feeling a sudden shift as I inwardly curse myself for having such a big mouth. "I, um . . ."

"Don't look away," he commands, his fingers grasping my jaw and forcing me to look at him. "There's nothing to be ashamed of. I just want to know. I *need* to know."

I swallow the knot in my throat and nod. "Yeah, um . . . I think I was close a few times but never could fully experience one, I guess. I thought maybe my body wasn't made for sex. Some women have sex, and it hurts all the time. I've read about it."

"Does sex hurt you?" Wolf's brows knit together with concern.

I shake my head. "No, I just . . . didn't particularly like it. Always seemed like something I couldn't wait to be over."

The muscle in his jaw works. "That Hilow guy is the only one you've ever slept with?"

I nod.

He shakes his head. "I could tell just by looking at him that he isn't exactly an orgasm maker. His name is Hilow, for Christ's sake."

"Okay, *Conri Wolf*," I jibe back, poking him in his meaty chest.

He grabs my hand and holds it to him, his jaw shifting from side to side. "I don't like that guy."

"Why? You barely know him."

"I know that he let those girls who hurt you into his home, and he's a fucking prat for not protecting you from that."

His defensiveness causes a pressure to form in my chest. It's a warm and cozy feeling of comfort. Of friendship. I appreciate it more than he knows. God, he's so much like his sister. But in the hot male form I want to have sex with, obviously.

"When we do this, I want you to tell me what you like constantly," Wolf says, dragging the backs of his fingers along my belly. "Something feels good, you let me know. Whether that's in the form of the noises you make or you flat out move my hand and tell me what you want me to do, you need to be in control of your pleasure as much as I am. Understand?"

I nod slowly. "Yeah, I think so."

"Nothing you can say to me will be too much." His eyes are severe.

"Okay."

"Nothing," he says one more time, his gaze flicking down to my lips and back up to my eyes. "In fact, the more you say . . . the more turned on I'll get."

"Well, okay then."

And in a rush, he lifts me up, forcing me to wrap my legs around his waist as he carries me over to the bed, laying me on my back and coming down beside me.

His hand trails over my breasts, my stomach, and the insides of my thighs. I squirm with need when his fingers slip under the glossy fabric of my panties, sliding along the seam of me as he blows warm air over my neck.

"How could you possibly think you're not meant for sex when you're always so fucking wet?" he growls, his tongue sliding against the shell of my ear and causing my body to shudder.

"I'm normally not like this."

He groans as if in pain. "Are you telling me you're just wet for me, Stretch?"

I huff out a silent laugh. "I'm not sure your ego needs the boost."

He chuckles softly. "Always so fucking mouthy."

He pushes a single digit into me as I arch upward, absorbing the invasion. "Why did you never try to play with yourself?"

I moan as he crooks his finger and grinds against a spot that feels illicit and naughty. "I don't know," I gasp, reaching down to grab his hand and grind it into me harder. "I guess I don't turn myself on."

"Fuck, Everly. You turn me on." He slowly pushes one more finger into me, stretching me, spreading my arousal over my clit. "Can I tell you the last time you turned me on at Trinity?"

I nod, my eyes closing as I process the fact that he even knew I existed at Trinity.

"It was at my rugby game when I looked up and saw you were wearing my shirt."

I pant and turn to look at him, his eyes hooded and drugged-looking. "I didn't know if you realized that was your shirt."

"I did," he gruffs, biting his lip as his eyes scan over my body. "It made me fucking crazy."

"Why?" I ask shakily as I feel myself climbing toward an uncomfortable place in my body.

He leans in and nibbles on my neck, his faint whiskers causing spasms on my skin. "Because you're you."

I moan and then gasp when he rubs his rough fingers over my clit with harsh, quick pressure. My hips jolt upward like they have a mind of their own. "Oh, my God, Conri," I squeal as he quickens his pressure. "This is too much. It's too—"

My release takes me by surprise, and I roll forward, my whole body coiled into a tight ball as I rupture down below. It's different than the one I had on his face in the barn. This one is sharp and violent. Edgy and electric. I feel tingly all over, like someone lit sparklers under my skin, every nerve fizzing and smoldering.

"Talk to me, Everly," Wolf says, his nose dragging along my jaw. "I need to hear what you're thinking."

"I'm thinking I'm really glad I didn't squirt again."

His body shakes with silent laughter as he turns my face to look at him. "That did not bother me one fucking bit."

"How could it not?"

"It's fucking hot," he says seriously. "It's the highest form of compliment for a guy."

I hold my hand over my face, and he pulls it down, pushing back the damp strands of hair that fall across my eyes. This is so weird. Talking through all this stuff with a guy who I swore hated me until very recently. I was in a relationship with Hilow for two years, and we never reached this level of intimacy.

"More. I want more." I reach down and cup Wolf's length inside his shorts. It's long and thick and feels like velvet-wrapped steel. "Can I?" I ask tentatively.

He turns onto his back and folds his hands behind his head. "By all means, help yourself."

I push down the waistband of Wolf's boxer briefs and barely hold back my gasp when I see the full length of him. "This is stupid big, right?" I ask, my eyes flicking up to him as I delicately stroke his flesh. "Like, don't-turn-around-too-fast-in-a-crowded-room big?"

Wolf's abs pop as he laughs, covering his face with his hands as he shakes his head. "It's not that big."

"Um . . . okay," I deadpan, disbelief all over my voice. "Granted, I don't have many to compare it to, but I feel like this is the kind of big that will make me walk funny tomorrow."

In a flash, Wolf's rippling body of muscle rolls over so he's on top of me, his palms braced on either side of my head as he blankets me in his heat. He smells like rain and some sort of natural testosterone-infused musk as he murmurs against my lips. "Trust me, it'll fit."

And just as I begin to enjoy the cage he's put me in, he's off me and pulling a condom out of the plastic bag on the floor. Flashbacks to that first aid he gave me in his bathroom hit me as he uses his teeth to open the package. He rolls it on with deft precision, and jealousy needles in my belly over how many girls have probably seen him like this.

"What?" he asks, his brows furrowed as his cock bobs toward me.

"Nothing."

He grips my chin and forces me to look at him. "What?"

I really hate how he always notices when my brain is braining.

"Just curious about your body count." I blink up at him, trying to feign confidence.

His brows lift as he tilts his head. "Does it matter?"

"You know mine. I guess I want to know yours."

"It was never anything serious," he says, his voice a low rumble as he drags his tongue along my neck, dropping soft kisses as he goes.

I grab his meaty shoulders so he's forced to look at me. "I'm not going to judge, I promise."

He sighs. "Keep in mind, I was a D and D nerd in primary school and most of secondary."

"Okay . . ."

"I really didn't get any female attention until uni and was kind of making up for lost time."

"Yeah, okay. So . . . what are we talking? Double digits? Triple?"

"Double, only double." Regret mars his smoldering face.

I shrug. "That doesn't surprise me at all. Sexy, tall, fit rugby player. I'm sure it was easy for you."

"I wouldn't say easy . . ." he drones, grabbing my wrists and pinning them above my head. "But I will say, none of them make me feel the way I feel every time you call me sexy." He growls into my chest, and I feel a sharp twinge as he sucks my skin into his mouth. "It was clear you would never look my way, and it drove me wild."

"What?" My jaw drops as I grab his hair to pull his face back up so I can look at him. "Why would you say that?"

"First year, you tried to set me up with someone else. That made it pretty obvious that you weren't interested." His brows lift.

"Oh, God, that's right," I groan and cover my face. "I was just trying to, I don't know. Make myself useful."

He shakes his head as his cock slides between my folds. "I could have found a number of other ways to make you feel useful." He reaches between our bodies and notches himself at my center, holding his length straight as he pushes his tip into me ever so slightly.

I gasp, body count conversation completely forgotten as a painful ache spreads low and deep.

"You okay?" he asks, his eyes full of concern.

I nod, and he pushes in a little more.

"Fuuuck," he groans, dropping his forehead onto my shoulder. "You're so tight."

"Just do it fast. I think that will be better."

His head jerks up. "Are you sure?"

"Yes, Conri. I want this. I want it to . . . hurt."

"Jesus, Everly," he mutters, like I've just asked him to cut out his own heart.

But he doesn't argue. He shifts back to line himself up again, his breath ragged in my ear as his jaw tightens, and with a groan, he drives deep into me, all at once.

I cry out at the sharp, shocked flare of pressure that's so painful and tingly I feel overstimulated. My body squirms with agitation. But it's exactly what I wanted. The sting, the stretch, the wanton abandon that comes from not thinking about it too much and just letting it happen.

My first time with Hilow was awful. It felt like he never even fully got inside me. I was dry, and everything felt wrong and awkward. Like two idiot kids who didn't know what they were doing. I suppose we were. This is different. *So, so different.*

"Christ," Wolf hisses, voice strangled. "You're killing me, Everly."

"Ditto," I whisper, digging my nails into his shoulders.

He stills, chest heaving, as if he's giving me a second to adjust, but I roll my hips up, greedy and impatient, the burn needing some relief, some friction, something.

With a groan, Conri pulls out and plunges deep back into me, his mouth on my ear, muttering filthy Irish curses I can barely understand but can definitely *feel*. Every thrust is heavy and sure, like he knows this is exactly what both of us want.

And it doesn't hurt anymore. It *burns*, sweet and raw, and I cling to him, aching for that release again. That moment of euphoria that comes with a climax I've only ever had with him. *Is this what sex is meant to be like? Because God, I don't know that I'll want to stop now.*

What would have happened if we'd have hooked up first year? How different would my life have turned out? What would Cliona have thought of me when we paired together as roommates, and I told her I fucked her brother?

Ugh, Cliona.

I can't believe I'm fucking my friend's brother. This is so wrong . . . so, so wrong.

"Conri . . ." I gasp as that wrongness, that naughty, deceitful shiver of rule-breaking swirls deliciously through my body while his cock slams deeper, stretching me so much I can barely breathe.

I drag my nails over his back hard enough to leave red marks, but he just grunts and fucks me harder, like he's trying to brand me from the inside out.

"Take it," he growls against my neck, and the filthy command shoots straight through me. "Take my cock, Everly."

My hips buck desperately at the lilt of his thick accent as I begin to crest over the edge. He slips his hand between our bodies, his fingers finding my clit to rub rough and raw, perfectly in time with his thrusts.

"Oh my God." My words are hoarse and tumble out as

pressure coils tight in my core, tighter, until it snaps—white-hot and violent.

I scream, biting onto his shoulder as my body shudders in agony, and my sex clenches around his. He groans in my ear as his body turns to stone, and he thrusts deep into me and stills, releasing his own earth-shattering climax right behind mine.

His body is damp and heavy, and I love every delicious ounce of pressure on top of me. Relish in it, even. He feels like the best kind of anxiety reducer. Who needs sleeping pills when you have a big-thighed, big-cock, grumpy rugby player in your bed?

I feel my stomach start to tighten as laughter bubbles up out of nowhere.

"What is so funny?" Wolf asks, out of breath as he pulls his head back to hit me with those glittering brown eyes of his.

I pat his slick back and shake my head. "Nothing. Nothing at all. Ten out of ten. No notes."

His chuckle is warm, and the way he looks back at me is panty-melting, if my panties weren't already melted on the floor.

My brows tweak. "Is it too much to ask when we can do it again?"

"Not too much. Just enough."

Chapter 25

Breakaway: *When a player suddenly bursts out of the pack and runs free. Pure escape vibes.*

Translation: *Run for your life, Wolfy.*

Wolf

The morning sun wakes me as it pours in through the giant windows of Everly's bedroom the next day. I frown at the wide-open curtains, wondering what time it is because it looks well past early morning. I glance at the nightstand for my mobile to check the time and am shocked to see it's almost eleven. I never sleep this late.

Last night comes rushing back in flashes. Her legs around my waist, her laugh going breathless as I nibbled her earlobe, the sounds she made when I fucked her from behind on our sides one more time before we were both lulled to sleep by the rain pounding on the roof.

Her bedroom smells like warm skin, jasmine, and the kind of sin you hate to wash off in the shower. Sleeping here was probably a bad idea. But so is fucking the girl I secretly stalked for nearly four years.

Everly is sleeping on her side, facing away from me. She's practically sideways in the bed, long limbs flung out everywhere, her blonde hair a nest and crusted to the side of her face. And I can't help but smile. She sleeps like a messy disaster. How very on-brand of her.

At some point, I need to tell Everly about my little trailing habit. She deserves to know the full scope of my dark obsession. I hinted to her last night that I noticed her at Trinity, but she deserves to know it all. Then she can decide if she wants to sic her uncles on me. I'd deserve it.

But when I think about it, I don't truly believe it was an obsession. It was just fear. I saw something in Everly that felt kindred. She reminded me of my mate Finn. Too pure for this harsh world. Protectively, I pull the blanket up over her naked back. I want her to be warm and safe and happy. I'm desperate for it.

Telling her all of that before we had sex would have freaked her the fuck out. And I don't even know what this all means. Is this just sex? Is it more? Fuck, I don't know. One second, I'm telling myself to never touch Everly again, the next I'm sucking her face off on the side of a mountain cliff.

The girl makes me crazy.

Guilt niggles as I think of my sister, who told me to give Everly a chance. I'm sure this isn't quite what she had in mind. I'm really fucking up on all fronts here.

My head jerks when I hear tires crunching on the gravel outside.

"Everly." I give her shoulder a nudge to try to rouse her, but she doesn't move a muscle. "Everly," I state louder, and she finally shifts a little before murmuring, "Sexy Irish tree trunks," and burrowing into her pillow.

My lips curve up into a smile. But when I hear car doors slamming outside, I know we need to figure out what the fuck is going on out there. "Everly, wake up." I shake her again, harsher this time. "There's someone outside."

She jerks up, hair wild, creases from her pillow streaked on her cheek. "Oh my God." She scrambles for her phone on the nightstand. "It's—Wolf, it's my parents."

"Seriously?"

"Yes. We're hosting brunch with the baby here today."

"What the fuck is that?"

"The whole family is gathering to . . . I don't know . . . brunch with the baby."

"They're all coming here?" I exclaim, my heart hammering in my chest as I swing my legs off the bed. "That might have been nice to know last night. I wouldn't have slept over."

"You would have just left?" she asks, hurt evident in her voice.

"I don't know," I growl, irritation prickling up my spine as I slip into my boxers and shorts, sliding my mobile into my pocket. "I don't know what we're doing exactly. We need to talk about that. But first, is there a back door in here?"

"No," she squeaks, grabbing her shirt up off the floor. "It's a cabin, not a panic room."

I eye her harshly for her snide tone. "Does the window open?"

"Of course the window opens. It's a window," she hisses, yanking on her shirt inside out.

"You're not a morning person, are you?" I state to the woman who was screaming my name into a pillow last night.

She bites her lip and sighs. "No . . . sorry. I need coffee."

"I'll remember that for next time."

Her brows lift. "So, there's going to be a next time?"

A knock rattles at the front door. "Ev? You up?" Everly's dad's voice calls, and I jump like he's about to walk right into her bedroom.

We scurry over to the window, and she slides it open, popping out the screen like she installed the bloody things herself. It's decent-sized, so I straddle it and hoist myself through it, shirtless and barefoot as I drop down onto the ground and pause when my feet touch the gravel.

She tosses my shoes out the window as she kneels in front

to be eye level with me. "Just pretend you were on one of your runs, and no one will be the wiser. I'll get your bag out of my car later."

"Okay," I reply, as I clutch my still-damp shirt in my hand.

She smirks, her messy bed head a stunning spray around her glittering eyes, all signs of makeup washed off in the rain last night. Christ, she's beautiful.

"Is it too much to ask for a goodbye kiss?" she asks, her blue eyes wide and anxious as we shine some daylight on whatever this is.

"So cringe," I murmur before reaching up and grabbing her face to crush my lips to hers.

She giggles against my mouth, and I feel suddenly frustrated that I have to go when all I want to do is climb back into her bed and taste every part of her body again.

Slightly dazed, I back up and yank my shirt down over my head. "I'll see you later, Stretch."

"See you later, Wolf."

I hop into my shoes and allow my feet to carry me over the mossy bank along the creek, up my normal path. I glance right and swear I see movement in the window from Luke's cabin but pray it's just my eyes playing tricks on me.

By the time I circle back to the barn, my lungs are burning, and my hair's plastered to my skull. I push open the dutch doors of the barn and step inside, using the hem of my T-shirt to wipe the sweat off my brow as Millie, Handsome, Butterscotch, and Reginald all peek their heads out from their gates. The goat bleats at me, long and loud, like it knows where I've been and is judging me. Harshly.

"Fuck off, you," I mumble as I lean back on the counter, heart still racing.

Whatever this thing with Everly is, it's happening. And I hope to fuck I'm able to survive it.

Chapter 26

Support Play: *When teammates run alongside the ball carrier, ready to catch a pass or protect.*

Translation: *The ladies of Fletcher Mountain have my back.*

Everly

Everly: My family wants me to invite you to the "baby brunch."

Wolf: Do they know what we did last night?

Everly: Of course, Wolf, I gave a full TED Talk over morning mimosas and baby cuddles. I even demonstrated some of our positions.

Wolf: Have you still not had your coffee?

Everly: No. And sorry. They're just trying to be nice, I think.

Wolf: So, what should I say?

Everly: My uncles are like bloodhounds. They'll take one look at us and know you defiled their niece.

Wolf: So, it's a no to brunch?

Everly: If you value your life, yes.

Wolf: What a shame, I was going to ask your father for your hand in marriage.

Everly: . . .

Wolf: A joke, Everly.

Everly: Did you forget I haven't had my coffee?

Wolf: Apologies. Have your coffee and when your family clears out, come over and pay a visit to your son who has been poorly neglected.

Everly: What?

Wolf: It's a giant red flag if you're a dead-beat Dragon Mommy.

Everly: OMG. Of course. Be there as soon as I can. Tell Rugby Mommy misses him!!!

Sitting amongst my wholesome family after being thoroughly railed the previous night is a very new thing for me.

Dare I say, an original experience.

While Luke and Addison fuss over Baby Levi on the area rug in the living room right in front of me, I'm sitting here sipping on a mimosa, recalling in great detail how easily Wolf lifted me last night. Like I weighed nothing. Like my body was made to fit in his hands, in his lap, against the wall with his mouth on mine.

I know this is a bad time to recall all those details, but it's hard not to think about it all when every time I shift on the sofa, there's a sharp ache that pulses between my legs.

God, I can't believe I'm sore from sex.

There is physical evidence of how he stretched me while whispering my name like it was both a prayer and a curse.

And God help me, it wasn't just the sex. It was how he looked at me after, his big brown eyes soft and sated as we both drifted off to sleep, totally unaware of what this whole thing is between us.

Man, it felt good to just not think for once. To not map out a plan of action or follow a tedious list. To just do something because I wanted to.

"You got laid," Dakota whispers quietly, ripping me out of my inner musings.

I gasp and turn to look at her. "Why would you say that?" I ask as she sits down beside me on the sofa with her own mimosa.

"You are literally smiling while Luke and Addison are wiping shit off their baby's back. The only thing that could make someone smile through something like that is a night of sweet, slow, passionate lovemaking."

Addison looks up from Levi and smirks knowingly at me. Does she know as well? My cheeks heat as I snap my gaze to Trista, who's helping Cozy in the kitchen, and I swear she's got a strange look in her eyes when she glances at me too. *What is happening right now?*

Thankfully, my dad, Ethan, Wyatt, and Calder are all playing *Mario Kart* like they have money on the game, so they seem oblivious. My grandma is hand-stitching something on Baby Levi's quilt she made him, so it doesn't look like I have to worry about her.

And Luke seems very stressed about the diaper explosion, so fingers crossed he's none the wiser.

But the ladies of Fletcher Mountain?

They must be freaky little mind readers!

I lift my hand to cover my mouth. "Is it really that obvious?"

"Don't worry, Mastermind," Dakota says primly while crossing her legs. "I'm your aunt now, so your secret is safe with me, but you need to wipe that smirk off your face if you don't want your uncles to sus you out."

I scrub my hand over my face, fighting back all my indecent thoughts. Stop thinking about sex. Stop thinking about Wolf. Stop thinking about his big hands.

Also, stop making it into such a big thing in your head, Everly.

It was just good sex. People have good sex all the time. It doesn't *mean* anything.

This thing with Wolf is casual. No big deal. Wolf is going back to Ireland at some point. He has a whole huge career in rugby to focus on. He was worried about me being a distraction, so I can't get all girlie and clingy and obsessed and totally freak him out. This is just a summer job up here on Fletcher Mountain.

We're just scratching an itch.

Nothing more.

But damn, did he scratch that itch good.

Ugh, I'm smiling again.

"Everly! How did yesterday with Wolf's rugby team go?" Trista asks, tearing my focus from my frantic thoughts to my family all around me.

"Oh . . . amazing! I have more sign-ups than I know what to do with," I peal, maybe a touch overly enthusiastic.

"Oh, awesome." Trista looks relieved.

"So does that mean we're off the hook?" Calder asks with a pleading look.

"Yes, Uncle Calder," I answer with a reassuring smile. "You and Wyatt and Luke will no longer be auctioned off to the highest bidders."

"Excuse me?" Luke asks, his head popping up as he holds a newly swaddled Levi against his chest.

"Don't worry about it." I wave Luke off.

He cuts me a dubious look. "Always scheming, aren't you, Evs."

"Why does Wolf never say yes to our dinner invites?" Wyatt asks, changing the subject, almost as if he knows the rugby player is on my mind constantly. "He said no to brunch today. He says no every time we invite him up to our cabin. What's his deal?"

I cut a knowing look to Dakota. "Why are you asking me?"

"Don't you see him a lot?" Wyatt's brows furrow.

"Yeah, but we're not like close or anything," I chirp loudly and stand, feeling my cheeks flush as I walk into the kitchen to help Cozy.

I try to make myself busy and can't help but notice the peculiar look on Addison's face as she strides over to wash her hands in the sink next to me.

"Me thinks thou doth protest too much," she sings under her breath to me as she shoots me a conspiratorial look. "You're being a little defensive, and I'm just trying to warn a girl. It's not like I saw a guy jumping out of your bedroom window this morning or anything."

"Oh my God." My entire body shivers with anxiety.

"Relax, I won't say a word." She smiles knowingly. "I got your back, girl."

She winks at me and walks back into the living room like she didn't just show me the sweetest gesture of sisterhood ever. My eyes move from Addison to Dakota to Trista. All three of these Fletcher Mountain ladies apparently have my back. And it makes me damn near burst into tears when I realize how perfect a choice I made for my uncles.

Damn, I love my family.

Chapter 27

Game Plan: *The overall strategy the coach sets for how the team will play that match.*

Translation: *"What are we?"*

Wolf

"Alright, Rugby, it's playtime. Don't get cheeky on me like last time. No more running under the bed. You're going to stay exactly where I can see you, got it?"

The lizard stares at me from his place under the heat lamp of his tank, looking bored and completely uninterested in whatever I'm saying. I've gotten to know my new pet the past few weeks, and he can be a stubborn sod when he wants to be. But I think we're starting to bond a bit more after I found a spot under his spikey chin that he likes having scratched. I know he likes it because every time I rub it, he closes his eyes like he's at a spa getting a massage.

After reading up on bearded dragons, I discovered playtime outside of their enclosure helps improve their mood, so that's what I've been attempting to do with him this week. Ready for round two, I slide the lid open and reach in. Rugby shoots forward through my hands, his earth-toned, pebbly scales scraping against my palm as I struggle to grab him.

When I finally get a decent grip, I lift his long body out and set him on the floor, where he stands, staring up at me like he's waiting for me to do something.

"Go on, then, stretch your legs."

And like a shot, he darts forward, his tail swishing behind him as he zigzags toward my sofa, his long claws clacking on the hardwood. I trail him like a proud father as he explores the space, pausing to puff his throat and bob his head like he's hunting for his next meal, even though he knows I'll feed him a load of freeze-dried crickets after this.

After a few laps around the flat, he ventures over to me, crawling up my foot until I reach down and pick him up. "Tired already?" I ask as I rub that spot under his chin.

His eyes close and then pop open when there's a knock on my door. Clutching him in my hands, I walk over and can't help the smile on my face when I find Everly on the other side of it with a foil-covered plate in her hands.

"Oh my God, Rugby," she gasps, pushing right past me to set the plate in my kitchen and free her hands. "I didn't know you ever got him out of his cage."

"It's kind of new." I hold him out to her as she runs her finger along his back. "Scratch under his chin. He likes that."

She squeals when his eyes close. "Oh my God, he does. You're a good Dragon Daddy."

I chuckle. "Do you want to hold him?"

She nods. "Show me what to do."

"Alright," I murmur, keeping my voice low so I don't spook him. "Try to stay calm. He gets freaked kind of easily. First time I had him out of his cage, he darted under the bed and hissed at me. I had to basically tear up my apartment to retrieve him."

"Aww . . . our poor baby. Maybe he just missed his Dragon Mommy."

With a smile, I step around to her side and hand him over, slow and steady. "Hold him under his chest, but don't squeeze. He's a tiny tank, but still—respect the tank."

"Of course." Everly's eyes are wide, and I can't help staring at her as she leans forward, hands hovering over mine as she slowly closes her fingers around him. Her touch is soft, careful, and slightly trembling.

"Nice and gentle. Wait for him to relax." I pull my own hand out, placing it lightly over hers, adjusting her grip just a fraction. I pause, catching her eyes on mine as a heaviness presses in on my chest.

Fuck, I think I missed her.

And it's only been a few hours.

I'm doomed.

I step back for some air and to let her take over completely, my chest tight in a way I don't want to reflect on. My gaze roams her body, dressed in a little white sundress and looking good enough to eat. She's careful and confident in that buzzy way of hers, and I can't help but think this is exactly the kind of person I'd want to co-parent a tiny spiky dragon with. *Who the fuck even am I?*

"I love him." She smiles brightly at me. "You're taking really good care of him."

"Did you ever doubt me?"

"After the camera roll of photos on your phone, never for a second." She giggles softly. "Are you going to want to keep him after you're done here?"

My smile falters at that abrupt question. "I don't know, I guess. Depends on where I end up." Anxiety prickles over me as thoughts of the future flood my mind, but I shake them away and try to focus on the now. "Do you want to sit down?"

She nods and follows me over to the sofa, lowering herself down like she's carrying a grenade.

"That's leftover brunch if you're hungry," she says, gesturing over to the plate she set on my counter.

"Thanks."

"No problem." She smiles wobbly at me, her teeth clamping down on her lower lip as her cheeks flush.

"Come on . . . just ask. I know you want to," I state, stretching my arm over the back of the sofa and pushing a strand of her hair back from her cheek.

"What?" she asks innocently.

"What are we?"

"I wasn't going to ask."

"Bollocks." I shoot her a skeptical look. "I know your mind has been racing all morning, so why don't you just tell me what you think we are, and I'll tell you if I agree with you."

Her shoulders shake with silent laughter as she looks down at the dragon in her hands, running her fingertip under his jaw in slow, steady strokes. "Well, I made a little list this morning."

"A list?" I ask, frowning at her. "Let me guess, you wrote it down in one of your little fuzzy notebooks."

Her eyes narrow. "No, just in my head . . . because I was surrounded by my family."

"Of course."

"But my list was of all the reasons we do not work."

"Let's hear them," I state, turning to give her my undivided attention.

"You're hoping to move back to Ireland. You're my best friend's brother. We're total opposites. We work together. We're super young."

You deserve better than me, I silently add.

"So, because of all that, it makes sense that this should just be a fun little summer fling. Casual. No labels."

"A no-labels label?" I ask, brows arched knowingly.

"Exactly." She nods and beams back at me. "Which is something new for me. And it's fun to try new things."

My eyes narrow as I nod, accepting her no-label label. Casual is good. If we're just a casual summer thing, then I don't have to worry about telling her about the past and how I used to follow her home on a regular basis. We can just focus on the now. And right now, I would really like to see her naked again.

"Right . . . well then. I think it would be *fun* for me to put Rugby back in his cage and fuck you for the next hour if that sounds alright to you."

Her cheeks flush a stunning ruddy color. "Works for me, Double D."

Chapter 28

Adjusting the Game Plan: *Often called by the captain or coach when responding to the flow of the game.*

Translation: *Time to make my own calls.*

Wolf

The line crackles, the faint hum of the Ballymun traffic outside my parents' shop bleeding through. Mam always takes calls out in front of the shop, and I can practically see her tall, slender frame leaning against the large display window.

"You sound tired," she says, no hello, no easing in. Straight to business, my mam.

I rub the back of my neck, staring out at my view of Fletcher Mountain, feeling guilty over the stark contrast of our two views right now. "Training is hard."

"Maybe taking your law exams would have been easier?" she shoots back, sharper than I expected. Christ, I've only been gone a bit over a month, and she's already on me about this.

I blow out a breath. "I'm thinking about applying for a different kind of job out here, actually."

There's a pause, and I can hear her light footsteps scrape on the pavement as she paces. "What kind of job?"

I swallow, feeling like a boy again instead of a twenty-something rugby player living on my own in a new country. "A rugby coaching gig for youths here in Denver. It's not a lot of money, but if I get an offer from the team, the two incomes could be decent."

Her inhale is soft, but it lands hard in my chest. "I thought this Colorado move was temporary."

"Well . . . getting back to Ireland is the long-term goal, but I'm not getting any calls from an Irish team yet, so . . ." I sigh heavily at that reality, hating that I might be letting my sister down if a call from Ireland never comes, but I can't base my life on the hope that they'll take a second look at me. I made my bed back home, and now I have to lie in it. At least here, I get to keep working in the sport of rugby in one way or another.

"All that hard schooling you did just to become a coach?" My mom sounds resolute. Disappointed.

"It wouldn't have to be forever." I try to keep the grumble in my throat, but it comes out thinner than I'd like. "It just feels like something I'm good at. I like helping kids, Ma. It feels important."

"Wish it paid you like it was," she harrumphs.

I sigh, feeling her dissatisfaction. "Maybe it's a bad idea."

She pauses for a moment, and her tone lightens when she asks, "Does this mean you like it over there?"

"Yeah, I do," I reply, the words heavy in my chest. "I like my team too. Fergie has become a proper mate."

"What about the host family?" she asks robotically.

I smile as I picture Trista and Stevie and all the rest of the family toddling around the mountain, living their lives. I pass Luke and Addison taking Levi out for walks in the stroller, Calder walking his bleedin' cats in these contraptions on his chest, Wyatt feeding carrots to his goat and all the other animals nearly daily. It's a good life up here on Fletcher Mountain. It's no wonder I've felt inspired to lay down some roots.

Then there's Everly.

Fuck.

I pinch the bridge of my nose as Everly's face instantly floods my vision. It's been three weeks of our casual no-label situationship or whatever you call it, and her bleedin' ripped sweatshirt is still hanging on the back of my bathroom door. It's pathetic how I stare at it every day while I'm in the shower. How I notice that it still smells like her. I tell myself I'll return it, but the truth is, I like the presence of her in my space. No matter how hard I try to keep things casual this summer, she's wormed her way into my space. My routine. My head. And if I'm honest—and Christ, I hate admitting this—I don't want that sweatshirt gone. Not yet. Maybe not ever.

"The family is decent. They treat me better than I deserve."

"I doubt that," Mam says, her tone terse. "You're a good boy, Conri."

"That's debatable," I laugh dryly as I take a deep breath in. "Do you think I'm foolish for applying for that job?"

"Yes." She sighs heavily. "And no."

My brows furrow.

"If it makes you happy, I suppose that's worth something."

My throat tightens. My ma doesn't use flowery language like this with ease. This is as close as we'd get to an *I'm proud of you.*

"What about Cliona?" I ask, my voice grave.

"What about her?" she snaps, and I can feel tension crawling through the line. I've always played a bit of a middleman between my mam and Cliona. They can often be like two lionesses battling to be queen of the pack. It's why Cliona and I are so close. I'm her protector, helping the two of them communicate when things get rough. Our ma means well, but her delivery can set my sister off.

"Are you letting her be happy?" I ask, my tone firm.

"'Course I am. What do ya mean by that?"

"Ma, she's doing brilliantly for Leinster. You need to let her off the law exam hook as well."

"Oh, fine, then. Both of you are grown now and know better than your da, and I, is that it?"

"No, I'm just saying that we need to start making some of our own decisions about our future. We've got a good education, and that's in large part thanks to you two. That's a foundation that will help us wherever we go. But at some point, we have to find our own way, don't you think?"

She grunts out a noise that doesn't sound altogether bad. "I suppose so."

I smile because this is as big a victory as I'll ever get with my mother. The woman is hard and soft at the same time. She's a good mam, even if she never fully embraced this rugby world of ours.

I know she's disappointed that I don't want to continue down the law pathway that she and Da urged me and Cliona to take. Da might even be furious. But had I not been raised by my hardheaded, determined, and hardworking parents, who I have always wanted to make proud, I may not have been confident to pursue anything other than their dreams.

But I can be more than a lawyer, even if it won't ever pay as much. And whatever I do will still be meaningful.

"I miss ya, Ma," I say because it's the truth, even if our relationship is a hard one at times.

"I miss you too, Conri," she says, her voice soft. "I just want you to be happy."

I smile warmly. "I'm working on that."

Chapter 29

Purple Patch: *An Irish sports term for a short period of great form or success during a match.*

Translation: *Honeymoon Phase.*

Everly

Cliona: Fletcher! I need a favor!!!

Everly: Name it.

Cliona: Can you recommend a place I can order a cake for my brother's birthday and then possibly go pick it up and surprise him with it next week? We have this cake tradition we do every year, and I want to make sure we still kind of do it, even if it's just via FaceTime.

Everly: OMG, I am a shit friend. I totally forgot you said you had a summer birthday.

Cliona: Since I was born. LOL.

Everly: I wish we could be together to celebrate.

Cliona: I know. I'm going through withdrawals from both you and my brother. But at least you can celebrate with my better half.

I smile at Cliona's last text to me. *Better half, indeed.*

Wolf and I have spent the past month sneaking around Fletcher Mountain like a couple of naughty teenagers. I swear

I'm wearing a path in the woods down below the mountain lookout point. The one where I was almost attacked by Fowl Pacino. Wolf and I have been using that as our gateway to each other a heck of a lot. The only nights we don't spend together are the nights when I'm busy with my family.

Real talk? I'm obsessed. I'm obsessed with the way he makes my body feel. I'm obsessed with how he talks me through everything we do together. I'm obsessed with the level of confidence I feel surging through me when he forces me to talk him through it.

I didn't know sex could be like this. I didn't know it would change the way I see the world. Like it's full of possibility, not just for the people I help but maybe even for me.

I'm even reevaluating my matchmaking manifesto. That's what good sex does! It gives you a new perspective on things.

Which is probably why I'm working down at Mount Millie today just so I can be near him. It's a grueling hot summer day, and he's out on the paddock with Stevie, rinsing down Clyde the Clydesdale.

I'm set up on a table in the barn alley with my laptop, barely focusing on the vendor emails I need to be sending out to get things finalized for the auction in two weeks, because it's more fun to watch Wolf and Stevie.

At one point, he directs the hose at Stevie, and the battle cry she squeals when the chilly water hits her brings Trista out of the feed room with a concerned-mother face, making sure her child is okay.

She is more than okay.

Both of us watch with big, dopey smiles as the sunlight slices through the trees, soft and golden, catching every droplet splattering between the big rugby boy and the curly-haired toddler. Wolf moves around the massive Clydesdale as he tries to spray Stevie, who hides behind an outdoor feeder. He's swapped out his standard sneakers and athletic shorts for jeans and boots, embracing his position as a farmhand completely. It suits him even better than his rugby kit, which I didn't think possible.

Wolf finally abandons the hose and tears after Stevie, snatching her up in his arms and tossing her over his shoulder to take her back over to Clyde. He sets her on his back, her tiny little boots kicking excitedly as he resumes the rinse, squirting her legs every so often to her utter delight.

The whole scene feels weightless and suspended. Like I'm watching a movie montage of complete and utter happiness. We've all magically settled into this natural routine on Fletcher Mountain. Wolf riding with my uncles three days a week to training. Me working from home or the barn. Trista and Stevie doing what they do best.

There's something insanely sexy about a guy who looks as dark and dangerous as Wolf be gentle and kind to animals and children. Something inside me tugs hard, the kind of thing I'd worry felt like love if I didn't know any better.

Trista breaks through my musings when she says, "I'm going to take Stevie up to the house for some lunch. Do you want me to bring you anything?"

"No, I'm okay, thanks," I say, struggling to tear my eyes away from Wolf.

Trista walks out to collect Stevie, and I watch in rapt fascination as Wolf walks Clyde back into his stable in the barn. His shirt is plastered to his body, clearly soaked from his little water fight, and I don't even try to hide the fact that I'm drinking in every square inch of him.

When he closes the gate, he makes his way toward me, giving me that we're-finally-alone sort of look. We waste no time meeting in the middle of the barn, lips, tongues, and hands roaming over each other like we didn't just spend the night together last night.

"You know, I think I need to add a rule about wet clothes in my matchmaking manifesto."

"Are you matchmaking us now?" he asks, moving to the other side of my neck, his hands palming my ass.

"Heavens no. This is just for other people's love lives," I groan when his cock presses into my belly.

"Of course," he murmurs before capturing my lips with his.

His tongue slides into my mouth, swift and all-consuming, and my knees buckle as he holds me up in his arms. God, this bad boy can kiss.

An intrusive thought hits me out of nowhere, and I shove him away. "Hey, were you going to tell me your birthday is coming up next week?" I ask, hitting the man who's seen me naked with a challenging glare.

He frowns back at me, the corner of his mouth lifted into a dismissive sneer.

"Why not?" I ask, propping my hands on my hips.

"Because it's just a day."

"It's not just a day," I exclaim with a gentle shake. "It's a day you share with your sister. My best friend. That's really cool."

His shoulders lift. "Yeah, I guess so."

I move in close, folding my fingers behind his neck. "So, what can I get you for your birthday?"

His hands sculpt around my ass. "I could think of a few things," he murmurs, pulling me in close.

A vibration pulses between us, and Wolf frowns, glancing down at his pocket. He pulls his phone out, and his brows furrow even further. "I just got a text from your uncle Wyatt."

"What does it say?"

"He invited me to poker night."

My heart lurches in my chest. "When?"

"Tomorrow."

"Shit," I hiss, pulling away from him and shoving my hair

out of my face. "I have plans with my grandma tomorrow night. We're going to dinner in Boulder."

"Why does that matter?" Wolf asks, smiling curiously at me.

"Well, I can't come to poker to . . . run interference. Maybe you should tell them you can't come. Tell them you're busy . . . giving Rugby a bath."

Wolf's shoulders shake with silent laughter. "I'm not afraid of a few mountain men, Stretch."

I shake my head slowly. "Famous last words, Wolfy."

Chapter 30

Spear Tackle: *A spear tackle is a dangerous tackle in which a player is picked up by the tackler and turned so that they are upside down. The tackler then drops or drives the player into the ground, often head-, neck-, or shoulder-first.*

Translation: *Hydrangea bushes hurt like a bitch.*

Wolf

I managed to live on Fletcher Mountain for almost two months without ever stepping foot inside Wyatt and Trista's home. I would have probably made it the whole summer dodging their host family invites had it not been for the fact that I'm sleeping with their niece.

Now, after becoming so close to Everly, refusing their invitation feels wrong. Disrespectful, even. Granted, they don't know we're sleeping together, but avoiding them is a weak move.

And I am not weak.

Which is how I find myself seated at a round kitchen table in Wyatt's cabin with all the Fletcher brothers shooting daggers at me for the past two hours. Everly's dad is the scariest of them. He's dressed in business casual, even though it's a Saturday night, and he looks at me like he knows what I'm doing with his daughter—when I know he doesn't. Wyatt, Calder, and Luke are in their signature flannels, eyeing me like a puzzle they've yet to piece together. Although in fairness, Luke's eyes are half-closed most of the night. I expect that newborn baby up the road is keeping him up at night these days.

And then there's me, dressed in jeans and a T-shirt as four sets of wary lumberjack eyes bore into me from across the table as I sit here and try not to think about how I fucked Everly against her hallway wall just hours ago.

"Call or fold?" Wyatt rumbles, his thick forearms flexing as he taps his cards on the table.

"All in," Stevie says confidently as she returns from the kitchen with her third bowl of popcorn. I growl at her as she attempts to climb back onto my lap. The little shit has been attached to my hip, refusing to go up to Calder and Dakota's cabin with her mother as soon as I arrived.

I told Trista I didn't mind. 'Cause I don't. If anything, Stevie is a nice buffer between me and these grumpy mountain men.

I lean in to whisper in Stevie's ear, and she sighs heavily like she disagrees with me but then says, "We call."

I throw in the correct amount of chips, and Calder narrows his eyes. "You feel good letting a three-year-old run your game? I thought you'd have the luck of the Irish on your side."

"I'm almost four," Stevie says perfectly clearly.

"Her luck is better than mine, I expect," I say, shifting this kid's bony ass on my knee.

The cards are laid out on the table, and as the pot builds, I cringe when my pocket sevens are no match for Wyatt's pocket aces.

"Ugh, we lost?" Stevie groans like she bet her whole toy collection on it.

"Yeah, we did. Thanks for nothing."

Calder hides his snicker as Stevie glares at me.

"I'm going to go watch my tablet," she announces and then takes off down the hall after running me clean out of money.

"So, how's your rugby camp going?" Max asks, his eyes fixed

on me as he sips his whiskey from a rocks glass and Calder shuffles the deck.

"It's going alright," I reply with a shrug.

"That doesn't sound very confident." Calder directs a look at me.

"I like the team well enough," I say with a swallow. "Just have to wait and see if they like me back."

"Do you have a tryout or something?" Wyatt asks, his eyes on me.

"Not exactly. But in a few weeks, there's a friendly match with another team that's on the schedule, and my coach made it clear that he'll make his decision on whether he's offering me a spot on the team or not after that."

"Can we come?" Luke asks, his eyes thoughtful.

I jerk my head back. "To the friendly?"

"Yeah. I'd love to see you play. Addison would too, I'm sure." Luke says the words like they're the most simple ones in the world.

But they're not simple.

Not to me.

"I'm in too," Calder adds. Max and Wyatt both nod, making it clear it's not just Luke asking to go.

It's all of them.

My chest tightens. "Um . . . yeah, I think they allow fans."

"Only if you don't mind," Luke adds, taking a sip of his beer. "If it's too much pressure—"

"It's not too much pressure," I cut him off, my heart pounding weirdly in my chest. "It'd be class if you guys came. I can text you the date and time."

"Class?" Luke asks,

"Ye know, deadly. Excellent," I explain. They nod.

"Right. Class," Calder says.

Max smiles and nods like it's a plan.

"I'm coming, Nana," Stevie yells from where she's seated in the hallway with her tablet, clearly not getting too far away from the group.

I laugh and glance over at her. "Couldn't do it without you, Steve."

The brothers all smile and get thoughtful looks on their faces before Luke says, "Steve was our father's name."

"Oh, I'm sorry. It's just what I've taken to calling her. I'll stick with Stevie."

"Don't be sorry," Max says, his jaw tight. "It's good to hear his name again."

Wyatt clears his throat loudly. "So do you think you have a real shot at making the team?"

"I hope so." I shrug and grip the back of my neck. "I'd hate to have to go back to Ireland after all of this."

"I think she'd hate it too," Wyatt says, gesturing back to his daughter.

I swallow the knot in my throat at the idea of saying goodbye to Stevie.

Or Everly.

Or the wee buggers at the rugby youth program. It's been amazing watching their attitudes and skill level change. Growing that bond with them. Some have even seemed to lower their guards and find mates to chat about life to. As much as young lads do.

It's fulfilling. As is working here. I can picture living in Colorado more than I ever thought I could. It's not home, as I'll always be an Irish lad at heart, but it's not as foreign anymore.

It's strange. I'm not sure when exactly the goal stopped being getting back to Ireland, but somewhere along the way during my time up here on Fletcher Mountain, my dreams have changed.

And I think it has little to do with the team I'm trying to find a place on and more to do with this family.

"Is rugby lucrative enough to not need a secondary income source?" Max asks, giving me that corporate look like I'm in the middle of a job interview.

"Not always," I state honestly. "In Ireland, professional players at the elite level do well, but it's nowhere near football salaries. And in America, it's even less. You mostly just get a stipend or part-time wage. It's why my parents were so insistent my sister and I prioritize our education. They wanted us to work in law eventually."

"What do you want to do?" Calder asks, staring thoughtfully at me. "I'm guessing Mount Millie isn't your dream job."

"No, definitely not," I reply with a laugh, chewing the inside of my cheek. "But the youth program that I'm a volunteer coach for is in the process of hiring for full-time coaches, and I put in an application." I pause as I feel their judgment in my bones. "I like coaching. It's not my long-term professional goal, but if I could do something that allows me to be a part of an outreach program, that would be my dream, I think. I like helping kids find ways to be more . . . themselves."

That answer earns me four identical grunts of approval. Which is a touch better of a reaction than I got with my mam on the phone last week. Truthfully, I'm not opposed to working in law someday, but right now, I'm not ready to let go of rugby. Nor the chance to help more young, troubled lads . . . *just like Coach Flannigan helped me when I started at Trinity.*

We get back to poker, and I exhale heavily, wondering if I shared too much or not enough. I haven't mentioned any of this to Everly, mostly because I'm terrified it will freak her out. Last I spoke to her about my goals, I was adamant about getting back to Dublin. But now, things are changing.

All I know is I owe it to myself to make that life choice on my own.

Everly

I've done a lot of crazy things in my life. Like standing outside a surrogacy clinic to try to hock potential surrogates to have my uncle's baby. Like hacking into my other uncle's dating profiles to sabotage his quest for random hookups. Or like becoming an expert on lumberjack competitions just to help my third uncle catch the attention of the woman he was madly in love with.

But spying on my uncles' poker night while they're sitting across from the man I'm currently having insanely amazing sex with?

This might be the crown jewel of crazy.

I'm pressed flat against the side of Uncle Wyatt's house, crouched like I'm preparing for a covert military op . . . except I'm wearing a sundress and wedges from my dinner out with Grandma earlier tonight. If I knew there would be climbing involved in my creeping, I would have changed my shoes.

But somehow, I've shimmied myself up the side of his deck and am perched a solid five feet off the ground on the railing, doing my best to see if there's any bloodshed inside.

I told Wolf I didn't want him to go tonight. I told him to make up an excuse. He told me he'd already refused multiple meals with Wyatt and Trista and that he couldn't say no again. And that he wasn't scared.

I'm scared.

Big scared.

My breath fogs up the window as I peer inside to see Wolf holding playing cards like he has nothing to lose. Which is a lie, because if my uncles catch even a whiff that I've been spending my nights with this hot, brooding rugby player, he's going to lose a lot more than a poker hand.

But from what I can tell . . . everything seems okay. Stevie is perched on Wolf's lap. My dad just handed Wolf a beer. And Uncle Calder seems to be behaving himself for quite possibly the first time in his entire life. Even grumpy Uncle Wyatt is cracking a grin every once in a while.

What is in the air tonight?

I lean just an inch closer to the window to see if I can hear what they're talking about, but my pulse is so loud in my ears I can't make out what they're saying.

I catch Wolf's voice, low and steady, when he says, "No, sir. My parents don't really care for rugby."

Oh, fantastic. They're prying into his parental issues. I'm sure he *loves* that.

I shift again, trying to see Wolf's face and if he's doing okay or if he needs a rescue, and that's when it happens.

The rom-com moment you see in movies, but it's all com, no rom.

My foot slips out of my wedge and off the deck railing, and for a split second, all I see is the night sky.

I make a horrifyingly undignified noise as I topple backward and land squarely in a hydrangea bush. My back instantly aches as branches stab my flesh, and my ankle throbs as my wedge hangs off it by the strap.

A thunder of chairs scrapes inside, and heavy footsteps come barreling toward me, but it's Wolf's voice I hear first.

"Fuck, Everly. Is that you?" His voice is sharp and severe, and I look up to see him vaulting over the edge in a natural, athletic way.

I bet that's exactly how I looked when I took my own tumble. Twinning!

He squats down beside me, immediately pulling my dress down to cover my exposed underwear that I didn't even realize were on full display. His hands rove over me, unsure where to touch first. "Are you hurt? What happened?"

"I'm fine," I groan, flailing like an upended turtle.

"No, you're not," he growls at me. Then he looks down at my swollen ankle, clearly raging pissed as he hauls me up out of the bush like I weigh nothing. His hands are warm on my waist as he steadies me on my feet, his eyes flashing between panic and anger. "What the fuck were you doing out here?"

"Nothing," I state through clenched teeth, trying to smile like this is silly and easy-breezy. "I was just picking some flowers. At night. With my face." I touch the side of my temple and feel a wet sliver of something trickling down my face. Why do I keep meeting this guy this way?

"Christ, love, you're bleeding," he murmurs, voice low enough to be intimate but not low enough to escape my uncles' notice.

Because when I glance up, four large male silhouettes are standing on the deck staring down at us, arms crossed, eyes suspiciously fixed on the scene before them.

"Why am I always patching you up?" Wolf asks, his tone frustrated and overly familiar. Which, to my uncles, probably sounds less like *concerned coworker* and more like *I've seen you naked*.

"I'm fine," I blurt, trying to shove Wolf's hands off me. Except he doesn't let go. He brushes a leaf from my hair and mutters, "Could've broken your neck sneaking around out here. Is your ankle okay?"

He slides his hands down my legs, and I can't even bring myself to look up at the men standing above us because I know what this looks like.

Luke calls out, "Do I need to grab a first aid kit?"

"Yes," Wolf growls at the same time I say, "No!"

Wyatt grunts, eyes flicking from me to Wolf like he's connecting very obvious dots.

I'm beet-red, leaves in my hair, dirt on my knees, and very,

very busted. Wolf slides an arm firmly around my back, steadying me, and says in that maddeningly calm voice, "I'm taking her home."

I swallow the knot in my throat because he's not asking permission. And weirdly, none of my uncles or my dad objects. *What parallel universe am I in that none of them are objecting or yelling at Wolf to put me down? Or demanding to come with me to see if I'm okay?*

They're just . . . letting us *be* whatever we are? Like adults? God, this is somehow *worse* than us just confessing. Because now all of them are exchanging looks that scream, *We know you guys are a thing, and we know it's not our business.*

I don't know how to behave in front of my family without them meddling in my business. That's like . . . our whole friggin' schtick!

I guess I'm grateful they're giving us this space because I'd have to tell them all me and Wolf are not a thing. Not really. We're no labels. And explaining that to my overbearing uncles and father would be my worst nightmare.

Luckily, or unluckily, I don't have a chance to overexplain because one second, I'm protesting that I can walk, and the next, Wolf's arm slides under my legs, and he one-arm carries me as he stomps across the gravel lane like carrying my six-foot-tall body is the easiest thing in the world.

At least this time I'm awake to enjoy it.

I fight back my girlie squeal as I clutch Wolf's broad shoulders and watch my uncles and father make their way back into the house as Calder calls to Wolf's back, "We'll let Stevie finish your hand. She'll probably do better than you anyways."

I try to laugh it off, but it comes out high-pitched and unconvincing. Nobody buys it. Least of all me.

Chapter 31

Hit Up Front: *Engaging the opposition head-on, not backing down.*

Translation: *Facing your fears.*

Wolf

"Why is it every time you hurt yourself, I want to fuck the ever-loving shite out of you?" I growl into Everly's ear as I finish cleaning her wound on her bathroom counter.

Her breath hitches as she shivers while my fingers are currently gliding up her thighs and under her dress. I can smell jasmine on her skin, warm and sweet and completely mouthwatering as my thumb teases the seam of her knickers. Yup, damp, as they almost always are when she's around me.

"I don't know," she whispers, her voice shaky but teasing. "Damsel in distress turns you on, maybe?"

"I feel like the one in distress right now," I mutter, grabbing her hand and pressing it to my cock.

Her lips part as she feels the ridge of my erection through my jeans. I hiss when she brings her other hand around and undoes them quickly, staring down at me as she grips my length with her bare hands. The skin-on-skin contact drives me absolutely wild as she pumps me, rubbing her thumb over my tip, syphoning out precum like it's her job.

"What were you doing outside the cabin, really?" I stare into her blue eyes, wanting to extract the truth from her before I fuck her into submission. "Because I know you weren't picking fucking flowers."

She shoots me a sheepish smile as she stares hungrily at my lips. "I was worried about you. I just . . . I didn't want them to scare you away."

My chest heaves with that admission as I nibble the shell of her ear and down her neck. I like that she worries about me. I worry about her too. I worry about her morning, noon, and night. She consumes me. I thought fucking her would lessen my obsession, but it hasn't. It's stoked a small flame into a raging bonfire, and Christ, do I just want to burn forever with this girl.

"You might find this hard to believe, love," I say, dropping a soft kiss to her bare shoulder. "But I think your family likes me."

The corner of her mouth quirks up. "That might change now that they know."

"Know what?"

"About us. About this." She squeezes my cock harshly, and I grunt with need.

"They don't know anything."

"You were pretty obvious," she says with a laugh that I kiss right off her face, my tongue plunging between her lips with a forceful pressure.

"And you were subtle stalking me through the window?"

She bites her lip coyly. "I liked watching you squirm."

I groan at that perversion in her voice. It's raw and unfiltered, and it makes me want to come right down her throat. "I'm about to make you squirm," I murmur against her mouth, desperate to be inside her, gripping her hips and pulling her toward me.

She pushes to the edge of the counter and drops down on her bare feet, grabbing me by the waist to trade spaces with me.

"What are you doing?" I ask as she presses me back against the counter.

"Apologizing," she whispers, stroking my length and staring down at my cock while she licks her lips.

I grip her chin and force her to look at me. "Apologizing for what?"

"For being too much tonight," she replies with a little smirk and then lowers to her knees.

Her lips graze the tip of my cock before I grunt and pull her up by the shoulders, forcing her to stand in front of me. "Don't apologize for that," I state, my voice low and rough as my cock bobs between us. "Suck my cock because you want to. Not because you think you're too much. Saying you're too much is like saying I could get enough of you. I can't get enough of you."

"I feel the same." She inhales a shaky breath and glances down at my length again.

My eyes half close as I watch her for a moment, her chest rising and falling with every labored breath. Her nipples pebble through the thin fabric of her dress. I lean closer, brushing my nose against hers, letting the tension thrum between us. "What do you want, love? Say it all for me. I need to hear it."

She bites her lip, charging herself up before she looks me boldly in the eyes. "Conri—" She releases a labored breath, her lips wet from her tongue. "—I want to suck your cock."

And with that, she drops down to her knees, her ankle magically healed as she pulls me into her mouth, giving me the best blow job of my fucking life.

Everly

"Is it too personal for me to ask you what your tattoo coordinates are?" I ask Wolf as he lies stretched out on my bed. We're both naked, tangled up in the sheets, my head on his chest, his right leg exposed in all its tattooed glory.

"After what we just did in your bathroom and then your shower, I expect 'too personal' isn't really a thing anymore," he murmurs, his voice low and dripping with sex as he squeezes my ass.

I smile and drag my finger over the lone wolf on his leg that's howling at a crescent moon before dragging down to the coordinates etched at the bottom.

"It's a pitch in my neighborhood of Ballymun," he offers, his voice soft and reserved.

I glance up at him curiously. "Like a rugby field?"

He nods.

"Any particular reason you got that field inked on your skin instead of Trinity?"

He shoots me a warm, almost tender look as he pushes a strand of hair off my face. "It's the first rugby pitch I ever played on. The first time I ever remember feeling truly strong." His answer hangs in the room, thick and meaningful, and my heart squeezes at the tortured look in his eyes.

I blink up at him, my mind full of intrigue as I play with the gold chain cross around his neck. "Is that why you like coaching kids so much? Do you feel like you can help them find themselves the way you did with rugby?"

His jaw flexes as he stares down at me. "I suppose so. Childhood is such a shite time for so many. If I'd found rugby earlier . . . maybe I would have learned to regulate my emotions better. Not lost my temper so much." He drags a deep breath in, raising his chest up high as he stares up at the ceiling. "A lot of these kids I've been coaching with Fergie don't have anyone showing up for them. No one at home who cares. My parents aren't exactly uncaring, but they aren't exactly hands-on either. And on a rugby pitch, you're never alone. Even the roughest gobshite on the team still knows what it feels like to be part of a team who will support him. I want to be a part of helping a kid find that kind of support. Give them teammates to fight for, not against. Maybe if we can work with them when they're young, they won't turn into little terrors like me."

"You're not a terror," I state defensively, propping my head on my hand to see him more clearly.

"The Trinity sports therapist begged to differ," he deadpans with a grim smile.

I frown. "Did the therapist ever tell you why you got angry so much?"

Wolf inhales deeply. "She said that certain high-stress moments in rugby trigger a retaliation instinct in me that I developed through years of bullying I experienced when I was smaller. She also felt like I had some unresolved guilt for abandoning my friend Finn when I started playing, and apparently, that guilt all manifests on the pitch, where physicality is justified."

I frown at that, absorbing the truckload of information he just dropped on me in a very simple, succinct way. "Do you keep in touch with your friend Finn still?"

He shakes his head. "No, sadly. But Cliona saw him last month and said he wanted to invite me to his wedding."

"Wow, that's really great, isn't it?" I offer him a wobbly smile.

Wolf shrugs. "I suppose. I probably won't be able to go anyways."

"Why not?"

"I don't even know where I'm going to be at the time. Cliona said the wedding is close to Christmastime. I'll be in season then, hopefully."

My throat feels tight. "You hope to be back in Ireland by then though, right?"

He looks down at me, a curious look on his face. "I don't know, I guess."

I chew my lower lip as I think about that. "Well, if you're home, you should try to go. I'm not a therapist, but I think it's important to face those fears we have head-on."

His eyes narrow on me. "What are your fears, Everly Fletcher?"

My body tenses at that question, so I turn to look away from him, not sure I'm ready to unpack whatever that fear might be. I didn't have years of therapy to help me define mine so simply.

Wolf's rough fingers grip my chin as he turns me back to look at him. "Tell me."

I inhale a shaky breath and admit the truth that I've never said out loud to anyone, let alone myself. "Of spending my whole life finding other people love while never finding it for myself."

Wolf's brows pinch. "Were you in love with Hilow when you two were together?"

"No . . . I never said the words." I lift one shoulder helplessly. "Which is crazy because after two years of being with him, if I couldn't say *I love you*, he clearly wasn't the right guy for me."

"Is there a timeline in your matchmaking manifesto for when you're supposed to feel love for someone you're with?"

I scrunch my nose. "No, my rules never go that far into a relationship. Probably for good reason. Maybe I'm broken when it gets to that point, so I shouldn't be giving out advice about it."

"I don't think you're broken," Wolf says, shifting onto his side. His arm slips around my waist as he pulls my back to his chest, fingers splayed low on my stomach like he's holding me together. "Most people fake being in love. I think it's cool that you didn't."

I turn my head to look over my shoulder. "I thought I was cringe, not cool."

"You're the perfect blend of both." He presses his lips to my shoulder, which sends butterflies all through my stomach.

"Is that your official diagnosis, Dr. Reilly?"

"Yes." His hand squeezes my belly. "And my anecdote for your fears is to remind you to be . . . you. Unapologetically. Be dramatic on purpose. Be extra with intention. Be Everly Fucking Fletcher without shame because then the right kind of love will find you."

A pressure builds in my chest. I'm not sure I want to kiss him or cry. I'll probably do both.

Chapter 32

Tackle: *A tackle takes place when one or more opposition players grasp onto the ball carrier and succeed in bringing them to ground and holding them there.*

Translation: *Bicyclists are no match for Irish rugby boys.*

Everly

"Cheers to rural mountain bars!" Claire says, clinking her glass to mine.

I smile and sip my drink. "I can't believe you haven't been to the Mercantile before."

"Well, I haven't exactly been legal for long," Claire replies, and I shake my head knowingly.

"Of course. I forget you're a year younger than me."

"Yeah, I still have a year left of school. Ugh," she whines and takes another drink. "I'm so jealous you're done."

"Don't be. Real life is confusing."

"Why?"

"'Cause now I have to like . . . decide my future and shit." I splay my hands out on the bar top and drop my head onto my arm.

"Is the rescue center not a long-term gig?"

I shake my head. "No. Honestly, I always saw it as temporary. A good transition job while I got settled back home."

"Do you not want to stay on the mountain long term?"

Claire asks, sipping her drink, her brown eyes wide and curious on me.

"In my dad's cabin? God, no," I croak and grab my drink. "Don't get me wrong, I love it up there, but I want to stand on my own two feet a bit more. Find a new adventure."

"I thought that was what Dublin was all about."

"Dublin was amazing, but it was also just a holding spot. Temporary. I'm ready to put down some roots that don't have an expiration date." I bite my lip as I ponder my next move.

"Where are you thinking you want to move to? Boulder?"

I lick my lips and shrug. "Maybe Denver or somewhere outside of Denver. I'm not fully sure. And don't tell anyone, but I've been kind of browsing online for jobs, and I saw this one for a digital agency in Denver that builds apps for clients. I feel like I could learn a lot in a job like that."

Claire tilts her head curiously. "I didn't think you were a techy type of person."

"The job is for a brand strategist, so not too techy, more marketing and data. But I like that it works closely with app development because I have ideas for an app that I think could be cool to launch someday."

"What kind of ideas?" Claire blinks back at me.

"Like a way to make my matchmaking thing more commercial. I want to create an app where your friends swipe for you instead of you swiping for yourself. And if it's not your friends, you can hire a matchmaker through the app to control your profile."

Claire's brows lift. "Um, this sounds really fun."

"Right! I've just been really inspired lately because of all this prep for the auction. And I want something for myself, you know? Oh, by the way. I think you should bid on a guy named Fergie at the auction next week," I state, changing the subject swiftly.

"Fergie?" Claire's nose wrinkles.

"He's Scottish, has red shaggy hair, and is a total puppy dog rugby hottie. You two would work so well together." I gesture to Claire's whole essence and can't help but see the vibes of him and her. Something tells me Fergie loves a girl with curves.

"You had me at Scottish," she giggles and downs the last of her drink.

I wave to Judy that we'll take another round, and she delivers them with a sly smile. "I'm still not used to seeing you at legal drinking age." Judy laughs as she sets a couple more cocktails down in front of me and Claire.

"I had to grow up at some point, Judy."

"Next thing I know, it'll be Stevie sitting in that seat ordering herself a round." Judy laughs, looking at the empty stool next to me. "I feel like she's going to be a beer drinker."

I smile and nod. "Or Fireball."

Judy laughs, and then her smile falls as her eyes move past us. "Ugh, cyclists." She leans across the bar, dropping her voice low. "Some of them are decent, but most are douche bags."

I cringe and glance over my shoulder as a group of thirty-something-year-old guys walk in, decked out in tight, brightly colored bicycle shorts and weird shoes that clip into their pedals.

"It's giving Tour de Dick," Claire giggles knowingly, and I cover my own snicker before turning back to the bar. She leans in and asks, "Aren't you even at least interested in seeing what these guys are packing?"

"No," I reply, biting my lip. "I prefer rugby shorts these days."

Claire gasps. "Oh my God. You did it."

"Did what?" I ask innocently.

"You're sleeping with the Irish guy!"

"Shhhh." I shush my friend and look around to see if I know anyone here. "I don't need it broadcasted all over Jamestown.

Although I'm pretty sure my uncles already know. Shockingly, they haven't killed him."

"Tell me everything," Claire says, leaning in close. "How long?"

"Like over a month."

"So that rumor I heard about at Hilow's party wasn't just a rumor?"

"That was sort of the beginning of it all." My cheeks heat with the memories of the past several weeks, and I have to take a drink to calm myself down.

"Eeep!" Claire kicks her feet excitedly. "Are you guys serious? Is it casual? A fling? What is it?"

"We're . . . not labeling it."

Claire's jaw drops. "I'm shocked."

"Why?"

"Because you're Miss DTR. Define the relationship. Isn't that in your matchmaking manifesto?"

"This isn't a matchmaking thing."

"I know, but like . . . it's still sort of your road map to healthy relationships, right?"

"This isn't a relationship. It's just . . . sex." I frown when I say that because it feels like a lie. But is it?

"Well, okay then." Claire shoots me a smug look. "Good for you, Everly Fletcher. Entering your Irish bad boy era, and I'm here for it."

I laugh and shake my head. "I'm just trying to have fun," I reply with a thoughtful smile. "My aunt Trista told me to put myself first for a bit more, and that's what I feel like this is." I realize I'm saying this to convince myself as much as Claire. "I have a huge surprise for his birthday in two days, and I cannot wait to give it to him."

Claire's brows lift. "Special birthday presents don't sound very casual."

I wave her off. "It's a gift for me too."

"Oh my God, is it something kinky?" she squeals, pressing her hand over her lips. "Are you two into freaky stuff? I could totally see that rugby player making you do like ice-plunge foreplay, and you're all like . . . no, I want manifestation dirty talk, please!"

I burst out laughing. But before I can dish on some of the dirty details, one of the spandex boys saunters over into our space, helmet hair and all, and leans his elbow on the bar way too close to me.

"Ladies," he says with a crooked grin that gives me the ick. "How's it going?"

"Fine," I mutter, giving him absolutely zero attention.

"You two local?"

Claire gives him a once-over. "Can you even breathe in those shorts?"

I snort, but apparently, that's taken as encouragement because suddenly Lycra Guy's arm is pressed up against mine. Not creepy, exactly, but forward enough that my smile wavers.

"We're just having a girls' night," I say, scooting closer to Claire. He moves with me and drapes his arm on the back of my stool, bathing me in his sweaty body odor and acting way too familiar.

"Let me buy you a drink," Helmet Hair insists as he reaches for my glass and brings it to his nose to smell. "What are you having?"

"Please don't touch my drink," I state firmly and then inhale sharply when he moves his hand to my lower back. It's a light touch, casual, but my whole body goes rigid. I open my mouth to say something, but I don't get a chance.

Because he's gone.

Correction.

He's *flying backward*, pulled away from me by a six-foot-five Irish rugby player with a penchant for red cards.

"Get your fucking hands off her," Wolf snarls, his accent slicing through the Mercantile like thunder. He looks like a storm in his black athletic shirt and shorts, ink rippling under his muscles, jaw tight, eyes blazing. He's a fucking masterpiece.

"What the hell?" The biker guy scrambles to regain his balance, but Wolf is already in his face, shoving him hard enough to back him toward the door.

"You touch her again, and you'll be picking your teeth out of the floorboards," Wolf growls.

The other cyclists then rush over, standing between Wolf and their friend.

Claire takes a big sip of her drink, like she's enjoying the show. "Everly, your boyfriend's about to fight a bunch of dudes in spandex. This is better than Pornhub!"

"He's not my—" I start, but it's drowned out by the *crash* of Wolf slamming one of the guys into the wall.

Judy comes barreling out from behind the bar with murder in her eyes. "Hey!" she barks, hands on her hips. "Any of you lay one more finger on anybody, I'm calling the cops!"

Wolf's shoulders rise and fall as his chest heaves while he glares at the bikers, who are all scrambling out the door and struggling to clip into their bikes.

Judy turns and thrusts a finger in my direction. "Get him out of here, Everly. Now."

I scramble off my stool, calling over my shoulder to Claire to sit tight while I deal with this. I don't know what I'm even dealing with, but whatever it is, I guess it's mine.

I wrap my hands around Wolf's large, hard-as-stone arm and yank him out the same door the bikers vacated, grateful to see they're all buzzing down the highway by the time we get out there.

The sun is setting behind the mountain, casting a large shadow on the Mercantile parking lot, where I'm standing with my rugby player, staring at him as I struggle to find the words to describe what just happened.

"Are you okay?" Wolf asks, scanning me up and down like he's making sure every piece of me is still intact.

"I'm fine," I exclaim, my heart spinning like a bicycle wheel in my chest. "What was that?"

"That guy was all over you," Wolf bites back at me, his square jaw ticking angrily.

"I was handling it . . . I thought." I glance back at the bar, trying to replay my actions in my mind.

"You weren't handling it very well," Wolf mutters through clenched teeth, his eyes dark and scary on me when he adds, "He touched your fucking drink."

"I wasn't going to drink it after that," I state defensively. "I'm not a total idiot."

He grumbles under his breath as he rakes a frustrated hand through his hair, his posture hunched and irritable.

"Where did you come from?" I ask, looking up the mountain.

"I was outside," he replies, wincing slightly.

"Doing what?"

He sighs heavily. "I was watching you."

"Why?" I blink back at him.

He growls again and begins pacing in the parking lot, shaking his arms out like he's preparing for a big workout or something. "Because it's what I do, Everly. It's what I've always done with you. I've been watching you since Trinity. Every stupid matchmaking session you ran, I showed up, and I followed you home."

"What?" I ask, my brain struggling to understand any of this. Wolf barely acknowledged my existence back then. And I would have noticed if he came to all those events . . . right? "Why would you do that?"

"Because you are painfully ignorant of how fucking beautiful you are." His voice is desperate and unhinged, his eyes haunted and boring into me like he's revealing something monumental to me. "You didn't even notice at your first event that a guy was trying to fuck with your drink."

"At Mulligans?"

"Yes."

I jerk back at that. "Well, why didn't you call the cops?"

"I don't know," he bites back. "Because I didn't have proof. It was just a feeling. I didn't like how he looked at you."

"How did he look at me?" I ask as my mind spins with this information, trying to recall what guy he's referring to. I don't know if that's even what I should be focusing on right now. I should probably be more curious as to why Wolf cared so much he followed me home for four years, but I'm just processing things as best I can right now.

"He looked at you like if he found you in a dark alley, he wouldn't care about consent," Wolf thunders, his entire body radiating rage.

"That's awful." My chin wobbles as fear slices through me. "But what about you?"

"What about me?" he pulls back, looking hurt.

"Weren't you also lurking in a dark alley when I was walking home from the pub?" I ask, heat flooding my cheeks as I picture what he's telling me.

He sighs heavily, a look of defeat marring his handsome, brooding features. "Yes, I was. And I get it. It's fucked-up. And it's fucked-up that I kept doing it. I didn't trust half the lads circling you. Not for a second."

"So, you were concerned?" I state, needing to test that word out.

"Yes," he growls, his nostrils flaring. "I needed to watch out for you."

"Okay." I swallow the knot in my throat. "Why didn't you just talk to me? Walk *with* me?"

"I didn't need to," he replies curtly. "I just needed to see you safe inside the Rubrics. Once you were in there, I could breathe again."

My mind reels with this strange information. *He needed me safely home so he could breathe again*. Holy shit. Firstly, how was I so oblivious, and secondly, what does that mean? "You followed me home since first year?"

"Yes."

"And then I was just randomly paired with your sister?"

His face twitches. "That wasn't totally random."

"What do you mean?" I ask, not sure I want to know the answer.

"I know a guy who works in housing. When my sister had to be moved because of her teammate, I called in a favor for her to live in your building. Figured then I could look out for both of you a bit easier. I didn't know they'd match you together. That was destiny's sick fucking joke, I guess."

"Holy shit, Conri," I croak, my body shivering as goose bumps erupt over my skin. "My mind is . . . blown."

"I know. I'm sick."

"Yes," I confirm and then take a step toward him to say the words right to his face. "You're a stalker."

"I know." He looks down, unable to meet my eyes as he says, "There's more."

"More?" I bellow, my blood pressure spiking. "I don't know if I can handle more."

"That guy you took to the ball who wrote a shitty Instagram post about you?"

"Yeah?"

He inhales deeply. "He got his phone smashed at the pub the next day."

"How do you . . ." Realization dawns on me. "That was *you*? I thought it was Cliona, but she wouldn't admit it!"

Wolf's mouth is tight and unapologetic. "Cliona made me promise not to touch him, but online bullies deserve worse if you ask me."

I open my mouth to say something back, but I don't know what I'd even say. My best friend's brother followed me home for four years and then broke some guy's phone who spoke poorly about me on the internet. What does any of this even mean? Four years. Four years of me walking into Mulligans with my furry notebook—and Wolf was there? Every time?

"Why did you do it?" I ask, my brain short-circuiting as I continue to process.

"To protect you."

"Okay, but why did you care so much?"

"I don't fucking know," he cries, his voice strained. "Because I'm *too much* as well, I guess." He lifts his hands in surrender. "I can't explain it, but I am sorry for not telling you sooner. I know it's fucked-up, and I don't blame you for ending whatever this is between us. I can even resign from the rescue center as well if you don't feel safe. Fuck, I'll go back to Dublin, and you never have to—"

"Stop talking," I say firmly, looking at Wolf hard in the eyes as my chest feels like it's going to explode. Half of me wants to scream and tell him he should kick rocks because what kind of normal person does that? It's creepy, Lifetime movie vibes for sure. My family would have a field day with this one.

But the other half of me . . . the stupid, reckless, possibly insane half . . . feels . . . touched? Like maybe I wasn't as invisible as I thought all four of those years at Trinity. Like maybe someone saw me when I was at my loneliest and decided I was worth looking out for?

The matchmaker in me wants to catalog it as some grand gesture, a fairy-tale moment that ends in happily ever after.

The girl in me . . . the one who secretly fears she'll never be someone's choice . . . wants to believe Wolf's been choosing me all along.

The most terrifying thought of all though . . . the one I'm a little scared to say out loud . . . is that there's something *erotic* about knowing he was there. Watching. Waiting. Protecting.

Holy shit.

"This is . . . easily the craziest, most fucked-up thing anyone has ever done for me." For me? Is it *for* me? Or *to* me?

"I know," he says, eyes cast downward.

"It's also . . . hot," I blurt out, laying all my cards on the table.

His head snaps up. "What?"

"It's . . . kind of hot." My skin prickles as an ache blooms between my legs that I am desperately trying to ignore. "Maybe that makes me crazy too, but all I'm hearing is that you saw me in a way I've never felt seen before."

Wolf leans in closer, his voice dropping. "I've always seen you, Everly."

I inhale a shaky breath as the air between us goes molten. My eyes sting with something that I can't quite name. "I see you too, Conri."

Suddenly, I can't remember why I'm supposed to be mad. This man, *even when he was still a boy*, saw me and made sure I was safe. That is such a contrast to how I thought he viewed me.

I just needed to see you safe inside the Rubrics. Once you were in there, I could breathe again.

It's the sort of thing I'd expect from my dad or my uncles. Always defending me. Always worried about me. Always feeling responsible.

But this . . . from Wolf . . . it feels bigger, more meaningful. More telling in ways I'm not sure how to process. All I can think about is him, inches away, that scent of his drawing me in like a moth to a flame.

We stare at each other for a long, unending moment before I say, "I want you to show me."

"Show you what?" he asks, his eyes brutal as they flick back and forth between mine.

"Show me what you looked like when you followed me home." My breath stutters as heat coils low in my belly. "I need to see it with my own eyes."

Wolf jerks away from me, his head shaking side to side. "No, Everly, this is sick. I'm sick."

"It's not sick. It's . . . I'm . . ." My voice falters. What I'm about to say feels absolutely batshit, but I just can't help myself. *"I'm turned on."*

Chapter 33

Dummy Runner: *An offensive tactic where a player on the attacking team runs toward the opposition as if running onto a pass, only for the ball to be passed to another player.*

Translation: *Cat and Mouse.*

Wolf

It's quiet in Everly's SUV after I've dropped Claire off back in Boulder. Both she and Everly had been drinking, so neither was in any condition to drive themselves anywhere.

I'm glad I showed up when I did.

The truth is, I'd been there for a while.

I didn't expect to feel so on edge when Everly told me she was going out with Claire tonight. In fact, I thought it would be good for her to go see her friend. We both need to come up for air and touch some grass. Figure out what the fuck we're doing because somewhere along the way, things between us have started to feel a lot less casual on Fletcher Mountain.

But as the sun went down, I felt myself growing more and more anxious. I started thinking about those nights at Trinity when she would run the dating clinics and how loads of guys would be there, surrounding her. Taking advantage of her kindness.

So . . . I decided to just go down the hill and grab some groceries. Maybe I'd stop by and say hello to her mate. Keep it casual. Keep it light. But before I even hit the car park, I saw the group of cyclists whizzing down the highway, parking their bikes in that cocky way that agitates me.

When you grow up being bullied a lot of your life, you can spot a bully quite easily. And those guys reeked of entitlement.

So, I watched them through the window. I positioned myself outside the pub, saw Everly and Claire at the bar talking to Judy, and told myself they would be fine. They didn't need me.

Until he touched Everly. My Everly.

The only word that came out of my mouth at the time was *"Mine."*

The rest is a bit of a blur, and it all ended in a way I never would have seen coming. Not for a million years.

I glance over at Everly as she stares out the window with a thoughtful look on her face. I wonder if she's regretting what she said to me earlier. Maybe it was the booze talking or the heightened emotions after the fight.

"Can I ask how many drinks you had tonight?"

Her head snaps to me. "I'm not drunk if that's what you mean," she replies defensively. "I had two drinks. Barely. Didn't finish the last one."

"Are you certain?" I ask, my brows furrowed. "Because I need to know if you meant what you said outside the Mercantile. I wouldn't mind if you wanted to take it back. It's not something—"

"I meant it," she says, cutting me off and releasing a heavy breath in the quiet of her car. "I want to experience the feeling of you following me in the dark." Her voice is low and husky, and I can't help but clock the way she's running her palms over her thighs. Like she's struggling with her own arousal as she adds softly, "Like if I go for a walk by the creek behind my cabin . . . I want to know what it would feel like to have you follow me or watch me . . ." She clears her throat. "Maybe even chase me."

Heat instantly crawls up my spine, my chest tight with a mixture of desire and restraint. "I think you're describing primal play, Everly."

She swallows thickly, her tongue darting out to wet her lips. "Maybe I am. Maybe that's my thing."

"Fuck," I groan, looking away from her as my cock thickens in my jeans. My girl doesn't do anything half-arsed. "You're playing with fire again, love."

Her lips twitch into a small smile. "Then turn me to ash, Conri."

The moon is a sliver tonight, pouring just a tiny glow over the creek that winds behind Everly's cabin. The air is heavy and still, the kind of balmy summer night that makes your skin feel damp.

I move quietly through the trees, trying not to step on any sticks, my breath slow and steady.

Everly's short blonde hair glows in the darkness, like a siren calling me in as I slowly make my way closer to her.

I'm rock fucking hard.

I have been since the moment she said, "Give me a twenty-second head start," and took off behind her house and up along the winding creek, well out of eyeline from any of the cabins.

I can see the faint sway of her white dress where the water catches it in flashes. Everly Fletcher, wandering in the woods at night like she hasn't a care in the world, is a fucking fantasy that I've lost sleep over.

Except now she knows I'm here, and she welcomes it.

It's a dangerous thing, being wanted for the most secret parts of yourself. But apparently, she's just as dark as me because this is all her idea. She wants me to follow her, catch her, and take her right here in the woods. *Christ.*

Her laugh drifts back through the trees, low and taunting, and it makes every muscle in my body snap tight. She knows I'm close. She's daring me to find her, but I like to watch.

I've learned a lot about this woman watching her all these years. She hides her loneliness by staying busy—always matchmaking, always helping—but when I'd watch her closely, I noticed she'd often seem like the odd one out in her own story. She'd be surrounded by people, yet sometimes she'd linger at the edge of a group like she didn't quite believe she belonged. I hated watching that, yet I liked it too. I liked that I could see beyond that glossy, sunshiny persona she displayed for everyone else.

I kept tabs on her, not just because I was worried about her, but because I yearned to see those little shadows she thought she was hiding. Those were my favorite parts.

As I've watched her these past several weeks on Fletcher Mountain, those dark spots are brighter now. She's more confident in her own skin. It's what made her even more impossible to resist. She's finally just being herself.

Branches whip at my forearms as I push through the brush, keeping my eyes locked on every rustle of her dress. She moves slowly, meandering along the water, not really trying to escape. No—she wants me to prowl after her in the dark like a starving animal hunting for a meal.

She pauses for a beat, maybe to see if she can feel where I am. Or maybe she's just teasing me with her silence. My cock aches at the thought of her glancing over her shoulder, knowing I'm somewhere out here, stalking her every move. I bet her nipples are hard under that wisp of a dress.

I step behind a tree and eye her bare legs under the moonlight, her dress riding high as she climbs up onto a boulder. She's breathing harder now, but still smiling, still tempting me like the wicked little siren she is. And all I can think is how much longer I'll let her play before I pin her against the rough bark of this tree and remind her exactly who's hunting whom.

She steps onto the shallow rock bed in the water, kicking her toes in the cool spring, and tilts herself just enough to show me the silhouette of her luscious curves.

Christ, she's good at this game.

I grip the tree, my fingers digging into the bark so much I feel a sliver lodge itself behind my nail. My breath catches when she pulls a strap of her dress down off her shoulder and then the other one, exposing her full, succulent breasts to me in a way that makes my cock throb.

A twig snaps under my boot, and her shoulders stiffen. "Who's there?" she gasps, role-playing to utter perfection.

Any bloke who would ever think this girl is too much doesn't deserve to live.

My blood heats with a familiar hot rush that I got every time I followed her home from Mulligans. If I'm being honest with myself, I was turned on then too. I did it for her protection, but the longer I did it without her knowing, the more I morphed into the beast I couldn't control. This hungry, feral beast that wanted to be fed.

I wanted to be caught. I wanted her to know I was there.

And in my fantasy . . . she wanted to be hunted.

She wanted to be mine.

Just like now.

"You lost, love?" My voice comes out low and rough, my arousal completely taking over.

Her hands reach up to cup her breasts, but she doesn't turn around. "No," she says softly, fingers sliding over her nipples. "But I think someone's following me."

My pulse kicks hard as I stalk closer, slow, deliberate, my boots loud in the quiet of night. She exhales like she's been holding her breath for me, and I can almost smell her arousal from here.

Christ, I bet she's dripping down her thighs.

"Maybe you should run," I murmur, sucking in a deep breath to prepare myself to chase if she takes off.

She turns around to face me, dropping her hands to show me her perfect teardrop breasts. My mouth waters at the sight of them. Of her. Of every square inch of her lush body.

"Maybe I want to be caught," she croaks, her voice as breathy as mine as her hard nipples point directly at me.

My control snaps, and in a flash, she's in my arms, legs wrapped tight around my waist, my hands roughly palming her breasts and ass as I feast on her lips like an animal eating its first kill of the season. The heat of her sex grinds against my cock, which is straining hard in my jeans. I carefully march us away from the creek to a nearby grassy area, and she cries out when I lay her down and reach between her legs to rip her soaked panties off her body.

She's feral as she opens my jeans and grips my cock with so much pressure I can't help but roar and thrust into her chest. She releases me to pull my weight down on top of her, nails digging into my back as my bare cock rubs between her folds.

"No condom," she rasps, her hand reaching down and positioning me at her opening. "I'm on the pill."

I die a little inside, muttering obscenities in Irish, but waste no time before thrusting into her, hard, fast, and deliciously bare.

"Fuck," I groan into her neck, my entire body vibrating with stimulation overload and feelings I can't even begin to understand. "Fuck, Everly, you feel so good."

"Yes, Conri," she cries, raking her nails down my back as her lips brush my jaw. "I'm going to come already. Oh my God."

She's wild and uncontrolled as I thrust in and out of her,

feeling her first climax grip me suddenly as I struggle to fight my own off. I want this to last. I want to remember this experience forever. I want to be with Everly forever.

Except I shouldn't want her forever. She's not mine to want.

She arches into me, and I growl low, throat tight. She's undoing me. I should pull back. Slow things down. Keep it safe. Distant. Watching from a distance kept me free. Stalking her kept me safe.

But I catch her eyes and see that same fire, that same hunger, that same crazy, desperate need to feel seen mirroring me back, and it has me undone. I've kept so much locked away. Anger, guilt, shame, insecurity . . . she's broken through all of that, and I let her. I welcomed it.

Maybe that makes me crazy too, but all I'm hearing is that you saw me in a way I've never felt seen before . . . I see you too, Conri.

The world outside disappears, and all that exists is her. Her scent, her laugh, the way she bites her lip when she wants me to kiss her. The way she makes me see the world in full color.

And when she shivers under me and holds me close as I release myself inside of her, giving her the very last bits of me that I've never given anyone, I know there's no turning back now.

And God help me, I don't think I want to.

Chapter 34

Blindside: *A blindside tackle happens when someone gets hit from an angle they didn't see coming. Figuratively, it's used to describe being caught off guard or surprised.*

Translation: *Birthday surprise incoming!*

Everly

The smirk I'm smirking as I watch Wolf feed the animals at Mount Millie is honestly disgusting. But we've been like this for the past two days. Unable to stop the smirking.

And it's because we're apparently both little freaks.

Stalking play. Primal play. Two phrases I'd never heard in my life until I did a little Google research after the most ridiculous set of orgasms of my life. In the woods. Behind my cabin.

I pray that whatever insane noises I made that night sounded like wild animals because the idea of my family hearing me like that is something that keeps me up at night if I think too much about it.

But damn, it was good.

Not something I need to do on a regular basis. But it was fun to experiment with.

To think I went from zero orgasms in my whole life to three orgasms in one sex scene with Wolf . . . that says a lot. That man gets me. He gets every little dirty part of me. And apparently, I get him too.

When we laid in bed and discussed our endeavors of that

evening, I felt so free and open. Like a butterfly emerging from its cocoon. And I felt terrible knowing that Wolf was so worried sick about revealing his habit of following me home at Trinity.

But honestly, maybe it's good he waited to tell me. Knowing his intense history with bullying and his strained friendship with Finn, I can understand why he felt called to look out for me.

Deep down, Wolf is a protector. He cares so much about people, maybe even to a fault. And doing it silently meant he didn't have to be vulnerable and tell me he cared.

Call me crazy, but I felt touched. He's the too-much, masculine version of me, and I'd be a hypocrite for not offering any type of understanding of that.

I feel closer to him than ever. So close that I am bursting with anticipation to give him his gift today. I can't wait to see his reaction.

"It's really sad to have to muck out pens on your birthday," I say with a heavy sigh, leaning on the gate with my arms crossed as I watch the hot, tall Irish boy I'm currently sleeping with work.

He shoots me a look over his shoulder, sweat beading at his temple. "You know, a good gift would be you coming in here and helping me."

I grin. "You said a birthday is just another day."

He huffs out a laugh, straightening up and leaning on the pitchfork. "I take it back. I love my birthday and would love some assistance, especially from you."

His eyes move up and down my body, so I offer, "If you beg nicely enough, maybe I'll see if Trista can give you the afternoon off."

He licks his lips, that dangerous little smirk tugging at his mouth. "If I'm begging on my knees, love, getting me time off won't be the first thing on your mind."

My cheeks heat instantly as I picture him on his knees for

me, but our little flirting session is interrupted by a phone call. Wolf pulls his phone out of his pocket and gets a curious look on his face before he answers the call. I walk over to where Stevie is positioned on her coloring table outside of the pen to give him some privacy.

He literally moves her coloring table from pen to pen so she can stay near him as he works. It's fucking adorable.

"I don't like how you talk to Nana," Stevie says, wrinkling her nose at me.

"How do I talk to him?" I ask, squatting down to eye her curiously.

She scowls at me. "Like you love him. Yuck."

I bark out a laugh and then hear Wolf say, "Are you serious, Coach?"

The tone of his voice snags my attention. It's sharp. Awake. Hopeful. Curious, I turn my head to see him pacing the edge of the pen, jaw tight, his massive frame wound with so much energy I can practically feel the air buzzing around him.

"No, I'm still training. Still fit. Denver's been good for me," he says into the phone, his accent thickening like it does when he talks to his sister. "Leinster? They're actually asking?"

My stomach dips.

Stevie holds up a drawing of a purple cow with four legs on one side of its body and none on the other, but I can't even force myself to smile. Because I already know, whatever's being said on the other end of that phone—it's not just a call. It's *the* call. A door opening.

And Wolf looks ready to run through it.

Wolf's pacing slows, but his voice doesn't lose that edge of barely contained adrenaline. "No offer from the Grizzlies yet . . . Okay . . . Yeah, I'll send over fitness and strength testing data, no problem. Of course I can take a meeting. I appreciate the call, Coach. Truly. Thank you. For everything."

He hangs up, shoving his phone into his pocket, and for the first time since he arrived here earlier this summer, Wolf looks lighter. Like his shoulders aren't carrying a mountain. Like he could run laps along the creek without breaking a sweat.

"What's going on?" I ask, pitching my voice to be bright and cheery. It's the voice I've perfected over the years of matchmaking everyone but myself.

His eyes are gleaming when they land on me. "Leinster had an injury to their number eight. They're lookin' for cover. My old coach thinks I might be in the running. It's . . . Jaysus, Everly, it's a chance I wasn't sure I'd ever actually get."

I clap my hands together, plastering on the biggest smile I can manage. "Wolf, that's amazing. I'm so happy for you!"

And I mean it—I do. My chest is full of warmth for him, seeing him so alive, so hopeful. This is what he's been working toward. He and his sister. He deserves this.

And I deserve . . . to not be a factor in any of it.

This was the agreement. A summer fling. A no-label label. He's obviously bursting with happiness, and I should be too.

But a sickness churns in my gut over the reality of it. Wolf going back to Dublin. Summer coming to an end. Of course he should go back. That's the goal. Not me. Not us. Not this bubble we're living in here.

I lean down to admire Stevie's lopsided cow, forcing a little laugh. "Look at this masterpiece," I croon, like my insides aren't twisting.

But I can still feel Wolf's eyes on me, can feel the pulse of his happiness echoing in my bones. And it hurts so much worse knowing how much I'm faking this.

"I need to call Cliona," Wolf says, shoving a trembling hand through his hair.

"That's going to need to wait, I'm afraid," Trista says, interrupting our moment as she strides down the aisle of the barn.

"I know it's your birthday today, but we have a new rescue coming in right now, and I'm sorry to inform you that it's another alpaca."

"Fuck." Wolf's face falls, dread overtaking his joyous mood instantly. He looks like how I feel as he says, "I know this isn't a kind thing to say, but I'm starting to understand why so many people abandon their alpacas. Alpacas are arseholes."

"Bad words," Stevie says from her coloring table near the pen Wolf is working at.

"Wyatt is bringing it up now, so if you could help him out when he gets here, that would be great," Trista says, turning to head back toward the feed room.

Wolf's brows furrow. "Why is Wyatt bringing the alpaca?"

I shrug and steel myself to shake off my mood as I casually reply, "No clue."

When my uncle's truck pulls up with his construction trailer, Wolf frowns curiously as he walks out to greet Wyatt, Calder, and Luke, who all pile out of the four-door truck.

"This one is a fucking wild one," Calder says, grabbing the handle on the trailer.

"You guys put it in your nice work rig? It's probably shitting all over in there," Wolf says, bracing himself outside the door.

"It's definitely full of shit," I murmur as I walk outside to join them, along with Trista and Stevie. Trista and Luke both wink knowingly at me.

Calder grunts, the door creaking open slowly, and when nothing moves inside, Wolf grows serious as he takes a step closer to peer inside.

"Surprise!" Cliona's voice peals loudly as she leaps out of the trailer and tackles her brother with all the athleticism of a professional rugby player.

Because she is.

"What the fuck?" Wolf exclaims, his voice hitting a high

pitch I've never heard before. "Cliona?" he asks, scrubbing his hand over his face as he rolls over to jump back up on his feet.

"Happy birthday, Moon!" she says, giving him a hard shove.

"Cliona . . . you're here. My sister is here," he says, his voice sounding almost childlike with shock, similar to his phone voice with his coach moments ago. He embraces her in a hard, bruising hug, and I watch the bond between them practically glow before my very eyes.

He buries his face in her shoulder, hiding his emotions, and when I spot the tears streaming down Cliona's face, I can't help but follow suit.

My throat burns as I press the back of my hand to my mouth, watching the two of them cling to each other like lifelines.

Seeing them reunited is beautiful and gutting.

Because this—this reunion—isn't just a hug. It's a reminder. A promise. A tether pulling him back across the ocean where he belongs. With her. With his family. With the team that he deserves to play for.

And what am I in all of this? A summer temptation. A temporary distraction that happened to fit between the cracks of his real life.

The ache grows sharper as I watch Cliona whisper something against his ear, his hand fisting in the back of her jacket like he'll never let go again. And I know—God, I know—he won't. He'll go back to Dublin. He'll pick up the pieces of everything he thinks he broke, everything he's convinced he abandoned. And he should. He deserves that healing.

But where does that leave me?

The tears blur my vision until the mountain and even Wolf's broad shoulders all blur into one hazy smear. I bite my lip hard enough to taste blood, desperate to keep the sob building in my chest from clawing free.

Because the truth is, I've finally found the thing I've been chasing for everyone else my whole damn life—a love so big it terrifies me. And it's already slipping through my fingers.

I sniff loudly, and Trista smiles and comes over to put her arm around me. "You did good, kid," she whispers, giving me a squeeze.

Wolf and Cliona break apart, marveling over each other. "I can't believe you're here."

"I didn't have much of a choice with this one," Cliona says, pointing at me. "She was about ready to call my coach to request a day off for me."

Wolf turns to look at me, his eyes red-rimmed and tear-streaked. "You did this?" he asks softly, intimately, like we're lying in bed together and not standing in front of most of my family.

I shrug. "I couldn't think of anything to give you, so I went with the obvious—"

My voice is cut off when Wolf eliminates the space between us and grabs my face, pressing his lips to mine in a shocking, jaw-dropping, heart-exploding, mind-boggling, earth-shattering stunner of a kiss.

Holy shit, Wolf is kissing me in front of everyone.

And holy shit, I'm letting him.

Because I don't know how many more of these I'm going to get.

Faintly, I hear a "yuck" from Stevie, and Wolf then finally pulls back, moving his hands from my face to my waist, holding me close like a flower he's not done smelling.

Cliona's voice breaks our little bubble when she says, "Well, that's one way to tell me you're shagging my brother."

I cover my mouth and turn to look at my friend. "Cliona, I'm so sorry, I—"

"Would you shut up and give me a hug?" she says, propping her hands on her hips. "I flew across a bleedin' ocean for you too, you know."

My face crumples as I close the distance between us and hug my friend. My dear friend who just months ago I spent every single day with and now haven't seen for weeks. My dear friend whose brother I'm now kissing in front of everyone, apparently. My dear friend who I can't tell that I've fallen in love with her brother . . .

Because that would ruin everything for everyone but me.

And that's not what I do.

Chapter 35

High Tackle: *When the tackler grasps the ball carrier above the line of the shoulders, most commonly around the neck or at the line of the chin and jaw. A high tackle is potentially dangerous and results in a yellow or red card.*

Translation: *A high tackle might be better than three mountain men.*

Wolf

I can't wipe the smile off my face as I watch Everly take my sister upstairs to my apartment to introduce her to Rugby, our dragon.

Our dragon.

More and more, I love the sound of that.

And I like the feeling of my sister seeing this life Everly and I have built over here. It feels meaningful and important, and I'm not sure Everly feels the same way or if this was just a fun birthday surprise and nothing more.

I ponder those thoughts as I muck the pens out in the barn below so we can prepare for a night out. Weeks ago, I would have been anxious and nervous about what my sister thought of me kissing her best friend—now, I just don't care.

She's become too important to me to prioritize anyone else. Even my twin. Which is exactly why I impulsively kissed her in front of her family.

I couldn't help myself.

The gift she gave me of surprising me with my sister in this moment . . . it couldn't have been more perfect. More right.

All is right in the world . . .

Until I push the wheelbarrow outside to dump it behind the barn, only to be stopped in my tracks by three brooding, scowling, angry-looking mountain men standing there waiting for me, like a bloody firing squad.

Calder's got his arms folded as he leans against the red barn. Wyatt's holding an axe eerily like a murder weapon, and Luke . . . Christ, Luke has a mug of coffee in his hands like this is a casual Tuesday afternoon and not an ambush.

I stand to my full height and pull my gloves off as I point to the pile of manure behind them. "Is this where you're planning to hide my body?"

Calder smiles. Wyatt scowls. Luke looks back at the mess like the idea just occurred to him.

Wyatt tips his chin toward me. "You have something to tell us, Wolf?"

I clear my throat and shrug. "If this is about the kiss—"

"It is," Luke interrupts, taking a long sip of coffee like he's got all day.

"Right." I plant my hands on my hips and force myself to meet their stares. I'm not about to shrink under their scrutiny. Their niece is an adult and can make her own mind up about who she spends time with. But perhaps I didn't need to shove it in all their faces without talking to her first, so a little humility here is probably in order. "I'm sorry for all of that down there . . . I guess I was just overwhelmed in the moment."

Calder barks out a laugh. "Overwhelmed? So, it meant nothing?"

"No." My brows furrow defensively.

"So, it meant something?" Luke asks, pinning me with a look.

"Yes . . . and no. Yes," I stammer, unsure how to answer that.

"What is it, then?" Wyatt bites, looking unimpressed by my wavering answers. "Because we all assumed something was going on after we saw you two at poker night, but we let you live because her dad was there, and Cozy threatened him with bodily harm if we did anything bad to you that night. Now you're just grabbing our niece right in front of us like she *belongs* to you or something."

"She does belong to me," I reply, my jaw tight.

All three of their eyes narrow, and I swear one of them growls.

"Come again?" Wyatt takes a step toward me, and my eyes flash down to his knuckles as they turn white around the axe handle.

"She . . ." I struggle to find the words but tip my chin up to feign confidence. "She's important to me."

Wyatt pauses, waiting for me to continue.

"She has been for a long time," I reply honestly, stating the words I have barely even said to myself. I feel a heat spread in my chest as I flash back to the past four years. It's like she's always been a part of me in some way or another. And now that I'm a part of her too, I refuse to be scared off. "I looked out for her at Trinity when she had no one, and I guess I'm doing the same thing here. I won't apologize for caring about her."

"Explain," Wyatt says, looking positively murderous.

I swallow the knot in my throat. "I just made sure she got home when she was out at night. That's it, I swear."

"Hmm," Luke huffs, his eyes introspective and giving me absolutely no indication if that's a good *hmm* or a bad *hmm*.

Calder tilts his head curiously. "So, what exactly are your intentions with our niece, then?"

That question brings me pause because a lot has gone down today. I got a call from my coach that an Irish team might want me, my sister showed up unexpectedly, and I kissed my girl in front of her whole family.

There are a lot of unknown variables at play here, which means I should dodge this question. Laugh it off or mutter something generic. That would be the smart thing to do. But the words don't come out that way. Instead, the truth slips loose before I can stop it.

"I'm trying not to fall in love with her, if you really want to know. And I'm doing a shite job of it."

All three pairs of eyes bore into me, and I hear Millie bleat from back inside the barn like she's eavesdropping on this whole conversation.

Wyatt shifts his axe, his jaw working. Calder studies me like he's weighing every word. Luke just lets out a low whistle.

"You sure about that?" Calder asks finally.

"Sure about what?"

"Falling for our niece. Girl's got a big heart for everyone else, but she keeps her own locked up pretty tight."

"I'm aware," I admit, and my chest tightens with fear because I don't even know where Everly's head is at with all of this either. I shrug helplessly. "Unfortunately, I'm not sure I have a choice in the matter. Just like that poker night with you guys, I'm all in, I think."

The silence stretches again. Then Calder finally cracks a grin. "Well, Wyatt, maybe you don't need your axe after all."

Luke chuckles, raising his coffee in a mock toast. "Been in a similar situation myself, and I can't say I have any good advice for you. Sorry, Rugby, but I do wish you luck."

"Thanks," I murmur and grip the back of my neck.

Wyatt still doesn't smile, but the edge in his stare softens just enough that I don't feel like I'm about to be chopped up into little pieces and buried under the goat shite. So at least I have that going for me.

They make their way past me, patting me on the back as they go like it's just a normal day on Fletcher Mountain. I exhale, shoulders loosening. I came down here to muck out stalls, but I think I mucked out some of my soul instead.

Everly

"Oh my God, he's huge!" Cliona squeals as she stares into the cage of our bearded dragon, Rugby.

"Do you want to hold him?" I ask, opening the top and reaching inside.

"No, I do not. Not even a little bit. In fact, I don't even want to be in the same room as him. I'm freaked-out!" She takes a large step back. "Fletcher, please tell me you don't have any lizards in your cabin where I'm sleeping tonight, or I'm going to go sleep in a stable down at Mount Millie."

I laugh and shake my head. "My cabin is animal-free."

Cliona's brows lift. "Except for my brother, apparently."

I glance toward the steps, where Wolf is currently downstairs, finishing the chores up so we can have a night out tonight for their birthday. "Are you mad?"

"No, I'm not mad," she replies with a laugh. "I'm a bit shocked, I guess. I didn't think you fancied him, but seeing you two together earlier, I don't know how I didn't see this before."

I frown at that. "Oh, it's not serious."

"What?"

"Me and Wolf . . . we're just . . . hanging out."

"Hanging out? What the fuck does that mean?" Cliona crosses her arms over her chest and watches me thoughtfully.

"I mean . . . we don't have a label. Like, we're not officially together or anything."

She hooks her thumb toward the window. "He snogged you pretty officially in front of your family a few moments ago."

An awkward laugh works its way up my throat. "I know,

but I think that was just him being so happy to see you. It was a big surprise, you know? He was grateful. But like . . . we're not making this a big thing. I know he wants to end up back in Ireland." I state the last part and look away, trying not to spill the beans about Wolf's big news to his sister because I'm sure he wants to be the one to tell her.

Cliona licks her lips and nods. "So, it's the distance you're worried about?"

"Um . . . yes and no. I just . . . I just know he doesn't see me like that." I force a laugh, but it sounds cracked.

"Like what?" Cliona asks, her eyes grave on me.

"Like a long-term thing." I shrug and try to smile through it, but the ache in my throat is severe. "He's told me before he's not a happily-ever-after type of guy, and that's kind of my whole identity. We are far too different."

This is the pep talk I need to get through the rest of this summer. Maybe that call from his coach came at just the right time. I was getting carried away. Forgetting who Wolf is. Who I am. He's not happily ever after. And I really only know how to help others with happily ever after.

"That's rubbish," she bites back at me, looking defensive.

"It's not rubbish. It's reality," I bite back, shoving my hands in my pockets. I love Cliona, but she doesn't know the full story yet, and when she does, she'll realize that this thing between me and Wolf can't be serious.

"Sorry to be blunt, but this thing between us is just sex, and that's okay. That's what I needed for the summer."

"What about what he needed?" Cliona asks, her brows pinched with concern.

"He needs to focus on rugby, and I know you can attest to that," I snipe, feeling my throat close with emotion that I've been doing a damn good job of hiding up until now. "I know he's your brother, so you want to defend him, but he's still figuring himself out, and I think I'm doing the same. I'm a matchmaker, and I know without a doubt that me and Wolf in a real relationship would be a horrible idea."

Cliona's head jerks at a sound, and we both turn to see Wolf's giant frame standing in the doorway with a stormy look on his face.

"Hey, Moon, we were just chatting about plans for tonight!" Cliona says with a forced, cheery voice. "I'm only here for twenty-four hours, so I want to see all the things you've been up to here in Colorado."

I clear my throat, my cheeks flushed red. "I think we do the Mercantile tonight. It's great in a rural-mountain-dive-bar sort of way."

"Sounds brilliant!" Cliona agrees. "Everly, maybe you can take me up to your cabin so I can get a shower and wash the stink of the plane off me?"

"Yeah, absolutely," I say and follow Cliona toward the door. I smile at Wolf as we walk by, but he refuses to make eye contact with me, and I'm suddenly having flashbacks of how he was toward me at Trinity.

Cold, distant, angry.

But I can't be surprised. If I heard him saying to Cliona what I just said, I'd be just as hurt. *Me and Wolf in a real relationship would be a horrible idea.* I don't actually believe that, but what choice do I have here? He wants to return to Ireland. He wants to play rugby and be the Reilly Rugby Twins. *I won't get in the way of that.*

So let him be angry.

Let him be distant.

It will just help us both get a head start on his departure.

Never mind the broken hearts along the way.

Chapter 36

Contract Call: *Informal call to join a team.*

Translation: *Decisions, decisions.*

Wolf

The entire Fletcher family comes out for my sister's and my birthday. Calder, Dakota, Luke, Addison, and Baby Levi. Then there's Wyatt, Trista, and Stevie, who was so excited to give me the birthday card she colored for me. Even Everly's grandmother, Max, Cozy, and Ethan came up from Boulder.

And if that wasn't enough, Fergie and Claire came up together as well after being matched up by Everly, apparently. Not for a date, more of a carpooling situation, but they're here, and we basically have the Mercantile bursting at the seams with our crew alone.

It's a proper party with my twin sister beside me. It should have me feeling incredible, bursting with the need to tell Cliona and everyone my Leinster news. I should be on cloud nine.

Only all I can feel is miserable.

Overhearing the way that Everly spoke about our relationship to Cliona earlier today cut me in a way I didn't expect. This isn't just a no-labels situationship we're in. According to Everly, we're just fucking. And her considering any type of future with me would be a *horrible idea.* So, whatever I thought I was feeling grow between us must have all been in my bloody head.

Good to know.

"Oy, mate . . . I got a present for ya," Fergie says, tossing a brown paper bag my way.

"Is this appropriate to open in front of children?" I ask with a frown at my teammate.

"Aye, of course it is. I'm not a complete animal. Most days," he says, shooting Claire a wink.

I open it and shake my head when I see a cowbell inside. "Seriously?"

Fergie throws his head back with a laugh. "I thought the farmhand needed a wee cowbell so the animals can all hear you coming."

I roll my eyes as a pit forms in my stomach over the idea of leaving him. God, he's a pain in the arse, but I grew closer to him in one summer than I did with anyone on my Trinity team in four years. He's just hard not to fall in love with. Like someone else I know.

"Oh, fine, you wee bairn. Here's your real gift." He pulls a larger box out from under the table that's intricately wrapped in burgundy and gold.

I frown and look up to see my sister with her phone pointed at me, like she knows what's inside the box.

"What is it?" I ask curiously.

"Open it and find out," she squeals, giving my arm a punch.

My eyes catch on Everly, who's frowning just as curiously as I am, clearly not in on whatever Fergie and my sister organized together. Strange.

When I pull the lid off, my jaw drops. "What is this?"

"It's your new kit, mate," Fergie says, pointing to the official Grizzlies jersey with the Reilly name in big block letters stitched on the back.

"But what does it mean?" I ask, heart racing inside my chest as I look at my teammate.

"It means that Coach wants you to check your email in the morning because you will have an official contract offer from the Denver Grizzlies waiting for you!"

The words are barely out of Fergie's mouth before I jump and clench my fists with relief. "Fuck yes, holy shit!"

Cliona squeals excitedly, jumping up onto her feet and wrapping me up in a big hug. "Congratulations, Moon! I didn't doubt you for a second."

I shake my head as I hold up the jersey, admiring my name on the back. "Fucking hell, I did it."

"You certainly did," Cliona says, wiping away her tears.

My eyes flash over to Everly in total shock because she's the only one who knows about my news from earlier today. Two team offers in one day. Leinster is not a full-fledged offer but definitely more hope than I had before. This is . . . this is . . . I don't know what the fuck this is.

"I got my spare room all ready for you, pal," Fergie says with a big shite-eating grin. "We are going to be proper roommates and take Denver by storm."

"Congratulations, Wolf," Wyatt says, coming over to give me a hearty handshake. "I know how hard you worked for this, and you should be very proud of yourself."

"Thank you, sir," I say, feeling my chest swell with pride as I accept congratulations from the whole Fletcher family one by one, getting an extra-long hug from Trista, who's a huge part of why this was all possible.

"Does this mean you're leaving me already, Wolf?" she asks, her eyes crinkled with happiness.

"Possibly, maybe. I don't know. I'm really overwhelmed," I reply regretfully, shaking my head. "I'm really sorry about all this."

"Don't you dare be sorry," Trista says, poking me in the

chest. "We will all be fine. This was the plan all along. I told you when you arrived that Fletcher Mountain has a way of healing things you didn't even know need healing."

My chest tightens with those words and how they can feel so utterly true and so utterly false at the same time. "I want you to know how grateful I am for everything. You all made me feel like I was a part of the family, and that means more to me than you'll ever know."

"You're a good kid, Wolf. A good man. I know you're going to do incredible things." She hugs me one more time, and when she lets me go, I find Everly standing off to the side, awkwardly awaiting her turn.

"Hey," she says, her voice wobbly. "What a day for you." She reaches up for a hug, and I hate how familiar and foreign it feels at the same time. It's familiar because I know this girl's body. I know every square inch of it. But it feels like another person hugging me right now.

I shouldn't have kissed her in front of her family. I freaked her out, and *maybe* that's why she said all of that to Cliona. Maybe she didn't mean it. Maybe she was just trying to downplay it because she wasn't ready to discuss it with my sister. I was fucking gutted when I heard her words, but it's not indifference I've seen in her face since then. *She's hurting.* And I'm wondering if she's hurting because of Coach's offer. Maybe she can't imagine me staying. *Or am I just fucking projecting?*

I want her to discuss it with me. I want to talk to her about it and apologize for being so impulsive in front of everyone, but I'm waiting until after Cliona leaves tomorrow. I don't need my sister worrying about me any more than she already does. I'm older by two minutes, but Cliona has always had the oldest-sibling vibes between us.

I need to sort this all out with Everly.

"Let me see," Stevie says, grabbing onto my shorts and tearing me away from the girl who consumes all my thoughts.

I squat down to the ground to show Stevie my jersey. "This means I'm going to be a Grizzly, Steve."

"No, you're Nana," she says with a frown.

"I'm a Grizzly, look," I say, turning the jersey so she can see the round bear logo on the arm.

"Nana," Stevie snaps back, scowling at me something fierce. *"You're my Nana."*

I roll my eyes. "Fine, I'm Nana."

She smiles victoriously before she runs back off to sit on her real nana's lap.

When I sit back down, my eyes swerve over to Judy, who's carrying two cakes toward our table, a spray of candles burning brightly on both of them. Cliona smiles warmly at me, making me feel right at home as she holds my hand under the table while the two cakes are placed in front of us.

Everyone in the pub starts singing loudly and horrifically off-key, making both me and my sister laugh. I'm so glad she's here. I was trying to put on a brave face over being apart for our birthdays, but it would have gutted me not to have her here. My parents didn't do a lot of things right with us, but our birthday, they always made special.

Two cakes.

Two sets of candles.

Two best friends.

People have asked me several times if I have that twin telepathy with Cliona where I can read her mind or feel her pain and vice versa. I always laughed and told them no, we're not magical.

We're bigger than that.

I was born into this world with an instant teammate. We share a bond that goes so deep I'd be lost without her.

When she first pushed me into playing rugby, she would show up at my matches and cheer so loudly I could hear her over all the other parents in the crowd. When my temper would get the best of me on the pitch, she didn't yell. Didn't lecture. She just sat with me until I stopped hating myself.

Having a twin is like walking around with two hearts. You don't make any life decisions without considering what the other heart will think. And the fact that I've let myself get so carried away with Everly without telling Cliona guts me a bit. I don't deserve her. I never will. But she's my blood. And it means so much to me to have her here today.

When they stop singing, it's Stevie who yells, "Blow the candles!"

My sister smiles knowingly at me as the two of us angle opposite directions to blow each other's candles out and make a silent wish for each other—a tradition that started when we were not much older than Stevie and a tradition I'll do for as long as I'm able.

For Cliona, I wish for a successful rookie season with Leinster. She works harder than anyone I know, and she deserves the best the world of rugby has to offer. She needs to take the world of rugby by storm. Not only on the women's side, but the men's side too.

I don't know what she wishes for me. Probably something similar, if I had to guess. But by the time the party ends and it's time to head up to Fletcher Mountain, she grabs me by the arm and says, "You know what I wished for, Wolf?"

"You're not supposed to tell me," I grumble, trying to release my arm from her grasp.

"I wished for you to be kind to yourself. I wished for you to stop seeing the worst in yourself. And I wished for you to see yourself as someone who deserves everything you want in life."

"That's three bleedin' wishes," I deadpan.

"Shut up, you knob," she says, punching me in the shoulder. "I mean it. I love you, and I want you to have everything you wish for."

"What if I save all my wishes for you?" I ask, hitting her with a soft, knowing look.

Her face twists as tears fill her eyes. "Then I'll save mine for you."

Chapter 37

Blowout: *A heavy defeat.*

Translation: *Shit just hit the fan.*

Wolf

It's after midnight, and I can't sleep, so I'm pacing my flat with Rugby on the loose, letting him stretch his legs for a bit, just to give me something else to focus on other than the fact that Everly was distant with me all night.

I'd have thought the Denver offer would make her happy, but she didn't seem happy. She seemed like she was done with me. Like having Cliona here was some sort of reality check she needed, and the past summer never meant anything to her.

Christ, was I really in this alone? Is she really still expecting this no-label label to hold? It's utter shite, and she has to know it.

I look out the window in my washroom, and my brows furrow when I see a blonde figure sitting on the lookout bench that sits above the path that Everly and I would use to walk to each other's places the past several weeks when we were hiding this from her family.

After tucking Rugby back into bed, I throw on a sweatshirt and make my way outside to her, anxious to hear what's on her mind that has her sitting outside alone at this hour. An ominous feeling creeps into my gut the closer I get.

Her head turns when a stick breaks under my foot.

"Don't worry, I'm not stalking you," I say with a soft smile that she returns, but it doesn't meet her eyes. "Mind if I join you?"

"Of course," Everly says, scooting over to make room for me. "It's your birthday. You should have whatever you want."

"It hasn't been my birthday for five whole minutes."

She lifts her brows cheekily. "Maybe you should celebrate birthday week."

"Please don't give that idea to my sister. She will run with it."

Everly laughs softly.

"Everly."

"What?"

"What is going on?" I ask, my tone resolute.

What do you mean?" she chirps back, causing my skin to crawl.

"Why are you doing this?"

"Doing what?"

"You're pulling away," I snap, my teeth clamped tightly together. "All that shite you said to my sister. Did you mean it?"

"I just said to her everything we said to each other when this whole thing between us started." Her lips press into a thin line as she stares out at the valley, her chin wobbling.

I sigh heavily. "Bollocks."

"What do you want from me, Conri?" she asks, her tone terse.

My chest concaves at the words on the tip of my tongue. I hate that I have to say them. I hate that she's not in this with me like I am with her. But fuck it, I have no more fight in me to give.

"I want you to ask me to stay," I say, my voice cracking.

Her eyes swerve to look at me, and they're red-rimmed and glossy. "I can't do that."

"Why not?" I beg.

"Because I know you'll sacrifice your own happiness for

mine, and I don't want that for you," she says, her voice trembling, revealing her true emotions at last. "I saw the light in your eyes when you got that call from your coach earlier today. You were like a big kid you were so excited. I won't let you walk away from that for me. You're self-sacrificing to a fault, Wolf."

"You're people-pleasing to a fault, Everly," I growl petulantly. "And that Leinster thing isn't even an official offer. This here in Denver, it's real. It even sounds like I'll get that youth coaching job I told you about."

She inhales a shaky breath, shooting me a wobbly smile. "Really?"

"Yes, they're bringing me in for a second interview. I didn't want to tell you until it was official."

She blinks rapidly at me. "That's what you've always wanted."

"I know," I reply, stretching my arm over the back of the bench, wishing Everly would curl into me, but she doesn't. "The pay is shite, but matching that with my rugby offer, I think I'll be alright living in Denver with Fergie. And hopefully something bigger will come out of the coaching job eventually."

She chews nervously on her lower lip, still processing everything. "But what about Leinster?" she asks, her eyes cast downward.

I stare at her, my chest burning when I reply, "Dublin doesn't have you."

Her lips part as a flush runs up her neck. "I don't want you making any big life decisions because of me," she says in a rushed, panicky voice.

"We could make them together," I state evenly, trying to get her to see.

"That's too much pressure." Her eyes dart all over the dark canyon. "If you end up going to Dublin and we're long distance, I'll need you too much. I'll want too much of you. *I'll be too much.*"

"Christ, if you say that to me *one more time*," I growl, dragging my hand through my hair. "I've told you a hundred different ways you're never too much for me. Everly . . . *I love you*."

I move to touch her, but she leaps from the bench, flinching like my words hurt her. "Don't say that."

"Why not?" I growl, my temper flaring as I stand as well.

"Because it just makes all this harder." Her throat moves as she struggles to swallow. "I told you I've never said that to anyone."

"I know."

"So, you can't just throw it out willy-nilly."

"I'm not," I grind out.

"Dammit, Wolf," she exclaims, covering her eyes. "You're ruining everything. This was just supposed to be casual. Not love. You're not thinking clearly. You're like drunk on Fletcher Mountain air or something. Eventually, you're going to snap out of this and realize this isn't what you want. *I'm* not what you want. Dublin is what you want. Playing rugby in Ireland is your dream. Being closer to your sister. You guys have goals. I don't want to get in the way of that."

I nod slowly, my heart heavy in my chest as I stalk closer to her, looming over her so she's forced to look up at me. "You think I could follow you home for four years . . . follow you here to Colorado . . . let you boss me around on this fucking mountain and not know what I want?" I bite, my tone guttural.

She shakes her head, refusing to accept my words, but I continue.

"I didn't love you at first. I hated you. I hated your optimism and privilege. I hated how easy it was for you to pry into people's personal lives. I hated how you wore a smile on your face every day, even though I could see that you were struggling. *I hated that*."

"How did you know?"

"Because I fucking *see you*, Everly," I roar, my chest aching with this pain inside me. "I see the anxiety you carry under those bright blue eyes and perfect smile. I see that you help people and matchmake and do things for others because then you don't have to reflect on what you truly want for yourself. Because if you admit what you want—if you let yourself say it out loud and make it real—then if it's taken from you, it hurts. Like your friends from high school or Hilow, or bloody hell, even your grandfather when he passed."

"Stop," she croaks, tears filling her eyes, but I can't stop. I haven't even got to the worst part.

"Somewhere along the way, you decided that if you don't name it, if you don't make it real, then nothing can ever hurt you, and you can go on being that happy, sunshiny girl you have convinced the world you are."

I step in close and breathe in her jasmine scent one last time. "But you're not happy, Everly. You're not sunshine. You're lying to yourself."

"You think you have me all figured out?"

"I've had a lot of years studying you to feel confident in that." My body stiffens with that realization.

The silence that follows is unbearable. The mountain seems to hold its breath, waiting for what happens next. Waiting to see if there's anything else I can say to turn things around.

But I don't want to have to convince her of this. I want her to see me the way I see her. And if she doesn't, then I can't keep chasing her. I can't keep following her and trailing her and trying to catch something that doesn't want to be caught.

This time up here on Fletcher Mountain was my shot. And my greatest fear has come true. I'm just not good enough. Everly and I are not endgame. We're no game.

"I need you to walk back to your cabin, please," I croak, my voice soft and broken. "I can't go inside if I know you're out here in the woods by yourself."

I hate that I still care, but it's not something I can just turn off. I'm not built like that.

Everly swipes away the tears on her cheeks before turning back toward her cabin. The moonlight catches in her hair, that pale blonde that's haunted me for years, and the words that come out of my mouth are harsh and punishing. "And don't worry . . . I won't be following you anymore. It was clearly a horrible idea from the start."

Her shoulders flinch as she pauses for a moment before continuing toward her cabin, leaving me on a cliff's edge back in the darkness, where I belong.

Chapter 38

Sin Bin: *The area where a player must remain for a minimum of ten minutes after being shown a yellow card. In high-level games, the sin bin is monitored by the fourth official.*

Translation: *The breakup.*

Everly

"Baby thief," my uncle Luke croaks as I turn on the lookout bench to glance over my shoulder at him approaching.

I smile and clutch Levi to my chest. "Shhh, my cousin is sleeping."

Luke laughs and walks around the bench to sit beside me. "Addison wanted me to check on you two."

"I'm keeping him covered under the shade, I promise." I shift to glance back at their cabin, where I popped by earlier and told Addison I'd take Levi for a bit so she could have a break. She mentioned making some sourdough muffins for the lumberyard or something. "I figured since you're back working in Boulder with Wyatt this week, she could use some extra help."

"You've been extremely helpful the last few days," Luke says, frowning curiously at me.

"Does that surprise you? I'm always helpful," I reply, smiling down at Levi's sweet button nose.

Luke harrumphs. "I just feel like this is extra helpful, even for you."

I shrug. "Just bonding with my cousin."

"And we appreciate it." Luke drapes his arm over the back of the bench as he leans close to admire his son. "I shouldn't be surprised you have the Midas touch with babies as well."

"He's perfect, Luke." I smile and press my lips to Levi's head, inhaling that sweet baby smell. "I still can't believe you're a dad."

"I know, right?" he says with a laugh. "It's been weeks now, and sometimes I'm still shocked they let us take him home."

I smile at my uncle. "How is it all going, really?" I ask, narrowing my eyes. Luke and I always have had the ability to go deep with each other very easily. He's like a big brother to me in a lot of ways.

"It's exhausting, tiring . . ." he sighs heavily ". . . incredible, magical, and the best thing I ever did after marrying Addison."

Tears well in my eyes at the grateful look on his face. "I'm so happy for you guys."

"Couldn't have done it without you, Eves," he says, chucking my chin.

I grin. "I think you and Addison would have ended up together eventually. I just helped speed things along."

Luke's hand moves behind me to trace over the engraving on the back of the bench. "Wish your grandpa were here to meet him."

A knot forms in my throat. "He's here," I state, glancing out at the beautiful canyon view in front of us. "He's all over this mountain. Don't you feel him?"

Luke looks around proudly. "Yeah, I do, actually."

I close my eyes and breathe in deeply, remembering what it felt like to hug my grandpa's big, tall frame. I'm the only grandchild who will have retained memories of him, and I try not to take that for granted.

"I heard Wolf's moving out tomorrow," Luke says, glancing down at the red barn.

"Oh, really," I reply, feeling my chest tighten.

Luke's brows furrow. "Something happen between you two?"

"No, why?"

He drops his chin. "Evs. Last week, he declared his feelings by kissing you in front of all of us, and we let him live because it seemed like you welcomed it. Now this week, you're acting like you don't even know that he's moving to Denver?"

"I don't know what you're talking about."

"Kid," Luke snaps, his voice firm. "It's your uncle Luke you're talking to. Don't bullshit me. What happened?"

I sigh heavily. "I failed, Luke."

"Failed what?"

"Failed at everything," I croak, my voice wobbly as anxiety builds in my chest. "I lied to you the whole time I was at Trinity. Acting like I was having the time of my life whenever you and I chatted. Living it up. I wasn't living it up. I was matchmaking. That's it."

"So what?"

"So what?" I snap, my eyes fierce on my uncle. "So, I don't know how to be in a relationship. My one boyfriend experience with Hilow was total bullshit. I thought I could do casual with Wolf, and I screwed that up completely, and he hates me now. So not only have I lost him romantically, but I've also lost him as a friend, which hurts so much more."

"Everly . . . did you lie about going to that Trinity Ball?" Luke asks pointedly.

"No."

"Did you lie about hanging out at Mulligans pub?"

"No."

"Did you lie about Cliona being your best friend?"

"No."

"Then what the fuck are you talking about?" he exclaims, pushing his shaggy hair out of his face. "Did you think you would only succeed in college if you fell in love with someone?"

I shrug. "Maybe."

"That's not what I challenged you to do. I challenged you to have fun. So, unless you were crying alone in your dorm room every night, I think you accomplished that."

I exhale heavily. "I guess so."

"Stop stressing so much about your love life," he says with a huff. "I know better than anyone that love is a long game."

He waves his hand, and I can't help but smile as I think about how long he waited for Addison to figure it out. And now I'm holding their little miracle in my arms.

"You're only twenty-two years old. You don't need to have things all figured out. Love will come on its own time."

I exhale through my nose. "Sometimes I'm worried that I don't know how to love someone."

Luke gapes at me. "Kid . . . you have the biggest heart of anyone I've ever known. You make this family work. You're the glue that holds us all together. You're the one who found all of us ridiculous uncles of yours and your father the *loves of our lives*. All our happy endings are because of you. To even entertain the idea that you don't know how to love is a fucking insult to my niece, and I won't stand for that kind of slander."

"Okay, chill," I giggle, feeling as if I need to protect my cousin in my arms from his own father, who's getting very angry right now. "I'm just contemplating lots of deep life thoughts right now. That's what you do at the lookout point here, right?"

"Yeah, I suppose." He reaches over and ruffles my hair. "I hate how grown-up you're getting. It's weirding me out."

"I know," I groan, shaking my head. "I'm thinking about moving to Denver, you know."

"What?" Luke stares back at me, his jaw dropped.

"Not right away, of course. I'd make sure Trista's rescue center is well established, but I'm thinking I need a change. Maybe a job in tech."

"Oh, Wyatt is going to be *mad* at you . . ." Luke puts a fist over his mouth in a teasing way.

"Shut up. You really think so?"

"Yes, and Calder. And your dad. He built a cabin up here just for you."

"Shut up, it wasn't just for me." I shove Luke with my free hand, and he chuckles warmly.

"I'm giving you shit, Evs. It's one of my favorite things to do."

"I'm aware."

He watches me thoughtfully. "I think Denver could be perfect for you. Close to home but still gets you some space from your dad and overprotective uncles. Close to some relationships you might want to pursue."

I sigh heavily and refuse to look down at the red barn. "I'm afraid I rugby red-carded myself there."

"Perhaps," Luke replies, his voice dubious. "But you in Denver will still decrease the odds of me seeing you suck face with any guys, so this move still seems like a win."

I elbow my uncle harshly, accidentally stirring Levi out of his peaceful slumber. He cries out, and I shoot a scathing look to Luke before putting the pacifier back in his mouth. Levi instantly settles, so I take a moment to look out at the view before me.

Living up here has allowed my snow globe of a head to be still for once. To stop pretending and stressing and fretting over everything I did or didn't do. I had a moment to just be comfortable in my own skin for a while and enjoy that calm before the storm.

And maybe moving away from here will just shake things

up and cause a blizzard in my head. But at least I'm admitting what I want, which a certain rugby player told me I never do.

The truth is, it's love that's the hard thing for me to wrap my brain around for myself. Wolf is right. I am afraid to admit how I feel because if it all goes belly up, I'll be crushed. And the odds of it going to shit are high. Wolf's whole identity is tied to rugby, to Dublin, to a world I might not fit in. If I admit I love him and then he leaves? It will fundamentally break me.

My "gift" has always been making *other people* happy. That's where I thrive. In many ways, my family has validated that I love being useful. How often have they praised me when I get shit done, or when I've helped solve a problem, or, of course, when I have connected the right pair? If I'm miserable and heartbroken, then I'll lose track of who I am and the good I want to do. I'll lose hope on love altogether. For me, having no relationship is safer than heartbreak.

Luke wraps his arm around me, and I rest my head on his shoulder. "Don't stress, Evie-girl. Love will find you when you're ready. And with a heart as big as yours, I'm certain you'll have no trouble shouting it from the mountaintop the exact moment you feel it."

Chapter 39

Full-Time Whistle: *Like the referee blowing the final whistle at the end of a match.*

Translation: *Exiting the Bad Boy Era.*

Wolf

"How's it going?" Cliona asks as I put my phone on speaker and set it on the dresser to keep both my hands free to hold Rugby to my chest.

"Fine," I reply tightly as I stare at my empty barn flat one more time.

She sighs heavily. "Have you talked to her?"

"No, Clio. Stop asking."

"You're both being stupid," she exclaims angrily. "And I don't mean you're stupid for turning down the Leinster opportunity. You're stupid for not working through this with Everly, especially after deciding to stay in Colorado. My God, this is world-class stupidity."

I blow a long breath out and pace my flat while holding Rugby. It was a huge decision to accept the Grizzlies offer and essentially decline the interest from Leinster. For years, that was the dream—Trinity to Leinster, Leinster to Ireland Caps, Ireland to the world. The Reilly Rugby Twins take over Ireland. Christ, it's all Cliona and I talked about.

But the truth is, Denver gave me a chance when no one else would. The team, the youth program, the mountain, the

Fletcher family—it's the first place that made me feel like more than just Conri the Convict. Like more than just a rugby player. To leave now would feel like I'm walking away from the man I want to become.

This decision has nothing to do with Everly. In fact, there's an argument I could make that choosing to stay is harder than deciding to leave. If I were back in Dublin, I'd have half a chance of forgetting her and moving on. Staying here will be an exercise in restraint. Especially with my past little habit of stalking.

"There's nothing to work through," I state flatly. "Everly doesn't want me."

"But she looked at you like you hung the bloody moon and then stapled ridiculous fairy lights in the sky for good measure."

I close my eyes and run my finger under Rugby's chin. My chest aches just thinking of her.

Cliona keeps going, relentless. "She's scared. That's all this is. You think you're the only one who's got demons? That girl may look like she lives a perfect life, but we're all fools in love. You're both just running away."

"Clio—"

"No, listen." Her voice sharpens again. "You've spent your whole life fighting for people, Wolf. Protecting them, even when they didn't know it. Maybe it's time you fight for yourself."

Rugby noses under my chin, like he knows I'm about to crack. My throat tightens, and I can't even get a word out.

Cliona sighs again, gentler now. "You can keep convincing yourself she doesn't want you, or you can do the scarier thing and show up anyway. But don't you dare tell me you love her and then just . . . vanish. That's not my brother. That's a coward."

The line goes quiet, and I swear I can hear my own heartbeat echoing in the emptiness of the flat. The flat that I'll miss more than I realized when I told Fergie I was ready to move in with him. This is all happening so fast, and for the first time in days, I wonder if she's right. If maybe the stupidest thing I've ever done isn't red-carding out of my final match at Trinity or turning down an opportunity to try out for a world-class rugby team in Dublin—maybe it's walking away from Fletcher Mountain too soon.

"Would you mind delivering Rugby up to Everly's cabin?" I ask, holding the large glass tank up at the front door of Trista's cabin.

"Yeah, no problem," Trista says, reaching out to take it from me.

Only I don't quite let it go. "Everly said she would take him, but if something changes, I'll take him back."

"Okay." Trista attempts to tug the enclosure out of my hands.

"Fergie's place doesn't really allow pets, but I'll figure something out if I need to." I struggle to let go.

"I understand," Trista says with a laugh and tries again to take my bearded dragon, but I refuse to let go.

"Just promise you won't put him up for adoption," I say in a rush, my body tense.

"I won't." Trista offers me a desperate smile. "We got him, Wolf. You're good."

I finally release the tank, and she moves to set it down on the dining room table inside. I stare at Rugby one last time, already having done my proper goodbyes to my dragon in my barn flat, like a real man . . . where I could weep in privacy.

Trista returns to the door and looks past me where Fergie is waiting in his vehicle with the last of my stuff. "You guys all loaded up now?"

"Yeah." I grip the back of my neck and look past Trista. "Does she still not want to say goodbye to me?"

"I don't know, you'll have to ask her yourself." Trista glances down at the wall beside the door, and I shift to see Stevie hiding behind the entry table, peering over at me with a sullen look on her face.

"Hey, Steve," I state, staring down at my summer shadow. "I'm taking off for real now."

She makes a little growling noise as she ducks behind the table, her small fingers digging into the wood as she refuses to look at me. She's been giving me the silent treatment since she found out I was leaving the mountain. It's been slowly breaking my heart. Just like another girl up the hill.

"Do you want to give me a quick hug, maybe?" I ask, squatting down in the doorway.

She shakes her head, her lower lip jutting out as she remains silent.

I swallow the knot in my throat. "What if I hug you hard enough for the both of us?"

Her little chin quivers as she steps out from behind the furniture and walks over to me. She doesn't lift her hands or look into my eyes. She just silently gives me access to her, and it fucking rips my heart right down the middle.

I grab her denim jacket and pull her into me, wrapping my arms around her tiny frame like my life depends on it. Her body melts against mine, her bones turning limp as I squeeze her, feeling her chest shake with silent cries.

God help me.

When I let go, her face twists with emotion, and she releases a loud sob that breaks through the last ounce of my control before she runs off, her cries fading into the distance as she hides herself away down the hall.

My lips curl as my own tears fall down my cheeks, my throat closing with all the emotions surging through me. If I'm this bad just moving to Denver, I can't imagine how bad I would be if I'd accepted the tryout offer from Leinster.

"She'll be okay," Trista offers, giving me a pat on the back as I swipe at my cheeks. "And we'll see you next weekend for the auction anyways, right?"

I nod and clear my throat as I stand, struggling to make eye contact. "Yeah, I'm happy to be here for that."

"Good. This is fine! This isn't goodbye, then. This is just see you later." Trista gives me a big hug before releasing me to turn and walk down the steps of her deck.

I pause to take in the view of Fletcher Mountain one more time. It's a sight I'll miss almost as much as that curly-haired toddler. But it's time for me to move on, even if it is the dumbest thing I've ever done.

I look up the hill of Fletcher Mountain, past all three cabins to the one at the very top. And that's where I see her.

Everly is standing on her deck, arms wrapped tightly around her body, watching me.

I lift my hand, silently waving my goodbye. She returns the gesture, a mirror image of what I'm giving her.

My body aches to go to her, to wrap her in my arms one more time. But I fear if I do that, I won't be strong enough to let go.

This is for the best.

From a distance.

Like it always should have been.

Chapter 40

Knock-On: *A mistake that stops the play.*

Translation: *Refusing reality.*

Everly

"Everly, how much corn is too much corn for the alpacas?" My walkie-talkie beeps on my hip with the voice of my uncle Calder.

I push my hair out of my face and pull the receiver up to my mouth. "That's a Trista question. Or Hilow. I know he's here somewhere."

"Roger that," Calder's voice cuts in again. "There's a pack of twelve-year-old girls in the barn, and I feel like Sir Poops a Lot is going to live up to his name if I let this go on much longer."

"Find Ethan," I beep back, swerving my eyes around Mount Millie. "If anyone can bust up a pack of girls, it's my brother."

"I have eyes on Ethan . . . We're good. Roger," Calder says, ending the communication.

I frown and shake my head at that abrupt end and look up to take in the space from my spot behind the silent auction table.

Mount Millie looks like a scene out of a Hallmark movie as the sun sets over the peak, casting a golden glow on the first Mountain Men for a Mission event. It's bursting at the seams with easily over a hundred people—most of whom are getting bused up here from the Mercantile in a sprinter van that I was able to get donated for the evening.

Twinkle lights are strung up between all the trees, and there's acoustic guitar music spilling out from the stage we set up directly in front of the barn. Smoke from the food vendors curls into the night air, carrying the smell of barbecue and fried food. There's a beer garden out by the paddock, along with several vendors selling various homemade goods from around the area and a long table of silent auction items I secured for the night.

Kids run wild from one jumping station to the next, faces painted and sticky from snow cones, while their parents pretend not to notice because they're too busy in the beer garden.

My uncles are stationed throughout the area, manning different parts of the center. Calder and Trista in the barn, Wyatt at the road entrance, and Luke at the beer tent. My dad and Cozy, as well as my aunties, are making everyone feel right at home, along with my grandma.

Everybody keeps giving me big thumbs-up, congratulating me on a beautiful event. Patrons ask for ways they can support the cause, and I have pamphlets with QR codes at the ready.

This event is launching Mount Millie Rescue Center to the next level, and I feel overwhelmed with pride over everything we've accomplished here in just a couple of months.

My hope is that we can raise enough money so Trista can hire someone else to take over for me, and I can move on to my job in Denver. I swore Luke to secrecy about me considering a move to Denver because I'm dreading telling Trista that I'm interested in moving on, especially after she just lost Wolf.

My heart sinks as I think about the rugby player who I can't get out of my head. I swear he had me take Rugby just to make it impossible for me to forget about him. Every time I look at our little bearded dragon, I can't help but picture Wolf watching me hold him. He had the most tender, adoring look in his eyes every time we played with Rugby. I should have known he loved me. It was written all over his face. But I can't say it back. I can't be the one to take away a life he should be living.

Cliona called and ripped me a new asshole. Told me I'm an idiot for taking her brother from her and then stomping all over his heart. Then she told me he's staying in Denver, and if I don't make this right, she'll never forgive me. I want to make it right, but I can't bring myself to call him yet. I'm fucking terrified of him rejecting me. Luke said love will find me, and I shouldn't worry, but I'm not sure he realizes how epically I fumbled this one.

I shake my head, snapping myself out of my inner spiral when I see another vanload of people arrive. I walk over to welcome them and nearly trip on my face when I spot a tall, dark, and tattooed rugby player that I know all too well. I'd better work on my poker face tonight, or I'll never survive this auction.

Wolf

"Holy shit, lad, this is a proper party, isn't it?" Fergie says, bouncing on his feet as we walk through the Mount Millie grounds.

I look around in amazement over the transformation this peak has gone through since I left. It's no longer the quiet little animal sanctuary I'd been working at the start of the summer. It's now a bustling, colorful, thriving destination alive with life and people.

And it's all because of Everly Fletcher.

I clench my jaw and try not to give a shite about any of it because caring hurts.

But I do care.

Fuck.

I care a whole hell of a lot. And not just because I respect Trista and what she's accomplished with this facility. But because this is Everly's hard work tonight. And even though she ripped my heart out and threw it down Fletcher Mountain, I'm still fiercely proud of her for organizing all of this. The girl is a force of nature.

"Nice to see you again, boys," a familiar voice sings, and my teammates and I all turn around to see the tall, stunning blonde before us. "I was worried you were going to stand me up."

"We'd never do that, pet," Fergie says, walking over to Everly and scooping her up into a big, spinning hug.

She squeals, and my jaw cracks with jealousy over the fact that my teammate can touch her, but I can't.

My eyes can't help but drink her in. She's stunning in a red-and-white-checkered sundress with cowboy boots, and I ache to tell her she looks beautiful. Just a week ago, I'd have been able to do that. I'd be able to pull her into the barn and steal a kiss before guests started showing up. I'd have been the one she bossed around on this mountain to set things up. I'd be the one zipping up her dress for her or breathing in the lush scent of whatever perfume she put on before we came down the peak.

I'd be the one taking her home at the end of the night and fucking her to sleep after a job well done. She'd be mine to cherish. To hold. To praise. To whisper how bloody proud of her I was and how in love with her I am for being so incredible.

But I can't do any of that.

She made her feelings very clear, and given that she didn't reach out this past week, it's obvious she's done with whatever we were. And I'm done trying to hope otherwise, even if that does make me a coward like my sister said.

I fucking love Everly. *How could I not?* I've probably loved her for years. But I lived in a fantasy in those years too. Even though knowing her more has surpassed my dreams or imaginings of who she is—wholesome, kind, spirited, sexy, fun—I can't hate her for not living up to *my* expectations that *I* projected on her. *She's not ready to entrust her heart to someone.* Sometimes love remains unrequited, and we have to fucking carry on.

That'll be harder since I'm staying in Colorado for the next year, at least, but I'm not staying with Everly Fletcher, and that's something I need to get used to.

I resisted her for four years. What's another lifetime?

"We have a little green room set up for you guys . . . and by green room, it's really just the feed room in the barn, but there's cold drinks and snacks, so please, come right this way. The auction will start in just ten minutes."

Everly's blue eyes catch mine as she gestures for the guys to walk ahead of her, and I cast my own down as I follow them, taking my place as just another one of the rugby players up for bid tonight.

Maybe I'll get lucky, and someone will win me who'll help me forget Everly Fletcher, full stop. A guy can dream, right?

Chapter 41

Hail Mary: *An American football term for a desperate long-shot pass at the end of a game.*

Translation: *Buckle up, bitches.*

Everly

"Welcome, everyone," I say into the mic, holding my hand up to shield my face from the giant yellow spotlight shining right at me. My eyes land on my grandma standing right by the stage and giving me a big, hearty thumbs-up. I glance around the rest of the audience and see my dad and Cozy standing together in one area, Calder and Dakota in another, and Wyatt, Trista, and Stevie propped against a nearby tree. Claire gives me a big wave from her area by the stage, and I exhale heavily.

The gang is all here to witness this ridiculously huge event I'm hosting, and the pressure is on.

I stare down into my furry notebook and begin to read my speech out loud. "I want to thank you all for coming this evening. I've never seen Mount Millie look so good, and that's saying something because she's been showing off for centuries."

The crowd laughs, thank goodness, so I press on.

"Tonight, every ticket, every drink you're holding, every piece of pie you've already eaten or face you had painted all goes straight into helping Mount Millie continue to do what she does best. Which is find happily ever afters for animals who have had a rocky start. Hopefully, you've had a chance to meet all our furry and wooly friends. There's one honorable mention that isn't here tonight, and that's Rugby, our bearded dragon, who lives up on Fletcher Mountain with me." I swallow the sharp pain in my throat over how abruptly our co-parenting ended.

"And speaking of Rugby . . . you are all in for a treat tonight. Come on up, boys," I call out and hold my breath as five giant, godlike rugby players come walking up onto the stage. They're all dressed in flannels and jeans, per my request, and they wave confidently at the crowd, who instantly start cheering.

My eyes linger on Wolf, who looks so much hotter than all of them. He's at least two or three inches taller, broader, and that brooding scowl he has on his face is just enough to make me forget everything I wrote in my notebook for these introductions.

I shake my head and turn back to the audience, forcing myself to focus on the task at hand.

"These are our mountain men friends, and they're here to help us raise money for Mount Millie. They're all players for the Denver Grizzlies Major League Rugby team, and I hope you all put in a bid for the season tickets on the silent auction table. I, for one, have seen one of these guys play, and it was . . . a memorable experience, to say the least."

I fan my face, feeling suddenly flushed.

"Now, how are these guys going to help us raise this money?" I cup my hand by my mouth and lower my voice to really ham it up. "With something very noble. Something very dignified. Something that's going to make my grandma blush."

The crowd laughs softly.

"Tonight, we're auctioning off a date with a professional rugby player! Yes, you heard that right. Actual, living, breathing athletes. Thick thighs included, egos sold separately."

Whistles and cheers sound off, loudest of all from my girl Claire in the front.

"Every bid you make tonight goes to funding feed and vet care for these animals, operation costs for the facility, and so much more. So please, bid like the future of Mount Millie depends on it, because it does.

"And if you end up with a very handsome dinner date who can teach you what the heck a sin bin is in the process . . . *don't worry, Grandma, that's an official rugby term*, well, that's just a good tax write-off."

I wink and earn another round of laughter and applause. "Let the bidding begin!"

The past couple of weeks, I worked up a small bio for each one of the guys, adding colorful anecdotes like it's a dating profile. As I roll through the first few guys, I'm pleasantly surprised by how quickly the dollar amount rises. I purposely save Fergie and Wolf for last because, well, arguably, they're the most attractive. And . . . hot accents have to bring in more money in these parts, right?

When Fergie steps up and I read off his bio, Claire's hand shoots up again and again and again. I smile because my girl knows how to take orders. However, when the price gets up over a thousand dollars, she gives me a despondent look, informing me she is out of funds.

My heart breaks for her, but I don't blame her one bit.

Fergie walks off the stage to join his date, a gorgeous twenty-something blonde who looks very excited about her win, and then it's just me and my lone Wolf standing there together.

"This is Conri Wolf Reilly, Trinity University's former star player from Dublin, Ireland. Wolf is a recent recruit for the Denver Grizzlies and looks forward to joining the community of Denver. He enjoys coaching youth rugby leagues, spending time with his twin sister, and taking his bearded dragon for walks. Let's start the bidding at one hundred dollars!"

I look out into the audience and am met with . . . *nothing*.

It's complete silence.

I frown at Wolf, who shifts nervously on his feet.

"Can I get one hundred dollars?"

A lone goat bleats in the distance as everyone stands out in front of me, saying nothing.

"Sorry, is this working?" I tap my microphone, causing it to squeal loudly.

"It's working, sweetie," Grandma calls back and gives me a big thumbs-up.

I frown and say, "Can we get fifty dollars? Fifty dollars for a date with this six-foot-five, tall, dark, and handsome rugby player who used to work right here at Mount Millie for us."

When I'm met with silence again, I nearly throw the microphone off the stage.

What. The. Actual. Fuck.

Wolf clears his throat, shaking his head in mortification, and I feel completely outraged on his behalf.

"What is going on with you people?" I say in a forced, joking tone. "Wait until you hear this Irish accent, and you'll be very glad you bid on him."

More. Silence.

If it were winter, the scream I would scream to start an avalanche and wipe out all of these assholes would be earth-shattering.

I step out from behind my podium and walk toward the edge of the stage, flagging Claire down. I hold my mic to the side and whisper, "Hey, bid on Wolf."

She shakes her head from side to side, and I look at her with murder in my eyes.

"Claire, it's fine. *Bid.*"

"No!" she squeaks back and then turns around to run away from me. *Well, that's weird as shit.*

My cheeks puff out as I blow out a long breath and turn a

pleading look to Wolf. His voice is low when he says, "Everly, it's okay. Just end the auction early. I'm fine."

"You're not fine," I snarl at Wolf like a rabid dog, my heart hammering in my chest over the utter failure of this moment. The failure to this man who doesn't deserve this.

All I can see is the scrawny little boy who used to get bullied. This is so fucking wrong. We're adults. We worked so hard on all of this. *He* worked so hard on all of this. He's the one who transformed this place into the beautiful facility it is, despite what a disappointment I've been to him.

"You're more than fine. You're wonderful." My voice comes out in a weird, breathy tone, and I feel my mind start to spin with anger, sadness, resentment, and all the feelings I've been bottling up for the past several days.

I hold my hand up and stare out into the abyss of the crowd, ready to make my rage their problem because they deserve it. They deserve all of it. Bringing the mic to my lips again, I say, "This person up here is extraordinary, and you should all be so ashamed for not recognizing that. He's a hard worker, showing up and doing any task that's ever asked of him, even if he's never even seen an alpaca before in his life."

I exhale heavily, my heart thundering in my chest.

"He pretends to be grumpy, but he really isn't. Most fights he's picked have been because he's defending other people. And he's usually smiling if you take the time to really look at his face. *He has a great smile.*" My eyes turn back to him, and he's looking at me in a way that makes me feel woozy. I love that look on him. It's that way he looks at me and makes me feel seen over and over.

"He listens more than he talks too, which is so rare in today's dating standards. And he is fiercely protective of those he cares about. If you find yourself in his inner circle, you can trust that he will always be looking out for you."

I catch a glimpse of Stevie in the crowd, and my heart skips a beat. "And, oh, my God, he's *incredible* with kids, but he does it in this cool, quiet way that's effortless. He talks to them like they're grown-ups, and he makes them feel seen in a way I've never witnessed before.

"He's insanely generous. So generous, he'll play his heart out for a sport he would probably rather coach just because his sister doesn't want to play without him, and he wants the best for her, so he'll sacrifice anything for her to succeed."

My breath comes out labored and hurried, my eyes welling with tears over the unfairness of this whole situation. "If you all knew him as I know him, then you'd love him like I do, and you'd know that he's worth ten times more bids than all those other rugby players."

My lips part as I realize what I just said. What just stumbled out of my mouth as easily as breathing.

I turn on my heel to look at Wolf, who looks equally as stunned.

"Did you just—" he asks, but I cut him off.

"I love you," I croak, tears falling down my face at the overcome look on his. "Oh my God, I'm in love with you."

"Everly—" Wolf makes a move to step toward me but stops dead in his tracks when a male voice yells out.

"Three hundred dollars!"

I swerve to look out into the audience and see my uncle Luke holding his hand up. He has Levi in a carrier on his chest and Addison holding on to his arm with a knowing smirk. I shake my head violently and then hear, "Five hundred!"

I snap my gaze over to that voice and see it's my uncle Calder bidding. He has his fucking tuxedo cat strapped to his front, and Dakota has their other cat strapped to hers. They have been the talk of the event today, wearing their cats like their babies. If I'd known what a spectacle they'd be, I would have put them in a booth and charged a cover . . . you know . . . for the charity.

I slice my fingers over my neck, silently telling Calder to stop so I can bid when another familiar voice calls out, "Eight hundred dollars."

"Wyatt, no," I snap, my voice severe. "He's mine."

"One thousand dollars," my dad says, stepping forward with a smug grin. Cozy and Ethan are near him, and they both cover their conspiratorial snickers.

"You need to stop," I stammer, my face flushed. "This isn't . . . I mean, it's not what . . ."

"Going once," Luke says loudly.

"Twelve hundred dollars!" I squeal into the mic, my hand and voice trembling in shock.

"Thirteen hundred," Wyatt calls out.

"Oh my God, you guys." I stomp over to the side of the stage. "Grandma, you do this."

"Do what?" she asks, her eyes bugging out of her face as I grab her hand and drag her up onto the stage.

"Be the auctioneer," I hiss, shoving her toward the podium and into the spotlight.

"Everly, honey, I—"

"Work with me, Grandma," I growl, my voice sounding positively possessed as I scuttle down the steps to take a place in the audience in front of my uncles.

"Fourteen hundred." I hold my hand up proudly.

Grandma jitters nervously. "Fourteen hundred, going once."

"Fifteen hundred," Calder says and shoots me an evil smile.

"I watched your cats for you two weeks ago!" I shriek, feeling the veins popping out on my forehead.

He shrugs like he doesn't have a care in the world.

"Sixteen hundred." I swallow the knot in my throat because I don't really have that kind of money. Like, I do, but it's in a trust or something. I don't really have access to it, but I'll figure that out later, I guess.

"My Nana!" Stevie cries out, shooting me a big, pouty lip as she crosses her arms and scowls at me like I'm trying to steal her boyfriend.

"Seventeen hundred," Wyatt says and shrugs in the fatherly way about him, like he's going to give his daughter whatever she wants, no matter the cost.

"Trista, control your family," I shriek when my eyes land on her.

She holds her hands up. "Payback is a bitch, kid."

"What?" I exhale heavily, completely confused with everything in existence right now, before I yell out, "Two thousand dollars."

"Sold!" Grandma sings, pointing a victorious finger at me. "Conri Reilly to Everly Fletcher for the highest bid of the night at two thousand dollars!"

The crowd erupts in a riotous cheer as I buckle over, propping my hands on my knees, fighting to catch my breath like I just ran up the mountain.

With a cursed mutter, I stand to walk over to my dad and Cozy and hold out my hand. "Dad, I need two thousand dollars."

His shoulders shake with silent laughter as I wipe literal sweat from my brow. "I'll get the checkbook out of my car."

Cozy pulls me into a hug. "Oh, sweetie, you need a Fireball shot after all of that."

"What the hell was that?" I ask, my eyes swerving around to all three of my uncles, who smile at me like the cat who got the cream.

She bites her lip and sighs. "Your uncles spent this entire event threatening every person here not to bid on Wolf so that you would end up having to bid on him."

My lips part. "They *what*?"

She smiles. "Matchmaking runs in the family, I think."

I shake my head, my mind swimming with the fact that those uncles of mine just nearly sabotaged my whole event just to get me a date with the boy I was too scared to say I love you to just a few days ago. Those brooding, burly, maddening, lovable, wonderful uncles of mine that I'm going to miss so fucking much when I move off this mountain.

Tears fall down my cheeks as I croak, "But why did they all start bidding against me?" I ask with a frown, sniffing my runny nose.

Cozy's brows furrow. "You know, I have no idea. I think maybe they're just dicks."

I erupt into manic giggles and fall into my stepmom in a hysterical mess of crying and laughing. "I am going to kill all of you. But first . . ." I wipe my tears away and turn around to find Wolf standing just five feet behind me, like I conjured him right where I wanted him.

He slides his hands into his pockets, looking perfect and boyish and so deliciously mine. "Hey, Stretch," he says, his voice low and dripping with something I recognize very well.

Love.

"Hey, Conri," I say back, pushing my hair off my face. I sigh and lift my shoulders. "You want to go on a really expensive date with me?"

His smile lights up his whole face. "I'm not sure I have much of a choice."

"Yeah." I wince and tilt my head at him. "That's the funny thing about love. It makes you do crazy things."

And this time, it's me kissing him in front of my family.

Chapter 42

Lineout Reset: *Restarting play cleanly after a disruption.*

Translation: *A metaphor for reconciliation.*

Wolf

"Your Dragon Daddy is home," I say, stroking my lizard under his chin from Everly's bedroom, where she's been keeping him.

"He's been depressed since you left," she says, her voice soft and teasing.

"He's not the only one," I murmur, closing the tank and sighing heavily.

I turn and lean on her dresser, grateful to be done with the event and finally allowed a moment alone with the girl who has consumed all my thoughts this week.

She's standing at the foot of her bed in her sweet little dress. Her skin glows from the bedside lamp, and the familiar scent of this space makes me ache inside.

"That was quite the show you put on down there tonight," I offer, flashing back to the frantic look on her face as she jumped off the stage and bid on me like her life depended on it.

"Tell me about it." She winces with an adorable, bemused expression. "Was it too much?"

I lose all sense of humor, my heart thundering in my chest at it. "You know it wasn't."

She sighs with relief as she eliminates the space between us, sliding her hands up around my neck.

"Does this mean the whole Fletcher family is Team Wolf?"

I ask as I recall the way her uncles all eyed me with knowing smirks as I held Everly's hand most of the night.

"I dare say yes." She presses her body against mine in a way that makes my blood heat. "I think they knew it before me, even. And I don't have any excuse other than everything you said to me at the bench. I was just scared."

"I'm scared too," I reply, running my hands up her sides, trying to soothe that furrow in her brow. "I've never been this vulnerable either, but recently, I decided to quit fighting my past and just let myself be happy with today."

"Oh yeah?" Everly's brows lift curiously. "What inspired this development?"

"You, Stretch." I lean in and press my lips to hers, drinking her in like a drug. "You inspire me in so many ways."

Her tongue teases mine in a light, sensual kiss. One of connection and understanding. She pulls away to say, "So what, now we're both going to end up in Denver and live happily ever after?"

My brows furrow. "Are you moving in with me?"

"What? No!" she sputters, her face turning red instantly.

I can't help but smile and squeeze her close. It's fun to watch her struggle through all this. The girl who has dedicated her life to helping people fall in love has trouble managing it all herself.

But I can be patient.

She's worth it.

"I am thinking of applying for this job in Denver with a tech company," she says by way of explanation.

I jerk my head back to get a good look at her because she hasn't mentioned this to me before. "Denver? Really?"

"Yeah, I mean . . . this job with Trista was always temporary. And obviously, I have to get the job first, but I think that's my next step."

I struggle to hide the fucking elation pulsing through my

body, my smile completely giving me away. To have Everly in Denver near me . . . it feels like a dream. Like somehow, I'm getting everything I want without having to fight for it. It's fucking incredible. I lean down and press a kiss to her lips, unable to keep myself off her after this news she just casually dropped. "So, you want to be in Denver, then? You could be happy there?"

"Yeah, for sure. It's close to home but not, like, in the backyard close. And I'm ready for a place of my own . . ." A dirty smile spreads across her face. "But I'm hoping you'll come by for sleepovers."

I groan as I pull her into my body, showing her just how much I like that plan.

She pushes back against me to continue talking. "But if you end up going back to Ireland for that other team, we can figure that out too," she says, her blue eyes wide and blinking rapidly as her brain enters that planning mode that it loves so much. "I mean it, Wolf. I don't want you turning down a dream team opportunity for me. I won't freak out. I love Ireland too . . . maybe I could even move there with you."

"With me?" My heart stutters inside my chest at the gauntlet she just dropped. "You'd do that? You'd move away from your whole family for me?"

"Yes." Her face twists in pain as she shrugs helplessly. "I love you." She adds it in an exasperated, surrendering tone. "I'm sorry I couldn't say it sooner," she rushes out, clearly registering the shock on my face. "One minute, I was just . . . doing what I always do. Talking. Selling. Playing the part of Everly the Matchmaker . . . and then suddenly . . ." She trails off, shaking her head with a laugh. "I wasn't talking about why other people should love you. I was admitting why *I already do*."

I drink in her words . . . letting them soothe a wound inside of me I've long suppressed.

For so long, I've carried this gnawing ache that I wasn't worth loving. That if I let someone close, I'd only hurt them, the way I once hurt Finn. The way I've hurt myself more times than I care to count. But in a way, it feels like Everly's been stitching me up from the inside without even realizing it. Letting myself fall for her has eased that fear and anger that I've carried since I was a kid too scrawny to stand up for myself. *And I've never wanted to kiss anyone so badly in my life.*

However, this girl I love still has more to say, apparently. "If we get serious, we could figure out a move to Ireland together," she continues, her brows furrowed deep in thought. "I'm sure I could find work out there, especially with a degree from Trinity. Or maybe I go back to school and get my master's."

"*If* we get serious?" I laugh and tilt my head at her. "Love, I've never been more serious about anyone in my life."

She quirks a brow, clearly pleased with that response. "That's good because we have a child to think of now."

My jaw drops as my heart comes to a dead stop in my chest.

"I can't be in love with a Deadbeat Dragon Daddy." She bites her lip and giggles, and I slowly close my eyes and shake my head. She squeezes me teasingly, and I growl as I press my forehead to hers and fight against the burn in my throat.

The burn isn't from holding back anger like it usually is. It's from relief. From this impossible, bone-deep comfort that settles over me as I hold her in my arms and listen to her laughter, accepting her teasing like a drug I can't get enough of.

I move in and capture her mouth with mine, no longer able to be patient. I need to feel this girl's skin on mine again. Being apart from her was more painful than I could have ever fathomed.

Fergie's flat felt like a prison cell as I lay in bed alone, thinking of her on Fletcher Mountain, at a place I grew to love this summer. I hated the idea of ending it all in such utter misery. Fletcher Mountain gave me a gift—a sense of family and connection that

I had never experienced before. To have it all end in such heartbreak of losing Everly felt like another painful loss.

But now, all is right in the world. She is mine . . . this place I've created here is mine, and it's going to take a hell of a lot more than her fear of being too much to push me away again.

Our tongues dance as I move us to the bed, leaving a trail of clothes all the way back to our dragon. She grips my cock, and I hiss into her shoulder, grumbling a noise deep in my chest as I let her push me onto the bed and watch as she climbs over top of me.

I inhale sharply as she positions me against her center, sliding my head along her slick heat. The familiar skin-on-skin contact between us jolts me back to life. Every breath, every heartbeat, every brush of skin is like a medication I was in desperate need of.

My body knows what it needs.

Her.

Always her.

She releases a stuttering breath as she inches me inside of her. "Come inside me, Conri. I want to feel you dripping out of me."

"Christ, love," I groan as I slide my hands up over her rib cage and around her breasts.

My grip tightens as I let her have this control when every instinct in me wants to take charge. To roll her over and fuck her until we can't see straight. But the way she looks at me . . . like I'm worth something, like I'm more than my mistakes . . . it's something I want to savor.

I glance down and watch her sink down onto me, seating herself fully on my lap. She's so wet I could come right here, right now. But I hold back. I fight off my own arousal as she grinds over me, her expression one of wanton abandon as she takes what she needs from me as well.

"Tell me you missed me," I command, my voice rough as I ache to hear her confirm everything I'm feeling.

"I missed you, baby," she pants, lifting herself up and slamming herself back down.

Baby.

It's intimate and pure. A term of endearment I've never had. And one I want forever.

My fingers flex on her hips. "Tell me you want me," I croak, needing even more.

"I want you," she says on command like the good girl she is.

My pulse thunders in my chest as I strain to hold myself back. "Tell me you love me," I say on a sigh, desperate to combine the lust and the love in this beautiful moment.

She stills on top of me, her closed eyes opening and finding mine in the warm lamplight. A small smile tugs at the corner of her mouth as she glides one hand over my cheek. "I love you so much."

And it's those words that snap my control. I roll her over and grip her wrists above her head and drive hard into her. She screams with pleasure as the sensation of her slick flesh drives me fucking feral. Her legs grip me, her cries frantic as her cunt tightens around me as I pump into her hard and fast. Having this girl in my arms, in this bed, around my cock—it's all too much. Too perfect. Too everything I always tried to never dream of. A wayward thought of putting a baby in her hits me out of nowhere, and I feel my heart explode in my chest.

But that's what this girl does to me. Everly Fletcher is endgame for me. She's the light to my dark, the optimism to my pessimism. She makes me dream about a future I didn't even consider for myself. And I want it all with her.

I cover her mouth with mine and feel the gasp behind her lips, knowing her orgasm is close. I drag my lips down her chest and pull her nipple into my mouth. The harsh suck causes her to cry out again.

"Conri . . . oh my God." Her nails dig into my back as she suddenly quakes around my length, her orgasm ripping through her as her limbs tighten around me.

The pressure of her flesh around mine forces all the blood to rush to my tip, and before I can stop it, she pulls my own release from me as well. I thrust hard into her one last time and give her what she asked for, pouring every bit of me inside of her. I want her to have it. Every part of me belongs to her now, and I don't want to know what life is without that reality.

I drape my sweat-soaked body over top of her, my head on her breast, chest burning with exertion as our hearts thunder in unison against each other.

I press a kiss to her pulse and murmur against her collarbone, "Not to risk freaking you out again, but I think you might be my soulmate, Everly Fletcher."

She makes a clicking sound with her tongue. "I'm afraid you're too late."

"What do you mean?" I lift my head to look down at her because I know there is no way she didn't feel everything I just felt.

A half smile teases her lips. "I can't be your soulmate because that title already belongs to your sister."

My brows furrow as I glare back at her. "In the future, can you possibly not mention my sister when I'm still inside of you?"

Her stomach shakes with laughter as she giggles in a way that erases all thoughts of my twin. I smile fondly at the girl I'm madly in love with. "And I can live with you not being my soulmate as long as you still love me as much as I love you."

She presses her lips to mine, murmuring against them, "I do, Conri. I love you way too much."

Chapter 43

Sold-Out Crowd: *Phrase used to describe a sold-out stadium for a rugby match.*

Translation: *Number one fan.*

Everly

The moment we step into the Denver Grizzlies stadium, I realize I've made a grave error in judgment.

Not because I'm at another rugby match, and I still think rugby is basically like human Jenga.

But because I allowed my entire Fletcher family to come with me. *Every single one of them.*

But Wolf said they could come! He said he'd told my dad and uncles at poker night they could attend this friendly match . . . whatever that means . . . and now, here we are.

It begs the question: are there unfriendly matches? Games that are organized with rival teams? Are they all rivals? What will be friendly about this match as opposed to the others? I already know there will be loads of hugging.

Regardless, my massive family all piles into our two rows of seats. There's my dad and Cozy, arguing with Ethan over the mustard he already spilled on his new rugby jersey with the name Reilly scrawled on the back. There's Calder, who's taken it upon himself to double-fist beers, much to Dakota's dismay. Luke and Addison are fussing over Baby Levi, who looks absolutely adorable in a little burgundy bucket hat. My grandma is here too, who showed me after we got through security that she snuck in Fireball shooters in her purse. *What the hell, Grandma?* Plus, my mom and Kailey are seated right behind me, and then there's Wyatt, Trista, and Stevie.

Stevie is on my bad side because she is fiercely competing with me as Wolf's number one fan, and I hate to lose. I'll let her claim him as her Nana. But that Irish bad boy is mine forever, even if he doesn't know it fully yet.

"Everly!" Dad shouts over the crowd as we squeeze into our seats. "Which one's Wolf again?"

"The big one," I yell back.

"They're *all* big!" Cozy calls from the other end of the row, clutching a foam finger. God, the merch sales from the Fletcher family alone are going to be paying Wolf's salary.

I point toward the field. "Number eight. Dark hair. The one who looks like he wants to fight someone."

"I like him better carrying alpacas, but I guess rugby balls work," Trista says with a laugh.

I smile as Wolf pauses his warm-ups long enough to look up into the stands, finally. I swear he's been avoiding looking up here, letting his worry that none of us would show up take control of him. His lips part in shock when he spots the sheer volume of us packed in here for him. I lift my hands and mouth, "Told you so."

I see emotion sweep over his face as he presses his hand to his chest and sighs before refocusing on his warm-ups.

I can't help but beam with pride. He was a nervous wreck this morning at my new Denver apartment. I forced him to talk to me before he left to go get ready for his match, and I'm so glad to show him that I was right all along.

"I'm not nervous about the match. I'm confident there," he says, his eyes swimming with worry as he holds me in his arms at my front door.

"Then what is it that has you all twitchy?" I ask, running my fingers through his hair.

I watch his Adam's apple move up and down his neck. "I've never had a group of people in the stands to watch me. Part of me wonders if they won't show up. It's ridiculous. I don't need them there, but—"

"Now you want them." I smile softly, knowing just how connected he became to my family this past summer. "It's okay to want that, Conri."

"I don't want to get my hopes up," he scoffs.

"Hey." I grab his face and force him to look at me. "We're done being afraid, right? Facing our fears. The Fletchers will show. I'd bet my life on it."

He licks his lush lips. "You're really lucky, love."

"We're lucky," I say, my lips turning down. "They love you just as much as they love me, you know."

"Steve does, at least," Wolf says with a laugh, referencing my clingy little cousin.

"And your parents care too . . . in their own way."

"I know." He exhales and closes his eyes for a moment, and when he opens them, he looks lighter and brighter, as if he used sheer willpower to change his mood. "I really love you, you know that?"

"Back at you, Wolfy."

He squeezes my ass, lifting me up off my feet as he growls into my neck. "Go take care of our dragon. I'll see you after the match."

"Score a goal for me."

He stops dead in his tracks, all smiles gone. "Love . . . it's a try, not a goal. We've been over this."

"Oh, that's right." I bite my lip coyly. "I might need another rugby lesson tonight."

"I could give you one right now if you want. I have the time."

"Scrum at me, bad boy."

With a growl, he tackles me, throwing me over his shoulder as he hauls me back to my bedroom, where we create our very own ten-minute sin bin.

The whistle blows, and the match kicks off, and even though Wolf gave me a solid lesson between the sheets this morning, I still wish Cliona were here to explain what's happening. Luckily, Addison seems to know a thing or two and is helping answer everyone's incessant questions about what's going on. I don't think everyone is appreciating the thighs like they should be because, in my humble opinion, that's the most important part of the match, but whatever, it's their loss.

By direct orders, I text Cliona updates on his match today every chance I get. She's also competing with me and Stevie as Wolf's number one fan, but as my soulmate, I'll forgive her.

A few minutes in, Wolf charges down the field, and my entire family leaps to their feet, me included.

My heart races when he gets tackled, jumping out of the pile of thick-thighed men like he didn't just take a beating.

"Oh my God," I exclaim as I glance down the row and see my uncle Calder standing on a chair and pumping his fist. "Calder, get down. Too much."

"Too much?" Grandma says. "He's your boyfriend, Everly. You should make sure he knows you're here! Wave or something."

"He knows," I mutter, horrified.

Grandma cups her hands around her mouth and yells, "Go, Wolf! We're all here for you!" Her voice cracks halfway through, but the sentiment lands.

A few rows down, a group of rugby fans turns around, shooting us judgy looks.

"Is that his mom?" one asks.

"Nope," I groan, covering my face. "Just his girlfriend's grandma."

The kid hits me with a puzzled look, and I can't say I blame him. This is the definition of "too much." You wonder where I got it.

My humiliation recedes as the game continues, things getting intense fast. I gasp when Wolf tackles someone and then somehow emerges with the ball, tearing down the field like he's running from the cops. My heart jumps into my throat when he dives into the end zone, scoring his team a try (learned that this morning), and my family goes completely feral, me included now. We're all on our feet. Ethan and Calder standing on their seats. Stevie abandoned on the ground. Luke holds his free hand out in a protective barrier around Levi. Cozy chucks her popcorn in the air as she screams like a banshee. And my mom jumps up and down, squealing with my grandma.

By the end, when they've easily won the game, I'm sweating like I played the match myself.

The team makes their way off the field, but not before Wolf's eyes find mine again. He makes a circle with his finger and holds it to his eye, like he's gazing at me through binoculars. If that's a nod to his stalking proclivities, then I enthusiastically approve. I mimic the gesture, and his dirty smirk causes my heart to flutter.

I mouth, *"I love you,"* and he waves to my entire family, offering an extra special one to Stevie before he takes off to join his team.

I'm so proud of him today. He looked completely in control, communicating effortlessly with teammates, remaining calm, even during tense moments. Confidence radiates off him, and everyone feeds off it—even his roommate, Fergie.

He's changed in so many tiny, quiet ways, and yet he's still that rugby bad boy that followed me around Trinity campus for years.

God, I'm so glad he red-carded himself back then. Or who knows what would have happened between us. My matchmaking heart likes to think we would have found each other eventually. But even I'm not sure I'm that powerful.

"You okay, Sea Monster?" Cozy asks, leaning over my dad to check on me as I swipe an errant happy tear away.

"I'm very okay," I reply with a dopey smile. "I'm going to marry that Irish boy someday."

It's pretty funny that after all these years of scheming and matchmaking, I've finally found the thing I didn't need to mastermind: my own love story. *Or rather, it found me.*

Chapter 44

Golden Point: *When a game goes into extra time and the first one to score wins the match immediately.*

Translation: *Officially entering the Good Girl Era.*

Wolf

A Few Months Later

I should've known the second she slid into the back seat of the Uber and fastened her seat belt that I was doomed. Everly Fletcher can't sit quietly in a moving vehicle for more than ten seconds without interviewing the driver like she's hosting her own dating podcast.

The driver named Shane barely got out, "Where you from?" before she was firing off relationship questions at him. We were barely half a mile down the road, and the guy had unloaded his whole breakup saga to my girlfriend.

"So, what you're telling me is that you're still healing," she says like she's some kind of relationship therapist. "You're better off without her, Shane. Larissa was the wrong fit for you. I think you need a good girl. Someone who won't play games, you know? You're clearly a hard worker and very responsible. I can tell from the way you use your blinker at every turn."

"Christ," I mutter under my breath, running a hand down my face.

She ignores me completely. "You said you had two dogs?"

"Uh . . . yeah," Shane replies, glancing back at us. "Lemon and Poppy."

"Perfect! I'm developing this app called PlusOne, where love is handpicked, not swiped. Basically, instead of people building their own profiles, your friends or family build for you. These people end up on a matchmaker leaderboard and can earn badges after successful matches. Anyways, if you want to be in my beta program, I'm sure I could find someone local for you. Oh my God, you could have your first date at a dog park! Wouldn't that be so sweet?"

She looks to me like I'm going to agree, and I can't help but roll my eyes. Ever since Everly landed a job with an app development company, she has become obsessed with developing her own app. The girl is always working.

"My dogs aren't good with other dogs," Shane says regretfully. "Dog-aggressive, you might say."

"Well, shit," Everly deadpans. "How about cats?"

"You're unbelievable," I chuckle and rub my hand along her back, which is exposed in a sexy little dress she's wearing for Finn's wedding.

I glance out the window, anticipation vibrating through me as I prepare to see my oldest friend for the first time in several years. I didn't want to go to this wedding. I wanted to send my regrets and wish him the best. But Everly needled at me a bit on it, and I eventually decided otherwise.

Out of the blue one day, I decided to call him. I didn't want the first time we'd seen each other in years to be at his actual wedding. I thought it would be light and just a simple catch-up.

It turned out to be so much more.

I confessed to him that I'd blamed myself for a lot of Finn's scars. Both physical and emotional. I said I felt responsible that he'd been bullied—*hurt*—and that I hadn't protected him. When I found the words to say that to him, he was silent. And then the fucker laughed.

Laughed.

The bleedin' shite.

"Conri Reilly, have ye really kept all that locked up in ye bleedin' head all this time? Do ye know who I hold responsible for the fucked-up shite done to us? Those feckin' eejits. Not you, ye plonker," Finn says.

"Well, man, if I wouldn't have gone off—"

"Stop. You were entitled to find some happiness, and I'm glad it was rugby that gave that to you. If I seemed distant, it was just because I was embarrassed. Not feckin' angry at ye. And then I figured you were embarrassed that I'd not found my own way. If only we'd bleedin' talked about it. Christ."

"God, Finn . . . I'm sorry, mate."

"Just get yer arse back to Ireland for me wedding and see for yourself how good my life is now, alright?"

"I'll do just that, Finn. But do ye think you can add a plus-one for me, then?"

The relief I'd felt had been palpable . . . our conversation more cathartic than all the therapy I'd had at Trinity.

Finn even made me send him a picture of Rugby and told me that if I didn't give him a bearded dragon as a wedding present, then all is not forgiven, after all.

I can't tell if he's kidding.

And it makes me smile every time I think of it.

Of course, Everly is also excited to meet my parents on this visit. I think it will be good to spend time with them as adults, not as kids. Show them how well I'm doing. Tell them about the kids I'm coaching and how much of a difference I'm making in their lives. Colorado was never in the cards for me, but now I can't really imagine my life anywhere else.

The added bonus is we'll get to catch one of Cliona's matches while we're here as well. I even convinced my parents to come with us to watch. I can't wait to see my sister crushing it in her rookie season. I know she's going to soar, and I want my parents to see that . . . for her.

We're packing a lot into this quick trip to Dublin, and then it's back to my spot with the Grizzlies. I was lucky they gave me leave to go in the first place.

I watch Everly chat with the driver as the autumn sunlight catches her cheekbones just right, and for a moment, I forget about the wedding, the city, even the noise of Dublin outside. All I can think about is how she's the first person I've wanted to show my whole self to, scars and all. And even though we've only been officially together for a few months, I'm confident that this thing between us . . . it's for the long haul.

I realize I'm staring. Really staring. And my chest aches with a kind of happiness I didn't know I was capable of. I reach for her hand, just for a second, and squeeze it. Not too tight, not too soft. Perfectly. And it feels like a promise I've been holding in my chest my whole life: that I'm finally done hiding in the shadows.

"Hey, Stretch . . . can you stop matchmaking long enough to enjoy the view? We're going by Trinity."

"Aww . . . where we met." Everly stops chatting with Shane and turns to look at the stunning architecture leading into the grounds of the Trinity campus entrance. Memories of watching Everly walking around here with her long blonde hair hit me full force, and I sigh and shake my head, still amazed that we somehow ended up here.

"Hey," she says, turning my attention back to her. "Do we have time to make a pit stop at the Rubrics building before the wedding? I'd love to take a picture with you there."

I glance at the time on my mobile and nod. "We have time, love."

"Hang a right up here, Shane," Everly calls out like she's known the driver her whole life. "Me and my boyfriend are going to go for a little walk on campus where we first met."

I smile warmly, thinking someday this might be the perfect spot to propose to this beautiful woman I get to call mine. Proposing to Everly Fletcher after only dating her for a few months might be too much. Or maybe it's *just enough*.

Either way, that's where I see our story going. This girl with her fluffy notebooks, her quiet but infectious joy, her crazy-arse, season-ticket-holding family, and her visions of growing love everywhere.

She's everything to me. And I can't wait to head into the new chapter of my life with her by my side. Even if she still can't tell me what the purpose of a scrum is. *Funny hugging thing, my arse.*

The End

Want to see Everly and Wolf get married and witness all the uncles crying in unison? Find their big beautiful wedding here: amydawsauthor.com/everly

Want more of Everly and her wild mountain family? The Mountain Men Matchmaker Series is complete! Check out the first book in the series, Nine Month Contract, *featuring Wyatt and Trista, available now wherever books are sold!*

Want to flashback to where Everly got her matchmaking start?
Read where it all began with Last on the List,
Max and Cozy's story, available now!

Read on for excerpts of both Nine Month Contract
and Last on the List*!*

★★★

Excerpt from Nine Month Contract

Help Wanted: Grumpy Mountain Man seeks baby momma to grow his seed. Uterus a must. Ovaries negotiable. Boobs not required but a nice bonus. Job is an incubator position only. No parenting allowed. Surrogate must be impervious to grunting in the form of communication and impartial to goat droppings. Rustic mountain range housing available upon request. Interested parties can text 555–5456. Murderers need not apply. Expect sizable payment and signed legal contracts before insemination commences. Also, must be cool with brotherly neighbors . . . and no, that isn't code for Why Choose.

Wyatt

Pet Goats: 1
Annoying Brothers: 3

"You fucking fuckers!" I roar as I slam my foot on the brakes in front of my brother's cabin, sending a dust storm of gravel swirling around my truck. Jumping out of the driver's seat, I charge up the steps toward my two siblings sitting on Calder's front porch and come to a stop between them. I glare at their relaxed frames stretched out on a couple of wooden rocking chairs with tin cups of coffee in hand.

Like it's just a normal Saturday fucking morning.

I hold up the piece of paper in my hand. "Which one of you posted this at the bar?"

"Easy there, Wyatt . . . you don't want to hit your daily word quota all before lunch." Calder laughs and sets his cup down on the end table beside him and snaps his fingers. "Although I guess *fuck* was redundant, so you have a few more words to burn."

Without warning, I reach out and grab his collar, yanking him out of his chair. I knew it was Calder. It's always fucking Calder. "Is my life some kind of joke to you?" I seethe, feeling every muscle in my arms flex as I hold my six-foot-three brother up on his tiptoes. I'm only an inch taller than him, so it's no easy task.

"How do you know it was me?" Calder's eyes dance with mirth. Mirth that I am two seconds away from punching off his smug face.

I glance over at Luke, the youngest of us, who seems perfectly at ease as he scratches his short beard and enjoys the show. I slant my gaze back to the most typical middle child on the face of this earth—never mind the fucker is thirty-five now. He was a pain in the ass when we were young, and he's a pain in the ass now. The only difference now is he has more disposable income and more "inspired" ideas for his shenanigans.

My voice is growly as I crumple the sheet between us. "*Impervious* was your word of the day last week, and you used it incorrectly for hours."

The corner of Calder's mouth tips up. "Pretty sure I got it right in that ad though, didn't I, Papa Bear?"

Rage spikes in my veins now that he's confirmed his guilt. "I'm going to throw you off this mountain and burn your cabin down."

I drag Calder's floundering body down the front steps of his porch toward the lookout point in front of my cabin, ignoring his raucous laughter that echoes off the foothills. I spent weeks clearing trees from this mountain vista when I bought this land to create this view before I even built my home. I wanted a place to quiet my thoughts and bring me peace.

This is the opposite of peace.

"Whoa, whoa, whoa," Luke calls out, his boots crunching on the gravel as he jogs past me to press a hand to my chest. "It's way too early in the day for manslaughter and arson threats."

"No shit," Calder scoffs, extricating himself from my grip. He steps back and straightens his flannel, concealing the ink scrawled across his chest. "This violent behavior will make finding you a Momma Bear very difficult, Papa Bear."

"Stop calling me Papa Bear," I hiss, ruing the day I ever thought it'd be a good idea to have my brothers build on this secluded mountain with me.

I fist the ridiculous ad in my hand and glance up the hill at the three cabins we all built together almost ten years ago. Three brothers living on a mountaintop I bought in rural Colorado sounded like a dream back then. We all worked side by side to develop this stretch of land and build self-sustaining cabins to survive up here on minimal energy resources. Even in the snowiest of winters, we have everything we need to survive for days without contact from the outside world. Weeks, even.

Sounds like fucking heaven.

Or it did . . . until something started to feel different for me. *As though some*thing *was missing.*

"This isn't a fucking joke," I grumble, running my hand over my short hair.

Calder's expression shifts from cocky to damn near somber as he pins me with a serious look. "I didn't make that ad as a joke, Wyatt. I made it because you're a damn fool for going back to that agency in Denver that's going to charge you six figures for a surrogate when there are decent women right here in Jamestown who will grow your baby for a fraction of the price."

"It's not about the cost, Calder," I boom for the hundredth time. "I'll pay whatever it takes to become a . . ." I hesitate to say the word out loud, my voice getting caught in my throat as the weight of it presses down on me.

Dad.

When will that word ever stop being difficult for me to say out loud? My eyes move over to the memorial bench Calder built and placed at the lookout point two years ago after our father passed unexpectedly. Our dad's favorite saying is inscribed on it: *We're not here for a long time, we're here for a good time.*

Dad was the salt of the earth—hardworking, protective, and challenging in all the best ways. I can close my eyes and still feel his presence all around me—his signature scent of Brut cologne, his chastising tone when my brothers and I were late to a jobsite, his bark of a laugh, or the way he never sneezed just once. It was always an attack of eight sneezes in a row. *Fuck, I miss him.*

And let's not even think about how hard it's been for my mom, who was just about to celebrate their forty-fifth wedding anniversary before he passed. Now, she's a widow who still cries at family events.

Dad was the definition of patriarch, and when we lost him, we lost our guide, our anchor, our voice of reason. The world got a little darker.

Now, I want to bring some light back into our lives. I want to see my mom hold my kid for once instead of my niece or nephew. I'm proud of what my brothers and I have built on this mountain, and I want to share that with a child of my own.

And I'll be damned if I let Calder fuck with my plan.

Calder playfully hits me on the arm, snapping my attention back to him. "You know, I might have some babies toddling around the foothills and not even know it. You're welcome to one of those if you can find one."

My jaw clenches, and I can't tell if this comment is better or worse than the other things he's said. A few months ago, Calder suggested I use Tinder and just go out and randomly knock someone up. And I admit that in a drunken stupor, I began to consider that idea but then remembered nobody goes to Calder for advice. Unless you want the name of a good sex club, maybe.

I open my mouth to argue with him for the hundredth time, but an approaching car forces all our heads to turn. I own the entire mountain, so all visitors are here for one of the three of us. When our eldest brother, Max's SUV appears on the horizon, we all murmur, "Fuck."

Max isn't a total asshole. He's just a different breed than us. And God love him, he can be a controlling, condescending fucker sometimes. He got even worse after Dad passed.

Back in the day, he worked construction for Dad's renovation business just like the rest of us, but Max always had different life goals. He broke off early, went to business school, and climbed the corporate ladder to eventually break out on his own. He owns his franchise development company and is likely the wealthiest man in Boulder, but I'm not doing too bad myself. I just choose to hide in the hills of Jamestown, the tiny community at the base of this mountain, rather than flaunt my money with a fancy house. I'm not Max rich by any means, but my land is worth a pretty penny, and the green cabins we've built up here make our lives very affordable.

Plus, flipping houses has been good to all of us. Our father taught us well, and we've managed to continue growing his business in his absence. Honestly, we're harder workers now than we ever were when he was here. His passing was a bit of a wake-up call. I only wish he were here to see it.

But the cash rolls the housing market has gifted to us for investments have been well taken care of the past decade, which is why I'm not concerned about how much it will cost for me to become a . . .

Dad.

Regardless of who has more money, Max likes to throw around that CEO boss energy everywhere he goes. And, well, we play by different rules on the mountain.

Like being able to cover up murder and arson relatively easily.

Max stands in front of the three of us and pulls his expensive sunglasses off his face to pinch the bridge of his nose. "Can someone please inform me why I just caught my teenage daughter making an Excel spreadsheet of viable candidates to be the baby momma for her uncle?" Max looks as confused as I feel.

"Oh, yeah." Calder grips the back of his neck and looks uneasy for the first time all morning. He clears his throat and stares down at his boots. "I posted that bar ad on Craigslist a few days ago and directed all calls to Everly."

"You what?" Max roars, and I lunge for Calder, only to be grabbed around the shoulders by Luke, who I struggle to shake off. He's not the biggest of the four of us, but he's a wiry little shit.

Max blows past us, and just before his fist connects with our annoying brother's face, Calder bellows, "This was Everly's idea!"

"Dick," Luke scoffs, looking disappointed. "Way to throw your niece under the bus. Super brave of you."

"One of them is going to kill me if I don't tell the truth," Calder snaps back defensively and turns back to me and Max. "She was determined to do this and asked for my help. And you know I can't say no to Evie-girl. I honestly didn't even know Craigslist was still a thing. Everly figured that out in all her research."

Max's stunned reaction causes him to pull back from Calder, his face cast in confusion. "Everly figured all this out?"

Calder straightens and tries to gain back an ounce of his manhood. "Yes."

Max, Luke, and I all gape at him, dumbfounded by this onslaught of new information. I had a long conversation with Everly several months ago about my plans to find a surrogate to carry my baby, but I had no idea she was this invested in the whole thing.

Max's voice is scathing as he turns accusing eyes at me. "You never should have told her, Wyatt. She's just a child. She doesn't even understand all this."

"She was relentless with her questions, Max," I argue, anxiety prickling the back of my neck at the possibility I did something that could have hurt her. "And she's eighteen—it's not like she doesn't know how babies are made. And hell, she's graduating from high school in a few months and moving overseas. If she's old enough to move away to a foreign country, she's old enough to understand all this." My tone is bitter.

"She's not moving away forever." Max's voice catches in his throat, revealing what we're all feeling as I look around to see the same sad, desperate look on our faces. The look we've all had since Everly told us she was going to Ireland for college several months ago.

Evie-girl is leaving us.

Another set of approaching tires breaks through our shared moment of depression, and when I see the familiar white Jeep truck pull up the lane, my heart aches all over again.

Everly Fletcher . . . my eldest brother's first kid, the sweet little girl Max had with his college girlfriend before they even graduated, gets out of her truck and walks toward us all with a look of determination.

I was only twenty when she was born, still just a kid myself.

Hell, Luke was barely a teenager. But the moment they placed that tiny pink bundle in my arms with a spray of fuzzy white hair and long slender little fingers that wrapped around my calloused thumb . . . I became a man.

And when Max and his wife split up when Everly was just two, she became all our responsibility. This little girl would want for nothing in life, and it was Calder's, Luke's, and my job to make sure she felt no pain from that break. My brothers and I have doted on her for the past eighteen years. We still take turns taking her out on weekly uncle dates when her busy teen schedule allows it. She and my brother's other kid, Ethan, who's seven now, get plenty of quality time with us. They love it.

We love them.

Flashbacks of Everly as a little tyke with blond braids bouncing around this mountaintop, begging to bottle-feed my goat, Millie, flash through my mind's eye. She would sleep over at one of our cabins every chance she got, which wasn't as often as we liked after my brother got divorced. Shared custody was a bitch for all of us.

This is why I want to do this fatherhood thing with a professional. With a contract. With no strings attached at the end. I don't want to share my time with my kid. Ever.

I'm still tormented at the thought of my only niece moving away. If I could take Everly to court and sue to keep her right here in Colorado, I would. Our girl in another country without all of us there to look out for her is unthinkable to me. My body tenses at the idea of something bad happening to her. Or hell, even someone just hurting her feelings. I can't believe Max said yes to letting her go that far away to college when perfectly good colleges exist right here in the same state.

"Dad," Everly exclaims, her tall six-foot frame striding toward us. "Don't you go blaming them for this . . . it was all my idea!"

"That's what I said," Calder confirms with a guilty shrug toward Everly. "Sorry, kid, but one broken nose in my lifetime is enough."

"You're welcome for that," Luke says with a smug grin. "Hi, Evie-girl."

"Hi, Uncle Luke," Everly says sweetly, then turns her attention to me, hitting me with those clear blue eyes I'd give my life for. "Uncle Wyatt . . . don't you be mad at Calder either. This was all me. You're not having any luck finding a surrogate in Denver. That agency clearly doesn't see you for all that you are, or you would have been matched by now, so I think it's time you tried a new plan."

"What plan?" I ask, feeling suddenly bone-tired at the idea of discussing this huge life-changing decision I've made with my entire family . . . *again*. I'm already exhausted by this process, and I only had to jack off into a cup once so far to ensure that my swimmers are good.

My boys are gold-medal swimmers . . . or so that old fertility doctor told me. But what's not earning me any medals is having to deal with my family's fucking input during nearly every step of this process.

"I think I can find you a surrogate," Everly says, her jaw taut with determination. "Someone who's perfect for this job."

"Evie," I say, but she holds her hand up to shush me. So, I shush.

"Just give me one week," she says, her youthful eyes flaring with so much grit I can't help but root for her. "Next week is my spring break, and I will interview the viable candidates who reply to the ad and see if anyone might be a good fit for this project. I'm certain I can find you someone special you'll never be able to say no to."

I shake my head. "Everly, I have another appointment at that agency on Monday. I could find someone then."

"Then we'll cancel my plan, and this will all be for nothing. No biggie."

"Everly," Max expels under his breath. "Finding a surrogate for Uncle Wyatt is a very big deal. It's real life, which is why he's going through the proper channels and trying to hire a professional from an agency. You're too inexperienced to understand all this."

"Please, Dad," Everly scoffs casually. "I'm not even a virgin."

Calder screams. Literally screams. It echoes off the foothills, likely sending all the wildlife scrambling.

Luke stumbles and nearly drops to the ground, his shoulders rising and falling as he braces himself on his knees and pants heavily, a look of disgust smeared across his face.

Max's jaw drops with horror as he stammers with what to say back to that very unexpected bomb his only daughter just dropped.

And I remain frozen, begging for a time machine to take this moment away immediately. Or, better yet, go back in time to whoever fucked my niece so I can kill that person before he has a chance to ever lay his eyes on her.

"Who is the fucker?" I rumble, my voice low and threatening. "Was it that Hilow prick who took you to prom last year? I thought you two broke up."

"We did," Everly exclaims defensively.

"Oh, my God," Max groans, looking like he's going to be violently ill at any second.

"It was a one-night stand?" Calder coughs as he rakes his hands through his hair. "I knew I was a bad influence on you. I never should have hung out with you so much. I'm a dirty, filthy, disgusting, rotten pig. I'm never having sex again. This is my vow to—"

"Uncle Calder . . . get over yourself," Everly drawls, her eyes rolling emphatically. "All of you, get over yourselves. This isn't about me. It's about Uncle Wyatt, who has dedicated so much of his life to making sure I was happy and loved and protected. Now it's my turn to do something for him."

My body stills with the weight of her words. Goddammit, when did she get so mature? The little girl we all helped raise is gone, and I'm looking at a woman now. A strong, independent, headstrong woman who I am so proud of my heart could burst. I turn around so she can't see the tears forming in my eyes, my jaw clenching with humiliation over the power this teenager has over me. It will kill me not to see her whenever I want next year.

Her footsteps are soft as she comes close and wraps her tiny manicured hands around my arm and rests her head on my shoulder. She used to have to stand on my feet to dance with me. This is so fucked.

"I know I won't be able to find you love, Uncle Wyatt. You've made it crystal clear that's not what you want in life. But please, let me be a part of helping you become a dad before I go." She stands on her tiptoes to kiss me on the cheek and whispers in my ear, "Because I know you will make an amazing one."

Well, fuck.

⋆ ⋆ ⋆ ⋆ ⋆

Nine Month Contract *is available now in all formats from Amy Daws and Canary Street Press wherever books are sold!*

Excerpt from Last on the List

Max Fletcher

A light knock on my door has me straightening in my desk chair. Everly doesn't knock, so I can only assume it's the nanny. I smooth down my new tie for the day and attempt to look busy as I call out, "Come in."

Cassandra walks into my bedroom, dressed in a long tie-dyed T-shirt and a pair of black leggings. She glances briefly at my bed and then forces her eyes on me.

"Can I have a word with you, Mr. Fletcher?" she asks, her hands playing with the hem of her shirt as she approaches my desk.

"Yes, of course. Where's Everly?"

"She's reading upstairs," she replies quickly, tucking her damp hair behind her ears.

The smell of coconut invades the room, and I wonder if she's just gotten out of the shower. Not that I should be thinking of my nanny in the fucking shower.

"I was wondering if maybe we could tell Everly I quit?" Cassandra quips, her tone sharp and contained.

My heart rate increases as I repeat her words in my head before I can mutter them out loud. "Quit?"

"Yeah . . ." she responds, her eyes staring down at the floor. "I'd rather she think I quit than blame herself for getting me fired. She keeps apologizing about the accident today, and I know it's breaking her little heart that she hurt me. If she thinks you let me go because of the pool incident, she'll never forgive herself."

I sit back in my chair, processing everything Cassandra has just said to me. She's known my kid for one freaking day, and she's willing to take the fall for her? I'm rarely speechless, but this situation makes forming a coherent sentence difficult.

I clear my throat. "Do you want to quit?"

"Not at all." Cassandra's round eyes lift to meet mine. The sunlight pouring in the windows behind me makes her eyes look greener than ever. "But I know that what happened today was terrifying for you and Everly. We were lucky you were here. I mean, I don't think I was going to drown. I was getting up to the top of the water before you jumped in. But I fully admit that it wasn't safe. Yes, it's true I'm not a great swimmer. I mean, I think I can save my own life, but if something like this happened to Everly, I'd be terrified of what that could look like. And with how much time you want us to spend in the pool this summer, I realize this makes me unqualified for the job I accepted. Therefore, I take full responsibility and will tender my resignation, Mr. Fletcher."

My head jerks back. *Tender her resignation?* That's pretty official language for someone whose past employer involved making footlong subs. I inhale a deep breath and stand, propping myself on the edge of the desk. "Let's take a breath here, Cassandra," I say, crossing my arms over my chest.

She nods and tucks her hands behind her back, her chest jutting out toward me. I flinch as I recall the feel of her extremely full breasts in my hands. How is it possible to be completely fucking terrified and half hard at the same time? That's really something I should talk to a therapist about someday. But not Josh's wife, Lynsey. Patient confidentiality or not, I don't need my best friend's wife to think I'm lusting after my kid's nanny.

"The truth is, Everly is an excellent swimmer," I continue, refocusing on the task at hand. "An incident like this never should have happened. Everly feels awful because she knows what she did was wrong. She usually has better impulse control than that, but I think she's really excited about hanging out with you this summer, and she got carried away."

"Hey, I've been there," Cassandra huffs with a laugh, her hand pushing into her dark hair as she gazes out the sliders behind me. "I remember pushing my sister off the dock at the lake once. She whacked her ankle on the boat hoist and screamed bloody murder for hours. Even had to get stitches."

I fight back a smile at that very random overshare. "Ouch."

"Yeah . . . the whole lake heard her battle cry. It was Awkward City. I immediately regretted my life choice that day."

I cringe knowingly, thankful for the turn in the conversation as the tension relaxes. "Kind of like your new boss regretting accidentally grabbing your chest as he attempted to save your life?" My shoulders lift with embarrassment.

"I mean, I was a kid, and you are a full-grown man, but I guess you can still relate." She lets out a soft giggle, and the tension eases between us as I watch her with downcast eyes.

"Awkward what?" I frown and watch her curiously, wanting to know more about her.

"City. Awkward City." The teasing smirk on her face makes it hard to keep scowling.

I click my tongue and sigh, trying to figure out the best way to resolve this. Giving up, I gesture toward her chest, trying hard not to look at it. "Well . . . I am sorry about that."

"It's fine. My tits get in the way a lot." She closes her eyes and shakes her head. "I shouldn't have said that. Can we stop talking about my breasts now?"

"Please," I agree, because now I can't stop looking at them and recalling how the weight of them felt in my hands. *Fucking hell . . . Awkward City, indeed.*

"Okay then." She pulls her shirt away from her chest as if she's trying to conceal her completely unconcealable breasts. "So are you saying I'm not fired?"

Last on the List *is available now wherever books are sold! The trade paperback from Amy Daws and Canary Street Press includes exclusive bonus material!*